'M   you, from the school? Yes. Well, I'm afraid you'll have to talk to the parents of the Barnes child. We did the best we could....'

'You did...what?' Dorothy said, and stared at her, her mouth half-open. 'What do you mean, talk to the parents of the child?'

'We couldn't get her into a respirator in time. I'm sorry. Stopped breathing, do you see. It's as well, perhaps. By the time we'd got her in it my guess is there'd have been brain damage. Anyway, there it is. I'll arrange for the necessary formalities and so forth – there'll be an inquest, of course, only in here an hour or so, so that's got to be dealt with – leave the parents to you, if I may? Pity, isn't it? Children dying – it always upsets people so much.'

The Virus Man

CLAIRE RAYNER

ARROW BOOKS

For Paul Sidey
A great friend and a great editor,
with love

Arrow Books Limited
62-65 Chandos Place, London WC2N 4NW

An imprint of Century Hutchinson Limited

London Melbourne Sydney Auckland
Johannesburg and agencies throughout
the world

First published by Century Hutchinson 1985
Arrow edition 1986

Printed and bound in Great Britain by
Anchor Brendon Limited, Tiptree, Essex

ISBN 0 09 946110 2

1

Miranda Hallam was found dead in her bed in Rose Dormitory at Bluegates School at seven o'clock on the morning of 31 October 1984. It was her twelfth birthday.

For Dorothy Cooper, the headmistress (she only used the hyphenated version of her name, Trant-Cooper, on the school prospectus, since she was always uneasily aware that someone might turn up who had known her in the old days before she had added that interesting embellishment) it was a personal affront, an event designed by Providence solely to cause problems for her, rather than an event to be grieved over. Of course, it was sad the child had died; the death of a young creature must always be regarded as sad, but why did she have to die in such a way and at such a time? Next week, when most of the other girls would have gone home for half-term, it wouldn't have caused a fraction of the fuss it was sure to cause now; already the other children were stirring, sitting up in their beds and staring uneasily at the very unusual sight of their dressing-gowned mistress in their midst at such an hour; wretched Miranda, she thought.

She stared down at the humped bundle in the bed, and then at the white face of Mary Spain, the young school matron who had actually discovered that the child was no longer breathing, and tried to decide what to do. Let the other children once realize that their dormitory companion was dead and heaven alone knew what would happen.

She bent and carefully wrapping the bedclothes round the child's body, said loudly, 'Oh, dear! We'd better get Miranda into the sickroom at once, Miss Spain. I dare say she'll feel better there.' And grunting only slightly under the weight, she picked up the bundle and carried it to the door. 'Now then, girls, time to be up! I want you all ready for breakfast on the dot of eight, now! No hanging about.' And she swept away, with Miss Spain scuttling after her, to deposit Miranda's corpse in the sickroom and then go on to telephone Dr Sayer.

Miss Cooper had never really liked Dr Sayer; she was a rather theatrical woman who made the most of every medical excitement that came her way, and there were few enough in Minster as a general rule. It had always been a healthy town (a fact which figured large in the school prospectus, which murmured soothingly of bracing air, so near the sea, and good country food provided amid tranquil surroundings), and Dr Sayer's practice therefore offered limited opportunities for the drama she so craved. That was why she had been so willing to take on the school's medical care when Dorothy Cooper had founded Bluegates back in the good palmy days of 1969. All the other local GPs had refused on the grounds of not wanting the added burden of seventy-five children aged between seven and sixteen living in the artificial atmosphere of a boarding school, and at first Miss Cooper had thought she had chosen well even though she'd chosen *faute de mieux*. But now she knew that Dr Sayer, who had in the past diagnosed everything from multiple sclerosis to malaria from an attack of a severe head cold, was more of a hindrance than an asset as far as the school's good name was concerned. She never minded how much fuss she made, and what effect it might have on nervous parents – many of them already over-anxious because of their guilt at sending their children away – and this, the first death on the premises, would be the most splendid of meat and drink to her. But what could the headmistress do? Dr Sayer was the school's official doctor, and that was it; she could not be bypassed. Dorothy Cooper was indeed in a very aggrieved state as she dialled Dr Sayer's number.

Jessie Hurst arrived at the hospital so early that Thursday morning that she actually had a choice of parking places. Usually she had to manoeuvre her heavy old Volvo back and forth as she sweated over the tight steering to get it into one of the really awkward places beside the boiler house, but this morning she was able to slide easily into the row just beyond the covered way that led to the pathology laboratory entrance, and that was a real boon on so blustery and wet a morning. But even that piece of good fortune didn't lift her mood.

She sat in the car for a few moments staring out at the rainwashed tarmac and its slither of fallen leaves and tried to switch off home and switch on work. It was a technique she had worked over for some time now, this deliberate separation of the segments of her life, and usually she managed it tolerably well: however irritable and depressed the hours spent with Peter at Purbeck Avenue had made her, she was able to start her day's work serene and alert, ready and able to cope with whatever might happen. Today, however, it was not so easy because last night Peter had started again and, unusually, had continued this morning. Generally he grumbled his way out of it in one session, and it was ominous that he had stuck so stubbornly to his theme this time.

'There's no need for it,' he'd said, over and over again. 'I keep telling you, I'm established. No matter how many cuts they make, *I'm* established. They can't make me redundant – I'm sitting pretty. And with the marvellous work this Government's done over inflation, we're better off than we've ever been. You don't have to do that ridiculous job. You should be taking it easy – staying at home – Mark off your hands and all; you should be taking it easy, your time of life – you don't have to be one of these women's libbers, not with the sort of home you've got, and the money I'm making – I'm sitting pretty.'

She had managed not to rise to any of it: didn't try to explain to him that she didn't work just for money (though God knew she valued having her own earnings in her pocket, rather than having to be aware as she always had been all through her married life that he was the source of the family cash), bit her tongue on her retort to his admiration for the Government, knowing how he would launch into a panegyric for Maggie Thatcher which would only make her lose her temper, and she certainly made no comment about the women's libber bit or the dig at her age. It wasn't worth it. It had been too long since they'd agreed on anything at all important, and certainly not on matters important to her. And she grinned sourly then at the wet leaves in the car park at the thought of Peter realizing that anything could be important to her; as far as he was concerned all that should matter to Jessie was what mattered to him and perhaps to Mark. That she might have needs of her own was a concept he just couldn't grasp. And it was no use getting angry about that, because he'd only stare at her with blank puzzlement if she did, and then shrug it off with some comment about women of her age and funny hormones.

She shook her head at herself then, working harder at

pushing Peter and the house away – it was getting more and more difficult to think of it as home, it was always the house in Purbeck Avenue in her mind – and concentrated instead on the job. She'd go in, in just a moment or two, unlock the laboratory, and switch on the lights and put on the coffee so that it would be ready when Ben – when everyone else arrived, and then go and start in the animal room, walking into the odorous damp warmth, murmuring to the rabbits and the little snuffling guinea pigs, talking to the two precious monkeys, Castor and Pollux, putting the food out; and slowly, as she visualized the hours that lay ahead, the knots in the muscles at the back of her neck relaxed and her irritation began to dissolve. It should be a good day, however badly it had started, as long as nothing tiresome came along to get in the way of Ben's plan for the day. They were to try the new batch of Contravert and that would be exciting and hopeful and – and at last she was able to get out of the car and slam the door shut and run across the car park to start some real living, some real *Jessie* living.

Ben was woken by the phone at eight o'clock, and swore furiously under his breath when he squinted at the clock and realized he'd overslept by over half an hour. *Bloody* June, he told himself, it's all her fault, and then, guilty at the thought, looked over his shoulder at her as he reached for the phone to stop its shrilling. But she was still fast asleep, her face puffy and miserable even in her unawareness, and he felt the old stab of distress. Poor June, not bloody June at all, poor June.

'Ben? Sorry if I woke you. Dan Stewart.'

'Been up for ages,' Ben lied and then wondered why he bothered. 'Well, just about. What's the matter?'

'Can you do a PM today? Sorry to push it at you, but it could be something important. Could be nothing of course, but I've got that bloody woman Sayer on my back, clucking like an idiot, bloody near orgasmic with excitement. I don't suppose it's anything much but there you are.'

'What is it?' Ben was sitting up now, and he looked down at June, still oblivious beside him, and turned his back on her so that he wouldn't wake her with his conversation. The longer she slept the better for both of them.

'Child at Bluegates – that poncey school over at Petts' Hill – boarding school, you know the place. One of the children was found dead this morning, and Sayer – she's their GP, God help 'em – says there's some sort of infection there that she reckons killed the kid. Load of rubbish if you ask me, but she's hoisted the flag, so what can I do? There'd have to be a PM anyway, of course, for the coroner, but with this suggestion there's some sort of infection there, it'd better be sooner than later. It's nearly half term, you see, the kids'll be going home next week, or supposed to be, for a break. So if there's anything nasty in their woodshed, I'd better know now, hmm? Can you manage it this morning? I can have the body over there before ten.'

'Shit,' Ben said and rubbed his chin, rasping his fingers against the stubble irritably. 'I've got an important animal trial starting this morning.'

'Sod your animals,' Dan said. 'This is a public health job. And have you seen this morning's *Guardian* yet? They're cutting umpteen million off research grants next year, so you're wasting your time anyway. I'll see you at the hospital around twelve or so. If I'm lucky.' And he rang off.

All the way to the hospital Ben's irritability simmered in him; he was tired of course by work, and that didn't help, but it wasn't surprising that his eyes felt gritty and his head stuffed with cotton wool. It had gone on until well after three o'clock, with June crying on and on until she had washed away all the last shreds of his sympathy for her and left behind only the weary bad temper that now filled him.

He'd known it was going to happen, of course. Her last period had been about five weeks ago and, as aware of her cycle as she was, he had realized with a sense of dull foreboding that she was almost a week overdue. Inevitably she had started getting excited the day she had expected this month's period to start, and when fully five days had gone by with no sign of it, she had been euphoric. He'd tried to warn her, to remind her that this had happened before, that she had to be a great deal more sure before she built up her hopes, but it was like dropping gravel into the sea, it made so little impact. And last night, when she'd gone to the loo after dinner and had come back with her face white and ravaged, he had almost literally braced his shoulders for the storm.

Fifteen years of it they'd had. Almost fifteen years. She'd started agitating about wanting babies almost from the day they'd married, though he'd tried even then to tell her that

9

there was no hurry, she was only twenty-one, she had lots of time, and that getting worked up about pregnancy could get in the way of conception, almost as though he'd had some sort of premonition of what was to come; but of course she hadn't listened, any more than she did now. June had always been like that; single-minded. Obstinate, he murmured to the swishing windscreen wipers in front of him as he turned the car into the long driveway that led to the hospital's car park. Bloody obstinate; but that wasn't really fair, or kind. She was a steady sort of person, that was the thing. What she started she finished; it made her reliable, loyal, all the things any man needed in a wife, especially a man with a job like his that kept him working at all sorts of odd hours, that absorbed so much of his energy. To complain because she had the faults of her virtues was unjust. Unjust, he repeated, as he pushed his car into the awkward space beside the boiler house – that bloody Martin from pharmacy had pinched his place again – because it was that certainty in her that had made him marry her in the first place. She was so comfortable to have around.

She isn't now, is she? It was sometimes as though there was another Ben Pitman who sat perched inside his head and commented sourly on what went on not only around the real Ben, but also deep inside him. She isn't now. She's hell to live with, every period bringing with it a scene out of Camille and the combined tragedies of Shakespeare, and then the bouts of desperate sex when she gave him no peace for fear of missing any chance of getting herself impregnated; she isn't easy to live with now.

And on top of all that an unscheduled PM on the one day he'd managed to clear so that he could start the new animal trial. It had taken weeks of planning to get to this, weeks of making sure that the animals were in tip-top condition – thank God, or whoever it was who arranged such things, for Jessie Hurst – of preparing the batch of Contravert, making sure that no one else but Jessie and himself knew what it was they were doing, and now all of it buggered up by Dan Stewart. But even as he whipped up his annoyance, he knew it wasn't Dan's fault any more than it was Susan Sayer's. It wasn't anyone's fault that a child had died. If there was doubt about the cause and it might be communicable then obviously the PM had to be done as soon as possible. But it was maddening all the same.

He pushed open the big swing doors to the pathology

laboratory with a loud swish, scattering the water from his overcoat all over the newly washed floor, and oddly, that made him feel better; as though he had, after all, some control over events, and he stood for a moment with his head up, reabsorbing himself into the place. The smell of the heavy pine disinfectant they used to scrub the floors and the overlay of formaldehyde and methylated spirit and the thick acrid bite of laboratory chemicals, all mixed up with the heavy warm scent of animals and straw and rabbit food filled his nostrils; not an attractive smell by any manner of means, but important to him. It meant peace, it meant busyness, it meant his own place; the worries that occupied him here were comfortable worries because he was in control of them: his own actions created any difficulties he might have, and his own actions could dispel them. It was never like that at home with June.

He stood for another moment or two to let the sense of security his laboratory gave him take over completely and then, with a small sigh, moved on to push open the further door into the biochemistry lab. One of these days he'd get the money he needed out of the district or even from the Medical Research Council and have a proper access to his own office built. It wasn't right always to have to walk through biochemistry to get to it, but at least there were compensations to the awkward geography of the place – an inevitable result of the way it had grown piecemeal over the years – and he valued them. The animal room could only be reached through his office, which meant it was much easier to control other people's access to it. The research was hard enough to organize as it was, without the complication of the world and his wife getting at his subjects.

The lab was already occupied. Harry Gentle, the senior blood technician, was sitting at a bench working over a sheaf of records, and there, beside the ramshackle table that had been rigged in the corner for coffee pots and biscuit tins, was Jessie. Her head was bent over the Cona machine so that her hair, with the streaks of grey in its heavy darkness, swung over her face, and as the door clicked closed behind him she looked up, and at the sight of him smiled widely.

The last shreds of his irritation went, June and her tears whirled away out of his mind; there was only today to be concerned with, and now he came to think of it, as long as Dan got that body to him at the time he said he would, he could get that PM done and maybe start the animal tests after all. As long as he had Jessie to help him, he'd get through, though it might mean working a great deal later than usual. But Jessie never minded that, and he smiled back at her and went to hang up his coat and pick up his coffee from Jessie. His eyes weren't gritty any more and he'd quite forgotten how little sleep he'd had.

Edna buttoned her coat as slowly as she could, loitering deliberately by the doorway, hoping he'd come back this way, maybe, and she could just say, casually, 'Oh, Dr Pitman, I'm glad I ran into you, could I just have a word?'

She smoothed the cloth of her coat over her hips, planning the rest of the conversation. 'Of course, Edna,' he'd say, smiling the nice way he did; always friendly, Dr Pitman, not at all stuck up like some of them. 'What can I do for you?'

'Well, sir,' she'd say, all relaxed and easy – Edna could see herself in her mind's eye being extremely relaxed and easy – 'It's nothing much really. It's just that I think this place needs a bit more cleaning than I've been able to give it. I'm not complaining, you understand, but the supervisor says I'm supposed to get it really clean in just two hours a morning, and I'm doing my best, but really, sir, it needs at least twice that. At least. I'd gladly do it, you understand, it's just that the supervisor, she says two hours is enough, much the silly . . . much *she* knows. So if you could have a word, sir, say you want me four hours a day, I reckon that'd mean I could do the job the way it ought to be done.'

Edna could see herself standing there, cool as you like, saying it all to Dr Pitman, could see him smiling and nodding and saying of course he would, anything you say, Edna, of course, and then going right away and telling that old bitch of a supervisor, and then she'd have to agree. That'd mean another twenty-one quid a week and though that wouldn't sort the whole thing out, it'd make a good difference, a very good difference.

Her coat was buttoned now, and there was no other reason she could have for hanging around, and she looked towards the door of Dr Pitman's office, and almost decided to take the bull by the horns, as it were, go and beard him in his den, stand up and be counted – the words twisted in her mind and she took a tentative step forwards, and then the door behind her was pushed open and Tomsett, the mortuary porter, put his head round it and shouted, 'Dr Pitman in yet?'

'In his office,' Jessie said. 'What is it?'

'There's an ambulance just come up, got an urgent PM, the driver said, and I told him he'd got it wrong, that I knew nothing about it, there was no PM booked for this morning, but he said there was, and got right cocky with it. But there isn't, is there? Because I'm not ready, no matter how you look at it. I'm not ready and won't be this side of . . . .'

'It's all right, Tomsett,' Jessie said soothingly. 'I dare say there's a simple explanation. You go and register the body in, I'll get Dr Pitman to come down and let you know what's happening.'

'Well, I can tell him now, and you too, if they've gone and arranged a PM without booking it the right way, all straight and proper in the book the way it ought to be, that I can't be held answerable for any . . . .'

'I told you, Tomsett, I'll sort it out,' Jessie said a little more sharply, and Harry Gentle looked up and grinned at her and Tomsett began to nag again and Edna sighed. Tomorrow maybe, tomorrow she'd be able to talk to Dr Pitman. She'd have to do something soon, because the way things were going she'd never get the money together. And here it was almost half past nine and the buses over to Petts' Hill going only every quarter hour if you were lucky. Nasty they got over there if you was late. I'll have to ask him tomorrow.

And she hurried out across the yard past the now crammed car park and the ambulance that had brought Miranda Hallam from Bluegates School to have a post–mortem on her twelfth birthday.

2

Peter Hurst was never late, but he was never too early either. He despised people who were so uncertain of themselves and their own value that they felt it necessary to get to their place of work before the appointed hour; sometimes he told Jessie that, when she was being particularly sullen about that silly job of hers. He knew she liked to get there long before nine, when she was supposed to start, and that irritated him. Bad enough she insisted on having a job at all; she didn't have to be so enthusiastic about it. Not that she ever paid any attention to what he said these days.

But no one could say he didn't apply his own rules to himself. He never appeared in his own office on the seventh floor of the new Civic Centre near the big new shopping precinct at Lovell's Cross before nine fifty-five, but by the same token he was never later than ten a.m. If it had been possible always to walk through the door on the tick, he would have done it, but idiots in car parks and the vagaries of the lifts made that virtually impossible. He had been thinking seriously lately about eschewing the lifts altogether and using the stairs since that would take some of the uncertainties out of the morning, but he hadn't reached a decision on that yet; it would be healthy, no doubt, but all the same, seven floors . . . .

This Thursday morning he managed to be as precise as he could have hoped for. His wrist watch was bleeping the hour as the big double doors that led to the Environmental Services section whispered open, and he nodded affably at Miss Price at the first desk as he went by, pleased with himself, and she stared bleakly back and knew they'd have a more than usually tiresome day with him. Mr Hurst when he was irritable was merely petulant or sulky like a small boy, and easy to ignore, but when he was pleased with himself he was inescapable, poking his nose into all the corners of the office which were none of his affair, covering up his inquisitiveness with a

14

massive jocularity that set her teeth on edge. And she'd had enough to put up with this morning already.

She followed him into his office to find his coat and hat already neatly disposed on the stand in the corner, and him standing beside the row of plants on his window sill, tweaking off the dead leaves and poking the compost in the pots to make sure she had watered them this morning.

'If you pull them around too much they'll die,' she said. 'And I've already done them today. There's a deputation waiting to see you. Seven of 'em, and you'll hate them all.' She said it with a gloomy relish that made his brows tighten for a moment.

'Deputation? What sort of deputation?'

'They're from the Animal Freedom Brigade,' she said, and grinned so that her narrow face seemed to split. 'Animal Freedom Brigade. A right mouthful, isn't it? You'll *hate* 'em.'

'Then I shan't see them.' He sat down at his desk and held out his hand with an air of calm decision. 'The post, if you please, Miss Price.'

'You'll have to see them.' Miss Price began to feel better as Peter Hurst's face started to lose its affability. 'They had an appointment to see Mr Wilmington and he sent down a message to say he's tied up getting the draft report ready for this afternoon's council meeting, and please will you deal with them. Shall I tell him you refuse, then?'

'Try not to be any more stupid than you have to,' Hurst said savagely. 'What is it they want anyway? What has animal freedom got to do with Env. Planning, for God's sake?'

'They've found out there's something going on somewhere, I fancy. They'll tell you all about it – try and stop 'em. I'll send them in, shall I?'

'Try and stop *you*,' Hurst said. 'They can wait. Bring in some coffee and the post and I'll see them when I've dealt with that.' But he knew, as she did, that he wouldn't dare to keep them waiting long. Not if Mr Wilmington had sent them to him. Wilmington might be only a grade senior to Peter Hurst, but he wielded his authority with great skill.

They filed in quietly and he peered at them over the top of the letter he was holding in his hand and ostensibly reading, trying to assess their strength, and began to feel better. Two men in neat business suits, much like his own, civilized looking chaps with briefcases. Older than himself, of course, could be retired, even, but sensible men. A couple of rather dumpy looking housewives, both of them with shopping bags as well as handbags clutched in their fists, neither worth a second look, but flanked by two girls very much worth a second look. Pretty, both of them, one in a pair of jeans so tight that they took your breath away – and it wasn't because you could imagine how they'd feel if you were wearing them yourself – and a floppy T-shirt that showed extremely clearly that she wasn't wearing a bra this chilly morning, and the other in a full-skirted flowered dress that showed a rim of lace petticoat beneath it, pretty as a picture. Lovely, both of them. Behind them a young man with a mop of black curly hair and a number of acne scars on his anxious round face stood uncertainly and then, as a grinning Miss Price closed the door on him, bobbed his head nervously and looked round at Peter Hurst with a slightly hunted expression on his face.

By now Hurst felt positively benevolent towards them; clearly harmless, they were no sort of threat to him.

'Good morning!' he said loudly, with the jolly tone in his voice he used for children and old people. 'A lovely autumn morning, isn't it? A touch blustery perhaps, and a bit of rain about, but very invigorating. Now, let me see, chairs for the ladies I *can* provide, but I'm afraid you chaps'll have to settle for your own feet. I'm sure you'll forgive me, but I don't normally enjoy so many visitors at a time. Now then, what can I do for you? What can the *department* do for you?'

Surprisingly, it was the curly-haired youth who was the spokesman, and he came and stood beside Hurst's desk, blinking a little nervously and rather obviously sweating, but his voice was clear and firm and his hands steady as he put a sheaf of paper down on the blotter.

'A petition, sir. That's what we've brought you here. You'll see when you study these documents at your leisure, that we, the Minster chapter of the Animal Freedom Brigade, have identified a vivisection centre here in the town. The main, indeed the entire aim of the AFB is to put an end to these vicious practices, alerting as many people as possible to the unspeakable cruelties that are perpetrated in these establishments and . . . .'

'Well, quite,' Hurst said heartily, not looking at the papers, but smiling round at the faces that stared solemnly back at him, lingering a little on the girl in the flowered dress; she really was very pretty with her soft curls and wide brown eyes. 'Quite, absolutely. Everyone with any imagination at all must . . . er . . . be concerned.' He began to back-pedal a little. It was all very well to be friendly, but it wouldn't do to be too enthusiastic about whatever it was they were in a lather about. 'But I'm not quite sure what this has to do with Env. Planning? I mean, we're involved in the business of building and insulation you know, and green belts and so forth.' He smiled at them, as though they were rather dim children in need of education. 'Nothing to do with animals, you see, nothing at all.'

'We want to know if this vivisection centre has been properly licensed. There are Home Office rules about these things, they're pretty bad rules, don't go nearly far enough – what we need in this country if we're to be regarded as civilized is a total ban on all live animal experiments with all medical research done only on tissue culture, not on helpless dumb animals that can't speak for themselves – but there are rules and they can be used, weak as they are, to help the cause.' He stopped and took a breath. 'And rules about how buildings are used are surely part of the work of your department.'

'Sorry, old boy.' Peter Hurst shook his head with every appearance of regret. 'Not our bag at all. We just scrutinize plans, consider requests for permission to build and make sure the buildings are up to scratch and so on. But we have little to do with how buildings are *used*.'

'Yes you do,' one of the dumpy housewives said sharply. 'When a shop on our parade over to Holmsley was sold and the new people wanted to run it as a fresh fish shop, they couldn't get permission . . . .'

'Quite a different department, my dear lady, *quite* a different department,' Peter Hurst said. He was beginning to feel more and more comfortable with these people; they'd soon be sent on their way. 'That's a matter for the rating authority, you see, and the people who deal with head leases and so forth; they have the say in usage of premises. We're part of overall planning here, you see, not individual projects. We have a good deal of responsibility for Minster and its environs but we're answerable to a different body: the council, you see, and its main committees. Very complex business, government, very complex. So you see, this . . . ah . . . no doubt very worthy petition of yours really isn't any affair of this department. I'm amazed that Mr Wilmington didn't make that clear when you asked for an appointment. Wasting your valuable time this way, it's too bad, really!'

'I think you'll find your department *is* involved, sir,' the young man said stolidly, blinking at him. 'We've already discussed this with the Environmental Health Officer on the second floor here, on grounds of health hazards, but he can't act, he says the place is properly run according to his knowledge, and it comes under your department, not his.'

'Environmental Health?' Hurst said, and lifted an eyebrow. 'Well, of course, that *is* part of Environmental Planning, but once again only in a very narrow way – they inspect restaurant kitchens, food shops, places like that. They don't have any wider responsibility for overall planning, so they take a rather more, well, blinkered, view than we would here. Where did you say this place was? Perhaps we can help you find just who is responsible for it. Home Office is my guess but . . . .'

'No, not the Home Office. We've dealt with them. They say it's not their department. The Health people say it isn't theirs, either, even though it's in NHS premises. They say it's Environmental Planning – you can object to misuse of premises which you've designated for certain uses – if you . . . .'

'I don't know that we ever had anything to do with designating any NHS premises in Minster . . .' Hurst began, trying to remember how many such establishments there were – health centres, clinics, hospitals, day centres – but the young man interrupted him, leaning forwards to rifle through his papers.

'If you look at these documents, sir,' he said with patient courtesy, 'you'll see that you did. Not you personally, of course, but this department. Long time ago, but all the same … there you are,' and he pointed out a paragraph on a tightly printed page and Hurst read it, frowning.

'I rather think, you know,' he said at length, 'that I'm going to have to take guidance on this matter. I'm not convinced even now that this is an Env. Planning affair, but . . . .'

'They all say that,' said the woman who had complained about the fish shop, her voice shrill and whining at the same time. 'Not my fault, nothing to do with me. Just like kids fighting over who broke the jam pot.'

'Shut up, Dora,' the young man said sharply. 'No need for that. We want to do everything right and proper. We won't turn to more active measures till we have to. Don't want any bad temper yet.'

'Quite,' Hurst said, and then looked at the young man sharply, who stared blankly back at him. 'What do you mean, active measures?'

'We're serious, sir,' the young man said, and smiled very sweetly, and suddenly looked no more than fifteen. 'We may seem a bit daft to you, sitting here, looking at all these pieces of paper. You may think we're just a bunch of cranks with nothing better to do than come here and make a nuisance of ourselves, but we're serious. We're trying to close down this place legally. There are Home Office rules and there are Department of the Environment rules, and we'll try to use them first. But if that doesn't work, then we'll have to take further steps.'

'Plan B,' said the pretty girl in the flowered dress, and giggled.

'What we plan doesn't matter,' the young man said quickly, and shot an angry glance at her. 'We're just going a step at a time. Seeing all the relevant authorities at all levels, that's what we're doing. That's the way the AFB always does things. We're not stupid, sir. We're just animal lovers.'

'I'm sure you are,' Hurst said, a little uneasily, and looked up at the damp face with its scatter of pockmarks, and then smiled. He really couldn't take such people seriously. Animal Freedom Brigade and Plan B – it was all out of a bad television show. 'Well, I'll see what I can do to help. I'll look at your documents, make further enquiries, and be in touch. Your address is on the papers? Excellent, excellent. I'll deal with it as soon as possible.'

'We'll come back if we don't hear from you in a couple of days,' the young man said. 'Shall we?'

'Well, a little longer than that, perhaps a few days longer!' Hurst said, and laughed boisterously. 'Big department here, you know, a lot of work going forward. But we'll get on with it as fast as we can. *Good* morning!'

After they'd gone he put their pile of documents in a file unread, and marked it 'Wilmington Urgent Action', and deliberately put it at the bottom of his 'In Abeyance' box. It would be a week or even a bit longer before it emerged and reached Wilmington, and by that time they'd be a lot less easy to deal with. And he himself would be in London for the week of the planning officers' conference and Wilmington would have to deal with them on his own. And serve him bloody well right.

The planning officers' conference; he sat and thought about that, his good humour at his ploy to embarrass Wilmington while getting rid of the AFB evaporating. Why the hell wouldn't she come with him? He only got his chance to go once in every four years, the way Wilmington always hogged it, and he'd been looking forward to it for months. And so should she have been; any other woman would give her eye teeth for a chance to spend a week in London with her husband. They'd organized all sorts of things for wives, so it wasn't as though she'd be bored. He'd shown her the programme, pointed out to her the lectures on herbs and French country cookery and the demonstrations of quilting, the evenings going to the theatre to see 'No Sex Please, We're British', and 'Singin' In The Rain', but she'd just looked at it poker-faced and said she really didn't want to bother.

Didn't want to bother! He sat with his back to his desk, his feet up on the radiator, staring out of the window at the block of the east wing of the Civic Centre, his face set in a scowl. She bothered enough over that stupid job; that was all she bothered about these days. If he'd known it would turn out like this, he'd never have let her go back to work in the first place. He'd only agreed because he'd been so busy at the time the job came up, and she'd been so off-hand about it, he hadn't thought it mattered all that much.

She'd shown him the advert in the local paper late one night last January when he was tired, ready for bed, and feeling a bit randy too. That had made him abstracted, stopped him really thinking about what she was saying. 'Laboratory technician wanted, general duties', the advert had read, and offered dreadful rates of salary, really dreadful, even if you didn't compare it to his own comfortable fifteen and a half thousand a year; but as she'd said, she didn't have much to offer, after all. She'd trained as a laboratory technician, but never really worked at the job, because when they got married he'd insisted she give up work. (And why not? he said, and had repeated it when she'd shown him the advert; why not? I was well able to keep my wife even then.) Then Mark had been born, and there'd never been the chance. But now, here it was, so why not? she said, echoing him, and smiled at him; that lopsided sort of grin she had that always made him feel randy, even when he wasn't already feeling the need, so he'd let her take the job, not really thinking about it properly, just wanting her to be happy.

And it had certainly seemed to cheer her up a lot, going off every day in her old car, and there was another side to it: it stopped her getting bored when he was out in the evenings at the photography club. In fact he'd been quite pleased about the fact that she often worked late; he'd felt a bit guilty at the way he was spending more and more evenings out now he was on the club committee, so it had all worked out pretty well. Until now.

He turned his chair sharply and pulled a file from the pile on his 'In' tray. There was work to be done, and he'd better do it, but it wasn't easy to concentrate on the pages in front of him. He couldn't pull his mind away from the fact that she wouldn't come to the conference in London with him. She said it was because there was so much going on at the laboratory, a lot of paperwork to get through, not enough time to deal with it during the day, but what could she be *doing* all day? He had only the haziest idea of what went on in a pathological laboratory anyway: he imagined she washed test tubes or something, carried specimens about in glass bottles; what else could there be for her to do that meant she couldn't get away to spend a week with her own husband as a wife should? It really was too bad of her; and he glared at the sheet of paper in his hand and promised himself he'd have it out with her tonight, one way or the other. It was time she gave up that damned stupid job and was herself again, quiet and comfortable to have around. She just wasn't his Jessie any more, and though he wouldn't have thought it possible that anything else she could do would ever make him unhappy, he had to admit that that thought was an uncomfortable one. She just wasn't his Jessie these days.

3

'I don't see any reason why we should let anyone know anything about it,' Dorothy Cooper said again, her voice pitched rather higher than it usually was; it was getting more difficult to keep her temper. 'What possible use can it be?'

'It would alert parents to the possibility of their child being affected, then they could keep an eye on them and make sure they got immediate medical help if there were any signs or symptoms,' Dr Sayer said, and she crossed her knees carefully and smoothed her skirt over them. 'You must agree, Dan, surely, that it's essential that we contain this epidemic? When we consider the possible effects?'

'There's no epidemic yet, Susan,' Dan Stewart said firmly. 'All we have is a collection of children with a few flu-like symptoms, and a child who died of unexpected and unexplained heart failure. You can hardly put those together and call them an epidemic.'

'Do what you want, Dr Sayer, and we really will have an epidemic on our hands: of frantic parents all rushing to take their children away from the school.'

'Well, of course, I do understand your anxiety about your investment, Miss Cooper,' Dr Sayer said. 'But really you can't put that before the health of . . . .'

'I'm not putting my investment anywhere,' Dorothy Cooper said, her face a sudden patchy red, but her temper still admirably under control – just. 'I am making the point that frantic parents won't be of much use to their children, that it's after the start of the academic year and getting new schools for them will cause a good deal of difficulty and upset, especially to the O level students. That is what I meant. And I repeat, I see no reason for all the fuss. As Dr Stewart says, a few sniffles and coughs don't add up to an epidemic – and as for Miranda – well, it's all very sad, but clearly the child was never as well cared-for as she might have been. We'd only had her a few months, but I can tell you, she was not a happy child, or a well child. Hardly likely she would be, with no one but a solicitor to show any interest in her, poor thing.'

'No relations at all?' Dan said. 'I know you told me her parents were dead, but I assumed there were relations somewhere, grandparents or something of the sort.'

'There was an aunt, a great-aunt. She died last year – that was why they sent Miranda here. No shortage of money, you see, but nowhere for the child to live. She went to the solicitor and his family for Christmas, and a venture camp for the summer holiday, and spent the other breaks here. If there had been any real relations, I might have had the chance to get to know more about her past medical history and so forth, but as it was, I never did. And of course *you* didn't spot anything wrong with her when you examined her on entry to the school, did you, Dr Sayer?'

'No, I did not, because there was nothing to find wrong.' Dr Sayer was red now, and her voice was much less in control than Dorothy Cooper's. 'I don't care what the PM report says – that child was in perfect health, no heart murmurs, nothing. She was a plump child, probably constitutionally so, but that wouldn't lead to heart failure. I am convinced that the child died of a virus infection, and that it's potentially lethal to other children. That's why I think it's our duty to notify all the relevant people, including the parents.'

'Not your duty, Susan,' Dan said. 'Mine.' He got to his feet and went to stand behind Dorothy Cooper, to look down at the register she had in front of her. '*I'm* the Health Authority's Community Physician here, and I'm not yet certain that I agree that this is more than a mild flu. How many of these children want to go home next week, Miss Cooper?'

'About half of them, I'd say,' she said, and ran her finger down the list. 'We've got a lot of diplomatics here – they go to their parents for the main holidays, not for the half-terms.' She shot a malicious glance at Dr Sayer. 'It's because they travel so far that Dr Sayer thought one of them had malaria last year. You remember, Dr Sayer? Turned out to be the early stages of measles as I recall.'

'It's difficult to be sure in the prodomal stages.' Dr Sayer was not at all abashed. 'I try always to be aware of the differential diagnoses. Malaria was a very real risk in a child who'd spent her summer holiday in South Africa – and I say that there is a real risk here of this being not flu but a much more virulent infection which carries a threat to life. We've already got one child dead of it, and I don't want us to risk another for want of a little foresight.'

'We have no evidence that the child did die of the infection. Her heart failed, that's all we know. Ben says in his report that there was some oedema at the base of the lungs, a bit of tissue puffiness, and it was probably fairly quick, perhaps half an hour or so, no more. And that's all he can say. There was nothing to indicate why, nothing at all. It could have been any one of a number of causes, as well you know.'

'The most likely is a toxic effect from an overwhelming virus infection.'

'And looking at the other children and their symptoms we don't seem to have anything like that,' Dan said, his voice thinning a little. It began to seem as though he would be the first to lose his temper. 'We've got a few snotty noses, some coughs, a bit of diarrhoea . . . .'

'A suggestion of neck stiffness.'

'But no headaches, no muscular involvement?'

'No,' Dr Sayer said, almost unwillingly.

'And how many have the suggested neck stiffness?'

'Just one,' Dorothy Cooper said loudly. 'Just one, and she's in the sickroom. And we all know about Jennifer Coultear. Both her parents are doctors, she gets very little attention from them except when she's ill, and she knows more about symptoms than any child I've ever come across. She's the most accomplished liar and malingerer, as you well know, Dr Sayer. She's had you in knots often enough.'

'Even malingerers get ill sometimes,' Dr Sayer was getting rattled now. 'And anyway that sort of behaviour is an illness in itself. An important psychological disorder and indicator of deep-lying distress and . . . .'

'But not,' Dan said wearily, 'of epidemics that need publicizing. No, Miss Cooper, I agree with you. There is no need to stop the girls going home for their half-term break next week, and no need to notify this outbreak, whatever it is. Flu, probably. There's been a lot this year, a couple of new strains moving in, and I'd be surprised if you didn't get a school showing some of it. We'll keep an eye on the children over the next few days but I don't for a moment think we've got anything here to worry about. Sorry to over-rule you,

Susan, but there it is.'

'You won't call Colindale?'

'No I will not. There's no need.'

'And if I do?'

'They'll refer you back to me, Susan, of course. You know that perfectly well. If there's a need to contact Colindale, I will, you can be sure.'

'What's Colindale all about?' Miss Cooper asked.

'Communicable diseases surveillance centre, Miss Cooper. They keep an eye on the whole country, know about trends in infectious illness, what's going the rounds. If this persists, I might contact them, see what they have to say about it, but there's no need to do it just now.'

'And do I need to . . . um . . . is it necessary to publicize the fact the child died here?' Miss Cooper looked up at him, her face red again. 'At the risk of being accused of being mercenary, I have to say it does worry me. Parents aren't exactly logical about these things. They get agitated over the most ridiculous things, and if they once knew a child was found dead in the dormitory – well, you can imagine. It wouldn't be good for the girls either. They get hysterical and excited – you know what children are.'

'But you can't deny the child died, Miss Cooper.' Dan grinned, then, a sharp edgy little grimace. 'I imagine even these children will notice if their schoolmate just disappears. Mightn't that cause more fuss?'

'Oh, of course, they'll have to know she's . . . er . . . gone,' Dorothy Cooper said. 'I just want to keep the drama out of it. We've had enough of that to last us a lifetime, one way and another.' She avoided looking at Susan Sayer so carefully it was as though she had shrieked at her. 'But they needn't know she died. I can tell them that she was ill, that she's gone home and won't be coming back to school. No need for more than that. They'll soon forget her, so long as they aren't made over-excited by being told too much.'

'Well, I see no reason to make a fuss about it,' Dan said, and stretched and went over to the chair by the door where he'd left his coat and hat. 'I'll say nothing about it, and I doubt you or your staff will. And I'm sure Dr Sayer will see the wisdom of a little discretion.' And he cocked a glance at her, and said, then, 'Can you give me a lift back to the office? I came up in a cab – my car's up the spout until tomorrow. My bloody daughter drove it into a wall, would you believe?'

Susan Sayer went pink and after a moment nodded. 'Glad to. I've only got a couple of calls to make, and they're on the other side of the town, and I can go past your place easily. Even find time for a cup of tea.' And she laughed, a little trill that made Miss Cooper look at her sharply, and made Dan look even more wooden than he usually did. He knew perfectly well that Susan Sayer had been dangling after him for the past three years, ever since his divorce, and usually he avoided her with all the skill he had, but he'd felt sorry for Dorothy Cooper, trying to protect her school in the face of the silly woman's fuss, and had acted on impulse; the request for a lift would distract Susan Sayer immediately, he'd known that, and it had worked, and even if it meant spending half an hour talking banalities with the wretched woman, he supposed it would be worth it to get her mind off her imaginary epidemic. So he opened the door and held it for her invitingly, and left Dorothy Cooper feeling for the first time since the morning had started so appallingly that things weren't, perhaps, so bad after all.

'But I *was* working!' Simon said. 'I was out looking for a story and I tell you, there is one there and . . . .'

'Your job isn't to go looking for stories, but to cover the ones you're told to cover,' Joe Lloyd said. 'And I bloody well told you to cover the courts this morning and what do you do but go buggering off on your own account? You do that once more and there'll be an advert going in the paper for your job – I'm warning you.'

'But there was nothing at the courts. Honest there wasn't, Mr Lloyd! There were a few speeding jobs, a half a dozen clobbered for parking, and a couple of shoplifters. And you say yourself half the time when I bring in about shoplifters that you'll spike it, no need to make their lives a misery, and who cares anyway, bloody supermarkets can afford it and they shouldn't leave the stuff where people can take it and . . . .'

'Stop changing the subject. It's my decision, not yours, whether I use the stories or not. What were they? Or didn't you bother to find out?'

'Of course I did! Here they are.' Simon reached for his notebook and squinted over his scribble of shorthand and abbreviations. 'A Mrs Lester, three kids, on supplementary, husband left her to look for work in London, never came back. They got her for pinching a frozen chicken and a bag of sprouts at the Buycheep supermarket. She'd put the chicken in the baby's pram and that made it cry with cold and try to chuck it out and that's how they got her. I thought, you'll never publish that. Poor thing, it wasn't her fault she couldn't afford to feed her family, was it?' And he looked hopefully at the old man over the edge of his notebook.

'That's all you know,' Lloyd said. 'Write it up, and I'll do a leader having a go at bloody Buycheep for being grasping and prosecuting a starving mother. That'll make a beauty. You see? You wouldn't know a story if it ran up your bloody trouser leg and chewed off your necessaries. What was the other one?'

'Other what?'

'Other shoplifter. You said a couple. In my day, when facts were sacred and reporting meant bringing in a story the minute you'd bloody well got it, a couple meant two. What was the other one?'

'A Mrs Laughton. Pinched a packet of sausages, three packs of biscuits, and a jar of jam and a tin of salmon from Barney's self-service. It was the salmon got up their noses, they said. They wouldn't've prosecuted for the other things, they were staples, but salmon, best red middle-cut, that was luxury goods and not on. So they brought proceedings.'

'I'll think about that one. Full name and address?'

'Mrs Edna Laughton, aged sixty-three. 5a Wessex Street, East Minster,' Simon gabbled. 'Now can I tell you about the story I've picked up?'

'Try and bloody stop you,' Lloyd said, and bent his head over the page he was checking, but Simon knew he was listening.

'Right. I went to the police station first. Nothing there.'

'Course there wasn't. Already checked – that's Roberts's patch. If he catches you poaching on his territory he'll have your guts for a seat belt.'

'Thought it was worth a go,' Simon said, and grinned. The old man wasn't half as mad as he was making out. He liked people with a bit of push and if there was one thing Simon had in vast quantities it was push. 'Then I went down to the ambulance station. They'd just had a call to go over to Bluegates School. Posh place over on Petts' Hill.'

'You don't have to tell me. I've been running this bloody paper thirty years, don't tell me what's in this bloody town.'

'So I went over there to see what was what. Hung about a bit, couldn't see a lot, but then they brought out a stretcher, all covered up.'

'Hardly leave the patient blowing in the breeze, would they? Bloody wet morning.'

'Not like that. *All* over, I meant, face and all.'

'Face and all? Like a body?'

'Oh, you're quick, Mr Lloyd, you're very quick.'

'None of your bloody cheek. Then what?'

'Followed it, didn't I? Followed the ambulance to the hospital. The Royal it went to, not the Eastern.'

'The Eastern doesn't have an accident department, half-wit. It wouldn't go there.'

'Might have done if it'd been some old person or other.'

'From a girls' school? Be your age! So it went to the Royal. Then what?'

'Didn't go to Accident and Emergency, did it?' Simon said triumphantly. 'Went the other way, to the car park area. Unloaded the ambulance at the path. lab. Mortuary entrance, that's where it went. What do you make of that, then?'

'Someone died,' Joe said. 'Like you will soon if you don't come up with something better'n this.'

'It was a kid, that's the thing,' Simon said. 'That's why I think it's a story, because I've heard nothing about a kid dying, have you? But they took a kid to the mortuary from Bluegates this morning. And when I tried to find out about it I got sent off with a flea in my ear, by some doctor or other.'

'A child?'

'Small body, you see, on the trolley.'

'Well, it didn't take me long to work that out, did it? I'm not exactly stupid, even if I don't go rushing around the streets chasing ambulances. Saw you off, did they?'

'Said I was Press, of course.' Simon swelled a little even in reporting the incident; he'd only been on the paper six months and still couldn't quite believe his own status as a reporter. 'But he said I was trespassing, there was nothing there for me, go and see the hospital secretary, so I did, and he denied all knowledge. So there you are. I think it's a story. What do you say?'

'I'll think about it. Now bugger off and write up that

mother and frozen chicken story. And keep away from the police station in future.'

'But this story – can't I keep on it? Let me go back, Mr Lloyd, please! I swear there's something in it.'

'There might be. But I'll deal with it myself. Now piss off out of it and get some real work done. I've got better things to do than waste bloody time with you.'

'Oh, Mr Lloyd, you can't take it away from me . . .'

'Yes, I bloody can, and I bloody will. Now go and get your work done!' And Simon, furious, went. There was nothing else he could do. But he found some comfort in seeing Joe Lloyd walk out of the office with his hat on less than ten minutes later. If he was following up the story himself, it must be a good one. And he had, after all, been the one to bring it in. Perhaps when Joe Lloyd had got it all written up, he'd remember that and do the honourable thing. After all, he'd been on the paper six months now. It was high time he was promoted.

4

Liz and Timmy were in the small garden in front of their flat when she arrived, scooping up the leaves that were swirling down from the plane tree in the adjoining garden; or rather Liz was trying to collect them while Timmy, shrieking with excitement, kicked them all up again, and June stood at the gate watching him and feeling the same degree of excitement lift in her at the sight of his fat round legs in their red wellington boots flashing in the burnt yellow of the leaves. He was altogether the most satisfying person to look at, in every way, and she felt her throat tighten with the emotion of it.

It was the same every time she came here, as warming and comforting to get her first glimpse of him as it had been the first time she had seen him three years ago, in the nursery at the maternity ward when he was six hours old. It was extraordinary really; whenever she saw other small children it wasn't pleasure she felt but the bite of fury; how dare such children exist when one of her own did not? How dare other women get pregnant when she could not? It was cruel, wicked, a deliberate punishment inflicted on her by . . . somebody. She could never bring herself actually to rail against God, even though she wasn't a churchgoer, couldn't even be angry with Providence, feeling obscurely that that was just God's other name – but she could feel hate for an unnamed someone, whoever that someone was who had decreed she shouldn't have children. Yet she never felt that when she saw Timothy.

It had been like that with Liz, too; usually she felt a matching hate for pregnant women, would cross the road to avoid them when she was out shopping, dropped any acquaintanceships when she heard that they had started a pregnancy, but she hadn't felt like that when Liz got pregnant. Right from the start she had been fiercely protective of her, watching what she ate, nagging her about her smoking, her occasional drink, her late nights, but never feeling that furious hatred; and that was odd because they'd never been close sisters. There'd been a good deal of jealousy between them in their young days, yet as soon as Liz came and told her she was pregnant – that the bastard had gone off as fast as his rotten legs could carry him as soon as he knew – all that had dissolved. June had taken over, fighting Liz's attempts to get an abortion, looking after her, paying all her bills, protecting her in every way she could – and had been rewarded with Timothy.

But still, underneath all that, the original rage seethed. She still crossed the road to avoid pregnant women, still looked at other small children with loathing, still gave Ben hell every month when she discovered that once again pregnancy had eluded her; it really was extraordinary how she could feel as she did about Timmy, and yet keep all those other horrible feelings intact.

He looked up then and saw her, and she felt her face crease into a wide involuntary smile, and she pushed the gate as he made a move to start forwards and come to meet her, just as Liz looked up and put out a hand to restrain him. And a trickle of chill moved into June's throat as she pushed the gate wider and, locking it carefully behind her, went up the narrow brick path towards them.

'Hello, Liz. Hello, Timmy,' she said as easily as she could, and Liz leaned on her rake and stared at her, her face unsmiling.

'I didn't think you'd come here again today,' she said. 'Third time this week!'

'Auntie June, Auntie June, Auntie June!' Timmy was tugging on her coat, and she bent to hug and kiss him and didn't have to answer. Liz was going through a bad patch, that was all; just reverting to the way she'd always been, scratchy and awkward. It didn't mean anything, nothing was going to change.

'I was shopping,' she said as easily as she could. 'Saw they had a sale at Hammond's and found this, so I thought I'd bring it over.' She reached into her bag and brought it out, the cheerful red plaid trousers with the matching braces that had cost her a great deal more than she would dream of admitting to Liz, and which certainly hadn't been in the sale. 'I thought they'd look rather good with that yellow sweater I made . . .'

'He doesn't like it,' Liz said, and bent over her rake again, drawing the rustling gold towards her in long sweeps. 'Says it makes his neck itch. Told you not to make a polo neck, didn't I?'

'I can fix that easily,' June said, and the cold in her throat increased, made her voice turn thin. 'Unpick it, make it crew neck. Would you like that better, Timmy? A different neck on your sweater?'

'What else, what else, what else?' Timothy carolled, and began to scrabble in her bag, and June felt the warmth begin to come back into her. 'What do you mean, what else, wicked one?' she said and laughed. 'What else should there be?'

'Whatever it is, he's not to have it,' Liz said sharply and stood up, her face flushed with her exertions. Or something. 'Really, June, this is getting ridiculous. Third time you've been here this week, and brought something for him every time. Do you want him to stop looking at your face and only at your hands? You're behaving more like a half-witted grandmother than . . . .'

She stopped and stared at June and then shrugged and took a sharp little breath in through her nose. 'You know what I mean,' and she bent her head back to her raking of the leaves. 'Don't want him spoiled.'

'I won't spoil him,' June said, and uneasily pulled her bag away from Timmy. The chocolate was at the bottom and he hadn't found it yet; better if he didn't, after all. She could keep it for him till next week. 'I just happened to see the trousers at the sale, that was all.'

'Yes,' Liz said. 'Well, yes . . . all right. Thanks.' And the grudging sound of her voice hung in the air between them as thick as the leaves still falling in the boisterous wind.

Please don't let her get awkward, a little voice gabbled inside June's head, don't let her get awkward, make her go on needing me, make it go on as it is, don't let her change, please don't . . . .

Not that it could change. She tried to quieten the chatter of the little voice with sensible thoughts as she watched Timmy start kicking up the leaves again, his face rosy with the excitement; how could it change? Liz had always been bad with money and she could never live on her Supplementary Benefit; not the way she wanted to live, eating and drinking the way she enjoyed, wearing the sort of clothes she liked. The rent of the flat alone took most of the income she got from the Welfare people; without June's regular allowance she'd never manage, and without June's extra gifts Timmy, and she, would go short of a great deal.

And without my help she'd never be able to see Nick, June whispered to herself, and that's got to be the most important of all to her. Who else would turn out to baby-sit at a moment's notice, who else would take Timmy off her hands any time she wanted?

And it slid even more deeply in her mind, the hope and dream that filled her more and more these days. Nick wanting to marry Liz, instead of just sleeping with her, Nick wanting to set up a proper home of his own, Nick not wanting Timmy, telling Liz she had to choose between them and Liz of course choosing Nick; why shouldn't she? She needed a man in her life, always had, and she could always have more children; why shouldn't she let Timmy go to the aunt who loved him so much, go away, start again, put the past and her child behind her — it was a picture that June never grew tired of contemplating.

Sometimes she elaborated the dream: sent Nick and Liz to Australia or South America where Nick could really make a fortune, a hard-living ambitious man like Nick, or discovered that not only did Nick not like Timmy, but that he already had a couple of other children of his own somewhere and told Liz that she'd be lumbered with them if she insisted on holding on to Timmy; once or twice she had even played with the thought of Nick and Liz out in that big noisy car of his, the Porsche he boasted about so much, and going too fast and the rain making the road slippery — but she had never been able to carry that one through. Thinking that way would be like being angry with God or Providence. Not to be allowed, it might turn round on her, make something dreadful happen to her, instead of to Liz . . . .

'Doing anything this weekend?' she asked, as casually as she could. The plan she had made this morning, lying in bed after Ben had gone to the hospital, lurked inside her head, a hopeful, joyful plan. 'Nick going to be around?'

'Not this weekend, he isn't,' Liz said, and went on raking. June's spirits began to lift. When Liz avoided looking at her it meant she wanted something. 'He's got some sort of deal he's sorting out. Might manage to come over for supper Sunday, but that's all — it's an important deal. Car parts, I gather. For Spain.'

'Spain,' June said carefully, keeping her voice colourless. 'Really? Will he have to go there?'

'Might,' Liz said, and raked more industriously than ever, to Timmy's noisy delight. 'On the fifth, he said.'

'That's not long now, is it?' June said, and bent to take the leaf that Timmy was pushing into her hand, smoothing its wetness to admire the pattern on it that had caught his eye. 'That sounds nice for him. Will you . . . er . . . will you go with him?'

Liz stopped raking and bent to Timmy to brush the leaves off his coat, holding him firmly as he squirmed between her hands. 'Well, he did mention it.'

'Whereabouts?'

'Majorca. They do a lot of business there, it seems.'

'Lovely in November there, I should imagine. You ought to go with him, you know. It'd do you good. You've been looking a bit peaky.'

'Have I?' Liz threw a quick glance at her and then looked back at Timmy, brushing his hair out of his eyes. 'We'd better go inside, darling. It's beginning to rain again.'

'Like it raining, like it, like it,' Timmy shouted, and pulled away from her and ran back to the leaves, stamping on them.

'It isn't good for you,' June said, and went over and scooped him up and held him high in the air. 'You'll catch a horrid cold if you get wet. Let's go inside and I'll play Lego with you and we'll all be dry. Come on.' And she turned back to Liz.

'Look, Liz, why shouldn't you go to Majorca with Nick, if he wants you to? Timmy can come to me, or if you'd rather I'll come and stay here with him. You need a holiday – do you all the good in the world.'

'Well, I suppose it would be nice. I could ask Nick if I could take Tim with us, of course . . . .'

'That's a thought,' June said as casually as she could. Easy, easy, her little voice whispered. Don't say the wrong thing, don't block her, easy does it . . . be careful . . . .

'But you know how he is,' Liz was clearly unhappy, clearly in a genuine dilemma, and for a brief moment June felt compunction for her streaking her concern for herself. 'It's not that he doesn't care for Timmy, of course. It isn't that.'

'Of course it isn't.'

'It's just that – you know, small children – and he's a hyperactive type. Timmy always was.'

'Oh, yes,' June said fervently. 'Bright, that's the thing. Bright children are always a handful. It's lovely.'

'Yes, lovely,' Liz said, and made a small grimace. 'It's no use kidding myself. Nick isn't crazy about him, never did like small children, Nick. He'll get better about him as Timmy gets older, of course, but right now . . . and a holiday would be good. I know he'd take me.'

'So why not go? It'd be no trouble to me.'

'I know,' Liz said with a sudden blaze of savagery in her voice. 'That's the bloody trouble, isn't it? And for Christ's sake, don't look at me like that. He'll have to learn sooner or later that people swear, and I'm his mother and I'm people, okay? I'm his mother and the sooner he knows what I am the better. If you had your way you'd rear him on Christopher Robin and Mabel Lucie Atwell and is there honey still for tea and all the rest of that sentimental crap. This is 1984, ducky, and people swear in front of children these days, and do a bloody sight more too, and the sooner you get that into your head the better for all of us.'

June stood blankly listening as Liz, still shouting at her, pushed open the front door of the flat, and then followed her in. Not a word, take it easy, she'll blow it out, not a word, her inner voice whispered. Just be quiet.

'I know you think I'm not fit to look after him, but Timmy doesn't, does he? Who loves Timmy?' Liz whirled and seized the child beneath the arms, tossing him high into the air so that he squealed and June watched with her eyes wide and her lips clamped tightly shut. 'Who loves Timmy?'

'Mummy loves Timmy!' the child roared. 'Mummy loves Timmy!'

'And who loves Mummy?'

'Timmy loves Mummy, Timmy loves Mummy!' bawled Timmy obligingly and shouted with laughter, and Liz pulled him close and hugged him tightly, staring at June over his shoulders with her eyes glittering. 'Timmy loves Mummy,' she said and it was an insult aimed at her and meant to hurt, and June knew it and felt the intended pain. 'Timmy loves Mummy.'

'Of course he does,' June said equably. 'Do you want some tea? I'll put the kettle on,' and she moved across the cluttered kitchen towards the sink.

'No, goddamn it,' Liz shouted, and put Timmy down so

abruptly that he began to cry. 'Whose goddammed kitchen is it? If I want tea, I'll make it myself.'

June stood very still and then turned back to the kitchen table and silently sat down. Timmy was standing in the middle of the floor whimpering and it took every atom of self-control she had not to go and pick him up, to croon to him and hug him and make him happy again.

Behind her Liz crashed among the pots on the stove, and then filled the kettle and came back, pushing past June to get to the dresser in the corner where the mugs were.

'Damn you, June,' she said viciously as she went by and thumped her shoulder, painfully, but June sat tight, saying nothing. 'You're the only person I know can make me act this way, you know that? The only bloody person. Even if lousy stinking Barry walked in here I wouldn't get so mad at him as I get at you.'

It was safe to talk now. June knew the pattern of Liz's anger, knew how fast it blew itself out. 'I know, love,' she said, and looked over her shoulder at her and tried to grin, and Liz looked back at her, her face twisted with exasperation. 'It's hell needing people, isn't it? I need you and Timmy, and there are times I could kill you for that.'

'Yes,' Liz said. 'Yes. So could I. The way you look at Timmy wears me out. And it isn't going to get any easier, is it?'

'I don't know,' June said, and bent her head, and her hair moved on her neck, parting to show the vulnerable nape. 'I don't know. How can I know?'

'Make the lousy tea,' Liz said brusquely. 'Bloody kettle'll boil in a minute.' And she went to Timmy, still standing snivelling in the middle of the room, to take off his raincoat and sou'wester and wellington boots.

The afternoon slid into its usual pattern, with Liz sitting at the table reading the paper while June helped Timmy make a Lego building, and then June washing up the tea things and discreetly tidying the messy kitchen while Liz sat on reading bits to her from the paper and talking about the people in the flat upstairs and the noise they made, and Nick and his business, none of which June really listened to; she didn't have to. Liz just needed to talk at her as much as she needed to be in the same room with Timmy as often and as much as possible.

She said not another word about the proposed visit to

Majorca, nor about the plan she had devised that morning to persuade Liz to go away for a few days on her own. She didn't have to; for once events were conspiring on her behalf rather than against her. Liz would go to Majorca and leave Timmy to be looked after by June. There was no doubt of that. Liz knew too; that was why she had become so suddenly, furiously, angry. All June had to do was sit tight and say nothing, and she'd have Timmy to herself for a full week. The idea was so exciting she couldn't even look at him.

5

'Truly, there'll be no problems,' Jessie said. 'Peter has a committee meeting tonight, and Mark's never at home these days – lives at his girlfriend's place mostly, as far as I can tell – so my time's my own. I want to stay. I'll be livid if you won't let me.'

'As long as there are no dramas,' Ben said, and peered into the bottom drawer of his desk. 'Damn it, I had a bottle of sherry here, I know I did. It tastes like French polish but it'd be better than nothing.'

'I found it,' Jessie said. 'It's over here, but I thought you might like this better on the nights you work late,' and she opened the stationery cupboard in the corner with the key from her ring, and took out a bottle of gin and cans of tonic water.

'You're bad news, Jessie, you know that? You'll make life much too comfortable here and then I'll never get home.'

'No dramas, please,' Jessie said, and after a moment he laughed, but the pause was an appreciable one and she was frightened. Stop it, you idiot, she told herself, stop it. Work, that's all it is. Work. 'There's some ice in the mortuary. Do you want some?'

'No thank you. Not mortuary ice. I'll do without it if there's nothing else.'

'It's only in the fridge,' Jessie said. 'Not in among the corpses, though I suppose . . . .'

'I know that.' He took the glass from her, and sniffed it appreciatively. 'Good girl. This'll pickle my gut nicely. Of course I know that, but I've never been able to fancy eating or drinking anything that's been around the mortuary. Ever since my first student days. They used to send into the hospital all the harvest festival stuff from the churches, for the poor impoverished nurses, you know? Trouble was the girls never saw it because the admin. staff used to snaffle the lot. They'd have it put in the mortuary till they had a chance to take it home when no one was looking, because that was the only place big enough and cool enough to keep it, there was so much – and the nurses used to get us out of the medical school to go and liberate the apples and pears and so forth. It put me off fruit for years. It's the same with ice.'

'I'd feel the same if that had happened to me,' she said, and twisted her own glass between her hands, watching the bubbles of tonic move lazily against the sides. 'I don't go there unless I have to. It does worry me a bit – that's why I try to be off-hand and use the fridge there as though it were the one in my kitchen at home. Silly, really, though.'

'Not silly at all. Death scares everyone. It's only idiots and liars who deny it. We spend most of our time trying to pretend it never happens, and you can't do that in a mortuary. Keep out, if you want to, Jessie. Let old Tomsett have it to himself. He likes to be melancholy and contemplate mortality.'

'That child this morning – that upset me.'

'Untimely death,' Ben said. 'Yes, it's upset me too. It always does, but children are the worst.'

'What happened to her?'

'Don't know. I mean, I know what happened, but not why. Heart failure, and nothing to say why. Bit of oedema at the lung bases – tissue sponginess and so forth – but she seemed a fit enough specimen. Unknown causes, I imagine the coroner will have to say.'

'How old was she?'

'Twelve.' He looked at her briefly, and then away. 'Today, as it happens. It was her birthday.'

Jessie's face creased. 'Oh, those poor parents!'

Ben smiled a little crookedly. 'How like you to be more bothered about her family than about her!'

'But she doesn't know, does she? She's dead. But her mother . . . you always remember what it was like producing a child, when a birthday happens. I remember about Mark being born every January. And when I smell mimosa. My room was full of it. And the one who died. I remember her too, every Easter and when there are daffodils – she was stillborn but I still remember. So, poor mother. It'll be hell for her.'

He was looking at her curiously. 'You needn't worry about her. She died last year according to Dan Stewart. I was concerned about the relatives too so I asked him – I didn't know you'd had a stillborn child.'

'Why should you? It's . . . there's no connection with my work, after all.'

'I didn't mean to intrude. I'm sorry.'

'You weren't intruding. Just probing. Oh, damn, I'm sorry, I didn't mean that. It sounded nasty. Did it? I hope not. I just mean . . . don't feel bad because you didn't know, because I didn't tell you. Anyway, it's all right now. I don't mind any more. It was fourteen years ago – a long time.'

'But you haven't forgotten.'

There was a little silence and then she said, 'No, I haven't forgotten. Um . . . what do you want me to deal with first, Ben? The batch of Contravert or the control animals, or perhaps the . . . .'

'Oh. Yes. Look, are you sure it's going to be all right to stay? I don't want to start the injections, you see, if we can't finish them. And that could take us well up to, I don't know, eleven or so, maybe later.'

'I told you, no hassle. I'll send a message to Peter, and that'll be that. What about you? Can you stay that late? Or do you want me to deal with the first bit on my own? I could, once you'd told me what you want.'

'I know you could.' He smiled, a wide glittering smile at which she could have warmed her hands. 'You're the best woman I've ever had here for doing as she's asked, but also for using a bit of intelligence to modify instructions when she has to. Bloody marvellous lady, that's you. But you aren't going to be on your own. I wouldn't miss out on this for the world. I can stay. I've talked to June, and she's baby-sitting for her sister tonight. So that's all right.'

'She'll feel better tomorrow, then.'

'I hope so,' he said after a moment, and then turned back to his desk. He hadn't meant to tell Jessie about June and her problems; he'd always believed very firmly in keeping work and home as two totally separate matters, but Jessie, after all, was Jessie. A sensible, listening lady, someone who was a mature and intelligent person in her own right, easy to talk to, and he'd told her months ago about June's obsessive pregnancy hunger and the way she used her nephew to comfort herself for her lack of babies of her own. He had told her not because she'd been curious or prying but because he'd been so desperately tired after a particularly bad night with June that he had had to tell someone, and Jessie had been there and a willing listener, and blessedly silent. She'd made no banal comments about one-day-it'll-just happen, nor offered silly advice about adoption. She'd just listened and nodded and said simply that she was sorry, and that had helped him enormously.

She was the only person he had ever told about his feelings, or about June's feelings; he had always rather scorned the clichéd idea that a trouble shared was a trouble eased – he had seen that as self-indulgence, a mean desire to load one's own misery on to someone else's shoulders – but he knew better now. Talking to Jessie had indeed helped him feel better about June, and tonight, discovering that Jessie too had had troubles having children had made her seem an even more trusted confidante. But they didn't have to talk about June and her behaviour any more for him to gain comfort from her; they had reached the stage of companionable shorthand speech, and that was most comforting of all.

'So!' Jessie set down her glass and folded her arms and looked at him. 'The others'll be in here soon to report before they go for the night. Is there time to tell me what you want me to do first? Or do we wait till they've all gone? It's . . . let me see. It's almost half past five. Another half hour, and that'll be that.'

'We'll wait,' he said, and reached for the top folder of a pile on the corner of the cluttered desk. 'But you can read this while you wait. It'll give you some more background. I'll go and do the checking rounds. Use my chair – I won't be long.' And he left her there, touching her shoulder companionably as he went past her. She managed to pretend he hadn't, but it wasn't easy. Being touched by Ben was becoming a rather agreeable experience, and as such, not to be dwelt upon when it happened.

She read the contents of the folder carefully; she knew a certain amount about what he was trying to do and felt she understood it pretty well, in broad principles if not in great detail. The years of training before she married had left her with a mind that was geared to understand biological theory, albeit a bit rusty from long disuse. But now, reading, she felt her thinking slip easily into the right grooves.

In essence, his theory was a simple one: ever since

interferon, the natural disease-fighter every living body has, had first been discovered, he had argued that it should be possible to stimulate its production in a predictable and reliable manner in order to give protection against all viral infections.

'Interferon,' he had explained to her, when she had first come to work with him. 'It is not one substance, you see. It's a group of proteins that body cells produce in response to invasion by a virus. They stop the virus replicating, and so prevent the illness it causes. Each type of cell produces its own type of interferon protein, so even if we could synthesize the stuff − which we can't at present − you'd need so many different types it would be impossible to use them therapeutically. And it's a treatment I'm after, Jessie, that's the long and short of it. A treatment.'

So, he'd gone on, he'd decided the answer had to be finding a substance that behaved as though it were an infective agent, but wasn't and therefore could do no harm to body cells, but which would trigger them into producing large amounts of the different proteins in interferon when it was needed. 'If I can do that, Jessie,' he'd said, 'then I've got the equivalent of antibiotics, only more so, because bacteria develop a resistance to antibiotics, of course, and you have to keep creating new ones to deal with new strains of bug. But my idea is to find something that doesn't respond to specific bacteria, or more particularly viruses, but to each cell's own needs. Do you see?'

She did, almost, though it was a struggle, but he seemed not to notice she was floundering just a bit.

'But if interferon's made by the body's own cells when viruses infect, why do you need to trigger production?' She had asked hesitantly, uncomfortable about displaying her ignorance, but wanting to understand. 'Don't the viruses do that anyway?'

'Absolutely!' he'd said, delighted by the question. 'Absolutely, but it seems to be a bit haphazard. Well, not really, of course: biological processes are never haphazard, but we do know it isn't always adequate. The most that seems to happen in nature is that a body attacked by one kind of virus won't be attacked by another at the same time because of the interferon production started off by the first virus to get to the scene. People don't get . . . oh, chicken pox and flu together, do they? And that's why: the chicken pox, if they get it first, stops them going down with the flu virus. What I want to do is produce something that'll be so powerful it'll repel the first invading virus as well as any subsequent ones. Do you see?'

She did, hazily, and she'd left the laboratory that day to go through to the library before going home, to collect all she could read on the subject of immunity, interferon and viruses in general, and for weeks after that her head had buzzed with information about polynucleotydes, phytohaemagglutinin, ribonucleic acid and deoxyribonucleic acid, lysozyme and heaven knows what else – but she had emerged with some grasp of what it was he was trying to do. To find a substance which would act as though it were a disease-causing virus and yet be harmless, and which would on introduction to a human body produce enough interferon to prevent potentially lethal viruses from having an effect – that was his search.

And it was a marvellously exciting search, she had decided, breathtaking in its possibilities; a cure-all for infections, no less, that was what he was seeking in his ramshackle animal room and ill-equipped laboratory, and she was to be part of it. Her spirits had boiled up into a froth of excitement that had made her go rushing into the laboratory one morning almost ablaze with it, to find him asleep with his head on his desk because he'd worked so late the night before, and hadn't got round to going home at all. And been deflated by his reaction, because he'd woken bad-tempered and very depressed. He'd realized during that long night's work that all he'd done for the past year had been useless.

'I've painted myself into a bloody corner, Jessie,' he'd said, staring at her from red-rimmed eyes. 'The last batch of the lousy stuff was contaminated. A year's work up the spout, would you believe? An entire bloody *year*. I'm giving up – it's a waste of time and money and effort and . . . I wish I'd never bloody well started it.'

It had taken her the best part of a week to coax him out of that crisis and by that time all her own blazing excitement had settled to a dull glow. She was still excited, but she no longer imagined the answer would come any minute, or even any year. The search and the work would go on for heaven knew how long – and, she realized then, that pleased her. Because the longer the work went on, the longer he would need her to work with him and the happier she would remain – but that was something not to be thought about, and she hadn't, settling instead to the steady day in day out grind of keeping the normal work of the laboratory going, and the research ticking over alongside it. It was no wonder that they worked till half way through the night on so many evenings each week. There was no other time available to do what was necessary, for his research was very much a side-line, not his main responsibility. But she was happy, and so, as far as she could tell, was he. And that was all she asked of life now.

Now, reading through the folder he'd given her while he moved around in the laboratory outside – she could hear his voice and Harry Gentle's, and Peter Moscrop's and their occasional laughter, and it was a good sound – she got her thoughts organized about the work that lay ahead. The animals were to be divided into three groups: the control, called X group, to be given nothing; the A group to be given the virus strain they were currently using, and the B group to be given that and also doses of the new batch of Contravert. It was an interesting new batch, based on prostaglandins (Ben had decided that was a useful line of enquiry, because of the role of prostaglandins in the inflammatory process), and they had plenty of it; there had always been problems in the past about finding an adequate source of supply, but now he was using material derived from placentae he was collecting from the maternity wards. There had been a time when they were collected to be sold to a pharmaceutical company for use in preparing a range of pills for hormone therapy, but that deal had ended when the company had found it cheaper to use a product imported from Holland. Ben had found out almost by accident that this valuable resource was being incinerated, in his own department's special disposal units, and had seized on it with enormous satisfaction, arranging to have the material he needed extracted by a small drug firm on the other side of the county which did the work for a remarkably low rate. This batch of his Contravert – and Jessie thought, surprised it had never occurred to her before, I must ask him why he named it that – was the first to use his new supply of the basic material. Altogether, it was going to be a fascinating stage of the research: a newer, much purer and therefore stronger drug, a selection of animals that really were at the peak of health – Jessie took great pride in that, for they were her special care – and plenty of time to do the necessary work.

She closed the folder with a sigh of sheer contentment as she

heard the far door to the main laboratory slam shut behind
Harry Gentle's shouted goodnight and Ben's footsteps
clattering over the terrazzo floor back to the office. The
evening ahead promised to be precisely the sort of evening she
most enjoyed. Let Peter fiddle with his photographs and his
committee meetings; let Mark spend all his time wrapped in
his girlfriend's arms and legs; she had much better things to do
than sit at home and wait for them.

6

Edna put the last spike of potatoes in the oven, turned the heat to 450 degrees and prayed no one would notice how late she'd put them on. As long as none of the teachers ate the horrible things – and they were always on diets, the stupid madams – maybe no one would notice they weren't cooked properly, and with no one ever paying any attention to anything the children said about their food, maybe she'd get away with it. But the way her luck was running she probably wouldn't; she got away with nothing these days, nothing at all.

Across the big cluttered kitchen Nancy McGrath was whipping up egg whites furiously, trying to get the froth to stand before the milk boiled; she was one of those people who never got things wrong, never had to get away with anything. She planned every detail of her work, never wasting a second, and Edna hated her for that. No one should ever be so well organized; it made everyone else, particularly herself, look stupid. And as Nancy looked up and caught her watching her she ducked her head and went back to the vegetable sink to start cleaning it. Once she'd done that, maybe they'd let her go, and she wouldn't be here when they came for the potatoes for their party, and then no one could say anything to her.

'Have you got the second batch of sausages ready to go in?' Nancy asked sharply.

'Sausages?' Edna said blankly. 'Was I supposed to do them an' all?'

'Oh, for Gawd's sake!' Nancy's movements never faltered even while she launched herself into one of her usual naggings at Edna. 'Have I got to do everything around here? Of course you were! I've got all these invalid diets to do and I can't do the party suppers as well, and it's not that hard to do, now is it? Baked potatoes with grated cheese, hot sausages, cups of broth. I suppose you've not grated the cheese either? I might have known it! Oh, get on with the sink, for heaven's sake. I'll take these up and then come and do your work as well as my own. I usually do – and I'm not putting up with it much longer. You come late and you do nothing – I'll be telling Miss Cooper, that I will . . .' and she stacked her tray with the glasses of egg nog and sprinkled nutmeg over each one with a deft twist of her wrist and swept out, leaving Edna mulishly washing up at the sink, and not doing it very well.

I'll tell them, I'll go into Miss Cooper's office and I'll say, now Madam, I'm not one to bear tales, really I'm not, as well you know, but really, what that woman in your kitchen gets up to, with her little parcels in her bag and all that, thinks I don't see, but I do, and Miss Cooper will say, oh, dear, Edna, how *dreadful*, sit down and tell me all about it – and her movements became more desultory still as she slid into a very satisfying vision of her whispered conversation with Miss Cooper about Nancy McGrath.

Up in Rose Dormitory Miss Cooper was checking the children, looking down their throats with a torch, a spatula and an air of great knowledgeableness even though she wasn't quite sure what she was looking for. But someone had to do it, with Mary Spain up to her ears and over looking after the children in the sick bay, and the overflow they'd had to put into Jasmine Dorm.

The girls stared solemnly back at her as they stood in front of her and one or two whimpered and tried to gag as she pushed their tongues down, but she glared back at them very firmly indeed and they soon stopped their fussing. Stopping their fussing, she told herself, as she patted Vanessa's shoulder and made her give way to Emma, that's what it's all about. They're far too suggestible, wretched girls, and they mustn't be allowed to get away with it.

'I feel awful, Miss Cooper, really I do,' Emma said in a shrill little whine, and looked at her mournfully with wide damp eyes. 'My legs are all wobbly and I think I'm just like Penelope was, and Lucy, and I want to . . . .'

'Nonsense,' Miss Cooper said firmly. 'Let me look at your throat, and we'll soon see what's going on there. Open up! Wider . . . that's it.'

Did the throat look inflamed? It was hard to tell. The child certainly seemed hot and sweaty (Miss Cooper could smell the faintly acrid scent of her) but the heating was turned up to its usual November level, even in this unseasonably warm weather, and she herself was feeling rather warm. She stared, frowning, at the pink cavern with the wobbling tongue floor, and tried to decide what to do. Allow the child to go to Miss Spain in the sick bay and she'd increase this silly drama they were all making, but insist she went down to join the others at the fireworks party and then discover that she did in fact have the blasted flu and she'd spread it even further – bloody hell, she thought viciously, and withdrew the spatula as Emma began to retch rather alarmingly.

'Well, Emma, I don't think there is anything in the least wrong with you, but if you want to make a fuss out of a little cold and go to bed and miss the fireworks, then it's up to you. No one will pay you any attention whatsoever, I can assure you, if you stay up here. Go to bed then, if you want to and think of all of us having a lovely time. There are baked potatoes and sausages . . . .'

But none of the children reacted with the expected oohs of greedy pleasure; they just stood clustered round her looking sideways at Emma as she went across to her bed and sat on it, and though they did not move Dorothy Cooper felt the frisson that went through them, almost saw it as though a wind had whispered over a cornfield and made the stalks shiver.

'My boyfriend Peter told me that Miranda Hallam was dead,' Vanessa said suddenly, not looking at Dorothy Cooper, but keeping her eyes fixed on Emma sitting drooping on her bed. 'He goes to school with a boy whose dad is a lawyer who looks after Miranda's money. He said Miranda was quite rich because her Mum and Dad were dead, and her Auntie, and he said she died and now no one knows where her money's going to go.'

'You are much too young to be talking of having boyfriends, Vanessa Maxwell, and it's exceedingly cheap of you into the bargain. What would your mother think of such things if she heard you?'

'She likes him,' Vanessa said, and still didn't look at her. 'His Dad's rolling in loot, she says, and she likes Peter. I've got a good chance with him. And Peter said Miranda died here, and you never told anyone.'

'Rubbish,' Miss Cooper said loudly and pulled the smallest child in the dorm, eleven-year-old Abigail, towards her. She hadn't meant to be rough but her alarm made her movements jerky, and the child was startled and began to wail, her face creasing piteously.

'Miranda had the bed next to me, Miranda had the bed next to me!' she wept, and suddenly sat down on the floor. 'My legs feel funny. I want Mummy . . .' and the tears began to flow in real earnest. 'I want to go home to my Mummy . . . .'

Now the frisson could be clearly seen as a couple of the children shrank away from Abigail on the floor and began to cry too, and Vanessa stood smiling to herself, pleased with the effect she'd created, as others began to whimper.

'Vanessa, you are a very stupid person,' Miss Cooper said furiously. 'Upsetting people with such nonsense! No one is dead and . . . .'

'Miranda was in the next bed to me,' bawled Abigail. 'I don't want to die like Miranda . . .' and Miss Cooper got to her feet, her face white with rage.

'Silence, all of you! One more word of this, and none of you go to the fireworks party, do you hear me? None of you! This is ridiculous rubbish, and I won't have another word of it.'

'What's the matter with Lucy and Penelope, then?' Vanessa was looking at her now, her chin up and her face smooth with insolence. 'They wouldn't have taken them to hospital if they weren't ill, would they? And the sick bay's full and people are in Jasmine being sick and saying their legs hurt and they wouldn't be if it was all rubbish, would they? I want to phone my Mum and tell her this place is a charnel house and she'd better take me home.'

'A charnel . . . .' Dorothy had to make a physical effort not to lash out at the girl with her hands. 'I never heard such rubbish in my life.'

'You keep saying that,' Vanessa said, and now the insolence was even more marked. 'But Penny and Lucy aren't rubbish, and they're in the hospital and that isn't rubbish and . . . .'

'Go away before I lose my temper with you,' Dorothy Cooper cried. 'If you want to go home in the middle of term and ruin your O level work, that's up to you, I wash my hands of you. Not that you'd get through anyway – you are a singularly stupid girl!'

'Much I care,' Vanessa said and went hipping over to the door. 'I'm not ending up a sour old virgin like some I could mention so I don't need your rotten exams.'

It was hopeless, Dorothy realized. There was nothing she

could do to stop the wailing, and she settled for physical action, harrying Abigail to her feet and half-dragging, half-carrying her to her bed, and sending the other girls downstairs to get ready for the evening's fireworks, before going to find Mary Spain to get Emma's and Abigail's temperatures checked. If they really were ill, and she had to get that bloody Sayer woman out again, that really would put the tin hat on it; every time she'd come this week – and it had had to be appallingly often – her face had looked more smug than ever. It was more than flesh and blood could bear, and at the moment Dorothy Cooper was very sensitive flesh and blood indeed.

'I don't like the way Pauline Barnes is breathing,' Mary Spain said as she came into the sick bay, and she made no effort to drop her voice and Dorothy again felt a surge of fury; was everyone determined to turn this minor run of flu into a dramatic epic in three acts? She frowned but Mary Spain, her face flushed and her hair in a tangle over her damp forehead, seemed unaware of her anger. 'It's the way they used to go when I was doing my fevers, the polios – I don't like it. I can't take the responsibility, Miss Cooper, and that's the truth of it. I'm SEN, you know, not SRN, and there's limits to what I can do on my own.'

'Do keep your voice down, Miss Spain!' Dorothy whispered furiously. 'I've got enough on my hands without the rest of them flying into hysterical panics. You've got Miss Ventnor and Miss Holly to help you – do stop fussing so much! And I'm here too. I can leave Miss Johnson and Miss Charring to deal with the fireworks party – and I wish to heaven I'd never agreed to that in the first place – so what do you want me to do?'

'I want you to send Pauline to hospital,' Mary Spain said, and set her lips in a sulky line, knowing the sort of response she'd get, but not caring. 'I can't be responsible, and that's a fact. It's no use you pretending there's nothing going on here. We've got a bad epidemic and I don't know what it is any more than you do, and that's the truth of it. It could be anything – polio, anything.'

'They've all had polio vaccine,' Dorothy said, looking over her shoulder at the bed in the corner of the sick bay where the child Pauline was lying. 'I don't accept them if they haven't. So it can't be that. All *right*. If you can't cope, I'll get better help for you. I'll call a nursing agency.'

'No,' Mary Spain said. 'No, Miss Cooper, I'm sorry, but I'm not staying here to be responsible, and I'm not waiting for any other nurses, and there you have it. That girl ought to be in hospital.'

'I'll take her,' Dorothy said, and now she sounded weary rather than angry. She'd done all she could to stop them all getting so excited and dramatic; no one knew better than she did how quickly hysterical notions could spread through a community made up largely of adolescent females. She had been quite certain that most of the illness was simple flu and the rest was tension and over-reaction fed into the children by Dr Sayer; but now, faced with a clearly frightened Mary Spain and a school full of children who were getting more and more agitated – and she thought venomously of the hateful Vanessa for a moment – she would have to give in. The time for firmness matched with soothing reassurance had gone. And she went down to her office to phone the hospital and explain that she had another child in a bad way, and was going to bring her in her car right away. They wouldn't be best pleased either, she thought as she went down the stairs; they'll fuss above having a referral from Susan Sayer, but I'm damned if I'm going to talk to that bloody woman tonight, I'm damned if I am.

'It's not poliomyelitis, I'm sure of that,' Lyall Davies said. 'Saw a lot of it, you know, in the States, when I was there in the fifties. Bad times, they were, bad times. You young men can have no idea what medicine was like in those days there, in the South. People died of the most appalling fevers you ever saw. Rocky Mountain Spotted, dengue, polio, the lot. Appalling. And I'm sure this isn't polio – not even sure that the paralysis is a real one, d'you see. Lots of girls together too much, get notions. Remember what happened at the Royal Free twenty-odd years ago? Intelligent enough, you might think, student nurses, but there it was, went down like flies they did, complained of paralysis, the lot, but most of it was hysteria.'

'That's what they said at the time. Later they agreed there had been an organic basis,' Dan Stewart said, irritated with the man even though what he was saying meshed with his own opinion; stupid old woman, he told himself.

51

'Organic basis of course!' Lyall Davies said. 'I'm not denying that. I'm just saying that there's an element of hysteria here. Psychological overlay, what? Yes, overlay.' He rolled the word round his tongue, relishing it. 'They get notions, girls do, make up their minds they've got something they haven't. Yes, there's an infection here, an enterovirus, I'd say, some diarrhoea, bit of nausea, some upper respiratory involvement, not all that unusual, you'll agree. But that's all – their reflexes are normal enough, don't you see, and you don't get the same response twice in a row when you examine 'em.'

'I know,' Dan said. 'But all the same, I don't like it. They've just brought in another from the school, and she's showing definite breathing problems. Could be some bulbar involvement. Can you arrange life support? Just in case?'

'Life support . . . trumpery language they use these days.' Lyall Davies shook his head and tutted. 'We've got a respirator here, of course – had ours for years, a good reliable piece of equipment too, not one of these fancy new jobs. They've got those at Farborough and Doxford, of course, but we don't have 'em here and wouldn't. Not part of our grading, d'you see. And you won't need such a thing anyway, you mark my words. You can have it if you want it, of course. Here to help, you know, always here to help. But I'll lay you odds you won't need it. Now, you've got the run of the place, Stewart, you know that, I'm off now, my grandson's fireworks party, don't you know, they won't have it without me, and there it is, but you stay here as long as you like. The boy I've got at the moment seems a pretty good chap for an Indian, Sanjib. That's his first name, you understand, but I can't get his surname round my poor old English tongue and he doesn't seem to mind so that's what we call him. You want anything, the nurses'll get Dr Sanjib out for you. But do remember it's Guy Fawkes tomorrow, won't you? Most of the fireworks parties'll be tonight, seeing it's a Sunday, so they'll be busy in Accident and Emergency and I've said they can borrow Sanjib if they're pushed. Goodnight, m'boy. I dare say you'll find your little girls are just fussing you.' And he went, leaving Dan standing in the corridor outside the ward, and chewing his lower lip.

Up to a point he agreed with the old boy. He might just be sitting out the days till his retirement, but still he'd had a lot of experience in his day and he must have had some fire in his belly once to have been appointed to a consultancy at all, but all the same . . . he shook his head and went into the ward, to find Dorothy Cooper sitting alone in the sister's office, the phone clamped to her ear.

'Yes, yes,' she was saying. 'Yes, absolutely. Once the display's over get them fed and to bed as soon as you can. And let them have their radios on if they want to. The more they've got to distract them the less likely they'll get to be agitated. Now, are you sure that you . . . fine. Thanks Wynn, thank God I've got you to keep your head there! I'll be back as soon as I possibly can.'

She cradled the phone and looked up at Dan and made a face. 'It's beginning to look as though Sayer's right, isn't it?'

'I'm still not sure,' Dan said. 'Lyall Davies thinks it's just an enterovirus of some sort.'

'Entero . . . .'

'A virus spread through the gut. They've had diarrhoea as well as the running noses and sore throats and tight chests, haven't they? And there's been some sickness as well.'

'Diarrhoea.' Dorothy dismissed that with a wave of her hand. 'That's always happening. Happened to me too, all this week, but it's nothing to make much of. I've had worse and I do know there's a lot of it about. Saw a piece in the paper – local GPs run off their feet apparently.'

'Yes, that's true, but we know pretty well what that is. It's not associated with these other symptoms your girls are getting, that's the thing. Especially not the muscular weakness.'

There was a little silence and then Dorothy said, 'I'm getting really worried, Dr Stewart. Do you think that child Miranda could . . . .'

He shook his head, not looking at her, the same anxiety chewing at the back of his own mind. 'I don't know. It could be. I didn't think so at the time, but . . . .'

'But Sayer made a fuss, so you agreed with me. And I could have been wrong.'

'Something like that.' He made a face and then said violently, 'Oh, shit!'

'That doesn't help.' She stood up. 'I'd better see how Pauline is. I gather Lucy and Penelope are doing well enough, but they weren't too happy about the child I just brought in. Will you come and see too?'

'Not much I can do,' Dan said. 'I want to see some of the path. reports. They've taken some swabs for culture – there might be something in them. And I've got to think about what to do about the school. I might have to send them home, you know, Miss Cooper. Close you down for a while. I'm sorry.'

'I know,' she said bleakly. 'I expect you will. I thought things were going too well. Only three empty places this term, the first time for years it's been so good. I thought, the way money is these days, no one'll be able to send their girls to me even though I'm one of the cheaper schools, but there it was, getting better. And now this. It's not fair, is it?'

He grinned for a moment. 'You sound like one of your own girls – not fair, not fair.'

'Do I? Well, there isn't all that much difference, is there? Except they've got time on their side. They're young.' And she turned to go to the door, but Sister appeared there, and stood staring at them both with a portentous look on her round face.

'Miss Cooper? You're the teacher, are you, from the school? Yes. Well, I'm afraid you'll have to talk to the parents of the Barnes child. We did the best we could . . . .'

'You did . . . what?' Dorothy said, and stared at her, her mouth half-open. 'What do you mean, talk to the parents of the child?'

'We couldn't get her into the respirator in time. I'm sorry. Stopped breathing, do you see. It's as well, perhaps. By the time we'd got her in it my guess is there'd have been brain damage. Anyway, there it is. I'll arrange for the necessary formalities and so forth – there'll be an inquest, of course, only in here an hour or so, so that's got to be dealt with – and leave the parents to you, if I may? Pity, isn't it? Children dying – it always upsets people so much.'

7

It upset the whole town. It really was quite remarkable how quickly the news spread; Dorothy Cooper would have been gratified to know just how much the people of the town knew about her school and how interested they were to talk about the happenings there, although she would have been less happy to hear the relish with which they passed on the information they were able to glean.

'Dying like flies,' the school milkman told every customer he could bring to the door on a trumped-up excuse as he made his slow way down Petts' Hill to the town centre. 'Rushin' 'em into the hospital fast as they can go, and they're all dead when they get there. Shocking, ain't it? Young girls like that.' And his eyes gleamed with lubricous excitement as his customers stopped to gossip with each other over the garden hedges and he went scuttling on, his very bottles glittering with the drama of it all, to spread the news further still.

At the hospital there was less excitement – death was, after all, a commonplace of the normal day – but certainly there was curiosity. Few of the nursing staff could remember the last time a respirator had been needed in the place; usually people showing signs of respiratory failure were bundled off as fast as ambulances could carry them to the Communicable Diseases Hospital at Farborough thirty miles down the motorway where they had modern life support systems, or to the neurological unit at Doxford, equally well-equipped. Minster was, after all, only a small local general hospital and did not run to the luxury of an intensive care unit, but as the day sister on the ward where Pauline had died said to the yawning night sister as she collected the report, 'That must have been one hell of a fast bug.' She cocked a sharp eye at the other woman. 'I did my fevers when I was at Great Ormond Street, of course.' She never missed an opportunity of reminding everyone how exalted a training she had had. 'And we saw a few of these bulbar paralyses, but we always had time to get them well ventilated. This one just collapsed, you say?'

'Just collapsed,' Night Sister said, sniffy at the implied rebuke. 'And yes, it *is* a fast bug. You can talk to Dr Stewart if you want to compare notes about the better quality bugs you had at Great Ormond Street. We had bugs in Leicester, too, of course, when I did my fevers, but they were just *ordinary* cases. So I never saw one like last night's. Child was barely in the ward and she was moribund. G'morning. Have a good day.' And she went to sit over her breakfast coffee and gossip with the remainder of the senior night staff about that bitch on Lyall Davies's ward and her snide comments.

Jessie, sitting at the next table over her own breakfast – with Peter away in London, and Mark never eating breakfast anyway, it was easier to come to the hospital to have her own meal than to bother to make something at home – heard the rumble of the night staff's conversation and at first paid no attention to them. She just sat staring sightlessly over the edge of the coffee cup she held in both hands, her elbows propped on the table, thinking about Peter.

That row they had had on Saturday when she had finally put her foot down and told him that no matter what he said or did she wasn't coming to his conference with him had been horrendous. They had never been a couple who argued, she and Peter. He had grumbled, God knew; all their married life there had been Peter's grumbling like an obbligato in the bass of a piece of familiar music to which you never really listened, but there had never been rows. She had been too pliant for that, always bending to what he wanted, silently letting him have his own way, never really saying what she wanted or how she wanted it. It had been less trouble that way, and it had actually given her what she did want more than anything else, which was peace and quiet. But for the first time there was something she had wanted more; to stay and work with Ben through the trial they had at last started was the most important thing in the world to her and nothing Peter could say or do would keep her from it.

So she had been adamant. Not that she had said that to him; she had just quietly said that she wasn't coming to London, thanks, and kept on repeating it as his grumbling turned into loud complaint and then built to a roar of fury. She had sat there at the dining table and let him shout and done nothing and said nothing until at last he'd blown out his rage and gone to bed.

And the next morning she had calmly packed his bag for the week, making sure he had plenty of clean socks and shirts – it never occurred to Peter that he could wash such things for himself in hotel bathrooms – and even took his car round to the garage to fill the tank, and had stood there at the door waiting to be kissed as he left; and he had shouted at her all through his breakfast and was still shouting as he marched through the door – kissing her cheek on the way as he always did, of course – and got into his car. But at last he had gone, white with fury and self-righteous sulkiness, and she had felt rather sorry for him.

Poor old Peter, how could he understand? He'd get over it, of course, once he got to London and his conference, and found lots of boring men to talk to all day and drink with all evening, probably going to one of those Soho shows he thought so sophisticated. He'd be happy enough when he got back, and she'd be extra nice to him and that would be that. And she would, for once, have done what *she* wanted. And she curled her fingers more tightly round her coffee cup and let her tight shoulders relax. A whole week on her own lay ahead; it was extraordinary how good that prospect made her feel. An uninterrupted day's work to look forward to, and four more to follow it. Lovely.

And then she became aware of the conversation at the next table, and her attention switched at once to what was being said and the implication of it for her own working day.

'Barely eleven she was, and only in the ward half an hour when she died. Came in through A and E, so of course there'll be a PM, and no one'll be more interested than I will to know what they find. There's that bitch suggesting almost in so many words it was because I didn't get her into a respirator in time, but I tell you, it was like greased lightning. Breathing a bit laboured but perfectly competent one minute and the next navy-blue face and no bloody pulse. Even Madam Great Ormond Street couldn't have done that much about that . . . .'

'A PM?' Jessie hadn't meant to speak, knowing how nurses enjoyed snubbing non-nursing staff – apart from doctors, of course – but she had to know; today's work had been carefully planned and the last thing they needed was an unscheduled post-mortem. 'Did you say you've got a PM today?'

Night Sister from Dr Lyall Davies's ward looked at her blankly, trying to decide whether to put her down as a pushy bloody technician or whether to be as charming as befitted a senior sister, and because Jessie looked worried rather than merely inquisitive, opted for charm.

'Mmm. Child died on my ward last night within an hour of her admission and there has to be an inquest. She came in from that boarding school.'

'Bluegates,' Jessie said, and frowned. 'Another one? That's awful . . . .'

'Another one?' Sister twisted her chair to look at her more closely, her face alight with interest. 'What do you mean, another one? Which department are you?'

'Path. lab,' Jessie said. 'I'm sorry. I didn't mean to be nosy – I don't usually listen to other people's conversations. It's just that . . . there was a child a week ago from there, died at the school and they brought her in for a PM. It was on her birthday she died. She was only twelve. And now . . . .'

'Well!' Sister said triumphantly, and turned back to her companions of the night. 'And there's that bitch trying to suggest it was because we were slow that the wretched child died! Not a word said about the fact there was another one that had died already, that there was information we didn't have, oh, no, not a word. Oh, I'll have her! Just you wait till I get on tonight! I'll get in early, so help me I will, just to have a go at her, not telling me . . . it's outrageous.'

'Perhaps she didn't know,' Jessie said, but the night nurses' table paid no attention to her at all; they were much too busy shredding the reputation of Day Sister, and Jessie got up and conscientiously stacked her dishes and took her tray back to the serving hatch before going along the trail of corridors back to the laboratory. She'd have to warn Ben there was another PM for an inquest and soothe Tomsett and then try to get on as fast as possible with the routine stuff so that perhaps, just perhaps, they could get through to the work on the trial they had scheduled for the day. It was all a mess, but never mind; Peter was in London, she could stay here all night if she wanted to, and that thought made every other one, however tiresome, an easy matter to deal with.

Ben knew about the PM before he got to the hospital. He had been just about to leave the house when the phone had rung and Dan Stewart had told him that there was another child from Bluegates in need of his investigation, and he had frowned but made no complaint, not this time. It was part of his job and he had no right to, and anyway, now he was interested. The death of one hitherto healthy child from uncertain causes could be regarded as an irritating intrusion on a heavy work load; the death of a second from the same school was something quite different. No wonder Dan sounded grim on the phone, he thought as he dialled a number and listened to it ring at the other end. In his shoes I'd be bloody worried too.

'Hello,' June sounded breathless but bubbling with excitement, and he grimaced at the sound of her voice. Looking after Timmy gave her a lot of pleasure, he knew that, and he'd been pleased for her when she told him Liz was going away for a week and wanted her to take care of the child in his own home, rather than sending him to their house. 'She thinks it's less unsettling for him, Ben,' June had said almost pleadingly. 'And I can't argue with her because she is his mother after all and . . . .' And you're terrified of doing anything to upset the damned woman, Ben had thought, furious for his vulnerable June, and so you let her get away with anything. But he'd said aloud, 'That's all right, love, if that's the way it has to be, that's the way it has to be. I'm busy at the hospital anyway, so it's just as well, maybe. I'll talk to you on the phone whenever I can.'

Now, listening to her babbling on about how good Timmy was being and how she'd managed to spring-clean the kitchen while he was at playgroup and how she planned to start on Timmy's bedroom today, he felt the irritation rising again; for God's sake, why couldn't she find something else to fill her life? Why this bloody obsession with the minutiae of domesticity and care of children when there was a whole bloody busy world out there for her? Yes, it was sad she couldn't have children, but why turn a disappointment into a tragedy by wallowing in it? She was telling him how much fun she and Timmy had had the afternoon before, baking gingerbread men in the sparkling clean kitchen, and what he'd said and what he'd done, and he interrupted more harshly than he meant to, wanting to cut off that tinkling babble, needing to bring her down to some sort of reality.

'I won't be able to call you this evening,' he said. 'I'll be working till God knows what time. I've got another child to post-mortem, not yet eleven years old this time, and it's likely to be a hectic day, what with that and everything else I've got on hand. So I'll call you tomorrow morning.' And he snapped the phone back on its cradle and slammed the front door behind him and went hurrying down the wet brick path, treacherous with fallen leaves and yesterday's rain; as though moving briskly and being obviously busy could make June, away on the other side of the town, realize how much her silliness irritated him. It was absurd behaviour and he knew it, but it made him feel a little better.

June went back to the kitchen after she hung up the phone and sat down slowly at the table, watching Timmy make patterns in his porridge and milk, feeling the coldness lift a little higher in her belly at the sight of his happiness. His cheeks, so round and downy, with just enough tan left from the past hot summer to give him the look of freshly buttered toast as the golden hairs glinted on the brown skin in the overhead light, his hands, pudgy and awkward as he grasped his spoon, his legs rhythmically kicking the chair legs; all were inexpressibly dear to her and she leaned forwards and gripped his arm suddenly, bursting with fearful love for him. He looked up at her, his milk-stained mouth open with surprise, and for a moment looked as though he might cry, but she laughed and said, 'Let's make a lake with your porridge, see how much of the lake you can drink up!' She guided his hands so that the grey sticky mass was pushed aside and the milk collected in the middle, and he laughed delightedly and stirred vigorously, and for a while she was able to forget the effect of Ben's words as she shared his pleasure.

But later, as she walked back from the playgroup at the church hall where she had left him, squealing busily with the other children over the miniature cars and the climbing frame, she remembered and felt sick. Children dying; they shouldn't die. It was horrible to think of. For a moment she hated Ben for having a dreadful job that put him in the position of knowing of the death of lovely children, of small people like Timmy; and unbidden an image lifted in her mind's eye of Ben holding a knife and slitting a child's body from neck to pubis, the way she'd seen in a picture in one of his medical books she had happened to pick up, and the image frightened her so that she broke into a little run, needing to get back to Liz's flat as fast as possible. It was awful, awful, and Ben was awful to have made her think about it. Why had he told her this morning he was a doing a post-mortem on a child? She hated him for upsetting her so and wanted to phone him and tell him so.

And knew she was being stupid and that he'd be furious with her, and rightly so. He was a busy man, worked hard, what with the lab and his research; she had no right to disturb him with her nonsense ideas, because they *were* nonsense ideas and she knew it. It was ridiculous to think that just hearing about a child's death was any sort of threat to Timmy; of course it wasn't, she was just being superstitious, and it had to stop . . . think about something else. Something else. Think about the other side of Ben's work, about his research.

But she couldn't even do that, because she knew nothing about it. He'd tried to tell her once but she'd been on the first day of a period and bitterly miserable and hadn't listened and after that he'd never tried again, so that had been that.

She pushed open the gate and went into the garden. Maybe when she'd finished cleaning the bedroom she'd collect some brown leaves and make an arrangement for the corner. Timmy would like that. And if she concentrated on that thought, she promised herself, maybe she'd be able to forget how frightened Ben's phone call had made her.

Joe Lloyd heard about the second death at Bluegates while he was having his breakfast at the Toque Blanche café in Schooner Street, just behind the office. He had been there every day of his working life in the past five years, ever since his wife had made it so painfully clear that the provision of any sort of service for him – culinary as well as sexual – was totally out of the question, and he was therefore as much part of the furniture there as the battered chairs and the Fablon-covered tables. Dimitri, who stood behind the steaming cluttered counter at the far end where he could watch with a scowl the shaven-headed boys who played with the Space Invader machines by the door, always had his usual   poached-egg-on-white-toast-tea-extra-slice-toast-marmalade ready for him as he walked in at nine o'clock each morning and never said more to him than a grunt; which was reasonable enough since that was all Joe ever said to him. They loathed each other, Joe hating Dimitri for his absurd airs and graces about his greasy establishment – Toque Blanche, indeed! – and Dimitri hating Joe for his ability to sneer in seven different facial expressions; but they needed each other, for regular customers were few and far between for Dimitri, and the place was the only one within reach of the office Joe felt able to afford on a daily basis

It was because he was so invisible to Dimitri and his friends – generally speaking it was only his personal friends who spent any time in his establishment – that Joe heard as much as he did about the child's death. The woman who was leaning against the counter talking volubly when he came in, collected his breakfast as usual, and slapped down the exact money for it as usual, didn't lose a syllable of her saga as he pushed past her. 'Phoned from the hospital she did, told Miss Ventnor, and she told Miss Spain, and she had an attack, she did, started carrying on, saying she couldn't be held responsible another minute she couldn't, she was walking out, and out she walked, and the others started trying to get the girls settled, and they was all excited over their fireworks and all that, and not a one of their potatoes did they eat, in spite of my work slaving over 'em all day, and then when they heard what had happened they started carrying on an' all.'

'So?' Dimitri passed a grey wet cloth over his counter, rearranging the grease into new patterns. 'So, girls carry on. Girls always carry on. It's what they're for.'

'So they starts falling down ill, that's what,' the woman said triumphantly. 'Going paralysed, crying they can't breathe, the lot. You never heard a row like it. I was busy gettin' their suppers ready, o' course. Cookin' sausages and potatoes, very busy I was.' She smirked at them and bobbed her head in self-satisfaction. 'But I heard what was going on. There isn't much Edna misses, I can tell you! And I'll tell you something more, there's something real bad going on down at that there Bluegates. I'm givin' up my job there, much as I need the money, and for all they begged me they did, that Nancy McGrath as works with me in the kitchen, told me with tears in her eyes she'd never get through the day without me to see things got done. Very attached to me, Nancy.' She leaned her elbows on the counter and looked winningly up at Dimitri. 'Gives me stuff to take home all the time, she does. Eggs and potatoes and that. Very attached to me, she is.'

'Then you'll miss her, won't you?' Dimitri winked at the man who had just come into the café, bringing a wash of cold air from the street outside. 'Her an' her eggs and potatoes. You'll have to go an' buy 'em like everyone else, won't you?'

'That's as may be.' The woman stood up straight and began to brush down the front of her coat. 'That's as may be. It's not all of us is as rich as some, businessman like you. What do you know about what it's like to have a family to look after?'

'And an old man always on the sugar stick,' the newcomer said, and the woman, ignoring him loftily, collected up her pile of tattered plastic bags and went, muttering a little under her breath, leaving Joe stirring his tea thoughtfully. There were things to be done, and ideas to be followed up, he told himself. One idea in particular.

The idea took him first to Bluegates, then to the hospital, and finally to the coroner's office on the third floor of the magistrates' court in Bentley Road, on the north side of the town. When he got to the office, just after eleven, he was unusually affable even to Simon Stone, who was tied to his desk subbing the obituaries, Joe Lloyd's favourite punishment for pushy reporters, and the first thing he did was to put in a call to London to the features editor of the *News* in Fleet Street. In all his career as a stringer, Joe had never had as promising a story to offer him, and he had every intention of making the best of it.

The story didn't reach Hugh Worsley until just before he left home to go to the chapter meeting. He'd had a busy day, an enthralling day, first writing the draft report of how Plan B had gone, as though they'd already carried it out, so that it would be all ready to send to the papers with a few alterations depending on how it all actually went, and then checking the actual plan step by step so that he could be sure at tonight's meeting that everyone had it really clear. If only he could do without Dora and Freda; the Reah sisters, they ought to be called, he'd once told Graham privately, expecting him to laugh, Pya and Dya, but Graham had given him a pudding-faced look and not been at all amused – he'd have to remember that he'd never been a student, had no idea what a joke was, poor devil, but how could he have, after all? Working in a bank all your life and then retiring even though you didn't want to doesn't exactly sharpen a man's sense of humour. Poor old Graham, Hugh thought magnanimously as he sat over his plan, not much use for anything really. Still, he was a supporter, and he did have a car and that helped a lot.

It was the woman from the ground-floor back room who told him, as he was standing in the ill-lit hall, wrapping his scarf round his neck. She peered out at him, alert as always for the sound of any human contact near her and said brightly, 'That's right. You wrap up proper. Don't want you falling down paralysed, do we?'

'What?' He stared at her, amazed as always at the incredible things she managed to say whenever he met her; she had an enviable ability to animate the most mundane of matters with her comments, and this one promised to be a classic.

'Epidemic there is, a new one, haven't you heard?' She came out of her room to stand leaning on the door jamb, propping the door open so that he could see the clutter inside: piles of newspapers and magazines, chairs toppling over with them, the floor littered. 'Up at that school at Petts' Hill, the posh one, all the girls there keep catching flu and getting paralysed. Dozen's of 'em died too, so they say, terrible it is. Only affects young people though, not old ones. Only young ones like you. So you wrap up warm.' And she grinned at him, pleased at the effect she was having.

'Dozens dead? Who said so?'

'Everyone said so. Milkman, everyone.'

'Ah, the milkman.' Hugh nodded sapiently, and buttoned his bomber jacket over his scarf, not caring at all that it made him look like a pouter pigeon. He picked up his precious folder and pushed that inside his jacket too; it would be safer there, and it kept the wind off him and that mattered a lot to a cyclist. 'Well, of course if *he* said so I'd better be careful, hadn't I? Goodnight Mrs Scarman,' and he went, enjoying the joke. He'd have that one nicely put together to tell the others when he got to the chapter meeting; they'd enjoy it, especially Gail. She liked a joke, did Gail. Maybe tonight he'd ask her back to his room. She'd come, of course. They always did. Other people at the poly might make cracks about his love-life, looking pointedly at his acne and so forth, but it never seemed to matter to girls. Personality counted, that was the thing, Hugh told himself as he climbed onto his bike and began the ten-minute journey to Graham's house in South Preston Road, just as it says in all the women's magazines. It's personality that's where it's at, and I've got lots of that. It'll be that that carries Plan B through, that and efficiency and single-mindedness of purpose and . . . falling down paralysed if you don't wrap up warm! A real Scarmanism, that one. He'd start the meeting by telling them, but then they'd settle down to making sure Plan B was ready for implementation and that would be marvellous. The evening should be as enjoyable as the day had been, he told himself as he cycled hard, head down, into the dark of the November night.

8

Tonight, Jessie thought, I'll leave the animal room to last. Usually she made sure she went in and fed them and checked the cages were clean at around six, but tonight, she told herself, they'll be able to hold on a little longer and come to no harm.

She would have been hard put to it to explain why she was unwilling to go in there while there were still other people around; there were no secrets about the research, after all. Harry Gentle knew about it, and so did Annie who did the bloods, and even young Errol who washed the glassware and generally cleaned up and couldn't care less about anything apart from his music. He spent all day with his earphones clamped to his head under his towering woolly hat, emitting faintly tinny noises and jigging as he worked, and she could have hung both the monkeys around his neck and he'd have paid no attention. Yet for all that, she felt uneasy, almost embarrassed, about it.

Maybe it was because she had been so occupied with the animals all week and therefore some of her usual work had to be shared out between the others? They hadn't complained unduly; they'd all been hectically busy anyway, too busy to notice who did what, perhaps, as this wretched epidemic took hold and more and more requests came in for swabs and blood counts and ESRs and even Paul Bunnell's. (One of the local GPs was totally convinced that the disease was just a rogue variant of mononucleosis and was telling all his patients soothingly that they only had glandular fever and clogging up the path. lab with the resulting blood-test demands.) But still it was important not to let anyone realize that she was putting so much time into the project, of that she was certain. It was nothing Ben had actually said, but she knew enough about the history of his work to know what worried him now. The long years of thinking about what he wanted to do, the struggle to squeeze minute grants of research money from wherever he could get them, the constant beavering away around the edges of busy working days to keep up the standard of his investigations – it had made him edgy and nervous, afraid that someone, somewhere, would see what he was doing and try to stop him on the grounds of economy. Cuts were the order of the day throughout the hospital; let anyone in charge of money once notice what Ben was doing, and who knew what might happen? It was no wonder to Jessie that Ben wanted to keep his head well below the parapet, and what he wanted, of course, she wanted.

She looked at her watch when she heard the outer door bang as Annie went defiantly to keep her date with the latest of her long line of housemen. (Her remarkable physical resemblance to Joan Collins ensured that lots of men found her entrancing to meet, while her total lack of interest in anything but her own appearance combined with a high degree of sexual prudery ensured that none of them took her out more than twice.) Harry still had his head down over his microscope as he finished the day's batch of urgent requests from the hospital itself. They'd managed, somehow, to clear the work that had come in from the GPs, having managed to offload some of it to Doxford Hospital, and now all that was left was perhaps another two or three hours of grinding labour to get the place clear for the flood that would arrive tomorrow morning.

'How's it going, Harry?' she asked. 'Can I take over some of it for you?'

Harry didn't look up, his right hand busily making entries on the paper beside him as he kept his eyes glued to the microscope.

'Can you? I wouldn't mind, I must say. I'm nearly on my uppers, one way and another. Where's our lord and master?'

'Still in histology. He's got to do the slides himself for both today's PMs and he's still got to dictate his reports. Here, Harry, you go. I can stay late tonight, no hassle. Better you go now and come in fresh in the morning than finish up with this damned flu yourself.'

'But I won't will I?' Harry straightened up and finished the report beside him before pulling the slide he'd been studying out of the microscope. 'It's only kids who get this one, not old bocks like me.'

'Yes . . .' Jessie took a sharp little breath in through her nose.

'It's horrible, isn't it? Have you ever come across anything like it before?'

Harry shook his head. 'Heard tales of course. There've been scares like this before, starting in schools; the literature's full of 'em. But I've never had to deal with one myself. I'll tell you this much, it's not that bloody man Winters's mononucleosis, that's for sure. If he sends in any more Paul Bunnells I'll go round to his bloody surgery and personally shove the blood right down his stupid throat.'

'I know,' Jessie slid into his chair as Harry stood up and stretched. 'I believe Ben's going to tell him. He said he would.'

'Ben,' Harry said in a considering voice, looking down at her as she unclipped the request from the next waiting specimen. 'You two having an affair?'

'Harry!' She stared up at him, scandalized. 'Harry, that's an awful thing to say!'

'Not at all.' Harry seemed in no hurry to go, leaning against the bench beside her and grinning down at her. 'You're a passable wench, Jessie, nothing wrong with you. Got a nice little arse there. I've seen him watch it as you go bustling about. And a nice face too, and a pleasant way with you as well as a head on your shoulders. A man needs a girl he can talk to after a little pokery. Gets boring with dunderheads, if you'll permit a bad pun. And he seems a nice enough sort of bloke. Me, I wouldn't know what turns women on.' He yawned suddenly, so that his jaw made audible clicking sounds. 'Christ, I'm knackered. I will go, ducks, if it's all the same to you. Have fun, you and your Ben.'

'Harry, don't you ever say such a thing again!' Jessie's face was crimson and she knew it and her distress about it made her even hotter. 'It's an awful thing to suggest. We just work together, and I like my job, that's all. I'm married and so's B . . . Dr Pitman and . . . .'

'What's that got to do with the price of bloody eggs?' Harry said. 'I'm married too and so's Sally, and there we are making lovely music together. It wouldn't be half as lovely if we were married to each other, I'm damn sure of that. Goodnight, Jessie. No, don't look like that. Not another word will pass the old lips if it makes you feel that bad. So you're virtuous, you'd never have an affair, and I'm sorry I ever said anything. Thanks for taking on that stuff for me. Goodnight, and I'll see you in the morning.' And he went, letting the door slam behind him as she sat there and stared after him, willing the tide of heat in her face to recede.

I'll have to leave, she thought, panicking, and felt her throat tighten at the very idea. I'll have to leave if they're saying things like that about me. Who's saying things? Harry? Who cares about Harry Gentle? He just likes to talk, that's all. Everyone in this damned hospital likes to talk. Gossip's more important to them than their pay packets. And seeing Ben every working day is more important to you than your pay packet, isn't it?

It's not, it's not! She almost said it aloud, she was so furious with herself, but she just sat there silently, staring at the door Harry had slammed behind him, trying to calm herself. It would be absurd to go off half-cocked just because of something one man had said, and a man notorious for his own casual sex-life at that. Everyone knew that Harry Gentle was working his way through the nursing staff, and that he'd already had affairs with most of the physios, so why pay any attention to him?

Will they start talking about me the way they talk about Harry? she thought bleakly. I will have to leave, won't I, if that happens? Why? It's not true, so no one can say anything. Why get agitated about something that just isn't true? Because you'd like it to be true, whispered a wicked little voice inside her head. You'd like it to be true; and she pushed back the chair on which she was sitting so sharply that it banged against the table and sent a row of test-tubes flying.

By the time she'd salvaged them and cleared up the mess, it was gone seven, and she could hear the distant chattering of Castor and Pollux; whatever work was waiting here to be done, they'd have to be attended to first, and she went round the lab, switching off the main overhead lights and leaving only the bench light burning over Harry's place. Saving every penny in the way of costs was becoming second nature now, and she went doggedly through the office and on into the animal room, thinking only of work, anything that would keep Harry Gentle's dreadful voice out of her ears. How dare he say it, how dare he? she thought, and heard that wicked inner voice whisper back – because even though it's not true, you'd like it to be, you'd like it to be.

The room was dim and warm and damp and she stood in the doorway for a moment absorbing its atmosphere, waiting for her thudding pulse to slow down. It was stupid to get so agitated over something so unimportant; think about the animals, just about the animals.

In the corner cage Castor and Pollux, aware of her presence, were leaping and swinging, demanding food furiously, and she went over to the fridge in the corner to collect their fruit and the excitement and chatter increased, almost drowning out the sound of the rain drumming on the roof. It was a ramshackle room, little more than a lean-to that had been built on to the side of the main block long ago for some sort of extra storage purpose, and ill-suited to the use to which Ben now put it, but she had made it snug enough since coming to join him, using strips of roofing felt to caulk the draughty corners and regularly cleaning the overhead skylight to improve the quality of daylight. But she hadn't been able to make it quiet, too, and now the rain pounded like machine-guns and made the animals stir restlessly in their straw, rustling and clicking uneasily.

Castor reached his hand out as she came to his cage and she looked at the tiny elegant fingers and the dun-coloured nails and wrinkled little knuckles, and set one finger in the palm the way she had been used to set a finger in Mark's hand when he was a baby, and at once the warm dry grip tightened and tugged and she had to laugh, looking up at the wide-eyed little face with its absurd tufts of hair.

The eyes, deeply brown, stared back at her solemnly and she thought – what's he thinking? Does he think? What happens behind those eyes when we're not here? Does he remember the jungle and the high trees and the reek of the dead undergrowth as the sun steams it? And then shook her head at her own silliness. That was sentimentalizing of the worst kind; these rhesus monkeys had been bred in captivity from a long line of captive primates reared specially for laboratory work. To assume that they thought and felt and yearned for home was – and she reached into her mind for the word, remembering Ben using it, and managed to retrieve it. Anthropomorphic. It was as bad to wonder what Castor was thinking as to believe that Rupert Bear actually existed and wore plaid trousers and a little yellow scarf.

And yet, as Castor let go her finger and reached eagerly for the bananas and apples she was carrying in her other hand, she still felt the melancholy of his situation. Would I like it, she wondered, even though I was warm and fed and clean and had a companion I cared about? Would I like to live in a cage? And Pollux came swinging across the cage from the back and began to shriek furiously at her mate as she tried to steal his food from him and Jessie grimaced at herself. She really was being very stupid tonight. As if we didn't all live in cages anyway, of one sort or another, and behave like monkeys ourselves, she thought; and remembered Peter shouting his way out of the house on the way to his conference last Sunday morning, and felt the dull heaviness that came as she remembered he was coming back tomorrow night.

But that was tomorrow's problem; now she had work to do and when she had fed the monkeys, and they had settled to picking the food over with their fastidious and busy little fingers, tucking the morsels they chose into their mouths with an air of daintiness, she began the rounds of the other cages.

First the group B rabbits, a breed of small albinos of the sort that Ben found easier to handle than the bigger ones (though dealing with the dissections on them was a little more complex because of their size), because they had the virtue of great fecundity. Litters of eight were not all that unusual from this breed.

These were the group that had been given the infective strain 737 together with the new batch of Contravert, and she looked down at them moving in jerky hops through their piled straw and noted that they'd eaten all their food from their midday feeding, and were as interested as they usually were in the cabbage stalk she had left for them to chew all afternoon. Their ears were not unduly floppy, their eyes clear and their fur lively, and she wrote that in the chart that hung on their pen before dragging out the soiled straw in the front and replacing it with a handful of clean. The main clean-out of the pens was done in the mornings, when daylight made it easier to get rid of the rubbish, because it was a long walk over to the incinerator, but she hated leaving them overnight without fresh straw, even though that made more work for her. She filled their dishes then with handfuls of pellets, and at once the five of them were scrabbling eagerly, pushing each other away, scattering their meal around the floor, and she chattered softly at them between her teeth as she fastened the pen door and crossed the room to the group A pens.

Here there were rabbits again, exactly the same breed as the other five and from the same litter, too. Ben had insisted on that, because, although it wasn't essential that a control group should match an experimental group genetically, it made the study more elegant; to be able to show that you had taken the trouble to rear your experimental subjects so specifically would bespeak a particular attention to detail, he'd told Jessie, when he explained to her why in his animal room he liked, where possible, to breed some of his own creatures.

'It's not just to save money buying them,' he'd told her. 'Though it is a bit cheaper to breed and I have to save every penny I can; it's just that it pleases me to do it. This way I get really standard groups for each trial – and there's also the fact that I'm forever having to collect new stock from the breeders. That's a fifty-mile round trip and it can be a wretched nuisance, so, if you work here, you'll have to be an animal midwife to an extent, Jessie.'

She'd never minded, and now as she reached for the light switch that illuminated this pen, she remembered this litter. It was the first that was her very own, really. Ben had been involved with most of her care of the rabbits at the beginning, but then, gradually, he'd handed over to her, and this particular group were the first to be born under her own eye. They had lain there, squirming in the observation nest, and she had watched them grow into the neat little bodies they now were with childish pleasure. It really was a tendency in herself she'd have to deal with, this affection for the animals. They were, after all, not pets. They had a purpose to their existence as far as the laboratory was concerned that went far beyond merely giving pleasure to humans. Or to themselves. They were here to find answers to important medical questions, and getting attached to them wouldn't help them do that – or help her to do her job, either.

The light swung a little as she switched it on, throwing long crazy shadows, and she steadied it with one hand and then looked down at the pen, and at first she couldn't believe what she was looking at.

There were five animals in this group, too, but these weren't pushing their noses through her straw, nor were they eating. The food she had put out for them at midday was scattered but largely uneaten and the straw looked undisturbed. She could see two of them lying in a small heap against the wire of the pen, and she crouched to look closer.

They were clearly dead, the limbs stiff and splayed and the eyes filmed over. They had scoured before they died, too, and were lying in their own ordure, and she reached for the straw rake from the corner and gingerly pushed it through the piles of straw to the back of the pen to look for the other animals.

There was another body in the same state, and the remaining two were clearly close to joining it. One was lying on its side, its legs jerking a little as it tried to breathe and she looked at its bulging little eyes and they stared back, and it was almost as though there was an expression in them, as though it was trying to talk to her, and suddenly she remembered a poem she hadn't thought of for years, one she'd learned at school:

> There is a rabbit in a snare . . .
> But I cannot tell from where
> He is calling out for aid;
> Crying on the frightened air . . .
> Little one! Oh, little one!
> I am searching everywhere!

That had made her cry when she was a schoolgirl and it made her eyes prick now as she looked down at the rabbit, its eyes glazing as its breathing became more laboured and then jerkier still.

She reached out to touch the dying creature, and then, almost automatically, pulled back. These were the group that had been injected with just the virus, not with the Contravert; touching them could be stupid. She'd better leave everything the way it was, and find Ben and tell him. At midday these animals had been fine and now they were . . . he had to be told at once.

And she went running out of the animal room, and out of Ben's office, leaving the doors not only unlocked but open. There was no one about at this time of night anyway, and it was important to get Ben here fast, before the last animals died. There might be evidence here he needed to observe for himself, because it was obvious, she told herself as she went pushing through the swing doors and turned right to hurry along to the mortuary and histology room alongside it, that his Contravert was doing something very remarkable indeed for the group B animals.

9

'I told you it would work!' Hugh said jubilantly, and slapped the photographs down on the table in front of them, and they all leaned forwards together, like a rather jerky chorus line in a bad musical, to look at them. 'You said I wouldn't get the evidence and there it is! And in under a week, too! I should have taken that bet with you, Graham – I'd have cleaned up!'

Graham looked morosely at the photographs, fanning them out on the table in front of him, and after a moment nodded. 'All right, so you were right and I was wrong, but frankly I never reckoned you'd get anything, even if you got into the place. This is . . . well, it's . . . what's going on there? In this one?'

'They're dead,' Hugh said, and made a face as on his other side Tracey, tonight looking singularly sweet in a Laura Ashley camisole over a billowing Indian batik skirt, burst into noisy tears. 'Look, Tracey, getting upset isn't going to help anyone. It's angry you've got to be, not upset! What good would you have been if we'd activated Plan B last night the way I wanted to, and the first thing you'd done had been to bawl? We'd have been in a right mess. As it is . . .' And he shot a malevolent glance at John and Graham, sitting side by side with their grey heads bent over the photographs. 'As it is, we wasted a marvellous opportunity. That woman went out, left the place unlocked and wide open. I just walked right in, looked around, got my pictures, walked out again. If we'd been at the Red Alert stage, we could have liberated the lot.'

'Not the dead ones,' Tracey said, and sniffed lusciously. 'Too late for them.'

'Well, we won't be too late for the others if we get a move on.' Hugh reached for the photographs, taking them firmly from Graham's fingers. 'I vote that we go into action tonight. If I could get in so easily last night, then we can do it again. Strike while the iron's hot and all that.'

'And what do we do when we get in there?' Graham said, and

73

leaned back in his chair, hooking his thumbs into his waistcoat armholes in the way Hugh most hated. How such a pair of dried old twigs as John and Graham had ever got involved in the chapter Hugh couldn't imagine. He should have blocked them out right from the start, brought in younger blood, but as he looked round at the rest of the meeting, he knew that was a vain hope. He'd spent long enough getting this lot together and a dreary enough bunch they were: Dora and Freda, a couple of old women as dismal as John and Graham were, and only Gail with any real meat on her bones; and he gave her a conspiratorial smile and she serenely returned it, very aware that Tracey had intercepted it and wasn't best pleased. It was easy to get people to agree that animal experimentation was a terrible thing and get them to sign petitions, but to get them to behave in a proper militant fashion – he took a deep breath in through his nose, closing his eyes for a moment as part of his self-control exercise; if he wasn't careful he'd lose his temper and then they'd all walk out on him.

'What we do is liberate the animals, break up the cages, destroy the paperwork we find, and render the place unusable. That's what we do. I've gone over and over Plan B with you and if you don't understand it by now . . . .'

'Well, I don't like your Plan B. It's a last step, as far as I'm concerned, and there are a lot of other steps we have to take long before we get to that.'

'A lot of other steps,' Hugh said scathingly. 'Niminy piminy, namby pamby, mincing along like a fairy queen steps, I suppose.'

'There's no need to be offensive. You may be the chairman and all that, but we're supposed to be a democratic organization. I've read the constitution they sent from headquarters if you haven't, and I know my rights. I joined the AFB because I want to do something about animal rights . . . .'

'What the bloody hell do you think I want?' Hugh shouted.

'Not because I want to play commandoes with a jumped-up schoolboy who thinks he knows more than anyone else. I fought in the war for the likes of you, sonny, and I know what real fighting is. You don't have to get me all stirred up with talking about playing soldiers and breaking into places, because I know what it's really like to get violent.' Graham stopped and grinned at Hugh, who was now white with rage, and then looked at John sitting silently beside him and at Dora and Freda, who sat, as they usually did, side by side and silent. 'So, let's put it to the vote, shall we, according to the AFB constitution of which we are a chapter? I vote we consider other steps before we go breaking into private property.'

'Private property?' Hugh almost shrieked it. 'What the hell has property got to do with anything? I want to save animals' lives and you're droning on about private bloody property and . . . .'

'It's a matter of the rule of law,' Graham said, clearly enjoying himself now, getting cooler as Hugh became ever more incandescent with fury. 'I think we do what's lawful first. Only if the law refuses to face up to the reality of our protest do we do anything like breaking in. I vote to publicize what's going on in this place, tell them how we found out, the lot, and use these photographs. I give you full credit for these – we could make a really powerful leaflet out of them, make people really sit up and take notice.'

'Leaflets are a waste of time,' Gail said unexpectedly. 'It's like those abortion ones they send round. The pictures are so hideous they make you feel sick, so you won't look and you won't think about it and you might go and have an abortion then, because you didn't know how awful it was. It's the same with animals. I keep seeing pictures of monkeys all wired up and all that and all it does is make me close my eyes. Leaflets are silly.'

'Thank God for a bit of commonsense,' Hugh said, and grinned at her. 'You're right, of course. It's the young people we've got to get involved and you won't get them by showing them pictures. That just upsets them the way it did Tracey. You can get money out of old people sending pictures round but what we want is action to save animals' lives . . . .'

'There's nothing wrong with old people,' Dora said loudly. 'There's too much of the young ones in this if you ask me. Going off breaking into places – it's not right! I joined to do something about the poor little animals but that doesn't mean I'm willing to break the law. And if this committee's going to turn into law-breakers, then it can do without me.'

'And me,' Freda said, as Dora nudged her. And Graham looked benevolently at them and said, 'Well, then, Hugh, time to take the vote, I'd say. Do we publicize these pictures – and I take Gail's point about a leaflet and withdraw the suggestion – or do we put your plan into action? And I'll tell you here and now, sonny, that if you do, I for one resign. I'll go and join the Animal Protection League where they've got a lot of sense and real democracy.'

'Me too,' said John, and Freda and Dora nodded like the pair of stuffed dogs that John kept in the back window of his car.

'Then I don't see that I have much choice,' Hugh said savagely, and then took a deep breath in through his nose again, remembering what he'd been taught about control last year when he was into yoga and meditation. 'Though I must say your view of democracy and mine don't match – what you're doing sounds more like bullying to me than honest voting. But I can be reasonable, and no one can ever say otherwise, right, Gail? OK, we vote publicity rather than action *at present*. If publicity fails we return to Plan B. I can't say fairer than that. All right?'

'All right,' Graham said, magnanimous in his success. 'It's up to you of course, old boy, chairman and all that. Through the chair, every time, hmm? Through the chair – and I vote for publicity. I know this boy, you see, son of a neighbour of mine – he'll be very useful.'

'I don't give a sod about bloody animals,' Joe said. 'As far as I'm concerned they're bloody nuisances that cover my shoes with shit. The only place I like to see 'em is stretched out on a butcher's slab waiting to be cooked. But they're a story, of course. I can't deny that. Where'd you get this stuff from?'

'Neighbour of ours,' Simon said eagerly, hovering over Joe, his hand half outstretched as though he was afraid the photographs he was holding might disappear into thin air. 'He was a bit mysterious about it, said he couldn't reveal his source, but he swore this place is inside Minster Hospital, and that they're abusing animals there. Those rabbits there, they're dead . . . .'

'I'm not a bloody half-wit,' Joe said. 'I can recognize a bloody dead rabbit when I see one.'

'And those monkeys, they're there too – they don't look too bad,' he added dubiously, bending even closer. 'It's like at a zoo, really. Still, they might be dead. Or ill-treated. Thing is, this chap says . . . .'

'What chap? Facts, boy, facts, how often have I got to bloody tell you?'

'His name's Graham Board, he's retired – made redundant from Hammonds last year – about sixty-odd I suppose. Goes out to a lot of meetings and such like, my Mum says. She's home all the time, so she knows everything the neighbours do.'

'Pity you aren't home all the time as well, then,' Joe grunted. 'I want a bit more information than just these polaroids. They could be anything, taken anywhere. I have to have chapter and verse, so if you want this story, go and get the chapter and verse. In your own time!' he added, as Simon grabbed the photographs and made for the door. 'Right now, get back to that subbing. I want that page locked up tonight, not next week.'

There might be something in it, Joe thought as he watched the boy go sulkily back to his desk. Cruelty to animals – it was a sure-fire peg for a bit of public excitement in this country. He could run features about the NSPCC till he was blue and no one paid a blind bit of notice, but show the punters one lousy rabbit with its toes turned up and say someone had done an experiment on it and they're out there baying for blood. Stupid bastards, Joe thought, hating his readers more and more with each passing day. I don't know why I stick with the stinking business.

He was still sore because of the lukewarm response he'd had from the *News* man on the Bluegates affair. There he'd been with a really hot story, two kids dead from one school, looked like an epidemic of some mysterious unnamed disease, and what did the bastard say? 'Keep it on the back burner, laddie. See how it shapes up.' See how it shapes up! Joe thought, and slammed another sheet of galleys on the spike. See how the story shapes up be buggered. It was already shapely enough for anyone with two shreds of brain to tuck between his bat ears, which was more than that bastard at the *News* had.

He leaned back in his chair and began to think. There must be a way to get the story into the nationals. He'd run his own piece of course, in last week's issue, about the deaths, full of sympathy for the bereaved parents, the whole bit, but he'd said little about the epidemic because at that stage there hadn't been all that much to worry about. A few kids with snotty noses, nothing much; but maybe by now there'd be a bit more? There was that talk he'd heard at Dimitri's – he should have followed that woman out, found out more from her; she needed tracking down, she did. He'd have to give some thought to that. If Dimitri were a civilized man instead of a half-witted orang-utan it'd be different; he could ask him who the woman was, but as it was – he stretched his memory, digging in it for the woman's name. Someone had used it, while he sat there mopping up his poached egg, and he'd registered it, out of force of habit, and now he closed his eyes and concentrated, trusting his trained memory to extricate it, and at last it did. 'There isn't much Edna misses, I can tell you!' Edna. That would do for openers.

It took them a long time to answer the phone at Bluegates, but at last they did, a breathless voice saying a little guardedly, 'Yes?', but not using the number or the name of the place as he would have expected.

'Hello,' he said, trying to sound affable. 'That Bluegates School?'

'Er . . . who is that?'

'Oh, I'm just Joe – wanted a word with Edna, d'you see. You know old Edna – works in your kitchens?' He dredged up a memory of the woman in Dimitri's in all her shabbiness. 'Middle-sized sort o' lady, looks a bit tired, like . . . .'

'Edna?' There was silence and then a sharp little breath. 'Oh, that's all right, then. Edna, yes, works in the kitchens? Can't say I do know exactly who you mean – teachers tend not to . . . well, yes. There's an extension through to the kitchen. I'll put you through. Just a moment.'

Joe grinned to himself, settling his haunches more deeply into his chair. This was what it was all about, the teasing out of the lines of a story. Never mind what the story was, the real fun was pulling it out of the tangle, strand by strand, and then laying the strands neatly to make a pattern. The pattern itself mightn't be the most exciting when it was finished but, oh, the delight of getting it right. And he listened to the clicking of the phone and waited.

'Mrs McGrath,' the phone barked at him, and he blinked. 'Hello? Who is that?'

'I'm trying to get hold of Edna,' Joe said, his voice relaxed and easy. 'Works with you? Got a bit of news for her, you see, and I can't find her at home. Just thought I'd try there . . . .'

'Edna?' The phone almost snorted at him. 'That woman is no longer in this kitchen's employ.'

'Oh, sorry to hear that,' Joe said, and moved the phone to his other ear, so that he could scratch his itching scalp. It always did that when he got really interested in something. 'Nothing wrong, I trust?'

'Who are you?' the phone said, deeply suspicious.

'Oh, just a person making enquiries, Mrs McGrath,' Joe said, and dropped his voice half an octave. 'Can't say too much, you understand. Just need to get hold of Edna.'

'Police, are you?' the woman said, and Joe raised his brows.

'Well, I can't say I'm surprised, the stuff she took out of here. Not that I'm prepared to be a witness, mind you, and you can't make me. I never said that.'

'No, of course,' Joe said soothingly. 'But you can say where I could find her? Maybe I got the wrong address? Could you just check your records? I'm sure they'll be very accurate. That's what we need, isn't it? Efficiency.'

If the phone could have bridled it would have but the woman's voice only said crisply, 'Hold on,' and then, after a moment recited, 'Mrs Edna Laughton, 5a Wessex Street, East Minster.'

'Mrs McGrath,' Joe said fervently. 'I thank you. You are a wonder. Good afternoon.' And he cradled the phone and again sat and stared at the wall for a moment, digging down once more into his memory. And then shouted for Simon.

'Those court stories you brought in a couple of weeks ago. Want 'em now. Get 'em.'

The boy gawped. 'Court stories? Which court stories?'

'Shoplifters, idiot, shoplifters! There was one called Laughton, lived in Wessex Street, East Minster. I want the notes. Now.'

'Wessex Street, East Minster,' Simon repeated and backed out, praying that he'd be able to find his notebook. He usually had three or four going at any one time, and the one he had been using a fortnight ago could be anywhere; and he went to hunt in the squalor of his desk drawers, awed as he always was by Joe Lloyd's remarkable memory, while Joe sat and waited, smiling gently to himself.

So, the *News* wasn't interested in two dead kids and an epidemic? He'd show 'em what a story was! They'd soon find how wrong they were not to pick up on it. Here he was in a position to get every bit of inside information there could possibly be from Bluegates; here was a source who'd be falling over herself to tell him everything there was to be told, from the kids' symptoms to the colour of the headmistress's knickers. A shoplifter! He couldn't believe his luck.

Dan Stewart sat at his desk for the first time that week, and stared down at the returns that had been hastily collected for him by his secretary and felt a little shiver of anxiety start in his belly and creep up into his shoulders.

There had been a more than a hundred per cent increase in the numbers of cases the GPs thought might fit into his tentative outline of the illness. He'd sent them all a confidential memo, telling them he wanted information on any virus infections that might present, and listing ten signs or symptoms, and offering them all simple checklists they could use to get the information to him. It was a simple method he'd devised years ago when he was young and energetic and new in the community health game for persuading busy or lazy doctors to get him the information he wanted with the least effort to themselves. It was a coarse-meshed screen, of course; plenty of the cases that had been added to the totals were likely to turn out to be chicken pox or German measles or just different strains of upper respiratory tract infection with a bit of coincidental diarrhoea and vomiting, but even allowing for that, there was enough here to make a man worry.

Could it be a raw new flu strain that had started there at Bluegates? And, if so, where had it come from? And he made a face at himself for being so stupid; half those kids were there because their parents worked overseas. Anyone could have brought Christ knows what in with them on their last trips home for the holidays. The new term hadn't been that old when it started. When was the first case? That child had died on – he flicked open his desk memo book – 31 October. And the school term had started on 17 September. That meant a . . . six-week incubation period. Not possible, he told himself. Not a flu strain. And not at the rate it's now seeming to spread. It's obvious it's a short incubator, not a long one. So we still don't know where it could have come from. Certainly not from overseas, unless a parent visited in the interim or a child came back late? He'd have to find out about that, and he made a note.

Not that that really faced up to the central problem he had to deal with. Was this a new bug, and had he encouraged its spread by not putting the school in quarantine? He'd let the kids go home for the half-term holiday, damn it, even when there'd been warnings that there might be something here that needed further investigation. He should have held on to them, swabbed the lot, seen what he could grow.

'Shit!' he said aloud, and reached for his phone. He'd have to talk to Dorothy Cooper, find out whether there could have been a source from overseas, and then get in touch with Colindale. It wasn't that there was anything really to worry about, he told himself, as optimistically as he could. The illness, whatever it was, might be keeping the doctors busy, but there was no reason to really worry . . .

Except for two dead children in as many weeks, an inner voice said sharply, and he swore under his breath with impatience as the phone rang tinnily in his ear, repeating itself infuriatingly. Where were the silly bitches? Why couldn't someone answer the bloody phone?

At last a breathless voice said, 'Hello?' guardedly, as though its owner was afraid someone would jump down the phone at her, and he said brusquely, 'Miss Cooper please.'

'I'm sorry, Miss Cooper's not available,' the breathless voice said, more nervous than ever now. 'Try tomorrow. She might be here then . . . .'

'Might be?' Stewart said and his voice sharpened. 'What's going on there? Who is that?'

'Nothing's going on,' the voice quavered. 'Er . . . are you a parent?'

'No, damn it, I'm Dr Stewart. And I have to speak to Miss Cooper.'

'Oh!' The voice drew a sharp little breath of relief. 'Oh, you should have said, Dr Stewart! This is Wynn Ventnor. Hasn't Miss Cooper called you? She said she was going to.'

'I've been out of my office all week,' Dan said, and sat up a little straighter. 'Why did she want me? Is there something . . . what is it?'

'Oh, Dr Stewart, we're so worried. Some of the girls are so ill, and now we've had to take Andrea Barnett into the hospital, she's like poor Pauline was, and we're so worried – the girls have been calling their parents and seventeen of them have gone already.'

'Gone? Gone where?'

'Home, or to their relatives in England if their parents are away. It's all so dreadful, Dr Stewart. Miss Cooper's being so strong, but honestly, I'm worried about it and . . . .'

'So am I,' Dan Stewart said. 'So am I bloody well worried. She's at the hospital? Good. I'll see her there.' And he slammed the phone down and ran for the door so fast his chair went sprawling.

10

'Well, it might be,' Ben said. 'It just might be,' and he tried to sound judicious, relaxed, very cool and professional, but Jessie could hear the excitement underneath the measured tones. 'I'll have to try another group, of course, replicate the whole thing. How is the other litter – the one in the corner pen? How many are there?'

'Only six in that one,' she said, feeling absurdly that it was somehow her fault that she hadn't had the skill to make the doe superfecund, able to produce vast numbers of small rabbits for Ben to work on. 'But there are two of them . . . I mean, do you remember what we did last time? We mated the same buck with two does from the same litter. The sister's in the pen beneath Castor and Pollux's cage. So you could use both litters, and they'd still be well matched, wouldn't they? It's not the same genetically as splitting one litter, but they're closely related.'

He thought for a moment and then shook his head. 'No, I don't think so. I'd rather replicate the experiment precisely. We've got some more of the same Contravert batch, haven't we? And the 737 – yes. So, we'll use one litter, even though it'll mean smaller groups.'

'We could do it twice,' she said. 'Both litters – split each one into groups A and B and use them as doubles.'

'We could . . . .' He sat and thought, staring blindly at the dead rabbit on the slab in front of him. 'We could – but I think I'd rather wait. I want to use the next generation of the virus as well, you see, for each experiment. Then we'll know if it becomes more virulent or if it attenuates as it progresses.'

'Then we've got to run parallel experiments,' Jessie said. 'One lot with the present virus strain of 737 as well as the Contravert, and another set with second and third generation 737 and Contravert. Otherwise you aren't replicating this experiment properly, are you? And we could use the sister litter for that easily.'

He grinned, delighted with her. 'Attagirl. Yes, that's the way we do it. You're quite right, of course. I'm trying to rush it. Hang on to my coat tails, Jessie – I'm getting excited and falling over my feet.'

'I'll hang on,' she said, and almost without thinking put her hand up and took hold of his upper sleeve and shook it slightly. 'Oh, I'll hang on. It's working, isn't it, Ben? We're going to do it – you'll be as famous as, I don't know, Alexander Fleming. We're going to do it.'

'I think we are.' He was still standing looking down at the rabbit lying stretched and rigid on the slab, waiting for its autopsy. 'Oh, Christ, Jessie, I think we are.' And he looked at her directly now, and she peered closer at him and said, uncertainly, 'Ben? Are you all right?'

'I'm shit scared,' he said, and she could see it even more clearly now, the dilated pupils and the pinching round his nostrils. 'I'm not sure what I've started here. I just thought it'd be interesting, useful; I thought – I'll find what I want, one of these days, and then everything'll be wonderful. I never really thought how it'd feel, what would actually happen. And now I think I might actually have found it, that it's one of these days today, right now, and I'm scared – I haven't felt this way since I was a child. When my father died . . . it's mad . . . .'

'Not mad,' Jessie took her hand away from his arm, suddenly very aware of the physical contact and acutely embarrassed by it. 'But a bit, well, illogical, for a scientist. What's there to be scared of?'

'You can be a scientist in one half of you, while the other half is still thirteen years old and just been told his father's going to die. Or that he's won a place at the best school in the county, or that he's got three A grade A levels or . . . logic has nothing to do with it. I just feel scared and excited and shaking inside and I don't know why for the life of me. Research shouldn't be like this. It's a long slow business – not dramatic and exciting and frightening. Or it shouldn't be so. I just don't know why I feel so . . . it's ridiculous. And I don't know why I'm talking so much rubbish. You're bad for me. You make the words come out of me whether I want them to or not.'

'That can't be bad,' she said as lightly as she could. 'I keep reading these articles that say people don't talk enough.'

'I dare say you're right.' He moved slightly away from her, turning his shoulder, visibly withdrawing. 'Now, the next stage. I'll section this one, make up the cultures and the slides, while you prepare the next. I have to do every animal, you see, and match the cultures. If they all died from the same strain of virus, we're all right. If there's an adventitious one, I'm getting excited and stupid over nothing. So, some real work. Will you start, then? I can manage here on my own.'

'Yes,' she said. 'Of course,' trying not to let the hurt of his withdrawal show. 'I'll finish Harry's stuff first, if you don't mind. Otherwise he'll come in in the morning and start asking awkward questions. I'll be ready well in time for you.'

'Yes,' he said. 'Fine . . .' and his voice was abstracted, his head already bent over the animal as he began to open the belly.

They worked all through the night. Once or twice Jessie looked up from what she was doing – getting the small bodies ready for him, clearing up after he'd finished each one, labelling the slides and the cultures, setting them in the incubator, writing up the charts – and once actually opened her mouth to suggest they stopped, went to get some sleep and then started again in the morning, but he was totally absorbed, enclosed in that absorption as though he were inside a transparent soundproof shell. So she closed her mouth again and said nothing, but went on doggedly working, her eyes hot and sandy and her skin feeling tight over her bones, but content for all that. It was as though there were no time, no world outside this small cluttered set of laboratories, no reality except in the faint reek of opened mammalian bellies, no sound but the ringing hiss of the overhead strip lights and the rumble of the fridges and the incubators; nothing but two silent people, working in a vacuum.

At half past seven, when she heard the rattle of the cleaners' buckets outside in the corridor, she straightened her back and made herself speak, and the effort made her voice sound loud and peremptory in her own ears.

'Ben, it's light. The cleaners'll be in here in a while, and they'll talk if it's obvious we've been here all night. I'm going over to the main hospital to get a shower and some breakfast. You ought to do the same.'

He looked up bleary eyed from the notes he had been writing busily for the past hour and blinked at her.

'What did you . . . what's the time?'

'Half past seven. Errol's due in an hour. I know he's usually late, but all the same . . .'

'Yes, of course. A shower and breakfast. Yes . . . coffee . . .' He sat and contemplated coffee and then grinned at her, his face alight with pleasure. 'Oh Jessie, isn't it marvellous? Haven't we had a marvellous time?'

'Yes,' she said. 'Yes, it's marvellous,' and she went to the corner of the office to reach into the locker and get out her bag and her coat. It was important to look as though she'd just arrived, rather than that she'd been here all night, and maybe putting her coat on . . . .

He stood up and stretched. 'I'll come over with you. Do you need your coat? It's not that cold, is it? I'm cooking.'

'That's lack of sleep,' she said. Her bag slipped in her hand, partly because she was so tired, but also because he was standing rather near to her, and that made her oddly shaky. The contents strewed themselves over the floor and she muttered under her breath and crouched to retrieve them. At once he crouched beside her, too, to help her, and together they scrabbled among loose change and lipsticks and tubes of aspirin and keys, and as they reached for the same thing their hands touched, and at once she pulled back as though his skin had been red hot and she had been scorched.

When she stood up, holding her bag awkwardly in front of her, pushing the things back into it, he stood up too, and now he was standing even closer, and she said breathlessly, 'Please. Don't . . . .'

'Don't what, Jessie?' He made no effort to move, standing there close to her, and she couldn't get away, for the locker was behind her and its open door blocked off any avenue of escape to the side.

And anyway, her mind shouted at her, why do you want to escape? There's nothing to escape from – don't be stupid, you're like a baby, a silly schoolgirl, getting all hot under the collar for nothing, stupid, stupid.

'Don't crowd me.' She tried to make it sound jocular, a light little comment any woman might make, but it came out in a squeak, and he ducked his head to look more closely at her, for she was standing with her head bent over her bag so that her hair fell forwards and hid her face.

'You said something before,' he said abruptly. 'I thought it odd then – you said that if the cleaners came in and saw us they'd know we'd been here all night and they'd talk. What did you mean?'

Still she stood looking into her bag, poking at it, pretending to look for something, pretending to tidy up its contents.

'Well, just that . . . you know what cleaners are. They love to gossip. Everyone in this bloody place loves to gossip.' And there was a sudden note of venom in her voice. 'And I'd rather they didn't. That's all.'

'Jessie, people in hospitals often work all night. Why should anyone gossip about it? You're not making sense. Or are you?'

'Probably not.' Again she tried the oh-so-light voice and now it was more successful, and she felt she could look up at him, if only briefly. 'Put it down to fatigue and stupidity. Sorry.'

'Why did you stay?' He said it abruptly and she looked at him, briefly, puzzled.

'What?'

'I said, why did you stay? Why didn't you tell me at ten o'clock, eleven o'clock, whenever it was you got tired, why didn't you tell me you were going home, and just go? Harry Gentle went, and so did Annie – why did you stay?'

'There was work to be done.'

'There's always work to be done. Any minute now the deliveries'll start and we'll be swamped with work. It never stops. Why did you stay, Jessie?'

'Because I wanted to.'

'Why?' He stood stolidly, not moving, so neither could she.

'I wanted to, I suppose . . . I don't know! It's important – the work I mean – and you were here and . . . .'

'The work's always important, but you don't usually stay all night to do it. You don't stay all night when I don't.'

'No, but . . . .'

'But what?'

'Stop it, Ben! You're nagging me! What have I done to make you bully me this way?' She was trying to drum up some anger, something that would help her push him out of the way so that she could escape, but it wasn't really working. She sounded merely petulant.

'I don't know,' he said, and moved of his own free will, going back to his desk to sit on the edge of it. 'I . . . was I bullying you? I'm sorry. It was just that I wanted to know.'

'What did you want to know?'

'Why you're behaving so oddly. Why I'm feeling so . . . .' He shook his head. 'I used to be able to stay up working all night and feel fine. Am I getting old? I'm a bit light-headed.'

She felt safe again; he wasn't so close any more and seemed to be less intense, and she moved forwards and pushed past him, forced to go close to him by the clutter in the small space, and he put out a hand and pulled on her upper arm, so that she had to half turn to face him.

'Am I getting old?'

'I imagine so,' she said, and managed a smile. 'I am. We all are.'

'How old are you, Jessie?'

'I'll be forty in January,' she said. 'Why?'

'Then I was an eighteen-month-old bouncer when you were born. Not much in it. If I felt as young as you look I'd be able to stay up all night and not notice it. You're an oddity, you know that?' He grinned at her, still holding her arm, and she knew she ought to pull away from him but she felt too tired to try. And anyway, she didn't want to. Before, she had been alarmed by his closeness; now she was relishing it. I'm mad, she thought, quite mad, and she stared at his face, so close to hers that she could see the hairs growing sparsely over his cheekbones, and liked what she saw even more than she usually did when she looked at him. Quite, quite mad.

'An oddity? Why?'

'Because you told me your age without a fuss. Most women make dramas or go all coy and stupid.'

'Men do that too. Peter's eight years older than I am and he gets livid if people find out.'

'Peter?'

'My husband.'

There was a little silence and she felt his hand on her arm slacken its grip, and she thought – that's it, he's remembered who he is and who I am and we've stopped being just ourselves and started to be other people's property again; and that thought made her angry, and she felt her cheeks redden a little.

'He's often stupid like that,' she said, and tilted her chin challengingly, as if she was daring him to be disgusted by her disloyalty. 'As if it mattered how old people are.'

'Yes,' he said, and stared down at her, and she watched his gaze move across her face, from her hairline, down the shape of her jaw to her chin, up to her mouth, her nose and finally to her eyes, and as their gaze met the redness in her cheeks rose, but it wasn't anger this time.

'This is bloody mad,' Ben said suddenly, very loudly, and let go of her arm. 'Up all night working and now standing here talking nonsense instead of getting ourselves wrapped round some coffee. We'd better go.'

'Yes,' she said, and as he let go of her arm, began to pull her coat on more tidily, fiddling with the buttons busily, again needing not to look at him. 'I'll go ahead, shall I? I want to get a shower, and I can in the physio's room. It should be unlocked by now.'

He was beside his own locker now, hanging up his white coat, pulling out his jacket, and he didn't look round as he spoke.

'Yes, fine. See you in the canteen . . . I won't be long.' And she turned and almost ran out of the laboratories and into the misty dampness of the morning air.

She felt extraordinary: light-headed and yet very alert, shaking as though she'd just been involved in some major physical exertion, like running up several flights of stairs, but at the same time both alarmed and elated. It was very strange, and she stopped running and stood still in the middle of the almost empty car park and stared up at the sky, taking deep breaths of the raw air to calm herself, to bring a sense of immediacy back into her body which felt like someone else's, so odd were the mixed sensations. She concentrated her mind on the sky, making a powerful effort to get rid of her confusing feelings, and gazed at the wide expanse fringed with the dark shapes of the hospital's scattered buildings. It was filled with grey rags of cloud moving swiftly against a darker greyness, and the last few leaves on the trees that edged the car park fluttered a little forlornly as the wind sliced through the tracery of naked branches. The feeling of being someone else, of inhabiting a strange body far from going away became more intense, and she stared harder at the moving clouds, still concentrating, and then suddenly the clouds seemed to stop moving; it was the ground she was standing on that was shifting, rushing away beneath her feet so fast that it made her giddy, and she swayed a little and almost fell, putting her hands out in front of her to hold herself still in a madly spinning world – and then he was there. He must have followed her more closely than she had expected him to, and been walking across the car park behind her, and now he held on to her so tightly that his fingers hurt her shoulders as she swayed in the chill morning air and tried to keep her balance.

'Here, you really are tired, aren't you? You'd better take the rest of the day off, Jessie. I shouldn't have let you stay so late . . . I'm sorry.'

'It doesn't matter,' she said. 'It's just . . . I was stupid. I was staring at the sky. It made me feel giddy. I'll be fine. A bit of breakfast and I'll be fine.'

'I'm sorry,' he said again, and she shook her head at him. It was fading now, the sense of confusion, the light-headedness. The world was again a stable solid place, not a ball spinning crazily, threatening to hurl her off into space.

'Not your fault. Come on. Breakfast.'

And he nodded, and tucked his hand into the crook of her elbow and half-led her, half-carried her towards the main block and the night staff canteen.

'You can have your shower after you've been fed,' he said as they pushed open the battered double plastic doors that led into the hospital via the Accident and Emergency Department. 'Your blood sugar's probably almost nil. I'm sure mine is. I lech after thick buttered toast and bacon as I've never leched before.'

'Yes,' she said, breathless with the speed of their progress. 'And coffee and marmalade and orange juice and . . . .'

'Then more toast and bacon. Come *on*. If we don't eat soon, I shall start biting lumps out of the next person who passes us.' And as one of the cleaners, a particularly large woman who waddled as she walked, passed them they both laughed, and at last she felt normal again. It was all right. She'd had a mad moment because she was tired, no more than that. Nothing special had happened between them. Nothing at all.

But though she kept telling herself that for the rest of that day, and for the days that followed, she didn't believe it. And she didn't really want to.

11

All the way up the motorway, Peter glowed with self-approval. When he'd left his hotel at six o'clock he'd already been pretty pleased with himself, bustling out of his room and down to the main lobby to chivvy the sleepy night receptionist to produce his bill, carefully checking it and querying dubious items, instead of just scribbling a cheque the way most people would at that hour of the morning, and then getting the car out of the car park and into the quiet street while it was still dark, but by the time he was really on his way he felt marvellous.

He'd shown her, that was the thing, he told himself over and over again as he threaded his way out of the tangle of streets round King's Cross, where he had found a hotel that had managed to be smart and yet not exorbitant – not for him the fancier establishments around Oxford Street preferred by some of his more extravagant colleagues – and on his way westwards to the motorway; he'd shown her. She must have had a really dreadful night, fretting over him, knowing how angry he was, because he'd promised to come home last night, and instead he'd chosen, of his own free will, he'd *chosen* to stay in London another night.

'I was asked to a rather high-level meeting, and then a party – a very select one,' he'd tell her, and he rehearsed the scene in his mind's eye, how he'd be sitting there at the breakfast table spruce and ready for a day's work while she was still bleary eyed, perhaps even tear-stained from her lonely worrying night without him. 'And I decided to go. You hadn't seemed to care whether you were with me or not, so I thought – well, why not? She won't mind if I stay away another night! Still, I came home early. Didn't want to fret you too much, my dear. Wouldn't do to upset you *too* much.'

Oh, he'd be magnanimous, affectionate, make her realize just how stupid she'd been not to go with him, to expose him to all those stupid men asking him where she was, giving him knowing winks when he said he'd decided to come on his own this year – oh, he'd make her realize, all right, but he'd be good about it.

That was the thing, to be good about it. And he let his mind slide agreeably further into the fantasy as he pushed through the heavier traffic going round Southampton and thickening as the darkness thinned in the eastern sky, and found himself seeing her throwing herself into his arms, crying on his neck, begging him to forgive her, promising never to let him go away without her again, promising to give up her stupid job – he might even have time to take her back to bed, just a half-hour quickie, that was all, before going to work – and he let his speed creep up a good ten miles past the speed limit at the thought. It was worth bending the law a little sometimes.

The house was very still as he turned the car into the drive and switched off the engine, and he got out and stood there, his case in his hand, listening. It was a quiet road, theirs – that was the way he liked to live, and he'd set out to find a house in a nice select sort of avenue – and usually he could hear sounds from inside his own home when he stood in the drive; the distant clatter of dishes in the kitchen, say, or the remote wail of Radio Three (and usually it irritated him that she always had that on; it was almost as though she was sneering at him because he didn't like that sort of music) but this morning there was nothing, and mentally he revised his scenario.

She wouldn't be sitting alone and forlorn in the kitchen, as he'd seen her all the way home; she'd be in bed still, sleeping the exhausted sleep of someone who has lain awake for hours weeping, and only dropped off eventually as the dawn chorus began, and he started to whistle softly between his teeth, and dug from his pocket his front-door keys and went rattling along the path briskly to let himself in.

The chain was up inside the front door, and he frowned sharply, and looked at his watch. It was just eight o'clock; surely, *surely* she couldn't have left for work already? It was crazy – she couldn't have, not after worrying why he hadn't come home last night at the time he said he would, not being able to find the hotel he was in – he'd deliberately not told her which it was, deliberately not phoned her himself – surely she couldn't just have gone off to her damned job as usual?

He set his suitcase down on the doorstep and leaned his thumb on the bell, listening to it pealing tinnily inside the empty house, and knowing there was no one there to answer, but wanting to display his right to make such a noise, peal after peal. The silence mocked him as he stood there afterwards, waiting, and he swore and went round to the side path to make his way to the back door. But the side gate was locked too and he stood there baffled. She, who always had forgotten to lock that gate however often he'd told her to, pointing out that though it might lead only to the back garden, still it could be a barrier to a would-be burglar, she who had told him he was a fusspot because he'd insisted on it, had chosen today, of all days, to remember!

He contemplated climbing over the fence in which the gate was so neatly and firmly set, and then abandoned that; not in a good office suit. And even if he did, what then? The back door to the house was probably locked too; if she'd chained the front door and left via the back door, she must surely have remembered to lock it even though she knew he didn't carry a back door key. Mustn't she?

But there was always the possibility she hadn't, and determined now to get in, no matter what, he went to the car and got out the big spanner with the jemmy end, the one he always carried in case he couldn't get the rims off a wheel when he had to change a flat, and forced open the back gate with it, working out how much it was going to cost to get it repaired even as he did it.

And of course the back door was locked, and the only way he could possibly get in would be by breaking a window, and surely that wasn't necessary?

She wasn't there, that was the thing, and for the first time since she'd started that bloody job, he cursed himself for not taking more of an interest in it. He didn't know exactly where in the hospital she worked; only that it was a Minster Hospital laboratory, and he had no intention of trailing round the place like a maudlin schoolboy looking for her. A phone call, perhaps; someone there surely should be able to track her down? He turned back to the house to look up at it, wanting badly to get in, to soothe his now thoroughly rattled sense of the rightness of things by being among his own possessions on his own territory, and he leaned against the kitchen window fiddling with the hinge, wondering if he could, perhaps, get that off, get in without doing too much damage; and then felt, rather than saw or heard, that Mrs Fenning next door had come out to her patio and was standing there listening, perhaps watching him through a chink in the heavy fence. And he took a deep breath and turned sharply on his heel and went back to the car.

He'd go to the office now; stop on the way at the King's Head for a bite of breakfast, the breakfast he'd planned to have with her, and then get to work dead on time as usual. Tonight he'd sort out this business with Jessie, but it wouldn't be the scene he'd planned. By God, it wouldn't. The magnanimity that had propelled him so happily up the motorway was quite dispelled. Tonight she'd be told to give up that damned job, and there was an end of it. He'd had more than enough, more than any decent man should have to put up with. And so he'd tell her.

Disastrous as the start of the day had been, there was worse to come. He had his breakfast at the King's Head, and singularly nasty it was – burnt bacon and leathery eggs and soggy toast – and he'd tried to complain about that, and all the satisfaction he'd got had been a mouthful of abuse from a tired and bored waitress, and that had made him later than he liked to be; and then, when he got to the car park, some idiot of a woman driver had managed to block the entrance by getting too close to the ticket machine and being too scared to drive either forwards or backwards. By the time she was extricated and he was able to park his own car, it was ten-oh-five, and then two lifts were out of order and he had to wait interminably to get up to the seventh floor. So he was thoroughly ruffled when he slammed in through the big double doors to the Environmental Services section at almost a quarter past ten to find Miss Price sitting at her desk and waiting for him with her eyes glinting with malicious pleasure.

'Mr Wilmington's asked for you three times already this morning,' she announced in that maddeningly off-hand voice she used when she had something really nasty to impart. 'He is steaming! I'd go straight in, if I were you.'

'But you're not, are you?' he snapped. 'Unfortunately for you, you lack the ability.' And he went down to his office, to take off his coat and hang it up with exaggerated slowness, refusing to be browbeaten by Wilmington or by that bitch Price; and then, in spite of himself, went hurrying along the corridor to Wilmington's office.

And found the usual annoyance he felt when he walked into it compounded twice over by the fact that the man had a new desk. It was bad enough he had twice as much floor space as Peter did, and an armchair and a coffee table to boot; he was only one grade senior, for God's sake, what right did they have to treat him as though he was the bloody Angel Gabriel? Now, seeing the large slab of excessively modern black-stained ash and chrome, Peter felt his face actually whiten as he controlled the fury that bubbled in him.

'Well?' he said as curtly as he could. 'I gather you wanted me? I've a lot to do . . . .'

'I imagine you have after a week off.' Wilmington leaned back in the fancy matching chair that complemented the hateful desk and lifted his brows at him. 'All the same, first things first.'

'I haven't been *off*,' Peter said furiously. 'I was at the annual conference, as you well know. Damned hard work it was too.'

'Go and tell that to Establishment branch. They might believe it. Me, I've been to these conferences, and I know what they are. Miller's Cat country, Miller's Cat. All wind and water. People leaping around spouting nonsense – they don't know, half of 'em, whether they're on this earth or Fuller's.' Wilmington had some time ago decided that archaic slang was the acme of wit, and used it constantly. 'Now, Hurst, I've got a large and meaty bone to pick with you.'

'Have you indeed,' Peter said savagely.

'Indeed I have,' Wilmington said, his high good humour showing in every line of his face. Peter Hurst usually managed to avoid situations which gave him any cause to exercise his authority, and now here he was with a real beauty with which to beat him about the head. 'You've dropped yourself right in it, my old squire, right in the jolly old mire. Two weeks ago, or thereabouts, I sent a memo to you asking you to see some people who wanted to present a petition about animals, remember?'

Peter stared at him, completely blank. He had no memory of it at all. 'Animals?' he said. 'What the hell do I have to do with animals?'

'Our furry friends, scientific research for the use of,' Wilmington said. 'These people were steamed up about it. Wanted to see me, but I had a council sub-committee meeting and couldn't see them. So I delegated to you, m'dear old boy.

Delegated to you. And what did you do?'

'Yes,' Peter said slowly. 'Yes, I remember. Bunch of old women, a couple of kids – I passed it back to you to deal with.'

'Oh, no you didn't, old man. That pig won't fly. Not nohow. You put it in your In Abeyance file, that's what you did. These people then went to the local paper, said they'd delivered this petition and had it ignored, and then took 'em some photographs they said they got of this place where furry friends, scientific research for the use of, were being clobbered by mad scientists. We've had that man Lloyd sniffing about and generally making a pest of himself, and he got himself into Chanter's office and made a great drama over it. So Chanter sends for the file and no one can find it for an hour, while Lloyd sits tight in his office generally wiping his eyes and reminding him that the paper supported him all through that sewage-farm drama and if he wants to go on getting local support he'd better pull out the proverbial digit. By the time your Miss Price extricates the file from the bottom of your In Abeyance, Chanter is fit to be tied and after your blood. Hoping to have your guts for garters.'

'Not mine,' Peter said promptly. 'Yours. It was *your* appointment and *you* signed it. I did my best, and passed the file back to you for action. As for saying it was in my In Abeyance file – rubbish. That damned Price woman obviously failed to act on an instruction and return it to you. I'll deal with her.'

'You'd better deal with Chanter too,' Wilmington said jovially. 'And the best of British luck to you, me old china, the best of British!'

The session with Chanter was even worse, and Peter emerged from his office at well after twelve white with contained fury – a man could be rude to a chap just one grade his senior, but Chanter, the head of the entire department, had to be treated much more circumspectly – to find that Miss Price had been tipped off by Wilmington that Peter was about to drop the blame on her, and was absent from her desk.

'Gone to see Mrs Porteous,' the junior said ominously and Peter felt sick; Porteous was the most militant shop-steward the damned secretaries' union had ever had. All he needed now was to trigger a typists' strike, and he'd really be in trouble. All he could do was swallow the reprimand he'd had from Chanter, swallow Wilmington's patent delight in his discomfort, and above all, swallow his natural instinct to be political and pass the buck on to Price. He clearly wasn't going to get away with that; might even have to apologize for his error. 'Christ all bloody mighty!' he shouted at his empty office as he slammed the door behind him, and didn't care who heard him.

The file was waiting on his desk, and he sat down and started to read it from cover to cover. He hadn't bothered last time, there had seemed little point, but now every single document was to be studied, and even the number of names on the petition counted (there were just over five hundred), so that if either that bloody Wilmington or even bloodier Chanter started to make a fuss again, he'd have every fact at his tongue's end.

He sent out for a sandwich for lunch, and that didn't help: the junior, despite being told he wanted mature cheddar cheese on wholemeal bread, chose to bring him processed rubbish on soggy white bread, and he didn't dare to complain, not with the union already alerted to him, and he chewed his way dispiritedly through it as he read page after page of AFB waffle.

It wasn't until he was half way through the file that he found the real information, and his eyebrows lifted as he read the details of the local establishment they wanted to close down. He'd never thought it would be at Minster Hospital. A hospital's a hospital, surely, he told himself, frowning now. They don't do original research using animals in hospitals, do they? I never heard they did. Unless it's for special tests? He had a vague notion that sometimes pregnancy tests involved rabbits or toads, but the documents he was reading said nothing about pregnancy tests. These people were talking about cruel operations and lethal infectious diseases, about animals being wired to electrical machines and heaven knew what other atrocities – all the usual stuff these people churned out. Surely they'd got it wrong? They must mean another place entirely, but he checked and it was quite clear. 'Within the Minster General Hospital complex,' the rather round childish handwriting ran. 'And therefore part of NHS premises. The DHSS deny any responsibility for this use and maintain that the local authority through its department of Environmental Planning should be approached,' and so on and on and on.

Minster General Hospital, he thought, and then remembered, suddenly, about Jessie. The morning had been such hell that she'd been pushed right out of his mind, and that made him suddenly doubly furious. As if he didn't have enough to put up with without Jessie being stupid; all the pent-up anger of the morning came bubbling up, and his fingers were actually shaking with it as he rifled through the pages of the local telephone directory and then dialled the hospital's number.

Only to discover she couldn't be found. 'Mrs Hurst?' the switchboard operator was clearly deeply bored by his demand to talk to her. 'Never heard of her – what department is she?'

'How the hell should I know?' Peter almost snarled it. 'Works in some bloody laboratory or other . . . .'

'If you're going to swear at me then I shan't deal with you,' the operator said promptly, for the first time showing some animation, and disconnected him, and by the time he had rechecked the phone number – having of course forgotten it and closed the damned directory – and redialled and demanded to speak to the switchboard supervisor and had an argument with her, finally managing to get the information that his wife worked in the pathological laboratories, it was too late. The man who answered the phone at the laboratories in a rather thick Jamaican accent told him cheerfully that everyone except himself was gone to lunch, man, and anyway Jessie, she wasn't goin' to be back today, not she, she had to go someplace this afternoon, so they told him, so don't you bother to call again, man, and hung up, leaving Peter with the phone buzzing in his hand and his throat so tight with his rage he could hardly swallow – and he needed to for the taste in his mouth, faintly sweet and disgusting, was making him feel sick.

He tried his home number, then, trying to convince himself she would be there, but of course she wasn't, and then even phoned his son at his job at the record shop, but that was a waste of time too. Mark had been at his girlfriend's house every night this week, didn't know where Mum was, hadn't even remembered his father was away, and Peter slammed the phone down on him too.

That boy; he'd washed his hands of him more times than he could remember, with his stupid passion for his gramophone records and his half-witted girlfriend, but he still had the power to infuriate him. Time he left home anyway. He was nineteen, and, as he was so fond of reminding his father, a legal adult; no one had any right to tell him how to run his life, he said – and that meant, Peter told himself savagely, that he had no right to expect his father to provide him with board and lodging when it happened to suit him. Time he went.

But none of this helped the way he was feeling about Jessie. There was still a huge anger in him at her absence from home, but now it had an undertow that he found very difficult to handle. He was frightened about her, and he'd never had cause to feel anything so unpleasant in connection with Jessie. To be frightened because of his own wife – it was crazy. And as soon as he got home he'd tell her so, because surely, *surely* she'd be there by then?

12

'Well, I say it again – I think she should be transferred to
Farborough,' Sister said loudly. 'I'm not equipped here, sir,
for fevers and I'm not happy about the way . . . .'

'Now, Sister, you're beginning to sound like one of these
modern whiners we have to put up with in the office upstairs.
All they worry about is newfangled notions like . . . what is it
they call it? Nursing process? Bah . . . they just *talk*, but they
need people like you and me to do the real work. Now, you
can't tell me I have to send a patient of mine to another hospital
just because you can't set up the right sort of barrier nursing!
You learned that, now, surely, when you were at Great
Ormond Street?' Lyall Davies set his head on one side and
looked at her with a heavy flirtatiousness to which she rose like
a trout to a feather.

'Of course I can manage the nursing, sir. It's not that I'm
worried about it, just that we simply don't have the equipment
here that we need. Ever since we were downgraded it's been
like pulling teeth to get the most basic equipment, let alone the
sort of ICU apparatus we need. We've got a resuscitation
trolley, of course, but that's all.'

'We've still got the respirator the League of Friends bought
for us. I remember that campaign well – I was chairman of the
committee and by Jove we did well, raised enough for the old
iron lung as we used to call it, you know, and a very good
name for it it was, and still had a bit over for this and that, nice
curtains for the nurses' home, as I recall. Yes, there's nothing
wrong with it, d'you see. It mayn't be as fancy as some of the
stuff they spend all that money on up at Farborough, but it
works, that's the thing. And this child can have it if she needs
it. I don't think she will – I still say there's a lot of hysteria in
this illness. Watch her when she doesn't know she's being
watched and she breathes perfectly normally. I'd put her in
that respirator a day or two just to see how she likes it. That'd

99

soon stop her fussing the way she does.'

'All the same, sir,' Sister said, and stopped and looked at Dan Stewart and Dorothy Cooper, who were sitting on the other side of her desk.

'I have to agree with Dr Lyall Davies,' Dorothy said. 'Andrea Barnett's one of those children who fuss all the time. Suggestible's not the word for it. She gets period pains every other week – anything to get out of doing games – and she can make herself vomit just by thinking about it. She's always complaining of something. If Miss Spain . . . if I'd had the right sort of nursing back-up at the school still I'd never have brought her in, but the damned staff are panicking as much as the children and it was better to get Andrea away – she was getting the others all stirred up. It's perfectly ridiculous – I'd really rather she wasn't transferred, I must say. Her father's in Hong Kong, works with Jardine's there, and I don't want to alarm him more than I need, and sending the girl to a communicable diseases hospital will make no end of a drama. And drama's the last thing we want.'

'I just wish I could get some hard evidence that this really is a new bug.' Dan got to his feet and went over to the chart trolley to pull out the folder with Andrea's name in it. 'Look at this – you've had all this blood work done, ESR, cultures, the lot, and not a thing to show for it. Just a generalized influenza-type illness is what it looks like, and I can't take up beds at Farborough for that – not unless I'm really sure there's a genuine need for it. They're full of salmonella there from the prison, and from that psychogeriatric unit at Wentdown Regis, and we've been warned not to put too much pressure on them. Why do these bloody things always have to happen at the same time? With the sort of evidence I've got so far on this bug, normally I *would* try to isolate patients, but the way things are . . . I don't know.'

He shook his head, still staring at the chart in his hands.

'Whatever I do I'm on a hiding to nothing. If I use my authority to send the child to Farborough and it's just a flu, they'll raise hell, and where's the sense of exposing her to salmonella, anyway? Careful as they are there, it could happen. And if I don't send her and it turns out to be a true bill – a really virulent whatever – then I'm up shit creek again. Sorry, Sister, I was just thinking aloud.'

'Look, Stewart, you're making too much of this altogether.

You heard the child's teacher – she's a bit of a malingerer, and now she's got a genuine flu and making the best of it. Those other two children who died were quite different – they probably had some sort of congenital heart anomaly that made them react so badly – after all, it used to be something we all expected, didn't we? Bad go of flu, well known, always knocked off the feeble, the young and the old.'

'Young babies, maybe, sir,' Dan said. 'Not hefty schoolgirls of twelve or so.'

'The young and the old,' Lyall Davies said firmly. 'But you'll notice that it's only children that are getting this particular flu. That's right, isn't it?'

'Yes,' Dan said, still looking down at Andrea's temperature chart with its wild spiky pattern.

'Then it's obviously nothing to get agitated about,' the old man said triumphantly. 'Obviously older people have an immunity. Must have been exposed before, so it's just a recurrence of an old flu strain. This business of paralysis and not breathing – this child's learned it – she's just going in for hysterical over-breathing. Putting it on, I'll lay you all Lombard Street to a China orange.'

Dan looked up at him sharply. 'You could be right, at that,' he said. 'We haven't had a single report in from the GPs of any cases over fifteen or so. When was the last major Asian flu?'

'There was one in 1979 – I remember I was knocked out with that one,' Sister said. 'Quite ill, I was.'

'And another in the winter of '69/'70.' Lyall Davies looked triumphantly round at them all. 'That one really was appalling. Remember, Stewart? Fifteen years ago, that one, we had seven deaths from it in one of the geriatric wards, seven! Fifteen years ago . . . that'd make sense, now, wouldn't it? Anyone under fifteen, no immunity. Anyone over it, no problems.'

'I don't remember that one,' Dan said. 'All before my time.'

'Well, I remember it,' Lyall Davies said. 'Like yesterday. You mark my words, that's all this is! It'll soon fizzle out.'

He got to his feet and leaned over and patted Sister on her shoulder in a very avuncular manner. 'Just you set up that respirator beside that child's bed, Sister, and see how soon she'll get over her fusses! And you go back to your school, Miss Cooper, and knock some sense into those silly little girls of yours. There's no epidemic here – just a lot of people who haven't the experience to know what they're looking at. Trust me, and stop all this worrying. I've got the experience, and I know. There's nothing to worry *about*.'

In spite of his obvious fatigue, and in spite of the fact that she said very little in response, Ben talked all through breakfast about the work. They had found a quiet table in the canteen, well away from listening ears, though Jessie was very aware of the sharp glances some of the night nurses threw in their direction; but it was only a few who showed any awareness of them. Lots of the people who came trailing in were too tired to be interested in anything but themselves. She wasn't the only person looking white and pinched with lack of sleep.

'The thing is, I need to speed up the tests. I've got a good deal of 737 and I'd hate to waste any of it. If only I had some more subjects to work on we could use not only the new batch of Contravert, but the next one they're making up for me – oh, Jessie, there's so much work to do! And the lab busier than we've been for months. Why does it all happen at the same time?'

'Epidemics are like that,' she said, almost mumbling it into her coffee cup. 'Always happen at awkward times. There was that flu thing six years ago – I went down with it while Peter was doing his last set of post-qualifying exams – it was awful. No one to do anything at home but me . . . .'

'Yes,' Ben frowned. 'Yes, there was one then, wasn't there? June was ill.' He sat silently for a while then, also staring into his coffee cup. He hadn't thought about June all night, and had forgotten to phone her the way he usually did at seven o'clock. She'd be worried. He'd better call her now; and he got to his feet.

'I'll be back in a minute,' he said. 'Just have to make a phone call. Try and think of a way we can increase the experiments – maybe you'll think of an answer. I can't.'

She did; as he came back to the table ten minutes later, his eyes looking huge in the shadows under them, she said, 'More animals,' even before he could sit down.

'What?' He was abstracted now; June had been tearful on the phone because she'd been so worried. His phone call was an hour late, fully an hour, she was sure something awful had happened to him, and though he'd managed to soothe her eventually, the irritation her dependence always created in him had broken through his words, and she'd known he was annoyed, and that made her worse than ever. Damn it, he thought as he saw Jessie sitting there at the table waiting for him. Why can't June be like her, calm and sensible and interested in my work?

'I said more animals,' Jessie repeated. 'Couldn't you afford some new stock? I could drive over for them this afternoon, if you don't mind doing the extra bloods with Harry, and get you some more from the breeders. Then we could start again tomorrow with four or even six groups. We've got the pens. Or you could, I suppose, use Castor and Pollux.'

He shook his head. 'They're too expensive. I ought to sell them really. I can't afford to use them, though I thought I could when I bought them. They're turning into damned pets, that's the trouble – no, it's got to be rabbits. Unless we've got enough of the guinea pigs?'

She shook her head. 'No, not yet. I've got several litters coming on nicely, but they're rather young. We used guinea pigs all last month, remember. It has to be the rabbits now. Anyway, you want to replicate the experiments and that means using the same type of subject.'

He rubbed his hand over his face and yawned. 'You're right, of course. I'm being stupid. Christ, I'm tired! I'll have to get some sleep, somehow, if I'm to be any use. You too. If you're going to drive over to Podgate this afternoon.'

'Glad to,' she said, pleased at his acceptance of her advice, happy to be given another useful job to do. 'I'll go and sleep at home, then. If I go now, I could sleep till about twelve and then start. Three hours or so should get me over the worst – what will you do? Go home too?'

He shook his head. 'I'd better not. I'll get a shakedown in the senior medical common room. Moscrop's back from his holiday today, thank God, so they should manage well enough till this afternoon – as long as I'm on call for anything urgent we'll be all right.'

'I'll go back and feed the animals then, and settle them for the day,' Jessie said. 'And I'll get back tonight as soon as I can with the new ones.'

'And we'll start again tomorrow. I'll have the cultures done by then, too, of last night's lot. Oh, Jessie, Jessie, so much happening, so much to *do*.'

'So you've already said,' she said a little tartly. 'Talking

103

about it won't get it done, will it?' And she went, making her way out of the hospital and across the courtyard again, to feed and clean out the animals before driving, very carefully, back to Purbeck Avenue.

When she got there and found the side door lock had been broken she considered calling the police; there had been several break-ins in this road recently, and her belly lurched as she saw the splintered panels and the gouged edge of the door jamb. But nothing else had been disturbed; the back door was as firmly locked as she had left it, and the front door still had its chain in place. So she didn't call the police. Leave it till tonight, she thought muzzily as she went upstairs and undressed. After I get back from the breeders. Then I'll call the police – or get Peter to do it. He'll be back tonight – and she rubbed her face wearily at that thought and pushed it to the back of her mind. Worry about Peter tonight, when he got home. That would be soon enough.

She slept remarkably heavily, after a hot shower, and woke with her pulses thumping with terror when the alarm clock went off at a quarter to twelve. For a moment she lay there, staring at the bright square of the window, too confused to know where she was or why she was there; one part of her mind knew it was midday, while another denied it, and she thought crazily, am I ill? and then, at last, remembered and lay still for another moment or two to let the rush of adrenalin subside before she got out of bed.

In spite of the big breakfast she had shared with Ben, she was ravenous, and she made a couple of cheese sandwiches to eat in the car, and picked up an apple before checking the kitchen was tidy, collecting her handbag and locking the house. She carefully pocketed the back-door key. Peter was always nagging about security; well, she'd done her best, and she jammed a piece of stone from the garden rockery against the side door as she went. It was silly, really; a would-be burglar would only have to pick it up and chuck it away to get access to the back of the house, she told herself, but at least it would slow him down. And she turned to get into the car, but stopped as she heard the phone ringing, muffled, from inside the house.

She considered for a moment going back, going through the laborious unlocking procedure to answer it, and then turned away. Whoever it was, they would give up long before she got to the phone and nothing was more irritating than having the thing go dead just as you picked it up; let them ring again. Probably only Mark wanting to borrow some money. She glanced at her watch; sure to be Mark. It was his lunch hour and that was the only time he ever tried to get hold of her.

It wasn't until she was almost out of the town on the Podgate road that she thought – that couldn't have been Mark. He knows I'm at work all day. He usually phones there if he wants anything. It couldn't have been Mark – and then dismissed the telephone she had left ringing in the empty house. It didn't matter any more. All that mattered was concentrating on driving, on being as fast as she safely could. She felt a deep need to get those animals back to the lab as soon as possible, to get the next trials in hand as fast as possible. I'm getting very like Ben, she told herself wryly. Impatient for answers, impatient to go charging on.

For the first twelve miles or so through the winding Dorset lanes she thought she was fine, that the three hours' sleep she had had was enough to stop her feeling weary; she ate one of her sandwiches, but it tasted dry and unappetizing, and she threw the other to the birds in the hedges that were flashing past the car window, and settled down to the last dozen miles doggedly. She'd ask for some coffee when she got there. That would make her feel better, and she could drink it while they put the animals in their boxes and took them out to the boot of the car.

She got there without mishap, and at first was comforted when she found she was expected. Ben had telephoned to say she was coming and to leave an order for the stock he wanted, and the animals were ready: they had been caught and set in the special boxes with the straw lining and neat airholes, and had only to be loaded into her car boot, while she signed the order form and arranged for the invoice to be sent to Ben. There was no time to ask for coffee or anything else, and she was back at the wheel within ten minutes or so of arriving. And then realized that it would have been wise to stop longer and ask for that coffee. She was more tired than she had realized.

But the flurry of activity that collecting the animals had caused brought her back to full alertness for a little while, and for five miles or so she drove well, glad to be on her way back with her errand done. The fields that lay on each side of the road that ran ahead of her were flat and brown in the afternoon glow, the last traces of the harvest still showing on some, and the faint blush of green on others showing where winter fodder was growing. Trees, almost naked of leaves now, stood stark and still, not a twig moving in the windless air, which was heavy, a little misty and far from cold, and she pulled over to the side of the road to take off her jacket. The old car's ventilation wasn't all it might be these days; she really ought to get it serviced, but meanwhile she had to find some way to cool herself. She opened the car window before she started off again, but had to close it as grit blew in and made her blink, and then found after she had closed it that her eyes were heavy and sandy and keeping them open more difficult than it ought to be.

The rest of the journey was hell; she tried putting the car radio on at full blast, but even that didn't help much. The noise just blended with the sound of the engine to make almost a lullaby, and once or twice she felt her neck jerk as her head sank forwards, out of her control.

She tried talking aloud to herself, to fight off the sleep that hung over her like a great threatening storm cloud, as though the sound of her voice was an actual force that could keep the greyness well away from her, and that worked for a while. But then her mouth felt dry and her tongue clumsy and she couldn't continue with it, and again she opened her window, preferring gritty streaming eyes and the blast created by her speed to the misery of the fear of sleep.

It was incredible that in fact she was nearly back at the hospital when it happened. There had been little traffic to worry about in the lanes, but now she was on the main road into the town there was more – lorries and vans and cars making for the motorway – and she had to hold on to the wheel tightly to keep herself on a straight line, for several of them already had their lights on in the early evening dusk, and their glow seemed to draw her veering off to the right, into their paths.

It was at a narrow part of the road that it happened; yet another lorry came blazing towards her, but this time she didn't seem able to stop the car from leaning towards it, and she was almost under its wheels, could actually hear its brakes screaming, when she managed to get her sluggish muscles into action again, and wrenched the wheel hard over. The car lurched and then skidded and her seat belt pulled viciously against her breasts, making her gasp for breath, and then held her tightly as the bonnet of the car hit a lamp post and the engine stalled.

She sat there blankly, staring out at the mess in front of her, aware that the lorry had stopped and that someone was running towards her, but not caring. All she knew was that the animals in the back of the car were safe because she could hear them rustling agitatedly in the back, and that she was no longer threatened with sleep. The impact had woken her completely, and she began to laugh, weakly at first and then more loudly as the lorry driver pulled open her car door and stared in at her.

13

'You see?' Hugh said triumphantly. 'Unless you do something really showy you get nowhere! Just look at this . . . and this . . . and this . . .'

They looked, glumly. Every one of the papers had front-page stories about an animal welfare group which had announced it had put poison in chocolate bars and distributed them to shops all over the country, because the makers of the chocolate funded research using animals, and Hugh, jabbing a peremptory forefinger, picked out the most dramatic comments and read them aloud as the others sat and said nothing.

'And what have we got about our activities in the local paper? Sweet bugger all, that's what! If you'd done as I wanted, we'd be the ones making the headlines, not this bunch of lunatics.'

'They're not lunatics,' Tracey said, and they all stared at her, for she rarely said anything very much, though she cried a good deal. 'I mean, they've done no harm to no one, but they've got people talking about the poor animals, haven't they? They haven't *hurt* any animals and they haven't broken into any private property – and I bet they haven't put poison in the chocolate bars anyway. They've only said they have to frighten people and make them think about poor little animals being used to make them.'

'They aren't using animals to make the chocolate, for God's sake,' Hugh said, his temper flaring. 'Don't be such a bloody stupid . . . .'

'Mr Chairman, there are ladies present,' growled Graham. 'Mind your tongue.' And Hugh flicked his eyes at him, and took a sharp breath in through his nose, working at controlling himself.

'It doesn't matter what they've done,' he said after a moment. 'I couldn't care less what they've done. All I care

108

about is what we haven't done. And we haven't got an atom of publicity for our work, while this other lot have got masses.'

'Then why don't you join them, if you don't like the AFB and the way we do things?' Graham said.

'I do like the AFB. I'm the founder member of this branch, remember! All I'm saying is we've had our noses wiped and it's all our own fault. You promised me you'd get us publicity for those photographs I took, and at considerable personal risk I'll have you know, and all you can tell us now is that you passed 'em on to the papers and that's the last you know about it! We haven't even got the pictures to show anyone else! And they were polaroids. No negatives.'

'I made no promises,' Graham said, unperturbed by Hugh's sweating anger, seeming almost to enjoy it. 'I said I'd try, and so I did. It isn't my fault that the pictures were of so little intrinsic interest. There was no proof in them that these animals there are being ill-treated, is there? It's not enough for you just to say so . . . .'

'No proof? What about the dead rabbits? What more proof do you want than that?'

'It's not enough,' Graham said with offensive patience. 'They could have been planted by you. It'd be the first thing they'd think you'd done. We've got to do better than that. Those pictures could have been forged somehow, that's what they'd say. I'm not saying they were, mind you, I'm just trying to show you how newspaper people think.'

'I think it's time to put it to the vote,' Hugh said loudly, sick of Graham and his pontification. 'The motion is that this meeting agrees to put Plan B into action. All those in favour say, "Aye".' And he glared first at Tracey and then at Gail, who both said, 'Aye', a little tremulously. And then he turned to Dora and Freda, and they stared back at him, in silence.

'Look, Dora,' he said in as conciliatory a voice as he could muster. 'I know how you feel about private property and all that, but it isn't really private property, is it? I mean, it's on NHS premises and that means it belongs to us, doesn't it? They take our taxes and they use them to build our hospitals and then they go and use our tax money to put animals to terrible torture in those buildings! We have every right to go in there and deal with the matter. We're paying for it, after all.'

Dora's face cleared and she nodded her head vigorously. 'He's right, Freda!' she said, nudging her neighbour, who still seemed dubious. 'He's right, you know. The taxes we pay, we ought to be consulted about how they spend our money. I think he's right. I'm going to say "aye".'

And after a moment Dora mumbled, 'Aye', as well and Hugh looked at Graham with his brows raised and his face smooth with satisfaction.

'Well, no need to bother you chaps to say anything, is there?' Graham stared stolidly back. 'Because we've got a majority for Plan B.'

'Direct action requires unanimous agreement on the part of all Brigade members in the branch,' Graham said urbanely. 'You know the constitution perfectly well. So you do need to hear from us, I'm afraid.'

'Then for heaven's sake, say something!' Hugh threw all his caution and his political skills, such as they were, to the wind, well aware that he was being outflanked. 'Because if we don't do anything the branch is dead anyway. So if you two want to kill it, then go ahead. I'll do the bloody job on my own, that's all.'

'No need,' Graham said. 'You can have your ayes from John and me on the understanding that you let us take charge of Plan B. We run the show, not you. We've got the experience, you see, laddy.' He said it so kindly that Hugh's cheeks burned with fury. 'We know how to organize these things properly. We've been thinking about it a good deal, got some stuff together – a couple of walkie-talkies, very handy that, a few tools, that sort of thing. All we need, once you agree that we're in charge, is you to bring that camera of yours to get evidence of what we're doing. Got to have a record of it, of course, or those other lot'll claim they did it, when the story gets out. As of course it will.'

'Plan B is mine. I developed it, I made the lists, I thought it all out, plotted it . . . .'

'And very well done too, with a few alterations John and I have made. Not as tactical as it might have been, you see, old boy, not as tactical as it ought to have been. 'Tis now, though. Needed the eye of experience, as John and I both agreed. Right, John?'

'Right,' said John obediently and looked owlishly at Hugh.

'Oh, sod you!' Hugh shouted, and when Graham tut-tutted at him lifted his hands as though he were about to strike him; but then subsided, and sat staring at Graham with eyes as malevolent in their gaze as a cat's at a mousehole.

'All right,' he said at length. 'All right. I'll do what's best for the branch. I'm above this sort of petty jockeying for position. I care only for the welfare of the group as a whole, not for my own glory.' He was beginning to feel better by the moment. 'So as long as you agree to Plan B, I'll agree that you lead the exercise. On the understanding that this is for this exercise only. Afterwards we return to the status quo, with me as the chairman, appointed by head office, remember.'

'We'll see about the future when it comes,' said Graham with a somewhat gnomic air. 'Now, details. John and I say tomorrow night. Midweek, you see, less likely to be good security. I imagine they lock up more carefully at weekends when the laboratory isn't operating. So, Wednesday is D Day . . . .' And he reached into his briefcase and with great aplomb pulled out his own version of Plan B, over which they all bent, as Hugh sat glowering over his folded arms, refusing, very obviously, to join in. I'll show the bastard, just wait and see how I'll show the bastard, he promised himself. Just you wait, Graham Bighead, I'll get you right into the shit, you see if I don't.

The room was one of the most heavily furnished Joe had ever been into in his life, and he'd been in a good many in his time as a leg-man. Against one wall stood a row of ornate birdcages filled with chattering whistling birds which rustled around their enclosed quarters nervously, swinging on fanciful trapezes, dodging round the miniature houses and turreted castles that cluttered their small available space, and filling the room with the smell of their birdseed.

The room outside the cages looked as cluttered and over-equipped as they did; there was a three-piece suite in heavy red mock leather, piled high with multi-coloured cushions. There was a dining table made of blond wood with insets of marquetry just visible under a vast china epergne filled with wax fruit, and six heavily carved chairs in the same marquetry. There were nests of tables, and a glass coffee table, and several stools and foot-rests, and every available surface, including the shelves that filled one wall, was covered with ornaments. There were shepherdesses and shepherds in fluted china, there were winsome kittens and impudent dogs in vivid colours, there were candlesticks and brass dishes and paper flowers and

Spanish dancer dolls with net skirts spread wide to show a
froth of red frills and musical boxes and bowls of sweets; and
Joe stared round and wanted to laugh. It was like falling head
first into a shop window on the day of the annual sale.

'Sit down, I'm sure,' Edna said, and stood hovering as he
inserted himself gingerly into an armchair. It was very
slippery and cold, and the chill struck up through his buttocks
and made it difficult for him to relax, though no sign of that
showed on his face as he smiled expansively at Edna.

'Nice place you've got here,' he said, his voice oozing
affability. 'Very cosy.'

She beamed complacently. 'Yes, I like a few nice things
about me. Makes a house a home, that's what I always say.
Not that the family appreciate it. I get all the nicest things I can
from my catalogue, you know, and then the cows never stay
home. You got daughters, Mr Lloyd? If you haven't, don't
bother, that's all I can say.'

'No children, sad to say, Mrs Laughton. I haven't been
blessed that way.'

'Then good luck to you,' she said and sat down herself,
leaning forwards with her hands on her knees. 'Now, you
wanted to talk to me, you said? From the paper? Have I won
that there competition? The one for the Christmas Hamper
full of Traditional Good Fayre and all that?'

'Not exactly, Mrs Laughton,' Joe said. 'Though you never
know, do you? Hasn't been drawn yet, that hasn't. They're
still marking the entries, but there's no knowing what
mightn't happen. No, I wanted to talk to you about
something different.'

He paused portentously. 'I was glad I was able to find you,
but then we had a record of you on our files.'

She frowned and pulled back a little. 'Record? What
record?'

'That unfortunate business last month, Mrs Laughton.
With Barney's self-service . . . er, let me see . . . a matter of a
packet of sausages, three packs of biscuits, a jar of jam and a tin
of very expensive top quality red salmon.'

'I never had nothing to do with it!' she said, trying to be
shrill and self-righteous, but producing only a whine. 'I told
them in the court I didn't.'

'I'm sure, Mrs Laughton, I'm sure you didn't. When I read
the report, I said to myself, there's more to this than meets the

eye, I said. So I won't publish it.' He smiled at her with great sweetness. 'Not yet, I won't.'

'I was scared it'd get in the paper and I'd lose my little jobs,' she said, staring at him with her eyes wide and watchful. 'I was that relieved when it didn't.'

'Well, Mrs Laughton,' he said expansively. 'It's me you've got to thank for that. So I hope I can count on you for a little help with my investigations.'

'What investigations?' She was comfortable now, suddenly aware of the power of her position, no longer the threatened suppliant, but the useful contact. She even preened a little. 'What can I do for you, Mr Lloyd?'

'Your little job you mentioned.'

'That's right. At the hospital – domestic supervisor I am, for the patha-whatsit laboratories. Very important job that, all those test-tubes and nasty things in bottles lying about.'

His brows lifted. 'The hospital? I didn't know you worked there.'

'Oh, yes, been there ages, I have. Seven months, it must be. Ever such a long time.'

'But I thought you worked at Bluegates School.'

'Oh, that.' She seemed to flatten and stared at him with suspicion again. 'Well, yes, I did agree to help 'em out a bit, just for a while . . . you know . . . .'

'How long for?'

'Oh, about three months it was, I suppose, till that rotten bloody woman . . . well, 'nuff said. No names, no pack drill.'

'What woman? It's not for publication, like your court case isn't at present. So you can tell me.'

'Mrs McGrath,' she said unwillingly. 'And nothing she told you is true, and I swear it. It was her took those things, and not much they were at that, a few leftovers, nothing else, but it was her that took it.'

'I don't know anything about leftovers.' Joe was enjoying himself hugely; this was better than a play. 'I'm interested in the epidemic they've got there. I need to know what it's like, how many girls have it, what they're doing about it; there seems to be some attempt to hush it up, you see.'

'The epidemic?' Her face cleared at once. 'Oh, that! Well, I must say it was really bad. One of the girls got sent home in no end of a hurry – Miranda her name was, I remember. I thought it was a real pretty name, Miranda, and she was took ill and

Miss Spain told me when I was collecting the dirty dishes from the sickroom, she told me the girl had got sent home because she was poorly. And then there was the others and the one that went to the hospital and died, and all the girls talking all the time about it. Not that they talked to me, stuck-up little madams that lot is, but I got ears in my head and I use 'em. They all said they was poorly the same way, got sore throats and snotty noses and headaches and that, and their legs gone all weak and paralysed and feeling terrible, and then they really got upset. It was the night they had their fireworks party. I remember I'd worked my fingers to the bone, I had, cooking their suppers and not one of them ate a thing as far as I could tell, not that it stopped that bitch McGrath saying as I hadn't cooked 'em right. Anyway, that was the worst time. All of them carrying on alarming. They've all gone home now, mostly. I stopped last week, and I know that since I left it's been no better. Girls getting ill and being took to hospital – it's probably the way they feed those poor children. Awful food they give 'em. All those raw vegetables and that, and only decent meat twice a week, rest of the time, it's fish, and that only grilled, never a nice piece fried with chips like all children like best. Not them, they eat all this muesli rubbish and bread like shoe leather . . . .'

'Yes,' Joe said, needing now to stem the flood he had unleashed. 'Let me get this down in a little more detail now. Give me dates and numbers as best you can, will you?'

For the next half hour he took her painstakingly through her story, noting each detail as he managed to get it, and the picture emerged of a healthy group of children being cared-for very well indeed and well fed and exercised, falling in increasing numbers into a flu-like illness that made them feel violently ill. They were feverish, they complained first of sore throats and headaches and later of leg pains. Then they said they couldn't move their legs and some of them seemed to have breathing difficulties. There had been one child with that – the one who, Mrs Laughton said, had been sent home, but which, Joe told himself, was almost certainly the first one to die – followed by three more, then eleven, then another fifteen, until virtually every person in the school had it, except the senior staff. It was the children and only the children who seemed to be at risk and he couldn't help but feel a surge of excitement as he contemplated that fact, seeing the headline

114

already: 'Child Killer Plague Sweeps South Coast School'. Lovely.

'Is there anything else you can tell me about the school then, Mrs Laughton?' He got to his feet, needing to unstick himself from the mock leather which had lost its chill rapidly, replacing it with a disagreeable sweatiness. 'No complaints from the girls as far as you ever heard? Got to be accurate about this, you know. Can't have people accusing us of bearing false witness and all that!' And he gave a jovial little laugh which made Mrs Laughton purse her lips and stop to think.

'Can't say as I ever heard of any,' she said regretfully. 'They seemed to like the place well enough, though it's unnatural I call it, taking little kids away from their loving mothers and putting them in boarding schools. Never did that with my three, you can be sure.' And she nodded with self-satisfied motherhood.

'Then they're not so bad, after all, your daughters?' Joe couldn't resist the dig and she looked put out for a moment and then said defiantly. 'They're like all young people nowadays. Got no respect for their elders. If I'd talked to my Mum, God rest her soul, the way they talk to me, and dressed the way they dress – well, I'd have been black and blue, and no error!'

'I'm sure you would,' Joe began to move to the door. The place was depressing him, not least because of the heavy smell of scented room deodorant coming from a plastic container set on a table near his chair. 'Well, thanks for your help. I hope I won't need to bother you again.'

'Yes, well, it's no bother, any time. Now, about that other matter . . . .'

'The little argument with Barney's and what the court said? Now, I wouldn't worry about that if I were you, Mrs Laughton. No need to make trouble, really, is there? You don't need to worry about the *Advertiser*, and that's a promise. Mind you, if something similar should happen I'd be hard put to it to . . . .'

'Oh, no, sir, there won't be nothing similar,' she said fervently, and scuttled after him to the door, her feet silent on the explosively patterned red, blue and yellow carpet. 'You can be sure of that. And if I can ever tell you anything else you want to know about the places where I has my little jobs, just say the word. I could be one of your . . . well, reporters, eh? I

115

dare say you pay a bit for news, eh? And there's me with a lot of debts, one way and another – losing me job at Bluegates and that, and all this catalogue stuff still to pay off, and the old man on the dole, and my girls not giving me a penny, greedy cows.'

'Well, I can't promise that,' Joe said hastily, and put his notebook firmly in his pocket. 'We have our regular reporters who deal with the hospital and all that – but I'll keep it in mind.'

'Regular reporters!' she said and sniffed, as he pulled open the front door, an action which set a series of bird mobiles hanging above it rattling and ringing. 'They don't know half what goes on there. What about the time that there monkey escaped, and they caught it down in the boiler house? I bet your reporter never knew about that!'

'Monkey?' Joe, who had been standing poised on the step to go, looked back at her sharply. 'What monkey?'

'One of those they keeps in the lab where I clean – where I'm domestic supervisor,' she said, sensing his interest and showing her triumph at it. 'Got all sorts there they have, monkeys and rabbits, all sorts.'

'What are they there for?'

'They do this here research on 'em, don't they? Gives 'em the flu and then gives 'em nasty injections to get rid of it. Ought to be put a stop to.' She smirked virtuously and held the door welcomingly wide. 'I've heard 'em talking about it, I have, early in the morning when there's just the two of them there. That there Dr Pitman and Mrs Hurst . . . .'

'And you worked there as well as at the kitchens at Bluegates? Where the animals are?' Joe said, and now all his instincts for a story were sitting up and begging for attention.

'Didn't I tell you? In the patha-whatsit laboratories, that's where I work. Where they test all these animals.'

'And you *saw* them? The animals? And you work there?'

'That's right,' she said. 'A woman's got to make a living, after all – no harm in that, is there?'

'I really wouldn't like to say,' Joe said savagely, and pulled his hat over his eyes and went marching down the path of the small council house, leaving the woman staring after him.

14

It had been quite dark for a long time when at last she drove into Purbeck Avenue. She was driving slowly, worried by the unfamiliarity of the controls: her own old Volvo had had a floor gearstick, but Harry Gentle's car had a steering-wheel change, and that took some getting used to, as did the size of the car. It was smaller than hers and oddly, that made her feel less sure about the sort of space she could get into and less sure about the distance needed to overtake another vehicle. And in addition to all that was the state she was in. No longer sleepy, that was for sure, but feeling as though she had been taken by head and heels and pulled out into a thread of tension: her eyes were hot and gritty, and her belly seemed to consist of a hard knot that trembled all the time. She felt faintly sick and on the edge of tears, which was an extraordinary way to feel, because she had never been a woman who wept easily.

The headlights cut a slit in the darkness in front of her, to show the pillar box, the landmark telling her she was just two doors from her own house. All the houses in Purbeck Avenue looked so alike that it was impossible to tell which was which until you were on top of them and could distinguish details like curtains and carriage lamps beside the front doors, but now she knew where she was, and gingerly she steered the car into the turn that would bring it into her own short driveway.

And stepped on the brakes just in time. The rear of Peter's car loomed up in the glare of her headlights and she sat there, both hands gripping the wheel until she caught her breath again. And then she switched off the engine and stared dully at the car in front, trying to understand why it was there.

He was coming back from London – when? He'd told her, of course he had, but suddenly she couldn't remember. Tomorrow, surely? Monday night he'd said. What day was it today? And she felt tears slide out of her hot eyes and slither greasily down her cheeks because she couldn't remember what day of the week it was.

'What the hell do you think you're doing?' Peter's voice was so loud, even through the car windows, that she jumped. 'This is a private driveway, damn you, and you've no right . . . Jessie? Jessie! What the hell are you doing in that thing? Where did you get it? Where's your Volvo? And where the bloody hell have you been?'

'Podgate,' she said stupidly, peering out at him, for he had now opened the door and was bending over staring at her. 'I had to go to Podgate for some rabbits – when did you get back? I didn't expect you yet . . . .'

'Didn't expect . . . Jesus Christ! I told you I'd be back last night! Last *night*! And you didn't expect me, now, twenty-four hours later? What the hell's the matter with you?'

She got out of the car, moving stiffly and slowly the way she sometimes dreamed she did, and stood with her back to the little car so that she could lean on it, looking up at Peter in the sickly yellow light thrown by the street lamp just outside their front gate.

'I'm sorry, Peter, but I . . . I didn't get much sleep last night. Didn't get any, actually. And then I had to drive to Podgate and on the way back I had an accident. Car's a write-off, I think. The police seemed to think so.'

'The car's a . . . .' He put one hand on her shoulder roughly and almost shook her. 'What do you mean, a write-off?'

'I hit a lamp post,' she said wearily. She'd already told the story over and over again: to the police who came to the scene, to the one who took her and her boxes of rabbits back to the hospital, to Harry Gentle who had been in charge of the laboratory in Ben's absence – and she still wasn't quite sure why he hadn't been there when she'd returned, for he had said he would be, when she brought back the animals – and to yet another policeman who came to check on the event. Now, telling Peter about it seemed too much effort altogether, and she shook her head and only repeated, 'I hit a lamp post.'

'You damned idiot!' Peter's voice lifted half an octave higher, and now she could hear the emotion in it, something more than just the irritation he had shown so far. 'You stupid woman! You don't deserve to have a car – to go driving into lamp posts and write it off, just like that – d'you think I'm made of money? Do you know how much my no-claim bonus is worth? And now you've gone and written it off!'

She stood very still, not looking at his face but straight ahead. She could see his tie, uncharacteristically unknotted and dangling its ends over the lapels of his jacket, and the light glinting off his shirt buttons. It was like looking at a carving, a part of her mind thought absurdly, not a person. A carving in coloured stone. And then his words really sank into her awareness and she took a deep breath and did look at him. 'What did you say?'

'I said you're a damned idiot . . . .'

'No. Not that. About . . . you were talking about your no-claim bonus? About money?'

'Well, of course I bloody was! What do you expect? Never an accident with either car for over five years – it's a substantial sum – are you all right? Were you hurt at all?'

But it was too late for that. She had pushed past him, pulling her bag from her shoulder as she went, rummaging in it for the back-door key, and he followed her.

'Jessie, are you all right? I was so angry when I got home and you weren't here – it was bad enough this morning, but not to find you here tonight – I've been sitting in the bloody car for over an hour waiting for you, do you know that? You put the chain on the front door, took the back-door key with you when you know I don't carry a spare – how was I supposed to get in? I had to break open the side door this morning as it was – did you want me to bash in the back door too? It'd cost a fortune to . . . .' And he stopped.

She had reached the back door by now and he was immediately behind her, and she opened it and reached in for the secondary switch that put on the light over the doorstep, and he stood waiting for her to make way for him. But she just slammed the door behind her and went out of the kitchen into the hallway, not even bothering to put on the overhead light as she went.

He followed her, cursing under his breath. Bloody woman, putting him in the wrong like this. He'd been frantic about her, positively frantic with worry. To have come home at six – and after such a pig of a day – and find she still wasn't there, to go over to Mark's girlfriend's house to check with his son whether he knew where she was to be found, and then to have come back to sit like an idiot in a cold car waiting for her – it was enough to make any man livid. And when you're angry you don't always say the things you mean, he told himself, tremulous with self-pity. Of course I should have asked her first if she was all right, of course I should, but I could see she was, she got out of the car didn't she, stood there? Obviously she was all right. I was entitled to complain about the damage she'd done.

He went into the hall and unchained the front door, and then went and switched on the lights in the living room. Normally he didn't like lights burning in unused rooms, because it was wasteful, but now he needed to see his home as bright and welcoming and safe, a place a man was happy to come back to after a bad day, and he stood in the doorway looking round for a moment before following Jessie, who had gone upstairs. He could hear her moving about up there.

The room, still and tidy, glowed at him in the lamplight, cream-coloured furniture on a beige carpet, bright cushions, well-polished tables, the whole smelling faintly of lemon-scented furniture polish and the big bronze chrysanthemums that she had set in a brass bowl on the coffee table. She had taste, Jessie, he told himself. It was a beautiful room, and he liked to look at it.

He heard a door slam above his head, and he took a deep breath and turned to the stairs. This had to be sorted out, and the sooner the better. He'd been an idiot to talk about money when she'd told him she'd been in an accident, an absolute idiot, and he'd say so handsomely. Get it all sorted out . . . .

She was in the bathroom, and he opened the door and went in, not bothering to knock, to find her picking up her bottles of bath salts and her cans of talcum powder.

'Listen, Jess, I'm sorry. I shouldn't have said that about the no-claim bonus. I should have asked you first how you were. But I could see you were okay, so . . . and I *was* pretty angry, you know. I had every right to be, didn't I? I was supposed to be back last night, and had to come back this morning instead, and you weren't here and . . . .'

'I got the days mixed up,' she said dully, not looking at him, and pushed past him to go back to the bedroom, carrying the bath salts and talcum and also her soap dish and toothbrush with her. 'I've been working all hours, so I got the days mixed. Not that it matters, does it? If you were supposed to come back last night, why didn't you let me know you were going to be late? If you'd phoned I would have known you were due back, known to leave the front door unchained. But you didn't call me, so . . . .' She shrugged. 'It's not worth talking about,' and she went over to the bed and dropped her things on it.

He stood in the doorway, staring at the bed. Her big blue suitcase was on it, and it was already half full. He could recognize her green check suit and the red trousers she always wore with the thick yellow sweater which made her look – he often thought but never told her – about sixteen.

'What are you doing?'

'I'm packing. Just a few things. I'll collect the rest another time.'

'Packing? What the hell are you talking about? Don't be stupid, what do you mean, packing?' Fear rose in him and made his voice rise, so that he was shouting. 'You're not going anywhere . . . .'

'Yes, I am,' she said, and went on putting her things neatly into the suitcase. 'I'm going. I don't know why I stayed this long. I'm so tired I can't think straight, and that's why I'm going. When you can't think straight you start to feel straight – you let the real feelings come out and that's why I'm going. I should have gone years ago, but I used to think too much. Now I haven't slept for thirty-six hours and it's made me high, you know that? High as a kite and flying just on feelings, and it's great. I'm *going* – I'll take Harry Gentle's car back to him and I'll get myself into a hotel in town and then you needn't bother about claiming on your bloody insurance for my car because I won't be here to need it. You can forget any of the money you spend on me, because you won't be doing it any more. You'll have it all to yourself, together with this horrible house.' And she snapped the case shut and hefted it off the bed and turned to stare at him with her head up, daring him to say anything.

He had never been a violent man, not physically. He'd always said that a man who had to use his fists to get what he wanted wasn't a real man. It took brains, a tongue well-employed, wisdom, an air of authority to operate as a man should, he would say when cases of wife-battering were talked about, and was as disgusted as anyone else by the stories told of injured women and frightened children. But now it was different. Now it was he who was being pushed by a provocative wife into behaviour that was obnoxious to him, the way he had heard it said some of these wife-beaters were, and as he hurled himself across the room at her somewhere inside his head a voice was shouting at him, you've got to stop her . . .

He hadn't even realized he'd lifted his hand; it was as though all the day's frustrations and fears had boiled up inside him to make a head of steam that operated his body of its own volition. Not until his hand hit her face with a stinging blow did he know he'd done it, and then, even as he watched his own hands in horror, the hitting went on, slapping her face from side to side so that her hair swung over her shoulders and her neck seemed as though it would crack under the strain of the movements.

She was crying aloud, screaming, and that made it worse, and he tried to pull the case from her hands, to throw her on to the bed, to show her he was master – that she couldn't just walk out on him, just because he'd talked about what any intelligent man would talk about when he heard his property had been damaged – but she used it to protect herself, shoving it hard against him, and the corner of the heavy case, with its cladding of protective metal, caught him in the crotch and made him squeal with pain and double over.

And then she was gone, running away from him, down the stairs and out of the front door. He could hear every step she took, heard the front door opened and left open, heard the slam of the car door as she threw herself into it and then its choked cough as she switched on the engine. By the time he was able to straighten up as the sickening wave of pain she had created slowly subsided, the car's sound was dwindling down the avenue.

It always looked so easy when they did it on a film or on TV: they would just stuff a handkerchief nonchalantly into the mouthpiece of the telephone and talk and what was heard at the other end was a clear but totally disguised voice. But it wasn't like that in real life.

The first time Hugh did it, pushing the money home as the pips started, asking for the editor, all he got was a bored voice at the other end repeating, 'Hello? Hello? Hello?' and then swearing and breaking the connection. The second time the voice said with marked asperity that he should try to get through via the operator because she couldn't hear a word, and again the connection was broken. So this time, very aware of spending ten-penny pieces as though they were going out of fashion, he abandoned the handkerchief ploy and decided to use an accent. He could do a fairly good Scottish one, but only when he said things like, 'Och, aye, the noo'; he wasn't sure he could sustain it for the amount he had to say. And then he was struck, he decided, by a touch of genius, and settled down to be as Irish as he knew how.

'The editor isn't here,' the now familiar voice of the switchboard operator said. 'I'll put you through to the editorial floor – someone there'll be able to help you, I dare say. Want to tell 'em about a wedding or a function do you? If it's a private function, it's our Mr Frost, but if it's a more public thing, like a play by a local group, it's our Mr Pullen.'

'It's a news story,' Hugh said grandly, and then remembering the need for consistency said it again. ''Tis a news story, begorrah,' and then as he listened to the click as the girl put him through thought uneasily – that's too stagey. I mustn't say that. Be careful.

His heart was thumping hard when at last someone answered the extension. '*Minster Advertiser*, Editorial,' the voice barked.

'Ah . . . yes . . .' Hugh swallowed, and coughed slightly. 'I'm after having a bit of a story for youse . . . .' Did that sound better? It seemed Irish enough to him, but it was hard to be sure.

'It's a bit late tonight, I'm afraid,' the voice said sharply. 'Weddings should be phoned in between ten and four to Mr Frost, events between ten and four to Mr Pullen. Goodnight.'

''Tis not a wedding, by gob!' Hugh shouted, almost feeling the way the phone was about to be hung up on him. ''Tis a warning, that it is . . . .'

There was a little silence and then the voice said at the other end. 'A warning? What sort of a warning?'

'That's better, now,' Hugh said, and relaxed. It wasn't going to be so difficult after all. ''Tis important ye pay me some attention, now.'

'I'm all bloody ears,' the voice said. 'What do you bloody well want?'

'There's no need to be swearing,' Hugh said indignantly, and then added quickly, 'at all, at all.' The voice at the other end of the phone snorted.

'Listen, I've better things to bloody do than sit here and be buggered about by some sort of practical joker. Tell me what you have to say, or I'm hanging up right now.'

'The hospital. There's to be a . . . um . . . a happening there, yes, a happening. Wednesday night. You be there, you and your cameras and your reporters as well, and you'll get something to your advantage. I can't say more than that. There's to be a happening.' He realized suddenly that he'd forgotten his accent, and added smoothly, 'Indeed to goodness', and remembered too late that it was Welsh.

'Who are you?'

'Now, you can't be expectin' me to be telling ye that! Call me a well-wisher.' Hugh shifted the phone to his other ear, painfully aware of the way he'd been pressing it too tightly to his head. 'Just a well-wisher, as wants to see daycent justice done. I'm after tellin' ye, there's to be a happening at the hospital on Wednesday night, about midnight. Be there.'

'What's the codeword?'

'Eh?' Hugh said, and swallowed hard. What had he overlooked?

'There's a bloody codeword the IRA uses when it's a true bill. You use it now and I'll bloody take you seriously.'

'Who said I was anythin' to do wid de IRA?' Hugh said, watching himself anxiously in the cracked and dirty mirror over the phone. 'Don't udder Oirhish groups . . . .'

'And they're bloody hoaxers too,' the voice said sharply, but Hugh wasn't put out now. He'd aroused this man's interest and he knew it.

'Well, I'm not one of 'em,' he said. 'Be at the hospital Wednesday and find out for yourself. You've nothing to lose but a great story.'

'Where at the hospital? It's a big place, covers a bit of acreage. Whereabouts?'

'By the pathological laboratories, that's whereabouts,' Hugh said, and then jumped half out of his skin at a loud tapping on the glass of the telephone kiosk. 'The laboratories at Minster Hospital, midnight Wednesday. You have been warned.' And he hung up and pushed his way out of the box past the bad-tempered old woman who was waiting outside.

He'd done it and if that didn't show that bastard Graham where he got off nothing would. All he had to do now was pray they'd take his call seriously and turn out. Tomorrow, perhaps, he'd call the TV people, get them to come too? But would they be able to be discreet, that was the question; he had rather hazy ideas about how many people were needed to make a TV show; would they come in dozens with batteries of lights, frighten Graham off? That would never do. No, leave well alone. Just hope that the man at the *Advertiser* would take it seriously, that was all. Just pray that he was a real journalist who knew when to sit up and take notice.

He need not have worried. Joe Lloyd had sat up very straight and had started to take a great deal of notice as soon as his caller had mentioned the laboratories. Now, as he sat and stared at the silent phone and whistled soundlessly through his teeth, he was trying to decide what to do: alert the police as any sober citizen should when he'd been given a warning by an Irish voice? No, he thought. No need to pre-empt my own scoop. That voice was as Irish as a palm-fringed lagoon; whatever this was, it wasn't a terrorist ploy. It had something to do with the laboratories at Minster, and that was where Edna Laughton worked when she wasn't working at Bluegates School, and Bluegates was where there was a mysterious epidemic, and the whole thing was Joe Lloyd's very own story. Someone up there actually loved him, for a change.

The whistling stopped being soundless and began to be a merry jig that made Simon Stone look up and ask himself whether this might not be a good time to talk to the old man about getting out and about. He was worth more than these horrible obituaries, he told himself. Much more. And the boss must surely realize it soon and give him the opportunities he deserved. And he got to his feet and went hopefully into Joe Lloyd's office.

15

June lay curled on the sofa, her head buried in the cushions, but still the sounds of her sobs made the air around him shiver, and Ben leaned forwards yet again to take her shoulders in both hands so that he could pull her towards him and hold her close and comfort her. But it was no use; she resisted him furiously, and after a moment he stopped trying. He was too tired to go on, for even that small action of reaching for her had made his arms and shoulders ache.

He knew he should feel unhappy for her, should feel remorse for letting her down as he had, but however hard he tried to drum up that feeling in him he couldn't. All he felt was a dull anger and that didn't help his general sense of ill-being. Bad enough he was exhausted by lack of sleep and the excitement of the new stage in his work; why did he have to face this as well?

He'd tried to explain that to her when she'd phoned him at the hospital, but it hadn't been any good. He'd been very deeply asleep in the night staff's room in the medical quarters, and when the phone had rung beside his ear he had felt like a drowning man struggling up from the depths of a vast ocean as he tried to wake enough to answer it; and then there had been Moscrop's voice in his ears, apparently apologetic but in fact rather amused, jeering, almost.

'Sorry to bother you, Ben,' the voice had clacked into his ear as he pulled himself half upright, in an effort to stop himself falling asleep again. 'Wouldn't have disturbed you for the world . . . .'

'What is it? Don't say it's an urgent PM because I don't think I could . . . .'

'Oh, no, nothing like that. We're coping rather well here, in spite of being two short. No, I'm afraid it's your wife.'

'My wife? What about her?'

'She's on the phone. Says she's got to talk to you, and when

126

I told her that you were asleep over in the medical quarters because you were up all night last night, she got very agitated and said she must talk to you right away. So I thought I'd better – she really is rather distressed. I've got her holding on the other line. Shall I have the call transferred?'

'Yes,' Ben said flatly, and held on to the phone, listening to the clicks as the operator made the connection, wishing he could see behind Moscrop's smooth façade. He suspected the man laughed at him for having a wife who called as often as June did, but he couldn't deny that she did make a nuisance of herself. If anyone else in the department had so many personal calls wouldn't he object in some way? Probably, he told himself, irritable suddenly, probably.

'Ben, darling?' The voice came tremulously into his ear and he blinked; he'd been on the point of falling asleep again.

'Yes, I'm here. Look, June, I wish you wouldn't do this, phoning all the time. It makes the work of the department so difficult.'

'But you're not working!' she said it shrilly. 'You're not, because that man Moscrop told me so. If he'd said you were doing a PM or something I'd have let it go, but he said you were only asleep.'

'Only asleep? Damn it, June, I was up all last night, remember? I told you that when I phoned you this morning – I've had . . . .' He squinted at the watch on his wrist. 'Just three hours sleep in the last thirty. I've got to get some rest, for God's sake.'

'Then, Ben, come home and rest.' Her voice was wheedling, no longer shrill or self-justifying. 'Come home, and I'll make you comfortable and you can sleep as much as you like. Once you're comfortable . . . .'

It was as though his heart had twisted in his chest, so sharp was the thump of apprehension that hit him. She couldn't mean it, could she? He tried to do the counting in his head, tried to remember when her last period had been, and again that thump of adrenalin hit him, but this time it left a sickly feeling behind.

'Look, June, I can't.' He tried to pretend he didn't know what she wanted. 'I'm exhausted, do you understand? I must get some more sleep, just till the end of the afternoon, and then go down to the department for a while to check on all I haven't done all day. I've got some new animals coming in and I've got to be there to receive them, and there are other things too – let me sleep now, and get everything done and I'll be home as soon as I can, I promise you.'

She had started weeping again, weeping so bitterly he could almost see the tears on her face. 'Please, Ben, I did the test, the mucus one – I know it's now, right now. By tonight I might be past it again, and that's another month gone – please Ben. Please . . . .'

His jaw had tightened. 'June, I've told you before, the fertile phase lasts at least two days. Later tonight will be fine – even tomorrow would, I promise you.'

'Now, Ben, *now* – I can't bear it if you don't come now – please Ben . . . .' And he had wanted to hang the phone up with a slam to get rid of her, but of course he hadn't. The strength of June's weakness was formidable: she could make the most determined people do anything she wanted just by standing there and weeping helplessly.

'I'm on my way,' he said, his voice expressionless, and hung up the phone carefully, with just a click. It would never do to lose control now, to indulge himself by attacking inanimate objects.

And much good it had done her, anyway, he thought now, standing in the kitchen and making black coffee for both of them, listening to her sobs coming from the living room. Much good it had done either of them. He'd known what would happen the moment he'd walked in through the door and seen the arrangements she'd made: the fire lit, even though it wasn't all that cold a day, the sofa pulled in front of it, herself decked out in the black negligee he'd given her two Christmasses ago and bitterly regretted buying; the whole scene had been more than he could bear.

'Christ, June,' he'd said as she came towards him, her arms outstretched. 'What d'you think I am? I'm not a stallion that you can turn on just when you want to! I'm a man, and right now I'm a very tired man, and there is no way I'm going to be able to do what you want. I'm exhausted, can't you see that?'

'No man's ever too exhausted to make love,' she said, and her face had begun to crumple ominously. 'All you've got to do is be with me, let me make you feel good.'

'I know you can make me feel good, June,' he said, talking as patiently as he would to a difficult child, and sat down on the sofa, deliberately planting himself in the corner of it so that he couldn't be made to lie down. 'You're clever in bed, you've learned a lot from all those wretched books you keep studying.'

'I only want to know how my body works!' she'd cried, sitting next to him as close as she could, so that he could feel easily that she had nothing on apart from the negligee; no nightdress beneath it at all. 'And how yours works so that we can make a baby – that's all I ask, Ben, only a baby – you can't refuse me.'

'I'm not refusing you,' he'd shouted despairingly. 'I'm not refusing you! I'm just telling you I can't! I could no more fuck you right now than fly to the moon, for God's sake! Can't you understand? I'm exhausted.'

But she hadn't listened. She'd thrown herself down on to the cushions and started to weep furiously, crying over and over again: 'You don't love me – you don't find me attractive any more – you don't love me,' and refusing to be comforted. It was as though she heard only what she wanted to hear, as though he hadn't told her how tired he was, how physically unable to please her he was; she had made up her mind to it that she was unloved and unlovable and there was only one way he'd be able to convince her otherwise.

He picked up the tray of coffee cups and carried it into the living room. Maybe the black coffee would help, maybe he could, after all, just manage it. If he concentrated very hard indeed.

'I said all along she was too ill to be kept here,' Sister said. 'And I for one won't take any responsibility for it if she dies.'

'What do you mean, responsibility?' Lyall Davies said. 'How can you be held responsible for my case? You're getting above yourself, Sister.'

'All the same, if it came to court I'd have to say . . . .'

'To court? What are you talking about, woman? How can it come to court?'

'If she were my child and she was as ill as this, I'd want to know why and what had been done for her and why she wasn't treated in a special centre, that's what's got into me. We do our best in this ward, but it just isn't possible to do all I want to do. Not with that clapped out old respirator and the general equipment we've got.'

'Have the parents shown any signs of being difficult? I don't want you going putting ideas into their heads, now.'

Sister looked at him witheringly. 'The fact I speak my mind to you, as a *colleague*, doesn't mean I'd say anything out of place to any parents, and well you know it, *sir*. You've no right to suggest I ever would. But I've every right to speak out when I see a situation I'm not happy about, and I'm not happy about Andrea, not a bit – and I have to worry the more on account of her parents are abroad. They can't come and see her, not from Hong Kong, can they? There's only that schoolteacher comes near her, and she doesn't do that often, the way things are at the school. There's barely three or four of the children not down with this whatever it is, and she's got her hands more than full. So have I. And I tell you, I'm not prepared to keep this child on my ward any longer. She ought to be in intensive care at Doxford or at Farborough and unless you do something positive about that, I shall go to the administrator and I shall . . . well, I shall say so to him.'

Lyall Davies scowled at her and then through the glass wall that looked out on the ward proper. He could see the screened corner where Andrea Barnett lay, could hear the restless hiss of the old respirator, and it was an oddly comforting sound. He'd heard it so often in the past, dealing with children very like this one, and again he scowled and turned back to Sister.

'I tell you frankly, Sister, I don't know what nursing's coming to, and that's a fact. There was a time when any ward sister who spoke to a consultant as you have would be immediately dismissed.'

'It's been a long time since the Stone Age,' Sister muttered, but he elected not to hear that.

'But I'm a fair man, and I want to help you feel better about your work for my patient. Now, I'll arrange for another round of cultures to be done – urgently, all right? And a repeat of all the blood work – then we can see if there are any changes needed in the antibiotic umbrella . . . .'

'Antibiotics,' she snorted. 'It's a *virus*! She's been on Septrin Forte right from the start – it hasn't touched her. Nor will it.'

'And I'll call the laboratory myself, immediately. I can't be fairer than that. But I'm not sending patients to Doxford or anywhere else without very good cause. And as far as I'm concerned there isn't enough cause.'

Sister looked at him, her mouth downturned with scorn. She knew perfectly well why he was so unwilling to transfer a patient, even one as obviously ill as this child. There had been that episode last year when one of the consultants at Doxford, a man half Lyall Davies's age, had been very scathing about a patient the old man had sent there, pointing out in acid terms that the diagnosis was totally wrong, and that even if it had been right, the treatment he had instituted would have been a disaster. That patient had survived and only been prevented from suing Lyall Davies by much soothing from the younger consultant. It would take a long time before Lyall Davies would risk exposing himself to anything like that again; even the threat of litigation here at his own hospital wasn't enough to budge him.

Not that Sister actually expected anyone to sue over Andrea, whether she lived or died. She'd only mentioned the possibility to rile the old man, to get him off his blasted backside and to get the child away, but it hadn't worked. And now she had to go through another round of blood collections and swabbings to get repeats of all the cultures and blood work that had already been done *ad nauseam*. And she went swishing out of her office and into the ward in a rustle of starched fury, leaving the old man to phone the laboratory.

When she came back she could hear him fussing and chuntering on the phone, complaining bitterly to whoever was unfortunate enough to be at the other end.

'Well, I'll not settle for any technicians on this work. No, I want Dr Pitman . . . need a fully qualified man and . . . I know you're a qualified technician, but that isn't the same, not at all the same. Might as well leave it to a nurse as leave it to you.' He'd caught sight of Sister coming back and enjoyed his moment of malice. 'So you tell me where he is, and I'll get him, if you're so scared of him. Right, right . . . yes, the number, man, I want the number.'

'What do you want Dr Pitman for?' she asked pugnaciously as he dialled another number.

'Take the bloods,' he grunted, not looking at her. 'Take the bloods. Child so collapsed it's impossible to get into a vein. Better leave it to one of these pathology johnnies. They do it better than any of us.'

'Oh, *yes*, sir,' she said with heavy emphasis, and this time he did look at her, full of loathing. Why did it have to be her who'd been there when he'd last tried to get blood out of a patient's arm and finished leaving it with a haemotoma five inches across? The sooner this bloody woman was got rid of the better, he thought furiously, as he heard the telephone ringing at the other end. She's the cause of all my problems here, every damned one of them. That was a comforting thought, and went a long way to blocking out the one that was pushing hardest against his mind: that he was too old for medicine now, that he'd lost his drive, his diagnostic acumen, his basic skills. That didn't bear thinking about, not at only sixty odd . . . .

'Yes?' the voice which answered the phone was husky, and sounded bored, and Lyall Davies snapped, 'Pitman?'

'Yes. Who's that?'

'Lyall Davies. I'm on Ward Seven B and I need some urgent blood work and cultures. Told me in your department you'd gone home, but this is urgent. Be glad if you could pop back and take the blood . . . .'

'Take the blood?' Ben said and now his voice sharpened. 'Come back and take *blood*? Dr Lyall Davies, I've been working flat out for over thirty-six hours, had no sleep at all yesterday – surely you don't have to drag me back at this hour of the evening just to take some blood? What about your houseman?'

'Sanjib's off sick,' Lyall Davies said. 'Bloody man. Got no stamina at all – and even if he were here this wouldn't be one for him. Child's almost moribund, very collapsed vessels, may need a cutdown to get the blood. I'm a physician, can't be doing with these knife and fork jobs. Better you do it.'

There was a little silence and then Ben said, 'All right. I'll be there. Ward Seven B, you say?'

'That's it. Child, name of Barnett. You've already done several cultures and the like on her. We've got the results here – Sister should be able to find them, I hope.' Again he shot a malevolent glance at Sister, now sitting at her desk and pretending to ignore him. 'I'll tell her you're on your way here then . . . .'

'Yes,' Ben said, and the phone went dead, and Lyall Davies cradled it with a satisfied expression on his face.

'Well, now, Sister, hope this doesn't keep you on duty too late – though I forgot – you people go off dead on time these days, don't you? Not like the old days when a ward sister stayed at her post until everything was just so – ah well, we've lost all that's best in nursing, just the way we have with everything else all over this country. Vandals and thugs and so forth.' And he stared at her for a moment and then said abruptly. 'Now, I have to go. I'm speaking at the Sydenham Society Dinner on diseases of the kidney, can't let 'em down. Booked it months ago, months. Got to get into my soup and fish and be there by eight, can't hang about. Pitman's on his way, he'll see to it that the child's blood is dealt with tonight. Tell him I want results by morning, no matter what. If there's anything urgent about the child you can reach me by phone. Here's the number – that's where the dinner is. Goodnight, Sister. *Thank* you for all your help.' And he went stumping out of the ward, leaving her looking after him with her face stiff with dislike and scorn, before she turned back to go up the ward to look once more at Andrea Barnett.

'If that child lasts the night,' she said to the staff nurse who was sitting beside her watching the respirator, 'I'll eat that bloody man's hat. And him too.'

16

Ben frowned as he put his key into the main laboratory door; it was already unlocked and he pushed it open cautiously. There had been problems a few months ago when some young people from the town had broken into the pharmacy in search of drugs; could the same thing have happened here tonight? But the place was silent, though all the lights except the one over Harry Gentle's bench were off, and everything appeared to be much the same as it usually was: the clutter of equipment on crowded benches, the hum of the refrigerators and incubators and the heavy smell of formalin and spirit. Obviously the last person to leave the laboratory that afternoon had just not bothered to lock up, and he frowned at that. Jessie was usually the last to go; she had a set of keys, because she needed to come in at weekends sometimes, to feed the animals, and for that reason she was the one who usually made sure the labs were secure at the end of the working day if he wasn't there late himself. What had happened to her today?

And then he remembered. She'd gone to Podgate to get some more rabbits, and he shook his head at himself; it seemed like a week since this morning when they'd made that arrangement and he'd promised to be here when she got back to take the animals from her. But June had phoned and that had been that.

He pushed the memory of what had happened at home this afternoon to the back of his mind, forcing himself to concentrate on the task in hand, on the culture dishes to be prepared, and the bloods to be started. It had been a hell of a job getting the specimens from the child, in the state the poor kid was in; there was a very real risk that unless he got the work in hand fast she'd be dead before any useful information the tests might reveal would be available, and he'd never forgive himself if that happened. Lyall Davies had been right to insist he came and took the bloods himself, right to insist on

134

getting results as soon as possible. I'm glad he called me . . . .

And at that thought the memory of the afternoon couldn't be held back; it flooded over him in a great wash, and he closed his eyes for a moment, standing there at the bench with a petri dish in one hand and a throat swab in the other. He'd been ashamed, that was the thing. He should have been relaxed, gratified that, after all, he had managed to please his wife. It had been a mechanical enough affair, a joyless forcing of arousal and a frantic thrusting and grunting that had paid scant attention to the object of its attention, but it had worked. He'd managed to give her what she wanted, which was not himself, not his tenderness or his concern or even his friendship; just a spoonful of cells that were all of him she seemed to value. Certainly she had shown in the most obvious way possible that that was all that mattered: she'd been obviously unaroused in any real sense when he started his dogged attempts, had been tight and dry, pale rather than flushed, dry-skinned rather than moistly excited, but the moment he had arched his back, almost painfully, as he reached his peak she had taken a great gasping breath and immediately gone into climax herself. And then had lain there with no sign of any remaining pleasure in her, her head turned to one side and making no attempt to kiss him, to fondle him, to do anything that showed she felt anything for him at all.

He had rolled off her, and at once she had reached for one of the sofa cushions and thrust it under her hips to raise them a few inches from the floor, and he had felt sick then. To be as calculating as that, to be thinking only of her need to give his secretions every help in reaching her bloody uterus – was that all he was to her? Just a prick on legs? Was that all she was to herself? A womb with a few attachments added?

That thought had made him angry, very angry, but not ashamed, not at that moment; the shame had come later, after he had dragged himself wearily upstairs to bed and fallen into a deep sleep to be woken again by a telephone call, this time from Lyall Davies. Then, after he had showered and driven himself, very carefully, back to the hospital, the shame had washed over him like a cold douche.

He had let her use him, had let her make him a sex object, a thing to be employed for her own purposes and with no reference to him as a person. He had, in effect, been raped. This must be how women felt when they were attacked and overcome by brute strength; he may have been defeated by the dreadful power of June's feebleness, rather than by muscle power, may have been coerced by fear of her reactions rather than by fear of physical pain into behaviour that was repugnant to him, but it was the same thing in the end. He had been appallingly used. What he should feel was anger, but what he did feel was guilt. It was his own fault that he had allowed himself to be so abused; he should have resisted, should have said no; but how could anyone resist June's pain, her hunger, her need? He'd have felt even more guilty now if he hadn't done what he had, surely?

'Painted into a corner,' he had murmured aloud as he parked the car in the almost empty car park. 'I was painted into a corner, on a hiding to nothing. Catch twenty-two . . . Christ, I'm tired. Thinking rubbish, behaving like a walking cliché. I need more sleep.'

He'd gone straight up to Ward Seven B and Night Sister had been waiting there for him with a tray ready to take the blood and the swabs, and he'd gone to work, and that had helped a lot. Having something concrete to do, a real physical action that showed tangible results in the shape of tubes of blood and used swabs, had taken his mind away from himself and back to where it belonged: being involved with outside matters, important matters, *real* matters.

He'd even managed to be concerned about the child – a thirteen-year-old who looked pale and for all her basic chubbiness had an attenuated air, as though her body was falling in on itself – and he said to Sister, 'This child should be on a drip, shouldn't she? Her veins are as collapsed as any I've had to get into. Why isn't she?'

'Dr Lyall Davies prefers the rectal route,' Sister said, her face expressionless. 'We're giving her a good deal of dextrose that way. I'd prefer a drip too, but he says . . . .' She shrugged. 'He prefers his own methods. It's not for me to say what the child should have, is it?'

He had sat at her desk after he'd got his specimens, reading the case-notes, and his brows had contracted. An odd history, with a somewhat surprising link with the two children whose post-mortems he had done – the school – and he had stared at the notes and then gone back to the child's bedside and looked down at her and thought, fulminating virus infection. The sort of patient who'd need Contravert, once I get it right. If I get it right. And he'd gone back to the laboratory thinking only about his research, and had felt good as a result; still tired, of course, but not sick at himself the way he'd been since this afternoon.

Until now. Now, as he forced himself to move again, setting his culture dishes in the incubator, racking the blood tubes, he tried to divorce his mind once again from the wash of memory that had tainted it; concentrating on the movements of his hands, watching his own actions as though he were at a cinema observing a strange person about his business, and that helped, just as dealing with the child on the ward had helped.

The refrigerator coughed and then went silent, as it so often did, and in the resulting quietness he could hear the distant chatter of Castor and Pollux and he thought – must go and see what Jessie did with the new animals. See what she's got – and after a last look at the bench to make sure he'd completed the work, apart from the writing of the report, he went into his office and through it to the animal room.

He saw at once why Castor and Pollux were chattering: usually they were quiet once it got dark, but now because all the overhead lights were burning they were swinging in their cage, sparring with each other, clearly tired and irritable, and he grinned at them, amused by the flash of fellow feeling that had come over him; poor buggers, he thought, poor tired buggers, we three . . . .

And then he saw her and it was so absurd, so unlikely, that he did something he thought people did only in fairy tales; he rubbed his eyes to make sure he was seeing clearly and stared again, but there she still was.

She had set a pile of the straw that was used for the animals' bedding against the far wall, and spread a car rug over it, and, covered by her coat, was lying on it fast alseep, and he moved closer, to peer down at her, to make sure she was asleep, and that there was nothing more sinister about her stillness.

As though she felt his nearness she stirred and turned over, leaving the skimpy covering of her coat to one side, and with one hand fumbled for it, to pull it over herself again, and he said uncertainly, 'Jessie? Jessie, what are you doing here?'

She opened her eyes at once, but didn't move, just lying staring with dilated pupils at the cage of guinea pigs that was in her line of vision, and he said again, 'Jessie?'

Now she did move, pulling herself upright to sit and stare at him, her face blank and her hair rumpled, and suddenly he laughed.

'You look like something out of a pantomime,' he said. 'Look at you.' And he reached forwards and pulled out the wisps of straw that were tangled over her temples, tugging none too gently, and she yelped and put her hand up to rub her scalp.

'I'm sorry,' he said, and crouched down to look at her. 'I didn't mean to hurt you. Jessie, what in the name of good sense are you doing here? I know you care about the work, my dear, but you don't have to *sleep* with the damned animals!'

She blinked and shook her head and put one hand up to her face gingerly and he looked closer, better able to see now, and said sharply, 'You've hurt yourself. Your face is bruised . . . what happened?'

'Bruised?' Her voice was husky. 'I didn't think he'd bruised . . . it does hurt, though . . . .' And she ran one finger down the line of her jaw, just where the bluish tinge that he had noticed was at its darkest.

'Who bruised you? What are you doing here instead of being at home? What happened?' He was getting agitated now, and put out a hand to help her to her feet, and they both stood there, she brushing down her crumpled clothes with her head bent, and he trying to see her face more clearly.

'I . . . it was nothing. Just a silly . . . it was nothing. I got the rabbits, Ben. I put them in separate pens, the two litters. They're a healthy lot . . . you'll be pleased, I think . . . they weren't hurt at all in the accident . . . .'

'Accident? For God's sake, Jessie, what are you on about? I don't know whether I'm . . . .'

'I'm sorry.' She rubbed her hands over her hair, trying to smooth it. 'Look, let's get out of here, and into the office. I need to sit down, I think . . . .' And at once he put a hand under her elbow and half-carried, half-led her to the office with its elderly but tolerably comfortable chairs.

'It's a complicated business,' she said after a moment. 'I'll do my best . . . I had an accident in the car coming back from Podgate. I was tired and . . . it was odd. The headlights coming towards me seemed to pull me into the middle of the road, do you know what I mean? Has it ever happened to you? I realized it was happening in time, or at least I thought it was in time, but I don't think I'd been in the middle after all because when I tried to steer back I hit a lamp post and the car was a write-off and the police said they'd be talking to me again, although I talked to so many of them, and one of them brought me back here with the animals. I wasn't hurt, you see, only a bit shaken up, so Harry Gentle lent me his car to go back to Purbeck Avenue then and . . . .' She stopped, suddenly seeing the pit she had dug for her own feet, but it was too late. He was sitting up very straight and staring at her.

'You went home. Then why are you here? You *did* go home?'

'Yes,' she said unwillingly. 'Since I'd settled the animals I went back to the house. I was so tired I didn't know what to do with myself, to tell the truth, and I just went. Moscrop had already gone by the time I went, and Harry said he'd lock up with my keys and leave them at the main-gate porter's lodge for me to pick up in the morning, and said he was going over to his girlfriend tonight and didn't need his car, and let me take it.'

'So why are you here now?'

She looked at him consideringly. All her instincts were to hide what had happened, to pretend her face was bruised because she'd walked into a door, or fallen over somewhere. To have been attacked by her own husband was a shameful thing to have to admit; much of the pity she had felt in the past when she had heard about wives who had been battered had been as much because of the injury to their pride as because of any injury to their bodies. How dreadful to have to display publicly by your injuries the fact that you were so much a failure as a woman that you couldn't even prevent a man from attacking you! Somewhere deep inside herself she had believed that women who were beaten by men had, to an extent, only themselves to blame. It wasn't something that happened to sensible, caring women like her. To have to tell anyone now that indeed it was, that she had been cast, against her will, into the role of victim; that was a disgrace that was hard to tolerate.

'But it wasn't my fault,' she said aloud. 'Was it? He said it was because he'd come back and I wasn't there and . . . . it's true I did get the days mixed up. I thought he wasn't coming back till tomorrow – not last night.' She rubbed her face with both hands, and laughed a little shakily. 'I'm still not sure where I am as far as time's concerned. It could be last night or tomorrow morning right now for all I know . . . .'

'You're not making sense, Jessie.' He said it as gently as he could but he knew there was a note of asperity in his voice and she reddened at the sound of it.

'I'm tired, damn it, and I'm confused and I was in an accident, and my husband hit me. What sort of sense d'you expect after that? An alphabetical list?'

'Your husband . . . what did you say?'

'You heard me,' she said wearily. 'Peter hit me. I suppose he was upset: he'd been waiting for me for ages, didn't know where I was, and then when I came and told him the car was a wreck . . . .' She shrugged. 'That upset him,' and she made her voice as colourless as she could.

'Upset or not, no man has the right to hit any woman,' Ben said strongly. 'My dear, I'm so sorry. Of course you had to get away from him – but why here? Why not go to a hotel or something?'

'It feels like home here,' she said simply, and there was a little silence between them, and then she looked at him and frowned, puzzled. 'Why are *you* here? What's the time?'

'Almost eleven,' he said. 'It's Wednesday night and it's almost eleven.' And then he laughed, softly at first and then more and more until there were tears on his cheeks as she stared at him until he caught his breath and said, 'I'm here for the same reason you are. I had to get away from a tiresome spouse.'

'Tiresome?' She blinked at the word and then laughed too. 'Well, you could say that being slapped by a man of Peter's size makes him tiresome, and he always had made me feel . . . well, perhaps you're right. But your wife? June? What . . . .' She stopped, embarrassed. The fact that she had told him of her own marital squabble didn't give her the right to ask him for details of his, and she withdrew into herself, suddenly fastidious. She didn't want to know. She'd had enough to put up with today already, wanted no more pain of any kind, even if it were someone else's and not her own. No more pain, she thought, so don't tell me . . . .

'It sounds crazy, and I know it's crazy, but I have to tell someone and you're . . . I can trust you. I'm not sure even now that I know what I'm talking about, or even thinking about. Being without sleep makes you do the oddest of things, doesn't it? It's just that I think June raped me.' Again he laughed, but there was no humour in it. 'I told you, crazy.

Forget I said that.'

There was a silence and then she said awkwardly, 'I'm sorry,' and realizing the inadequacy of it smiled at him, and he managed to smile back. 'That's silly. I suppose it's my lack of sleep making me talk nonsense too. Look, Ben, I'm sorry I bothered you with my . . . with what happened, and I'd rather you didn't tell me about . . . anything about June and you because it'll make things complicated. Just let's be as we are, can't we? Working and busy and talking about work and enjoying it and . . . .'

'Yes,' he said at once. 'Absolutely yes. Look, you need some more sleep. So do I. You can't sleep with the animals, can you? So . . . .'

'I can, you know. It was lovely. I just sort of did it. I hadn't meant to but I thought I ought to leave a note for Harry saying I'd brought the car back and telling him where I'd parked it, so I picked up the keys and came over here. And then somehow it seemed too much trouble to go anywhere else. I'd meant to go to a hotel, really I had. I had a suitcase and everything, but the animals were there and they smelled so . . . so animal, you know? I like that smell. Earthy and musty and . . . . it's life, isn't it? Dry straw and corn and lettuce leaves. Nice. And when I'd fixed up the pile of straw and lay on it it made a lovely sound, whispering when I breathed. I slept beautifully. Till you came.'

'But you were afraid to switch off the lights.' It was a statement, not a question.

'Yes,' she said after a moment. 'I suppose I was.'

'Take the couch here,' he said. 'No, really. I've still got some work to do so I shan't need it and . . . .'

She looked across the office at the battered old horsehair sofa that stood against the wall. It was usually covered with piles of books and papers, but he sometimes cleared it to sleep on when he had worked particularly late and wanted to start early next morning; he only did that when June was spending her nights looking after small Timmy at her sister's flat, she knew that, but all the same it was his, and she shook her head.

'What about you? You need sleep as much as I do. And you're not going home either.' Now it was her turn to make a statement rather than ask a question.

'No, I'm not going home. But I can go over to the hospital to sleep in the medical quarters. You can't. So it makes sense.

Sleep here, Jessie, and I'll get those bloods reported and then I'll go over to the hospital. There's a child there in Seven B I'm interested in, and I'd like to look at her before I go to bed and . . . well, I want to get the work done on her now. She's got a virus infection.'

She quirked her head at him and managed a smile, weary though she was. 'Got you excited, has she? Are you going to give her Contravert?'

'Hardly! I've not completed the animal trials yet, for heaven's sake, let alone human ones. No, of course not – but she's the sort of case it'll be useful for, when . . . if we manage to get it right. So I want to see how she gets on. I'm interested.'

'No matter what else happens, there's always work,' she said with sudden fervour. 'Thank God for work.'

'Yes. Thank God for work.' He got to his feet and went over to the sofa and began to take the papers off it, stacking them methodically on the floor. 'You'd be better off if you undressed, you know. You can't really sleep like that. I've got a couple of blankets here somewhere, so you'll be warm enough.'

'I've got my case with me, so I've got nighties and things.' She said it mechanically, watching him drag blankets from a cardboard box in the corner, and wad one up to make a pillow; she was now too exhausted to move, to go and do as he said and change in the little shower room beside the mortuary where he and visiting pathologists cleaned up after working in the PM room. But then he looked over his shoulder at her and said curtly, 'Go on. You need all the sleep you can get.'

'Yes,' she said obediently, and with a great effort of will got to her feet and went over to the corner in the office where she had left her big blue suitcase, and rummaged in it for a nightdress and cardigan to put over it. 'You're right, of course you're right. I'll just go and change.'

At the door she stopped and looked back at him. 'Ben, will it all be the same again tomorrow? I mean, will it be like it usually is? Comfortable and . . . busy and, well, comfortable? You won't let what I told you spoil anything?'

'Spoil what?'

'I don't know. I just feel frightened. I need everything here to go on as it always has. Work and being quiet with you and just getting on with it. Only getting excited and hopeful and worried about work, not about me or about . . . not being personal. Am I making sense?'

He was silent for a moment and then continued arranging her bed, not looking at her. 'Yes, you're making sense. I know what you mean. I'll forget anything you said tonight – or I'll try to if you'll do the same. Not about yourself, of course. You've got to decide what to do about Peter and whether you're staying away from him for always or just for tonight. About me, I suppose I mean. I shouldn't have said what I said about June.'

'Then you didn't say it.' She managed to smile at him and went out, leaving the door open behind her, padding along the cold corridor in her stockinged feet, glad of the sudden chill. It gave her the added spurt of energy she needed to get herself undressed and back to that infinitely welcoming sofa. He didn't say it, she told herself, so I shan't think about it.

But all the same, when she had gone back to the office and lay at last curled up under the rough red blankets, hearing him moving about in the laboratory outside, she knew she wouldn't forget the bleak look on his face when he'd said, 'It's just that I think June raped me.' Nor would she forget the rush of feeling that, weary as she was, had filled her body at the images that statement had conjured up. After what Peter had done to her that night, thoughts like that just weren't thinkable.

17

They met again at breakfast at half past seven in the night nurses' canteen, both looking a little haggard, but rested all the same. It was as though the extraordinary week that lay behind them had not really happened, and as she collected bacon and toast from the bored hotplate cook and poured cups of strong black coffee for them both she ran the events of those days before her memory's eyes.

It had all really started with the dead rabbits, and the fact that the other litter was alive and well, and she took her tray over to the table where he was finishing his bowl of cereal and set it down and said, 'Ben . . . I was thinking . . . about the results we got with that group B litter. It *is* true, isn't it? They *did* all survive the 737 virus? I mean, there couldn't have been any mistake, could there?'

'I know just how you feel.' He pushed his bowl away and seized a plate of bacon greedily. 'I was thinking the same this morning, while I shaved. Did it happen? But it did. We've really cracked it. I'm still scared of it all but not as much as I was. I *know* I've managed it and I feel bloody incredible about it. No matter what else happens, this is wonderful.'

He looked at her for a moment and then away, and she knew what he meant as clearly as if he'd said it: forget personal things, forget what I said last night, what you said. Forget it.

'And I know we're on to it now. There's no doubt in my mind at all. The stuff is good and it works. And the marvellous thing is I've got a lot of this batch of Contravert. Enough to do any number of repeat trials, *and* enough to get it properly analysed, to make sure we can standardize it in the future. I'll talk to Don Clough about that this morning . . . .'

'Who?'

'You remember. He's the chap at Charrington's, the people who do the extraction from the placentae.'

'Yes, of course,' she said. 'They make the Contravert for you.'

'Not make it. They just extract it. They're incredibly good there, I must say, for such a small set-up. Clough's one of these really pernickety old women – hell to deal with, but he delivers what I need, which is a standard product every time. Don't know how he does it. I must call him today and get him going on a new batch that matches this one exactly. However much I've got, I can't have too much. It's exciting, marvellously exciting.'

He had gobbled his bacon and was now drinking his coffee, holding the cup in both hands while his elbows rested on the table, and staring at her with eyes glittering with excitement. She looked back at him, but only briefly. It was as though she were shy of him, very suddenly, the way a schoolgirl is shy if she meets a person she has always hero-worshipped; her pulses were banging thickly in her ears, and she was furious with herself because of it. It's only because of what happened last night with Peter, that's all; I'm grateful to him, no more. Don't be so silly – it's not even a crush, just an attack of acute gratitude. And she refused to consider the undeniable fact that she had been feeling like this about him, if not so intensely, even before her confrontation with Peter.

'Yes,' she said now, and managed to look at him again. 'It *is* marvellous. You'll be able to start treating people with it soon, won't you? How soon do you think, Ben?' That's the way to get my head clear, she thought. Talk about work. Be cool and scientific instead of stupid and emotional.

'People? Human trials, you mean? Heavens, I can't say. I'll need to put a proposal to the ethical committee here, I imagine, and maybe at area level too before I can do that. It's one thing to work on animals, quite another to start dealing with human lives.'

'Do you *have* to get permission from a committee? What happens if you don't? Do you get into trouble?'

He shook his head at her, amused. 'It's not a legal thing – it's an ethical matter. It's just not done to go ahead and do what you fancy doing with a new drug without getting the opinion and judgement of other people in the field. Or at least in adjacent fields. And in medicine you know as well as I do that people worry a hell of a lot more about what other doctors think of 'em than they do about legal sanctions.'

'It's just that I was reading somewhere about the first anti-cancer drugs. They were used on people who were so ill they couldn't recover anyway, just to see what would happen, weren't they?'

'Yes, I suppose they were. There was a consultant at the Northern in London when I was a student there – years ago, it was – who'd developed some sort of jungle juice based on one of the nitrogenous mustards, I seem to recall. No one really approved of what he was doing, but as they said, when patients were obviously dying anyway they couldn't be hurt by a new medication, and there was always a remote possibility they'd be helped . . . .'

'Were they? Helped, I mean?'

He shook his head. 'No, they all died, and then the poor devil got a carcinoma himself, and so the research stopped anyway. And I have to be fair – eventually they did develop anti-cancer drugs though we all used to jeer at the old man at the time. And they cracked it by using them on people so ill they were willing to take a chance on anything.'

'So you could try Contravert the same way.'

He shook his head. 'Not yet, not yet by any means. I've had one successful animal trial and that's all. I couldn't start a human one for ages yet. It just wouldn't be ethical.' He looked at his watch and then got to his feet. 'Look, Jessie, I want to go up to Ward Seven B, see what's happening with that child – will you go and start things off at the lab? I won't be long, and then we can start on the new litters.'

'Of course.' She got to her feet too, and together they walked out of the canteen. 'I'll do the pharmacy order, too, shall I? It's Wednesday, isn't it? They make such a fuss if you don't get the requisition in before nine and if you're going to a ward . . . .'

'God, is it Wednesday already? Whatever happened to Monday and Tuesday? What happened to the year, come to that? Nearly Christmas, damn it, and I swear it was Easter last week. Yes, please, do the order. I left the rough list on my desk – hope you can find it. I'll try not to be too long . . . .' And he was gone, loping along the corridor towards the main ward block.

She watched him go, liking the way his rather shabby white coat slapped against the back of his legs, and the odd lurching gait he always showed when he was in a hurry; he's like a child rushing to get to an exciting party, she thought fondly, and then made a face at her own imbecility and went hurrying off herself to the laboratory. There were things to be done and other more important thoughts to be thought; such as what she was to do about Peter. Her bruises were covered now with a little discreet make-up and looked little more than shadows, but they were there all the same, and they had to be considered. Was she going back to Purbeck Avenue tonight? Was she going back ever? Some time today she'd have to face those questions, but not quite yet. First the animals to be fed, the pharmacy requisition to be written, a new animal trial of Contravert to be started; her familiar technique for separating personal matters from work matters struggled and at last triumphed and Peter left her thoughts altogether. There was only work now, and lots of it.

Half an hour later the phone on Ben's desk shrilled, and she dropped the last handful of food in the group B pen and made a cheerful clucking sound at the rabbits, who looked as perky and as bright-eyed as they ever had, and went to answer it.

'Jessie? Is Errol there yet? I want him to bring something over to Seven B for me . . . .'

'I sent him to the pharmacy with the requisition, Ben. I told him to come straight back but you know what a villain he is. He could be ages yet. What is it you want?'

'I left some of the reports I wrote on the bloods I did last night for this child – Barnett. They're on Harry's bench. Is he there yet?'

She laughed. 'Bit early for him! Moscrop's in though . . . .'

There was a little silence at the end of the phone. 'I hate asking him to do anything out of the way. He's such a supercilious bastard.' And she grinned.

'I know what you mean. He's already complaining because there was a huge book of requests in from the GPs this morning. Look, I'll bring it over. I've fed the animals, and the rest of my work can hang on for the few minutes it'll take me. Seven B, you said? I won't be long.'

When she got to the ward she stood at the door for a moment looking down its polished length, and felt an odd little tug of anxiety at the sight of the glassed-in cubicles with their quartets of beds and the few patients moving slowly and clumsily around in their thick quilted dressing-gowns and floor-slapping slippers. It was an adult female medical ward, and several of the patients were elderly women with the yellowish parchment faces of terminal illness, and despite the brisk smell of disinfectant and fresh flowers in the air there was an under-smell, too, of disease and death, and she breathed through her mouth instead of her nose, not wanting to admit to the fear the smell brought with it.

There was a screened bed in the far corner cubicle and after a moment she walked over towards it, seeing a nurse standing there, and said, 'Dr Pitman?'

'In here,' the nurse said and went away, leaving her standing there. The other three beds in the cubicle were empty, and for a moment she thought there was no one there behind the curtains either, but then she heard the murmur of voices and heard a faint bubbling sound and again the little surge of anxiety rose in her, and irritated at her own foolishness, she moved forwards as briskly as she could and slipped behind the curtains.

The child on the bed had a gently humming cuirass respirator round her chest, and a tube running in via her nose. There was another tube beside the bed that disappeared under the covers in the region of her hips, and she could see also that there was a tracheotomy tube in position in her throat. As she watched, the sister who was standing on the other side of the bed, with Ben and another older man behind her, reached over and disconnected it, and began to apply a suction nozzle. The machine bubbled revoltingly, and then at last hissed clear and the sister removed the nozzle and said decisively, 'I don't give her above another few hours. Not at this rate.' And she turned and looked over her shoulder at the old man standing behind her. 'I've called the school, told the headmistress, and she's notifying the parents. But it'll be too late by the time they get here, if they come at all. It's a long flight from Hong Kong.'

'You're so pessimistic, Sister, I sometimes wonder why you bother to get up in the morning,' the old man grunted, and pushed her aside to lean over the child. Looking at her face, with its deeply shadowed temples and the hectic flush over the cheekbones, Jessie felt her belly contract with pity; she was a pretty child, meant to be round-faced and ebullient, but now she looked as helpless as a fish on a marble slab, a travesty of a young human, and Jessie wanted to lean over her, to touch her, hug her, force her to wake up instead of lying there with her eyelids only half-closed so that a rim of white showed beneath them.

She made herself look away and said quietly, 'Dr Pitman, I brought the reports you wanted.'

'Ah, thank you, Jessie. Look, sir, here you can see what I mean. Read this one . . . and this one . . . it's more than just the ESR, isn't it? It's every one of the readings. And it seems to be increasing.'

'I told you she should be in intensive care somewhere else,' the sister snapped, and went rustling away. 'I'll send the staff nurse to special her. I've got other patients here to look after.' And the old man looked after her with such an expression of dislike on his face that even in these circumstances and with the dying child between them, Jessie wanted to laugh.

'Bloody woman,' he muttered, and then looked back at the reports Ben was holding. 'Listen, Pitman, you're the pathologist. Not a clinical man, I know, but you know a lot about disease processes. Do you think this child needs intensive care? She's all right in that respirator – it's an old one, but it works – and she's holding her own . . . .'

'Barely. Sister's right, you know. It's a matter of hours, if that,' Ben said, and then added, 'She looks very like the children I had to PM. It worries me that I could find no obvious cause of death in them.'

'What's that?' The old man frowned.

'Two other children I did post-mortems on recently came from the same school. It's a nasty business, nothing to see but evidence of a highly malignant virus infection, lots of kids down with it and one or two – well, three, counting this one – knocked out altogether. And no way of knowing what the virus is.'

Jessie was never to know what prompted what she did then, was never able to decide whether she had been wrong or right to do it. All she knew was that suddenly she was listening to her own voice, while Ben and the other doctor stared at her, Ben with his face blank with astonishment, and the old man looking almost foxy in his mounting interest in what she was saying.

'Contravert,' she heard herself saying. 'Ben, if she's as ill as you say, and as ill as sister says – and nurses are usually right about things like this, aren't they? – well, why not try Contravert? I know we're still doing animal trials but if the poor little scrap's dying anyway – remember what we were saying before? About the way they tried out the anti-cancer drugs? Well, why not your Contravert? I . . . it's marvellous stuff, Ben, and it'd be wrong, surely, to have something that could help this child and not use it?'

'What's she talking about, Pitman?' The old man turned and stared at Ben. 'Hey?'

'I . . . .' Ben took a deep breath and threw Jessie a look that was composed of dismay and undoubted anger, but also something else she couldn't quite identify; excitement, perhaps, she thought. Yes, that's what it is; he's excited by the idea of using Contravert now, wants to do it. He's angry with me for suggesting it, but he wants to do it.

'I've been working on an antiviral agent,' he said gruffly. 'It's been something I've been interested in for years, and now – well, I have something that might just possibly be effective. We've had one very small-scale animal trial that was successful.' Again he threw that sharp glance at Jessie. 'But it was only a small trial, and it has to be replicated several times before it could safely be used for a human trial. I have to get the ethical committee on it and . . . .'

'Ethical committee my foot,' the old man said strongly. 'Listen, m'boy, I knew Fleming, you know. Old man at the time, and I was just a student at Mary's, but I knew him, and I'm here to tell you that if he'd waited for any blasted ethical committees nothing useful would ever have happened at St Mary's. He tried his stuff out on a chap with septicaemia, dying chap, moribund, he was, and everyone knew it, gave him his stuff, went away, next morning chap's sitting up gobbling up his breakfast. Now, what is this you've got? What did she say it was called? Contra something?'

'Contravert. It's a neologism of my own. It's . . . I based the work on interferon theory. That's produced in a cascade when cells are triggered by viruses and . . . .'

'Don't give me the science, m'boy. Not my field. I'm a clinical chap. All I want to know is have you got an active antiviral drug that's as active as the antibiotics?'

'I think so,' Ben said. 'I hope so,' and though he seemed unwilling to have the admission dragged from him the excitement was unmistakably there in his voice now, and Jessie looked at him and lifted her eyebrows, grimacing her apology at him, but knowing he wasn't as annoyed as she had thought he was at first.

'Then for God's sake, man, let me have some for this child!

What are you waiting for? If you've got an answer, it's got to be used.'

'Dr Lyall Davies, I *can't*,' Ben said, and he put one hand on the old man's arm and shook it slightly to emphasize his words. 'I've done just one animal trial. It was a good one, I admit. The two sets of animals were exposed to the same infection, and the control group all died of the bug, and the treated group all survived. But that's only one test. I've got to do more, lots more, before I can possibly try it on people . . . .'

'Even a dying child?' Jessie heard her own voice again with the same sense of surprise, and then stopped caring about whether she had any right to be joining in on the discussion at all. 'Her parents aren't here so they can't say what they want to happen. But I've got a child – well, he's not a child now – but if that had been Mike like that when he was small, I'd have wanted something done for him. Anything. If he died anyway then that would be my tragedy – but at least I'd know that everything possible had been done. It's what doesn't happen that hurts most. And if this child dies just because you want to wait for ethical committees and more trials . . . .' She didn't attempt to finish the sentence and her words hung in the air between them as the respirator behind them hissed and hummed, and the child lay still within it.

'Where is the stuff?' Lyall Davies said, and poked his face into Ben's. 'Hey? Where is it?' He turned on Jessie. 'Do you know?'

'Yes,' Jessie said, and didn't move.

'Then go and get it for me. I'll use it if he won't. Then I'll get the blame if anything goes wrong,' the old man said.

Jessie shook her head. 'No. It's Ben's and Ben has to use it. It'd be wrong to just hand it over to you, as bad, almost, as not using it at all. Ben has to decide freely. Otherwise . . . .' She shook her head, confused. 'I don't know why. I just know it would be wrong. I'll get it if Ben says he wants me to. Ben?'

He looked at her, his face smooth and expressionless as he thought, and then he turned back to the bedside and looked down on the child. The half-closed eyes seemed to peer slyly up at him and he reached forwards and pulled the lids down gently, to close them fully, and it was that action that seemed to make him reach his decision. Watching him, Jessie thought – that's what they do to dead bodies, and she knew the same thought had come into Ben's mind because he turned and looked at her and said harshly, 'All right. It can't do any harm, I suppose. And it might help – go and get it. The bottle marked A5 on the third shelf of the small fridge . . . .'

She looked at him almost indignantly. 'As if I'd forget!' and turned and went, running through the ward, leaving the ward sister staring after her in disapproval, along the corridor and down the stairs, not stopping until she was so out of breath she could run no more. Ben was going to use Contravert on a sick child, and it was all her fault. If the child dies, she thought, as she reached the laboratory and hurried to the small refrigerator to get the A5 bottle, if she dies, what then? Will I be able to live with myself after that? And will Ben? And for a moment she stood there with the bottle in her hand, staring down at it, trying to find the strength to put it back in the fridge, to go back to Ben and tell him she was wrong to have suggested it. She was sorry, she hadn't brought it after all, forget all about it, please . . . .

And then she wrapped the bottle in a dressing towel, very carefully, and carried it back to Ward Seven B.

18

Peter took the piece of crumpled paper out of the waste-paper bin and smoothed it on his desk, bending over to see it more easily in the light thrown by his desk anglepoise. What was the good of being stupid and emotional over this? If she wanted to be absurd, it didn't help matters to be equally absurd himself. To have crushed it in both hands and thrown it away had been childish. Start again, he told himself, be strong and sensible and don't bring yourself down to her level.

It started without preamble. 'I've thought a good deal today about what happened last night, but I need more time to think. I just can't make any decisions yet about what I'm going to do, but I also can't just go on living at Purbeck Avenue as though nothing has happened. It did happen, and it has to be dealt with. I'm staying away for a few days, but I'll be in touch when I feel able to. We'll see where we go from there.' And she had signed it with just her initials, J.H.

It was that which had frightened him most, that which had made him crumple up the note and hurl it into the bin. If she'd signed it 'Jessie' or used the old familiar 'Jess' that he'd always called her when they were first married and now used when he was feeling particularly affectionate, it would have been all right. He'd have known this was just one of those stupid states women got themselves into, especially middle-aged women (at thirty-nine Jessie must surely be getting to that difficult stage?), but the chill remoteness of those initials took it all well beyond that. She was really angry, coldly and bitterly angry in a way she had never shown before, and he couldn't understand why.

He leaned back in his chair and stared at the piece of paper glowing under his desk light. So, all right, he'd hit her. No decent man should ever hit a woman, everyone knew that, but surely there's a point at which provocation justifies an overflow of anger? He'd been driven as far as any man could be driven, he told himself, feeling his throat tighten with the sadness of his situation: away for a week, not getting any of the comforts a married man is entitled to expect, and clearly so far out of mind as well as out of sight that she didn't even remember what day he was due back. How could any man not be driven to a state of fury by that? And then on top of it driving like a lunatic and destroying his car – what did she expect him to do? Say, 'There, there, ducky', and kiss her better?

At that thought he felt his face go a dull hot red. Kiss her – Christ, but he was feeling the need of that! He'd always been the most faithful of men; all his married life he'd kept himself solely and wholly for her. None of the bits on the side other men went in for, not for Peter Hurst, and this was all the thanks he got! It would serve her right if he started an affair, and he sat and brooded about that possibility, reviewing the women he knew who could be considered for the role of mistress, and felt worse than ever. Miss Price? Heavens no – and she was one of the least unpleasant and ugly of the women around the office; and it wasn't much better at the photographic club. Though there was that new woman who had come with Dave Lettner last week – he sat up straight again and picked up the piece of paper and this time crumpled it very deliberately and threw it back into the bin. She'd let him know when she was ready to talk to him? Sod the bitch! He had better things to do than sit around and mope, waiting for her to come crawling back. Next time she sent her bloody jigging black messenger with one of her insolent notes he wouldn't be around to read it so quickly. She'd soon change her damned tune.

And he took his coat and hat and went out of the office, ignoring Miss Price's sardonic goodnight and glance at the clock – because it was still not quite five thirty – and went to get a drink at the George Hotel before going to the committee meeting of the photographic club. Maybe Dave and his friend would be in the mood to go out for dinner.

The best thing to do, Hugh told himself, is to cover every possibility. It wasn't enough just to tell them he'd got a rotten cold; he'd act it out, with all the trimmings, and then he'd be that much more convincing. There was always the risk that that bastard Graham wouldn't believe him and would make an excuse to come round and see for himself; well, if he does, Hugh thought gleefully, he'll find out.

He bought a can of chicken noodle soup and a packet of cream crackers from the supermarket, and an inhalant, a bottle of cough medicine and a highly aromatic chest rub at the chemist's, and wrapping his scarf firmly around his neck, even though it was a mild evening for all it was the middle of November, went trudging along the road back to his flat, breathing through his mouth as though his nose was blocked up and telling himself how awful he felt. And it seemed to work, because as he let himself into the house and Mrs Scarman popped out of her room like a doll in a Swiss weather house, as she usually did, the first thing she said as she peered at him was, 'What's the matter with you then? Got this nasty flu, have you? I told you it was going around, didn't I tell you, warn you to wrap up warm? Won't be told, you young people, won't be told.'

He looked at her lugubriously over the edge of his scarf and sighed deeply, enjoying himself. 'You're right, Mrs Scarman,' he said, making his voice as thick and nasal as he could. 'You're absolutely right, of course. I'm feeling awful. What I'd like to do is go to bed and sleep it off with some aspirin and that . . . .'

'You do it – the best thing you could do, that is, sweat it out; I always say, feed a cold and sweat a fever.'

'Trouble is I've got an urgent appointment for tonight. I really ought to go out. I'll be letting people down if I don't and that worries me. Maybe I ought to go anyway, though it'll keep me out till well after two or even later . . . .'

'You can't do that!' Mrs Scarman said, scandalized, as his voice became ever thicker with every word he spoke. 'If I was your mother, I'd see to it you didn't go anywhere but to your bed!'

'I wish you were,' he said wanly, standing there with his shoulders drooping, clutching his parcels. 'If my Mum was here instead of in Newcastle she'd just phone them up and tell them I couldn't come.'

'Then I will, gladly,' she said at once, and he managed not to grin his pleasure. 'You tell me who to phone and I'll do it.' And she went bustling into her room to come out with a pad of paper and pencil and a little box marked 'Telephone Calls'.

'You write down the name and number then and I'll call them,' she said busily and gave him the box to hold in what was meant to be an absent-minded manner, and he dug into his pocket and fished out a ten-penny piece thinking – mean bitch! But it was worth letting her get away with her grasping ways unrebuked just to get her help; he could have hugged himself with pride at his manipulative skills as he heard her dialling, and then listened to her side of the conversation.

'Oh, no, Mr Board, he's ever so poorly. You should see him, eyes as red as they can be and nose running like a tap and that hoarse you can hardly hear him. I warned him he'd get ill, and there he is, just like I said he'd be . . . .'

Lovely, he thought as he went up the stairs, remembering to trudge as heavily as an invalid would. Perfect. If that doesn't convince him and he comes round here, he'll see how ill I am. And then God help the bloody lot of 'em when the balloon goes up. And it should go as high as the moon; surely that newspaper man *would* have warned the police? He'd thought hard and long about tipping them off himself, but had baulked at the risk. He had hazy notions about the police ability to track down phone calls. Safer not to get near them; let the newspaper chappie do the necessary. He must have done it, must have got the police organized. Any decent citizen would, let alone a journalist. No, he'd done all he needed to; no need for more.

And he settled himself in bed with a hot-water bottle at his feet to make him hot enough to sweat, after smearing the chest rub all over a handkerchief and waving it round to spread the smell of it, his hot soup and his cream crackers ostentatiously displayed in a tray next to him with the inhalant and cough mixture well in evidence beside it. The stage was well and truly set and it would be Graham Board, meddling bastard, who'd act the fool on it.

'Why should he mind?' June said. 'It's not as though you're strangers, is it? You're family, and of course I have to help if I'm needed.'

'I wouldn't like to have a husband willing to let me be away as much as you are,' Liz said and shot her a mocking glance in the mirror as she carefully applied mascara to her lashes. 'I'm better off without a bloody husband, I reckon, than one as off-hand as your Ben is. Always acts the high and mighty with me, and what is he, at that? A right chauvinist pig, walks all over you . . . .'

'He isn't!' June's face crumpled a little. 'It's just that his work . . . he's always very busy, so if I have to be away it's not as bad as it would be for a man who worked ordinary hours at an ordinary job. And he's not a pig at all – no more than your Nick is,' she added daringly, not wanting to upset Liz but needing to defend Ben.

'Oh, Christ, Nick's the biggest MCP there is – but he's a rich one. He gets the benefits of being a macho bastard, and that means I get them too. This American thing . . . .' She dropped her mascara brush and cursed and then sat and stared at June through the mirror. 'That's what makes me so mad about Ben. He treats you like furniture, takes you for granted, and doesn't even make much money for you.'

'He makes enough,' June mumbled, not looking at her, not wanting to risk reminding her that the extra money that she handed over for Liz and Timmy's keep originated from Ben, knowing how much that would enrage her sister. 'I don't care for money that much.'

'Then the more bloody fool you,' Liz snapped, and began to do her eyelashes again. 'More fool you. You haven't got much else, let's face it. You might as well be miserable in comfort. Why do you stay with him? You're not that happy – he can't even give you a baby.'

'Stop it,' June said, and her voice was almost a wail. 'You know I don't want to . . . .'

'Well, how do you know it's not his fault? How long since *he* had a test? It's always you that gets in a sweat over it.'

'He never had any problems. Nor did I, that's the stupid thing. You know all that, Liz – don't go on about it . . . .'

'Well, he's not much of a lousy doctor if he can't find out what's the matter with his own bloody wife. Here's me worrying myself sick over the stinking Pill and you getting in a sweat – oh, all *right*!' For June had begun to weep helplessly, the tears rolling down her cheeks. 'For Christ's sake shut up or you won't be fit to look after Timmy. I won't go unless you pull yourself together so you'd better get a hold on yourself.'

She was in a high good humour now; she always was when she'd manage to needle June, and June knew it, and therefore felt better too. This was just another of the rituals they went through, just another of Liz's ways of reminding her that she owned Timmy, the person June loved most in the world, that he was Liz's, and that was something never to be forgotten.

Now, with the message rammed well and truly home she looked sleek and cheerful as June blew her nose and dried her eyes.

'Will I do?' Liz asked, standing up in front of her mirror now and twisting and turning to get a close look at herself from every angle. 'I've managed to lose three pounds this week – I thought I'd better get a bit off before we go to America – *if* we go.'

'If?' June's alarm showed in her voice. 'I thought it was all agreed . . . .'

'Not if you go getting yourself in such a sweat every time I come out with a few home truths about you and your bloody Ben. I can't leave Timmy with you if you're in a state.'

'I'm not in a state. I'm fine,' June said, and leaned back in her chair, to show how calm she was. 'It's you going on about Ben. He's all right really, you know. It's just that he's up to his neck in his work.'

'I'll bet he is. And up to his neck in some fancy little nurses, I'll bet that too. Oh, all right, I'll lay off. He just makes me so mad, that's all. Still, it's none of my affair. He's your bloke, and I wouldn't have him as a gift.'

'You don't need him. You've got Nick.' June managed a smile and Liz glanced at her and grinned too.

'Haven't I just! I'll get him to the bloody tape yet, you see if I don't. You know he wants us to be away for Christmas? It's not just a week he wants to go for, not like Majorca.'

'I told you, it'll be fine. Timmy's too young to know exactly what Christmas is anyway, and I'll see to it he has all the toys and his stocking and all. He'll be fine.'

'I know he'll be bloody fine,' Liz said savagely, and reached for her bag as the doorbell rang. 'That's what makes me so sick, you stupid bitch, don't you know that? I'll be back around three. Bye.' And she was gone in a gale of Patou's Joy; Nick was giving her more and more expensive presents these days.

June sat on for a while in the bedroom after the front door had slammed and then went quietly in to look at Timmy, asleep in the corner of the other bedroom. He was lying on his back, his hands flung up above his head and his mouth half open, snoring gently. He looked softly flushed and his upper lip was beaded with a light sweat, and she wanted badly to pick him up and hold him close, but she controlled that, contenting herself with leaning over the cot and looking at him, eating him with her eyes, taking in the warm smell of him and the sound of his breathing. She could stay like that for a quarter of an hour or more at a time, usually, but tonight she moved away after a few minutes and went heavily into the living room to sit down in front of the TV set with its sound turned low, so that she could hear Timmy if he called, and tried not to think about what Liz had said.

The American trip must be on: Liz had told her that Nick was determined to take her, that he'd booked tickets on the People Express, that he had a lot of deals cooking there in New York, he needed her with him, and there was no reason to think that would change. It *was* all right; she would have Timmy for Christmas, and it would be wonderful.

But there was still a tug of anxiety in her and she thought back over their conversation, hearing Liz's high flippant voice again, and tried to identify what it was and then felt sick as she heard Liz's voice in her mind's ear saying it again. 'And up to his neck in some fancy little nurses . . . .' Why had she said that? Does she know something about Ben that I don't? Is she trying to warn me? Is that why Ben was so horrid yesterday, why he said he didn't want to make love, why I had to coax him so? Was that it? Was there someone else at the hospital who . . . .

She sat up straight and stared determinedly at the flickering shadows on the TV screen, refusing to think any more about what Liz had said. She'd just been up to her usual tricks, trying to upset me, paying me back for loving Timmy so much, paying me back because she needs me so badly. That was all it was. Wasn't it?

'I don't know what's going to happen,' Joe said again. 'If I knew I'd bloody tell you, wouldn't I? Don't keep bloody nagging. All I can tell you is I've had a tip-off that something's happening at Minster Hospital tonight. It could be all my eye and Betty Martin, but you don't get good stories thinking that and going home to an early night and your Horlicks. You've got to gamble. And what the hell do you care anyway? Paying you, aren't I? You're getting your bloody overtime.'

'I wasn't complaining,' the photographer said, unruffled. Everyone was used to Joe Lloyd's pose of extreme irascibility. 'Just asking. It helps to know what sort of film I need. How much light there'll be and all that.'

'Expect no light and you won't be disappointed. Lots of flash, that's what this'll be, Ronny, a lot of flash.'

'Sexy stuff, eh?' And the photographer giggled and Joe Lloyd looked at him witheringly and then at Simon.

'As for you, keep your eyes skinned and your bloody mouth shut. I don't want you goin' off half cocked. I wouldn't have you there at all if I didn't have to, but that bloody lab's too far away from the hospital building proper to keep an eye on both at the same time, so I want you there by the hospital. You see or hear anything, you let me know, right? If anything does happen it'll be at the labs, I'm sure of that much – but we've got to cover every possibility.'

'What's going to happen, sir?' Simon was so bright-eyed and eager he was sweating with it. 'Haven't you any idea? Didn't this tip-off say anything about . . . .'

'You know as much as I do,' Joe said. 'Now shut up. We'll meet at the hospital at eleven thirty. The tip-off said midnight, but we'll be early.'

'I'll get there at eleven,' Simon said eagerly, and Joe glared at him.

'No you bloody won't. Hang around there too long and someone'll see you, big ugly lump like you. Eleven thirty I said, and eleven thirty I meant. No earlier, no later. And you . . . .' He jerked his head at the photographer. 'Plenty of film. I've got a gut feeling about this one. Don't forget.'

After they'd gone he sat in the office chewing his ham sandwich and drinking the stewed ink that passed for coffee from the machine in the corner and thinking. Should he have told the police there was something in the wind tonight, got them to turn out too? No, he had been right with his first thought. Get those lummoxes in and they'd ruin it, whatever it was. Soon enough to call 'em afterwards, when he knew the strength of it. He'd have evidence for them, photographs, his own eye-witness status – and the thought of himself in a witness box pleased him. He'd be making the news yet, and not just reporting it.

But there wasn't only the question of the rights or wrongs of notifying the police about tonight's affair; he still hadn't decided what to do about the Edna Laughton business. The epidemic story seemed to be petering out a bit – there'd been no more reports of trouble at Bluegates, though seeing most of the girls had been sent home perhaps that wasn't surprising; was he right to do what he was doing, which was waiting to see if there was any more illness around the town? Perhaps the fact that Edna Laughton worked at the hospital with those animals wasn't as significant as he'd first thought?

He'd got this idea she'd picked up some sort of germ there and taken it back to the school, like that story he vaguely remembered about Typhoid Mary. She'd been a disease-carrier who'd worked in school kitchens somewhere and spread her plague to thousands of people, hadn't she? He couldn't quite remember; he just had this feeling in his guts that he'd got hold of an important story and wasn't quite sure how to use it. Go off half-cocked and all he'd do was make a fool of himself at best, and trouble for a stupid but well enough meaning old woman at worst. Handle it right and it could be his big scoop, his chance to get out of this shit-hole of a town and up to London at last. It was never too late, was it, to make the top? He was wasted here, always had been, and there was nothing to hold him in Minster; not with a wife like his, for Christ's sake . . . .

He sat on, brooding, for a long time, and then picked up the phone book and began to leaf through it, looking for a number. He was a fool. There was someone he could talk to about this, of course there was. Why hadn't he thought of Dan Stewart sooner? He was the local health chappie; he'd be able to tell him the strength of his hunch, and if he said Joe had got it all arse about-face, what would it matter? Doctors never told on you, did they?

Dr Stewart, he discovered after a couple of phone calls, had gone out and was not expected back for some time. Any urgent messages could be left for him, but Joe cradled the phone without leaving any messages at all and thought that perhaps after all there was no point in chasing Dr Stewart right now. Tomorrow would do – after he had found out what tonight's events at the hospital were to be. Tomorrow would be soon enough.

19

I'll never sleep, she thought, and turned over again, listening to the creak of the old springs beneath her, and feeling already the stiffness creeping into her shoulders from the sofa's unyielding lumpiness. I want to be over there with the rest of them, want to watch that child, see what happens, but Ben had been adamant.

'There's no sense in both of us being worn out. I need you to be in good nick tomorrow – I've neglected the department appallingly this past few days, and that worries me. If you get a decent night's sleep then at least you'll be fit to see what's what, even if I'm not. Anyway, there's no guarantee I won't be getting to bed myself pretty soon. We've given her the first dose and we can't do more. I'll wait till midnight to give her the next – and we'll keep on with a four-hourly regime – and then I'll go to bed in the medical staff quarters. So, you go now, please, Jess. I promise you you'll know every detail of what happens when I see you tomorrow, but be sensible now.'

So she had gone, leaving the ward with just one more backward look over her shoulder at the child in the screened corner bed. She'd been given the first dose of Contravert at eight o'clock in the evening, after the whole day had been spent in discussion and checking and rechecking of the test results, both of the child's blood and of the cultures of her throat and nasal swabs, and after a long discussion between Lyall Davies and Ben, during which Ben's resistance to the idea of using his remedy had at last been worn down. She had sat there between the two men in Sister's office, listening to them arguing, and trying very hard indeed to understand why it was Ben was so unwilling.

He had a remedy for a dying child, she had told herself as she looked at his troubled face; why does he worry so about wretched ethics? Surely you have to forget such things in a situation as desperate as this one? But then Ben had said to

Lyall Davies, spelling it out as though to a dim child rather than to an eminent colleague, 'But it's never been fully tried on animals, yet, let alone humans – I've taken the work to no ethical committee, I've had no over-view from any outsider, just my own hunches and ideas to go by. How do I know that the stuff isn't dangerous? How do I know it doesn't have side-effects that are worse than the condition it's supposed to be ameliorating? It's just too big a responsibility to ask one man to risk a child's life with something he simply doesn't know enough about . . . .' And she had been swayed by his obvious distress almost to agree with him.

Until Lyall Davies had said with vigour, 'Nonsense! The child's moribund – you can't do any more harm to her than her disease is doing. If she's going to die whatever you do, then where's the worry about side-effects? There's no risk-benefit ratio here – it's all too obvious. Give the child the stuff, man. It can't do harm, might do good, what more can you ask for? To refuse on the grounds you're using is ridiculous.' And she had had to agree with him.

And eventually he had won, overwhelming Ben with the force of his argument, and Ben had looked at her almost appealingly, seeming to want her to back him up. But she had sat dumb, unable to do so. She had agreed with Lyall Davies; that child was too ill for there to be any argument, and she no longer felt any guilt about having put the idea of using Contravert into old Lyall Davies's mind, so turning him into the *force majeure* to which Ben was now succumbing. It had had been right to think of it, right to do it, and she had watched as Ben had sat working out a dosage for the child, checking her body weight against the number of Contravert units, just as he did for dosing the rabbits, and then had drawn up the first syringe full of the straw-coloured liquid.

He had decided to use it intramuscularly, as he had for the rabbits, though Lyall Davies had tried to persuade him to put it directly into a vein.

'That'd surely be quicker, m'boy,' he'd said, watching eagerly as Ben checked the measurement lines on the syringe. 'Time's running out, no doubt about it. It's amazin' she's held on as long as this, tenacious little thing that she is. But just look at her . . . .' And indeed the child looked worse than ever, if that were possible, her face crimson over the cheeks but waxen pale over the brow and the temples, and even more deeply unconscious than she had been. She no longer responded to painful stimuli and it was clear that her breathing was now totally controlled by the cuirass respirator. Earlier there had been signs that she was struggling to breathe unaided, but they had gone now.

But Ben had shaken his head. 'Intravenously could be too quick. If there is any impurity in the stuff it won't be held back the way it might be, to an extent, by the intramuscular route. I prefer the slower way, it's relatively safer . . . .' And he'd been immovable on that, though Lyall Davies had made another attempt to persuade him.

And then there had been nothing. Lying now sleepless on the couch in the office at the lab, Jessie felt again the sense of anti-climax that followed Ben's injection into the child's thigh, as Lyall Davies had stood there staring down at her and then announced gruffly that there was no sense sitting here; he'd be at home if he was wanted, and he'd gone out to speak to the night sister who had now arrived on duty, leaving Ben and Jessie alone in the cubicle.

'If she dies I'll blame myself, now,' Ben had said, not looking at her, not taking his eyes from the child's oblivious face. 'You do know that, don't you? It's ridiculous, of course, since it's obvious she's too ill to recover whatever we do, but I'll blame myself.'

'I . . . .' She took a deep breath. 'But suppose she *does* recover? Have you thought about what that will mean? Because I have. I think she will – I saw the rabbits in group A, remember, and I know how ill they were. That strain of 737 is a very virulent one, and they were damned ill. And the group B rabbits didn't die. So maybe this child won't. Think about that, not about the negative things.'

'I ought to be furious with you,' he said, and now he did look at her. 'Dropping me in it like this.'

'Yes, I did, didn't I?' She lifted her chin defiantly. 'Well, I'm not going to apologize for it. I think it was right. I'm glad I told him.'

'I wish I knew how I felt about it,' he said, looking back at the child. 'I think I'm numb, now . . . .'

'I think you're hungry,' she'd said. 'You've been on this ward all day and not eaten a thing. Come to think of it, neither have I. Come and have some supper.'

He had looked at her and said with an air of surprise, 'You're right. I'm starving.'

'I'll tell Sister where you'll be,' she said, and took his elbow and urged him out of the corner cubicle the way she would have urged a recalcitrant child. 'She'll call you if there's any change. Come on . . . .'

Sister had been obviously glad to be rid of them, promising she would send a senior student nurse to special Andrea, assuring them a little testily that the child wouldn't be left for a moment, and that all the regular observations would be taken – half-hourly blood pressure, temperature, pulse and respiration readings, the lot – only go, was the unspoken invitation, and they both heard it. And went.

They chose to go to the night staff canteen again, beginning to feel like regulars now, and collected tired hamburgers and soggy chips from the hotplate and managed to eat them, they were so hungry, and then sat over cups of coffee, tired and silent. Until Ben had stirred himself and said, 'You ought to go home, Jess.'

She pushed away the lift of excitement she felt when he had used the diminutive of her name, refusing to respond to it.

'I'm not going home,' she said flatly. 'Not for a while, at any rate. May I sleep in the office again tonight? For a few nights till I sort things out? I could go to a hotel but . . . .' She had grinned at him then, albeit a little crookedly. 'I think it might be an idea to save money where I can for the future, and hotels are expensive. I checked on the phone earlier today – they want £35 a night for bed and breakfast even at the cheapest of them. Do that for a week, and I could be in trouble. I have a little of my own, but it won't go far – I'm going to have to depend on my salary. And it isn't all that big . . . .'

He had looked up at her sharply and then made a face. 'Oh, Jess, I'm sorry. I'd forgotten. That's dreadful of me, to have forgotten something so . . . .'

'Not at all,' she said swiftly. 'For God's sake, Ben, we're here to work, not to . . . not for anything else. Just to work, and work comes first. Of course you forgot.' She grinned then. 'So did I, for a lot of the day. It was great – I just forgot.' And she touched her jawline gently, to remind herself of the bruise that still ached there. 'I actually forgot. Work's marvellous, isn't it?'

'It has its moments,' he said dryly. 'Look, Jess, I don't mind you bunking down in the lab, of course I don't. But it's not very salubrious – that squalid office and the reek of the animals and the chemicals and no real bathroom, just that nasty old shower, and . . . .'

'I like it,' she said. 'It makes me feel comfortable.' Near you, murmured a voice deep in her mind, but she ignored it.

'You're right about hotels, of course, but – haven't you any friends you could stay with? People who'd understand and would . . . .'

She made a small grimace. 'I've lived in this town for over twenty years, and I have to say no. Oh, I know people, of course I do. Neighbours in Purbeck Avenue.' She managed a smile then. 'They'd be shocked to the core to think I'd want a bed anywhere except with Peter. I keep reading how marriage is breaking down and one couple in three are divorcing – well, I don't know where that's happening. Not in Purbeck Avenue it isn't. Everyone I know is an incredibly respectable wife and neighbour. There isn't one of 'em I can think of who'd be able to cope with me, a woman whose husband hit her.'

There was a little silence and then he said gruffly, 'You sound very lonely.'

She thought about that for a while, passing in review the people she knew in the town, the office friends of Peter's that he sometimes brought back to dinner, the people from the photographic club, the neighbours in the polite stretches of Purbeck Avenue, the women she had known in the days when Mark was a schoolboy and parents met each other at Open Evenings and Sports' Days, and she said almost wonderingly, 'Yes. Very lonely. I never really thought about it before. I just . . . .' She shrugged. 'I got up in the morning and did the house and shopped and cooked and went to bed in the evening. Read a little in between, watched some TV, did a bit of knitting, and then – yes. Lonely. But not any more.'

He had lifted his brows at her in disbelief and she had laughed.

'I already said it – work's marvellous, isn't it?'

'It's not enough for you, though, is it, surely? It is for me, but it's different for me. I've got the research and . . . .' He stopped and as though he had said it aloud she knew what he had thought. 'I mean, there's home as well, of course.'

'Of course,' she said and smiled at him briefly and then looked away, embarrassed. 'But why shouldn't work be enough for me? I enjoy it, hugely. For the first time for years, in all my life, really, I feel I'm doing something useful, something that really matters. When Mark was very small I felt useful, but that didn't last. Once he started school and pushed me into the back seat . . . I didn't mind that, you understand. I never wanted to be the sort of woman who squashed a child. I was glad he was . . . glad he was so independent, took over his own life as soon as he did. I still am. It's just that I've not felt very useful for a very long time, and now I do. I don't think I want anything else now. If I could just find somewhere small and cheap to live, and be here all the time otherwise . . . .'

She took a deep breath and stopped. She had been on the brink of displaying the most private of her fantasies, her image of herself as a busy career woman, no longer involved at all with husband or son, totally involved only in her own interests, her own needs and her own life, and that was dangerous.

'So don't worry about me. I'm fine. But it'd help if I could sleep at the lab for a few nights, if that's not too illegal. I'll be perfectly comfortable and it will help me a lot as far as money's concerned.'

'Then do it,' he'd said. 'If anyone from the admin. side wants to know, then you're there to keep an eye on the animals.'

She laughed. 'But Ben, you've said we've got to keep a very low profile about the animals. You remember the fuss when Castor got out, and they started nosing about from the admin office . . . .'

'Well, yes. But it'll be different now. If that child actually gets better . . . .'

She pounced on that. 'Then you do think it's possible?'

He reddened. 'Well, it's not beyond the bounds of possibility, is it? Ill as she is, she's clearly got a tough little constitution – looking at her I'd have thought she'd have died any time this past twenty-four hours, and the sister on the ward, who's a downy old bird in these matters, she thought the same. So she's held her own when no one expected it. So, maybe she'll recover when no one expects it – and the Contravert did work for the rabbits, after all.'

'Didn't it just,' she said joyously. 'Oh, Ben, didn't it just!'

'You're getting excited,' he said as dampeningly as he could. 'Bad science, that, to get excited. But . . . .' He shook

167

his head. 'Every time anyone walks in that door or the phone rings over there I think it's the ward telling us the child's dead. But it's over two hours now since she had the first dose and she's still going. I'm going back to see her, Jess. No, not you. I need you fit to work tomorrow. Go to bed now, there's a good girl. I'll sleep over here, and see you in the morning. By then we'll know where we are. Where that child is . . . .'

He stopped at the door and looked back at her as he went and she opened her mouth to call after him, 'Don't forget to phone your wife . . .' but then closed it again. It was none of her business what he did about his wife any more than it was any of his what she did about Peter. And lying in her cocoon of rough hospital blankets now, trying to sleep, she tried to push all such thoughts out of her mind, thoughts about his wife, her husband, thoughts even about work. She had to sleep, because tomorrow would need to find her alert and able to cope. Go to sleep now, now, now, now . . . .

She wasn't sure whether she had in fact been on the edge of sleep or as wide awake as she now was, but suddenly she was sitting bolt upright and listening. There had been an odd sound from outside, not from the animal room, where there were the usual scuttlings and whisperings the animals made at all hours of the day and night, but from beyond the office door, in the lab, and she sat with her head strained upwards, struggling to hear.

It came again, a creaking sound and then a sort of soft rippling noise, and she slid out of her bundle of blankets and pulled on her coat over her nightdress and, barefoot for want of the pair of slippers which were still somewhere inside her big blue suitcase in the corner, went out into the laboratory.

It wasn't completely dark, because there was a faint glow of moonlight coming through the high windows, and her eyes were accustomed to the dimness, for she had been lying with her lids closed for a long time, and she reached for the light switch but then with an innate sense of prudence stopped and left the big room as it was, big and shadowy.

She went padding along the cold tiled floor towards the source of the noise, which was the main door into the laboratory from outside. Tonight, she had locked it, on Ben's instructions; he had been worried, he had told her firmly, finding the door unlocked when he had come in the other night, and if she was going to sleep at the lab, then she must lock herself in.

'They've had break-ins at the pharmacy, remember,' he told her. 'We don't want any such thing happening here. We've got no drugs here, but these people don't know that, and they might try it on. So, for heaven's sake, lock up.'

She could just see the key sticking out of the door as a faint moonbeam caught it and then, as she stared, the door shook and the key fell out of the lock, clattering to the floor. Someone's breaking the door down, she thought frantically; Ben was right, someone *is* trying to get in, and she took a deep breath and shrank back as the door rattled again and with the same rippling noise she had heard before, rocked and shifted in the dim light.

There were voices now, hoarse and low, speaking in indistinguishable words, and someone gave a little squeal that made another voice out there lift in fury, and she felt a lift of terror inside herself to match it, and turned, wanting to run back to the office to barricade herself in and phone for help. But as she turned she caught her bare foot on the projecting leg of a lab stool and the pain that seared through her made her gasp and stop still unable, for a sick moment, to move.

And that was the point at which the door finally gave way and banged open behind her. There was more confused noise then as someone shouted, 'Lights,' and someone else cried, 'Can't find the switch,' and then suddenly lights blazed on, and she began to run, hobbling towards the office door.

'Goddam it, there's someone here! Hold her, John, easy now, just stop her.' And she turned, desperately, to fight off the attack she was sure was coming and saw them: a huddle of figures, their faces blank and smooth and horrible, and she felt a great surge of fear now as she looked at them, and then realized somewhere deep inside her mind that they were wearing stocking masks and weren't at all as inhuman and robotic as they looked, and she opened her mouth to shout. But one of them grabbed her and put his hand over her face and she couldn't shout and indeed couldn't breathe either, as she struggled to fight him off, beating her hands against his restraining arm, and kicking out with her bare feet, unaware now of the pain she was inflicting on herself.

'Over there,' one of them shouted, a man's voice again. 'Over there, go on, open the bloody door and let 'em out, over *there,*' and she heard a squeal from a much higher-pitched voice and then a rush of footsteps.

There were other sounds now, coming from further away, but it was hard to be sure what she was hearing, or whether some of the strangeness was coming from within herself, because her struggles to get air through the hand in the thick glove that was clamped over her mouth and nose were getting her nowhere. She was beginning to feel dizzy, to feel the uproar around her receding to somewhere deep inside her mind. The world seemed to be shrinking to a dot of noise and then stopped existing at all.

20

She could hear someone retching painfully, could actually feel
the pain they were experiencing, the tightness in their chest,
and she felt a deep pity for whoever it was, and then, as the
retching started again, realized it was her own body that was
being racked so agonizingly, and she opened her mouth as
wide as she could to take a deep breath and to shout for help.
But all that happened was the retching started again, and now
she felt the cold of the tiled floor beneath her already bruised
cheek and the hot tears that were coursing down her face to
splash on it.

'You all right, Miss?' a voice said above her head, and then
there was someone kneeling beside her, slipping an arm
beneath her shoulder. 'Get this one, Ronny, long shot,
closeup's a bit messy, good atmosphere stuff, you all right,
Miss? What happened? What were you doing in here? Did you
hear them break in?'

The retching had stopped, blessedly, but she still couldn't
speak, feeling the nausea lurking just below the level of her
throat and she shook her head slightly, trying to breathe
slowly and deeply, and then struggling to sit up.

The man with his arm round her head helped her, shouting over
her head, at the still invisible Ronny. 'Get the lab, and then the
room in there that they broke into. There're cages and all
sorts, make sure you get good shots of all of them, and then a
wide angle one that shows the whole place. Will you bloody
move, man, the police'll be here any minute, and then we'll
not be able to get anything. You feel able to stand up, Miss?
Come on, now, we'll get you sitting down.'

'What happened?' She managed to get the words out and
was amazed at the sound of her own voice, thick and husky.
'What . . . where are those people?'

'Gone,' the man said. 'Left their calling-card though . . .'
and he thrust a large sheet of paper in front of her. It was torn

from a roll of wallpaper and on the reverse had been painted in large black letters, 'The Animal Freedom Brigade was here. Captive animals have now been freed. We will return if more animals are put to torture and free them. You have been warned.'

She stared at it, her face crumpled with amazement. She was feeling steadily better now as she managed to fill her lungs with good air, and the nausea at last began to subside.

'I don't understand,' she whispered, and then aware that the man was still holding her, pulled away and looked up at him. He looked a very commonplace sort of person, wearing an ordinary suit and tie, though rather messy shabby ones, and she frowned at the sight of him.

'Who are you? What are you doing here?'

'Joe Lloyd, *Minster Advertiser* news desk. Got a tip-off there'd be trouble here tonight so we were here with a photographer.'

'You got a . . . you knew someone was going to break in here?'

'Knew something was going to happen. Didn't know what, of course, but we . . . .'

'And you didn't warn us?'

He didn't look perturbed. 'How could we warn you when we didn't know what it was that might happen? It was just a general sort of thing – could have been a hoax. Called the police as soon as we saw what was going on, though. Got our pictures of them running and then called the police right away. They shouldn't be too long, even that shower of . . . not too long.'

'You knew and you didn't warn us,' Jessie said again, feeling the fury rising in her. 'How dare you be so . . . .'

'There's still the monkeys in here, Joe. They opened the cage but the little buggers never moved. All the others are empty though.'

'What did you say?' Jessie whirled on him and he stood there and stared at her with his mouth half open, startled by the passion in her voice. 'What did you say?'

'I said the monkeys are still there.'

She got to her feet, shaky but determined, and pushing away Joe Lloyd's protective arm went to the animal room to stand in the doorway staring in. The place was in a shambles; the sides of the pens had been torn down and the closed cages that had been on the walls ripped down and left lying, empty, on their sides in the middle of the clutter. There was no rabbits or guinea pigs to be seen and she stared round, wildly, making the little clucking noises in her throat she used when she fed the animals and which they had seemed to her to know. But there was no sound but the chatter of Castor and Pollux who were swinging wildly in their cage but making no attempt to leave it, preferring to remain safely high up among their swinging rails.

'But how did they get out?' She said it as much to herself as to the two men who were now standing staring over her shoulder at the mess. 'They wouldn't be able to run that far. They must be in the laboratory – this is the only door out . . . .' And she turned to go back to the lab to look for them but the photographer shook his head.

'They put 'em in sacks and carried 'em out,' he said. 'Every one of 'em. Shoved 'em in sacks and carried 'em out. Seein' they're supposed to be animal lovers, I wasn't that impressed, I can tell you. I read as it's wrong to pick up rabbits by their ears, and there they was, dragging the poor little bleeders up that way, shovin' 'em into sacks and draggin' 'em out . . . .'

'And you didn't stop them, you idiot?' she blazed. 'You let them do it? How can you be such a bloody fool?'

'I got the pictures,' he said, aggrieved. 'There was no call for me to be playing no bleedin' hero. Not with six of 'em rushing around all excited. But I got the pictures and they'll be good ones, you see if they won't. You'll be pleased with 'em, Mr Lloyd, they're really good . . . .'

Outside in the laboratory there was a rush of feet and then loud voices and Jessie turned to see the place full of people; uniformed policemen and the night security guard from the hospital, and they were all talking at once and Jessie felt her head spin and swayed slightly, and Joe, alert as ever, caught her by the elbow and led her back to the laboratory to sit her down on Harry Gentle's seat beside his bench.

'Right.' The most senior of the policemen was standing above her. 'You were here, madam? Can you give me some information? Your name, first, and your business here.'

'Jessie Hurst,' she said dully. Her head was beginning to ache abominably and she felt cold, and she pulled her coat more closely around her, suddenly very aware of being in her nightdress. 'I work here. Senior technical assistant – I look after the animals as well . . . .'

'Ah, yes, the animals. I gather there's been some damage done to them?'

'They've gone.' She almost whispered it, and she pulled her shoulders up, wanting to hide her distress from this impersonal man and the other people standing around and staring at her, feeling the tears pressing needle sharp in her throat and behind her nose. 'All my rabbits and guinea pigs have gone – all of them . . . .'

'What were they here for, madam?' The policeman sounded stolid, seemingly unaware of her distress, but she felt there was a kindness about him for all that and she looked up at him and he smiled at her encouragingly. 'Their purpose, madam? Pets were they, or . . . .?'

She managed to smile. 'Pets? Hardly. Though Castor and Pollux were a bit, I suppose. We didn't use them much – so expensive and it wasn't the right work for them anyway . . . .'

'Castor and who, madam?'

'The monkeys. Rhesus monkeys, very expensive research animals.' She said it wearily, wanting them all to go away and leave her alone to grieve over her loss.

'Ah, they were research animals, were they?' The policeman nodded and wrote in his notebook. 'Now, madam, they've all gone, is that right?' He looked over her shoulder and nodded at one of his men who had emerged from the office. 'Yes, according to my chap they've all gone. Now, we'll need some information of a technical nature. Is there any risk in any of these animals being out of captivity?'

'What?'

'Any risk, madam? Are they carrying any notifiable disease, are they infected with any organism that belongs to the group that has to be reported to the public health authorities?'

She was staring up at him now with her face blank with horror. She hadn't thought about anything yet apart from the loss of her animals; these small things which had no real personalities, no individual names and yet which had become so very important to her. She wasn't being sentimental, of course she wasn't, but she'd been fond of them and their loss was an emotional blow. But now, staring at the calm face of the policeman standing there with his cap tucked neatly under one arm and his pen poised over his notebook, she felt all the reality of the situation and opened her mouth to speak and then closed it again and then swallowed hard.

'I might have some information on that . . . .' Joe Lloyd said and stepped forwards, and she turned and glared at him, daring him to say anything. No one was to say anything at all, no one, until Ben was here. Ben had to be here, in *his* lab, talking to this policeman about *his* animals. They weren't hers at all, they were Ben's and she needed him here so badly she could have cried his name aloud.

But she didn't. She said, as calmly as she could, 'I think we'd better get Dr Pitman to answer that, Sergeant . . . ah . . . Inspector. The work here in this laboratory is . . . er . . . it's special work and I'm not qualified to speak of it. No one is qualified to speak of it but Dr Pitman. He's sleeping, I think in the medical quarters tonight. If I could just phone him and get him over here, I'm sure he'll be glad to help.'

And he'll have to do something fast about getting them back. Oh, God, he must get them back, and suddenly she heard her own voice talking to Ben earlier that afternoon, up on Ward Seven B. 'That strain of 737 is a very virulent one, and they were damned ill,' and could see there in the mind's eye the dead and dying group A animals the night she had found them there – oh, God, Ben, get here!

'I'll call him,' she said and tried to get to her feet, but the policeman was all solicitude and wouldn't hear of it. 'I'll send one of my men to get him, Miss Hurst – no need for you to disturb yourself – Coppins, you go, will you? The night guard there'll show you the way, no doubt. And Jenson, Curry, Pastern, you go and search for the animals, will you? I doubt there's any sign of them now, but there may be some indication of the way they went. See what you can identify. Now, sir,' and he turned to Joe Lloyd. 'You said you had something to say about the health of these animals?'

She looked at Joe with her eyes as wide and eloquent at she could make them. She had no idea what it was he wanted to say, had no way of knowing whether he had any information at all, but she was certain of one thing: no one must say anything at all until Ben came, and as Joe opened his mouth to answer, clearly ignoring her silent appeal, she said loudly, 'This man can't know anything about this laboratory or the work that is done in it. He's some sort of newspaper reporter. And I want to make a complaint about him. He said he had a warning that these people were going to break in and yet he didn't tell us.'

The policeman lifted his brows at her and then turned to stare at Joe. 'Really, sir? Perhaps we can leave the matter of the animals to one side for the moment, then, till the doctor gets here. What is this, then? Why are you here?'

'Listen, let's be clear on one thing,' Joe said with an air of great pugnacity. 'I was the one that bloody well called you, so don't you go coming the old acid with me. I behaved as any decent citizen should. The minute I knew there was any call to get the law in, I got the law in. Before that if I'd called you I'd have been labelled a time-waster and a hoaxer, and well you know it, so we'll have no nonsense.'

'What was the nature of the information you had that you didn't see fit to pass on to us, sir?'

'A call from a bloke who said there was something planned to happen here tonight. He wouldn't give any details apart from it was here at the laboratories, midnight, Wednesday. So I gave the matter a good deal of thought and decided the best course of action was not unnecessarily to waste police time on what might well be a hoax but to come out myself, in the middle of the night, *outside* my normal working hours, to see what I could do to help if anything should happen to occur.' He lifted his chin at the policeman and stared him straight in the eyes. 'And if you say I was wrong, then I will add that as a journalist I have every right to protect my sources of information.'

'But not to collude in the commission of a crime,' the policeman said in a pleasant voice. 'Eh, Mr Lloyd? I know the law as well as you do, I imagine. Not if your silence allows the commission of a crime.'

'Hardly a major crime, Inspector,' Joe said. 'A handful of rabbits and guinea pigs and the like running round loose, back in their natural habitat? You can't call that a crime. What happened here tonight was more in the nature of a demonstration. People have the right to make political statements of this nature in this democracy of ours.' He almost smirked as he said it.

'A *law*-abiding democracy, Mr Lloyd.' The policeman shut his notebook. 'Well, it's not for me to decide whether you were right or wrong to say nothing to us about the information you had. I leave it to higher than me to consider what happens about that. Meanwhile, what information is it you have about these animals in a health sense?'

Joe stared at him, his mouth set in a sullen line, and the policeman sighed and said, 'I'd let us have it all, Mr Lloyd, if I were you, I really would. Could make all the difference to the reactions people might have to your sitting on that warning.'

'Are you threatening me?' Joe said, and the policeman smiled.

'Mr Lloyd, now, you ought to have more sense than that! As if . . . ah, now, this would be Dr Pitman, I take it?'

Jessie got to her feet and ran across the laboratory to seize Ben by the arm. 'Ben,' she said urgently. 'Did they tell you?'

He nodded. His face was grim and he looked over her shoulder at the policeman. 'Some idiots let my animals out?'

'Hard to say, sir,' the policeman said. 'We do know they were taken out of here in sacks, but whether they've been let loose is another matter. If they are, is there any information we ought to have about them? Are they carrying any notifiable disease or organism that . . . .'

'I'll say they bloody are,' Joe Lloyd said loudly. 'I'll say they are. The bloke you ought to have here is Dan Stewart, Inspector, as well as this one. He's the one who knows what's going on. I talked to him not all that long ago and he couldn't deny there's a hell of an epidemic building up, that there's a very nasty strain of flu that's a real killer that started showing itself at the school on Petts' Hill and . . . .'

'Now, just a minute, just a minute,' the policeman said patiently and held up one hand. 'All this is too fast for me. Dr Stewart, you say? Our Public Health chap?'

'That's the one,' Joe said. 'You ask him what's going on at Bluegates. Ask him about the two kids that died there. Ask him how he feels about the sort of reports that are coming in from here and there about the spread of the illness. And then ask this fella what sort of research he was doing with those animals of his. You might find you've got a bigger case to deal with than just the theft of a few bunnies, and so I bloody well tell you . . . .'

21

Joe sat at his usual table at Dimitri's with all the national papers spread out in front of him over the remains of his breakfast and wanted to shout his excitement from the rooftops. There it was, his story, all over them. In spite of the plethora of heavy news, ranging from famine in Ethiopia via chemical pollution killing thousands in Bhopal and miners' strikes to political fury over university student grants, the headlines were.

'Mystery epidemic in top private school – hospital researcher blamed', was about the mildest in the *Daily Telegraph* as the tabloids shrieked their versions of the story at a much higher pitch. 'Child killer plague hits South Coast'; 'Lethal animals loosed on helpless children by animal rights extremists'; 'Hospitals warned. New children's disease ravages South Coast', and so on and on. Last night's – or rather this morning's – phone calls had paid off.

Two of the stories had his by-lines on them and he pored over those with particular glee. He'd made it; he'd got his toe in the Fleet Street door, and it was just a matter of biding his time – choosing which of the offers that must come his way he would accept – and the story wasn't over yet, by a long chalk. He had more to offer them, much more. There were colour pieces to be done about Bluegates School; parents of the girls to be tracked down and interviewed; the Animal Freedom Brigade people to be found somehow – and the pictures might help him get hold of them, if he was lucky; those stocking masks didn't always disguise people as much as they thought – and altogether a lot of work to be done. He hadn't looked forward to a day's work so much for years.

Simon Stone was hovering at the door of the news room as he got there, waiting to pounce, but Joe shook his head at him as he went bustling by, refusing to stop and talk to him.

'Got a lot to do, too much to waste time talking to bloody you,' he shouted over his shoulder in high good humour. 'But

I'm in a reasonable mood, so you can do the courts today, and let Robert do the obits and the hatch and match pages – get on your way, boy!'

'But Mr Lloyd, I've got a story for you . . .' Simon went trotting after him. 'At the hospital last night . . . you told me to wait over at the hospital and there wasn't anything happening so I was asking around, got talking to one of the night nurses and there's a story, I think you'll . . . .'

'I was there last night, I got all there was to get,' Joe said, and swept his desk clear of its drift of paper and assorted proofs so that he could pull his typewriter towards him. 'So go away and do as you're told, unless you actually *want* to do the bloody obits again . . . .'

'No, of course I don't. But I do want to tell you about what this night nurse told me about this treatment they're using – it's new, you see, and . . . .'

'I'm sure. Later, son, later. Right now I've got a bloody follow-up story to write and if I don't get on with it I'll miss the early editions and I might even miss tomorrow's editions. I made the late news pages this morning, but tomorrow I want news *and* features – so go away and stop pestering . . . .'

And Simon, knowing when he was defeated, went away, but he was simmering with frustration. He knew he had a story; what had happened to that child on Ward Seven B was a *super* story, and even Joe Lloyd would have to admit it. Once the bastard sat still long enough to hear it. But until he did there wasn't a thing Simon could do. If only, he thought gloomily as he collected his notebook to go to the courts, if only there was another paper in Minster I could work for . . . .

'Now, let me get this clear. Dr Stewart, you say there's no blame to be attached to the hospital over this, and you, Inspector, seem to think there is. So, where do I go from here?' Mrs Cloudesley folded her hands neatly on her desk blotter and stared at them owlishly. 'I have to know what to put in my report, d'you see. I have to take the meeting's guidance – it isn't something I can decide just on my own, is it?'

'I don't see why it matters who's to blame,' Ben said. 'The real problem is what we do about the fact that those animals are out and could be spreading 737. If we're lucky, they'll die soon, and I think we could be lucky. They're all bred in captivity, not really capable of fending for themselves in the wild, even a wild as tame as the country around this town, and they're also not hardened to winter conditions out of doors.'

'We're having a singularly mild winter so far,' Dan Stewart said sourly. 'And we've had a hot summer and a very fine autumn. The earth'll be pretty warm still. It'll need one hell of a sudden cold snap to kill off those animals, and there're no signs of that happening, going by the weather charts. I checked this morning because I was thinking along the same lines. That fish won't bite, Ben. We have to work on the basis that the animals will survive and will interact with animals in the wild and with their bugs.'

'In the wild then. But there's no reason to suppose they'll interact with humans . . . .'

'Like bloody hell,' Dan said forcibly. 'One dog goes after a rabbit, takes it, goes wagging its arse back to its cosy little suburban kennel and the kids welcome it home with kisses. Like bloody hell they won't interact.'

'There's no need to be coarse, Dr Stewart,' Mrs Cloudesley said. 'And you still haven't answered my question. Who's to blame?'

'What the hell does it matter who's to blame?' Stewart almost shouted it. 'I don't give a three ha'penny curse about that. So you can whine – "It's all his fault" – what difference will that make? It won't bring the lousy animals back, won't stop Ben's bloody 737 spreading itself all over the place. That's all I care about . . . .'

'There may be a case to answer,' Inspector Cahill said. 'There are laws governing the control of infectious agents, as well you know, Dr Stewart. If I have reason to believe a law has been broken it's my duty to inform the necessary authority and . . . .'

'And I have to send a report to my authority, so it does matter, Dr Stewart,' Mrs Cloudesley said. 'Though of course I do agree you have a health problem in dealing with any unfortunate sequelae of this distressing incident.'

'Unfortunate sequelae . . .' Dan said disgustedly, and then took a deep breath. 'All right, all *right*, I here offer my opinion. Ben was not behaving in any way improperly in doing the work he was doing in the lab. He made all the necessary efforts to contain the animals and the materials he was using, and from what he says, he's had it all well in control this past four years. Four years, for God's sake! It's obvious it isn't his fault there's this panic now. It's those bloody idiot animal rights people or whatever they call themselves. I never heard such crap as they dish out.'

'That's hardly just,' Mrs Cloudesley said unexpectedly. 'I'm a supporter of the RSPCA myself and I can understand what they feel. They acted wrongly of course, breaking into private property, stealing the animals, but all the same, you can't blame them.'

'Can't blame them? Can't blame . . . you're trying to drop one of your own medical staff in the shit because of some sentimental half-baked rubbish to do with so-called animal welfare? I never heard of anything so . . . you've got children, Mrs Cloudesley, as I well know. Are you telling me that you didn't have them immunized against polio, against whooping cough and all the rest of it? None of those would have been available without responsible animal research of the sort Ben has been doing, and now you go and try to . . . .'

'I'm not trying to do anything.' Mrs Cloudesley was getting white about the mouth now. 'I'm just trying to ascertain the facts here, that's all. And I'm as entitled to express an opinion as anyone else, and I tell you frankly if I'd had any idea, as senior administrator of this hospital, what you were doing there in the lab, Dr Pitman, I would have been most disturbed. Most disturbed.'

'I never tried to hide what I was doing,' Ben said. He sounded weary, and Jessie looked at him sharply. 'I was pursuing some private research alongside my hospital work and I never used any hospital funds for what I was doing. I raised what little money I had from other sources.'

'But I gather you were using material obtained from the hospital – from another department – to make your product.' Mrs Cloudesley looked more owlish than ever. 'I would have thought that was less than . . . well, I would have thought you could have discussed the cost of that material with my department and we would have reached some sort of arrangement.'

'Material from the hospital?' Ben said forcefully. 'That is nonsense! I was asked to dispose of placentae from the maternity unit, as part of my department's activity. I could have spent hospital money on running the incinerator, but instead, I took that waste and turned it to practical use for my research. I'm damned if I'm going to be told I've behaved in any way dishonestly over that. I *saved* money. I didn't lose it for you.'

'All this is a waste of time,' Dan said and got to his feet. 'And I'm buggered if I'm sitting here any longer when I've got so much to do. I've got to check every damned report from every damned GP in this town and I've got a session with Colindale to think of too. This is shaping up to be a hell of an epidemic – the local cases may have been comparatively few, but the pattern's consistent. An initial spread, a lull, and then another crop of cases, all rather more ill. The bug's probably becoming more virulent as it moves on from host to host. It could be a hell of a thing – especially now those goddammed animals are out. As vectors go, they're going to be bloody efficient, if you ask me. But I've given my opinion and I'll stand by it in a court of law. Ben has not misbehaved in any way, in his handling of his material or in his dealings with the hospital and its funds and equipment. He's not like me – he's got so much bloody probity it hurts. If anyone has to be blamed here it's not Ben.'

'I don't want to delay you, Dr Stewart,' Inspector Cahill said. 'But there's something here I'm not very clear about. As I understand it, you're worried that these animals, if they have been released, will carry their germs with them to the population?'

'You got it in one. Very quick of you, Inspector,' Dan said, and the policeman glanced at him briefly but showed no awareness of the insulting tone in Stewart's voice.

'Then in that case, why is there already this mention of epidemics and so forth? Why are you checking on GPs' reports and having sessions at Colindale? The animals were stolen last night and my understanding is that it takes a longer time than that for germs to be passed on.'

There was a little silence and Jessie looked at him, feeling alert for the first time today. She had been trying to get her head clear, trying to sort out her own confused thinking all through the meeting, attending it only because Inspector Cahill had insisted she should as one who had been present in the lab during the break-in, although she would have been much happier to find a bed somewhere to crawl into. She ached with fatigue, for she had slept little in what remained of the night after the police had gone and Ben had returned to the hospital block, but that same question had been worrying her, at the back of her mind. Hearing it put into words by this flat-voiced policeman sharpened the sense of foreboding in her belly.

'The thing is,' Inspector Cahill went on stolidly, 'is this epidemic you talk about the same one as the infection these animals were given? This 737 you talk about? If it isn't, fair enough, it's just a coincidence – though I have to tell you I don't go much on coincidences. They don't happen very often, in my experience. If it is the same infection, though, I want to know how it is that it's already out and about. Last night's break-in didn't do it, surely?'

'I don't know.' Dan Stewart said unwillingly and threw a sharp glance at Ben. 'I have to check on all the cases we've had so far . . . .'

'I've been worrying myself stupid about it,' Ben said, his head bent and his eyes fixed on the floor as he sat with his hands thrust deep into the pockets of his white coat. 'All bloody night long – I just don't *know* if it's the same. I didn't look for the organism when I did the post-mortems on those kids, but I suppose there were features which could have been linked with 737. A mild petechial rash – I put it down to a generalized virus infection, never thought it could be 737 – my own strain of 737, that is. Why should I?' He looked up now at Dan, talking to him as though there were no one else present, just two doctors talking shop. 'How could I have thought of the possibility? There's no connection between the school and my lab, is there? No way it could have got out.'

'Mrs Edna Laughton,' Inspector Cahill said, reading from his notebook, his voice expressionless. '5a Wessex Street, East Minster. Worked here as a cleaner, part-time. Worked at Bluegates, as a kitchen hand, part-time . . . .'

There was a stunned little silence and then Dan said slowly, 'Oh, Christ. You've got to be kidding. A kitchen hand? You can't be right about that.'

'I saw Mrs Laughton this morning, acting on information received,' Inspector Cahill looked up. 'From Joe Lloyd of the *Advertiser*. He found it out. Interesting how that man finds out things, isn't it? He was the only one knew there was to be a break-in here last night. We're looking into him, of course. But he got it right. I saw her this morning.' He looked reminiscent for a moment. 'Fussed a bit, but she told me in the end. It's the link, I imagine.'

'Edna?' Jessie said suddenly and they all turned and looked

at her. 'Nonsense. It can't be.'

'You know the woman?' the Inspector said.

'Of course I do. The cleaner – a rather stupid woman – lazy. Never did any more than she had to. Always fussing over every little job. But she never went into the animal rooms. It was my department and only mine. I did all the cleaning in there. She never had cause to go near them.'

'May not have had cause, Madam, but I fear she did,' Inspector Cahill said. 'I had some trouble getting the information from her, but I managed it. Rather a sticky-fingered lady, I reckon. Helped herself to whatever was lying around. She keeps budgies, and now and again admitted to taking a handful of the rabbit food from your animal room for them.'

'Budgies don't eat rabbit food,' Jessie said, aware as she made her objection how pointless and stupid it was but needing to say something.

'Edna Laughton's do,' Inspector Cahill said dryly. 'It's my guess they take what they're given and glad to get it. The point is, Madam, she got into your animal room.'

'And then went to Bluegates School kitchen,' Dan said. 'Oh, shit. I feel sick.'

'You'll feel worse by the time all this is over,' Mrs Cloudesley said with an air of triumph, and got to her feet. 'Well, I don't see that I need keep you here any longer. I'll get my report in and we'll see where we go from there.'

'But . . .' Ben began and then stopped as they all heard it: the sound of voices raised in excitement and Mrs Cloudesley's secretary crying, 'No, sir, really, they're having a very important meeting. I can't disturb Mrs Cloudesley . . .', and then the door opened and Lyall Davies was standing there, looking round at them with an air of barely suppressed excitement about him.

'Is Dr Pitman here? Ah, there you are, m'boy! Been trying to get hold of you all morning – phoned your department over and over and at last found someone who had the wit to say you were over here. Morning, Mrs Cloudesley – damn near afternoon, isn't it? Yes. Good afternoon. Now, I know you'll forgive me because I have some very important news for you, for all of us. Very exciting it is, and likely to bring this hospital's name into a lot of attention – papers'll be full of it, television too, I don't doubt.' He looked sleek and happy and beamed at them with all the jollity of a well-paid Santa Claus.

'We've had enough of that already,' Mrs Cloudesley said. 'Haven't you seen the papers this morning already, Doctor? There isn't one of them doesn't have something about the break-in last night, not one.'

'Break-in – what break-in? These damned louts after drugs again? Well, never mind them – they're always being written about. No, this is something much better, much better! It's the sort of thing we all like to see in public – does the profession good, does the hospital good, and it'll do us good, Pitman, the pair of us.'

Ben was staring at him, not really listening to what he was saying, and it was Jessie who suddenly realized why Lyall Davies was looking so pleased with himself. In all the hubbub of last night and this morning's aftermath they had managed to forget what was happening on Ward Seven B.

'Andrea,' she said. 'What's happened? Is she responding?'

The old man looked at her, his eyes almost lost in the creases round his eyes because he was grinning so broadly. 'Is she responding? Well, you could say that!'

'What's happened?' Ben was on his feet now, and standing over Lyall Davies. 'Has her fever subsided? Is she holding on well?'

'My dear chap, she's doing all that and more! Little wretch is sitting up in bed over there demanding scrambled eggs. As I live and breathe, m'dear boy, scrambled eggs! Fully conscious, if weak, no signs of any brain damage, even after such long unconsciousness, breathing without the respirator, and asking for scrambled eggs!'

'Oh, thank heavens,' Jessie said, and leaned back in her chair, feeling her legs shaking too much to be able to hold her if she stood up. 'Thank heavens and all the . . . it worked.'

'What are you talking about, Dr Lyall Davies? If you please?' Mrs Cloudesley's tone was acid. 'We were in the middle of an important meeting, and we find ourselves somewhat confused by all this . . . .'

'Not going to apologize, m'dear lady,' Lyall Davies said with great jocularity. 'No apology needed, because this is the best thing that's happened to this hospital since . . . well, the best thing ever! I told the boy to use his stuff, had to push him, and insist, but I had my way and now we've got as remarkable a cure as any I've ever seen. Scrambled eggs, would you believe, scrambled eggs!'

'Is this the child on Seven B that was so ill?' Stewart asked sharply. 'The one who had the same infection as the others from Bluegates?'

'Andrea Barnett,' Lyall Davies said, still enjoying himself hugely. 'That child's name'll go down in the annals, believe me it will, down in the annals!'

'It's your stuff, Ben?' Stewart turned on Ben and stared at him. 'The stuff you've been working on?'

'Yes,' Ben said and put both hands to his face and rubbed it as though it were numb and he was trying to bring it back to sensation. 'My stuff.'

'The same that you used for the rabbits you gave your 737 to?'

'Of course the same. What else could it be?'

'Then you blessed old idiot, we're all right. Thank the Good God we're all right! The bloody rabbits and their bugs may be out or they may not – but you've got the answer to the infection. So the problem's over before it's begun, isn't it? We've no real worries at all . . . .'

22

It took several days for the excitement to reach a peak but once it did there was no holding it. Every paper pushed all other stories off the front page and ran the South Coast Plague for all it was worth. It led every radio news broadcast and made the main story on the national television news both on the BBC and on the independent network for days on end. The serious weeklies ran specially commissioned articles from Nobel prizewinners on the scientific background, the heavy newspapers went in for leaders ranging from the ponderous whither-science type to the starry eyed this-is-the-twenty-first-century rave, and the tabloids started funds to help the families of the children stricken by the disease, while simultaneously managing to make it clear that because of the great new British Wonder Drug Breakthrough they were all going to get well at once anyway.

Hugh Worsley sat in the canteen at the poly reading his way through the headlines and wanting to explode with the frustration of it all. That bloody newspaper man had cocked it up completely. If he'd behaved as a responsible citizen should, he'd have alerted the police, had them there ready to arrest Graham and his idiots before they could do anything. As it was, Graham had been catapulted to a level of self-satisfaction that was galling to behold, and which had made Hugh sick with impotent rage. He squirmed now at the memory of the way the man had sat there beside his bed the day after the event, telling him all about it in glowing self-congratulatory detail. How they'd broken in with the minimum of fuss; how the woman who'd been there had been safely but firmly dealt with and prevented from raising the alarm; how the newspaper people had been enabled to get really good photographs, and Graham had managed delicately to imply that he had himself mobilized the press coverage – and Hugh had had to sit there and listen to him, able to say nothing to label him the lousy liar he was – and had then magnanimously told Hugh that he'd be welcome at the next meeting if he fancied dropping in and was well enough, but they could manage quite nicely without him, thanks all the same.

'We took the animals out to the Nature Reserve heath,' he said then. 'Tracey, dear child, made a nice little ritual of it, letting each animal run free individually. It was really touching to see it, and off they went hopping, happy as Larry. So there you are, dear boy. Plan B, with my modifications, went ahead as smoothly as hot butter over a toasted crumpet. Such a pity you couldn't be there to join in the fun.' He had patted Hugh's hand kindly. 'But you must take care of your health first, of course – so you stay there until your little cold is better and don't you worry about a thing. We're getting on excellently well. We've already planned the next operation – there's a place that breeds these laboratory animals over at Podgate, we've discovered. That's our next target. I'll run the operation of course. Got campaign experience, now, after all, so you can hardly expect anyone else to deal with it, can you? I've been in touch with the area organizer of the Brigade, of course – must be constitutional, mustn't we? – and he fully agrees. I'm running the branch now, but I don't suppose you'll mind too much, being ill as you have been, and having your studies to think of and so forth.'

And he had smiled triumphantly and gone away, and Hugh had got up and dressed and gone down to the poly to see what he could salvage out of the mess; maybe he could raise a few extra numbers, take over the branch again, get bloody Graham and his wets outnumbered. But no one had been particularly concerned. The political flavour of the month seemed to be raising Christmas money for the families of striking miners, and no one had much energy or interest for anything else. Perhaps, Hugh thought, I ought to change tack, start up a Trotskyist cell here. Now, that could be interesting: most of the students here were the wettest of wet liberals, and could do with a bit of stirring up; it was clearly worth considering, and he had to consider something, that was for sure. Life was altogether too gloomy and boring at the moment, one way and another, because to cap it all he had that tickling feeling behind his nose that warned him he was about to get a real cold. And the way his luck was running at the moment, it'd probably be a stinker.

Dorothy Cooper sat in her flat at the top of Bluegates and listened to the radio with her heart sinking ever more deeply. She'd had one offer only for the school as a going concern, and it was a poor one, but after all this there was no way even that offer would stand. It was odds on they'd withdraw it, and then where would she be? Every penny she had was tied up in the bloody place, and if she didn't get it off her hands soon she could be in major financial trouble.

Perhaps the answer was just to sell the building as suitable for institutional use? A nursing home, maybe: with a bit of judicious partitioning of the dormitories they could create a sizeable number of individual rooms – well, cubicles anyway – that would do nicely for elderly people. Or, if she couldn't find a buyer for such a project, perhaps she could consider a change of use for the place on her own account? There was always a demand for homes for the old, wasn't there? People wanted them off their hands, but wanted them well cared-for, so perhaps if she could find a trained nurse with a little money of her own they could convert the place, rename it, set up in a different line of business altogether? Old people couldn't be any harder to deal with than those damned children had been, and any problems in old-age homes attracted much less fuss than things affecting children. People were so soppily sentimental about the young; if they knew them as well as I do, she thought bitterly, they'd be a bit less daft.

She reached for the phone. It might be worth talking to the estate agent along those lines, and also there were people she knew from the old days in Birmingham who might be worth contacting again. A nursing home for the elderly – the idea was getting ever more attractive. One thing, though, she told herself as she dialled the first number. The last person I'll have here is that bloody Sayer woman. A man doctor next time, someone I can handle, that's what I'll have. Not one of those busybody types who make more trouble than they resolve. And she took a deep breath as she listened to the distant burr of the ringing phone and tried to keep her energy marshalled into a usable stream; it was getting harder these days to keep herself going, to prevent herself from just giving in and not bothering any more. It wasn't so easy once you'd passed your fiftieth birthday. A bit of you might be for ever fifteen, but the rest of you – perhaps you should have married that man after all; what was his name? Ernest, that was it. Ernest Barker. Being

Mrs Ernest Barker had seemed the dreariest possible fate in 1958. Now it would be wonderfully comfortable; better surely, than trying to make a living on your own as sixty stared at you from over the all-too-close horizon.

Peter Hurst was sorry for himself, too. It wasn't until all the newspapers shrieked the town's name at him and he read the short breathless paragraphs beneath the black excitement of the headlines that he finally made the connection between Jessie's job and the people he had that row about with Wilmington. Christ, he thought as he sat at his desk bent over the pages, Christ, but she was devious, as crooked as a person could be, really deceitful. Why hadn't she told him what was going on there, told him she was one of these damned vivisectionists? He'd have done something, found a way to deal with what was going on, stopped the research smartly, long before all this fuss could have started. His own wife, working in a place about which people sent delegations to his department! It was appalling, wickedly selfish, and he sat and brooded over the papers, almost in tears over her duplicity. What had he done to be treated like that by her? Hadn't he worked hard to make her living all these years? Hadn't he been all that a husband should be? And look how she repaid him! Walking out on him, hiding important facts about what she was doing, bringing him into disrepute in his own department, ruining his career, for all he knew; it was too bad, too dreadfully bad, and his throat tightened with the misery of it all.

But most of all with the loneliness. Before she had actually gone, it wouldn't have seemed possible to him that he could miss her so much. It wasn't as though they'd been together all that often even when she was there, but there had been an indefinable something about the house when she was living in it that was no longer there. It wasn't just that now there was a sheen of dust on the furniture and dead flowers smelled disgustingly in the vases; it wasn't that there were no meals ready when he came in and that clean shirts no longer appeared on his bed. These things were tiresome, but surmountable. Food could be had in restaurants, shirts could be dropped in at the same-day cleaners on the corner of Arndale Street and collected again a week later; but none of that dealt with the cold core of the problem, that emptiness in the house, that brooding silence that made his flesh creep, sometimes, and made him put on the television set at full blast, just to keep it at bay.

He'd tried to persuade Mark to spend more time at home, but that had only the effect of making him display his terminal selfishness in all its glory.

'Not on your Nelly, mate,' he'd said in the false cockney accent that he used these days, and which his father so loathed. 'Not on your bleedin' Nelly. Sharon's Mum and Dad have given us their two back upstairs rooms, and I've fitted one up as a kitchen – I tell yer, squire, it's a right little palace we got there! Wouldn't come back 'ere for a pension – Mum gone, 'as she? Well, yer can't blame 'er, reelly. Must 'ave felt like she was dead, livin' 'ere –' And he'd looked at his father with the bright-eyed insolence that Peter had always found so difficult to deal with and gone off whistling, taking the last of his possessions with him to his repellent Sharon's house, and Peter had watched him go and thought savagely, let him rot. Not a penny does he ever get from me again – and turned back to the empty house and the growing fear it created in him.

Now, sitting in his office and reading about his wife's boss and his wife's hospital and his wife's hospital laboratory and for all he knew, his wife's damned epidemic, the fear grew and changed inside him, became a deep dull anger that would take a lot of controlling. He'd never been an aggressive man, but there was no doubt that this woman he had lived with and loved all these years was bringing out in him a vein of violence that he never knew existed. Indeed, it never had existed; she had created it, she had fed it, and she would be the recipient of it. That was the only comfort he could give himself.

Edna Laughton needed no comfort. The fact that she was being described by the papers as the prime source of the epidemic that had killed two children and almost killed another passed over her head, leaving behind not an atom of anxiety. She knew she'd done nothing wrong; she knew she'd been as good to those children as anyone could be, cooking them their potatoes and sausages and all that; she knew that the papers had it all cockeyed and were blaming her for something that wasn't her fault. But she didn't mind that at all, because the important thing was that the papers were talking about her. There was her name. There were the photographs that

young man had come and taken, of her smiling and pointing at
the budgies she had fed with stuff she'd got at the laboratory.
There was her address as clear as anything for all to see. There
had to be something in it for her, she had told herself happily,
there had to be. And all morning she sat there at home waiting
for the phone to ring and journalists to talk to her; and didn't
have to wait a great deal, because they started quite early and
went on a long time, and she chattered busily while taking care
to allow lots of time for them to offer her the money she knew
was her due.

But they didn't, and after several calls, during all of which
she had told her story faithfully, adding only the most minor
of embellishments here and there, she made up her mind that
this couldn't go on. Someone, somewhere, should be paying
her, and the best thing to do was go and ask for it, and the only
person who could be asked was Joe Lloyd. So she'd ask him.

Joe Lloyd was sitting in his office at the *Advertiser*, also waiting
for phone calls. He'd filed his copy to every possible desk
where he could hope to sell, and seen his stories appearing
(though now they were using his by-line less than they had the
day the story first broke) so by now the offers should be
coming. But they weren't and he was seriously considering
taking the tide into his own hands, as it were, and asking for a
Fleet Street berth. It would be more satisfying to wait for the
offers, of course, to weigh one against another, but if it wasn't
going to work out that way, he'd have to do something fast. In
the newspaper business today's front-page splash is
tomorrow's three-inch single on the bottom of a left-hand
page at the back of the book; today's great men become
tomorrow's 'Who's he?' faster than they ever did, he told
himself, and began to work out a strategy, planning exactly
how he would put himself across to the men who had the
power to give him what he wanted.

The door of his office opened without a preliminary knock
and Simon Stone put his head round. 'I thought you'd want to
see Mrs Laughton,' he said brightly, and ushered the woman
in, grinning like a monkey with pride at his own cleverness. 'I
know she's part of this story of yours so I wouldn't let her go
till she had the chance to talk to you,' and he stood back,
waiting for a nod of approval. 'She said it was important, so I
brought her right in . . . .'

'So I see.' Lloyd cradled the telephone with a little clatter and scowled at the woman. 'Well, madam, and what do you want? I've talked to you for hours, got all you had to say, so there can't be much to add.'

'To add? Well, that's as may be,' Edna said, and stood twisting her bag in her hands and staring at him. ''Oo's to know what else I know about that hospital? Worked there long enough, I did, and for all you know I could have lots more information for you.'

'You didn't tell me much I didn't know already,' Joe said, and glared at Simon. 'Well, what do you want?'

Simon reddened. 'I thought you'd be pleased to see Mrs Laughton . . . and . . . .'

'Yes. Sure, very pleased. Anything else?'

'Not really . . . .'

'Nothing about miracle cures you forgot to mention?'

Simon went even redder. 'That's not fair, Mr Lloyd! I tried to tell you, you know I did, but you just wouldn't listen to me and . . . .'

'Ah, go away,' Joe said disgustedly. 'And take your Mrs Laughton with you. I've got better things to do than waste any more time on the pair of you . . . .'

'You got it in the end, Mr Lloyd!' Simon was feeling deeply aggrieved at the injustice of Joe's complaints now. 'I mean, it didn't make any difference. You got the story in . . . .'

'Oh, didn't I just! When you were about to sell it on your own to the bloody agencies, and don't say you weren't . . . .'

'Not sell it, I swear!' Simon said. 'I just knew it was a story and you said you didn't want to know so I thought I'd put it on the wire and let anyone who wanted it have it . . . .'

'Call yourself a journalist, you half-witted newt, you? Ah, piss off and leave me alone, will you? If it weren't for the bloody union, I'd have you out on the street for what you did . . . go on, get out of my sight.' And he glared at Edna Laughton then. 'You too. I've done with you and . . . .'

'Have you, then? And what about my money, then?' Edna cried shrilly. 'It's all very well you go putting me all over the papers like you have but here's me with not a penny to show for it!'

'Money?' Joe stared at her. 'What bloody money? You've got no money coming to you . . . .'

'After all I told you? After all the papers what you told what

I told you? Course I have! Got to have . . . I'll make a complaint, I will, if you don't make sure I get everything what's due to me . . . .'

'A complaint? Who to?' Joe began to laugh then. 'Who bloody to?'

'The authorities,' Edna said passionately. 'The authorities, that's who to.'

'Go and make it,' Joe said with a vast scorn, and picked up his phone. 'Right now. Go and make it and stop wasting my time. I've got work to do,' and he began to dial, not looking at either of them. 'If you and this woman aren't out of here in one minute flat, you'll wish you were never born,' he said, and Simon pulled on Edna's arm and jerked his head at her and took her away, risking slamming the door on Joe as he did so. But the old man didn't look up and went on dealing with his telephone.

'You might as well do as he says, Mrs Laughton,' he said, and looked at the woman with his face creased with commiseration. 'Go away, I mean. There's no way anyone's going to give you any money, you know.'

'What, and me told them all that stuff to put in the papers? Course there's got to be money for me! It stands to reason there is . . . .'

'Well, there isn't. It's what's called a free press. And that means no money for anyone like you. Not much for me, either, come to that. I'd forget it if I were you. You won't get anywhere.'

And when he had at last coaxed her to the lift and seen her on her whining way out of the building he went back to his own desk, telling himself gloomily that he could do worse than take his own advice. Forget the newspaper business, that's what I ought to do. Bastards like Lloyd and the obits and the damned courts – where's the point in it all? I'd have a better time selling eggs at Safeways.

'Call for you,' Robert said as he got back to his desk. 'The agency you were talking to the other day – when Lloyd heard you and did his nut. They want to talk to you – they didn't say about what. Make sure the old bugger doesn't hear you this time . . . .'

What they wanted to talk about made Simon change his mind completely about his choice of career. He was the right man in the right-shaped hole after all. How could it be otherwise when he'd been offered a job with a Fleet Street news agency, who had an eye for a young man who could pick up good stories and feed them in to them? He sat there at his desk, his phone clamped to his ear, watching Joe Lloyd through the glass of his door occupied in the same way. But Lloyd wasn't grinning at all, and Simon was.

'June? I'm sorry I didn't call sooner,' Ben said. 'It's been absolutely awful, all of it. I hope you haven't been too upset by it all . . . .'

'Upset?' June frowned and shook her head, watching Timmy all the time as he bumbled about the room on his fairy tricycle. It made an awful mess when he did that, but it was too wet for him to play outside today, and he wanted to ride his tricycle, so what else could she do? But it took constant watchfulness to prevent him breaking things as he went barging about the cramped space. 'No, I haven't been . . . oh, Ben, hold on a moment . . . no, Timmy darling, not like that. Go slowly, sweetheart, or you'll break Mummy's sideboard and then what will she say? No, don't cry, darling, just wait till Auntie's finished on the silly old phone and then I'll play with you . . . I won't be a moment . . . Ben, I am sorry . . . it's just so difficult, with Timmy not being able to play outside . . . it's been raining all morning, you see, and I don't want him catching cold.'

'I said I hope you haven't been worried about all the fuss.'

'What fuss?'

There was a little silence and then Ben said carefully, 'You haven't seen the papers?'

'Papers? Oh, no, darling, not with Timmy to look after! How could I? I try to see them when he goes to bed, perhaps, though by then I'm usually too tired to bother. Why? What's in them?'

'Nor heard the radio? Seen the news on TV?'

'What is this, Ben? You know I'm looking after Timmy! I did tell you I'd be staying here a few days, bringing him over to our place just a bit at a time so he settles better and enjoys Christmas with us . . . .'

'Oh, yes, Christmas,' Ben said and laughed. 'I'd forgotten about Christmas. Look, it'll take me too long to explain now. But find a moment to read the papers. The *Guardian* has got it about the best – all the others are madly inaccurate, making a great drama out of it all – but read the *Guardian*. And then tonight, I'm on *Probe* and . . . .'

'*Probe*? That TV programme?'

'That TV programme, June, yes. I'll be staying in London overnight, and I'll be back tomorrow, I hope. I'll talk to you then. Give my love to Timmy,' and he hung up carefully and gently, controlling his irritation as much as he could, because he wanted to be fair to her. After all, he was as obsessed with what he was doing as she was with Timmy; to be annoyed with her because she wasn't aware of what was happening in his life was hardly just, but all the same, he was annoyed and he had to work hard to contain it.

But there were worse things than that to worry over and he sat and stared at the wall of his cluttered comfortable office trying to order his confused thoughts. So much to be done – the animal room to be restructured and restocked, the trials of Contravert to be started again, the child on Ward Seven B to be monitored, and above all the publicity to be handled – yet all he could do was sit and stare at the wall and do nothing. What he should be feeling was the elation of the scientist who has made his leap forward, the rich academic excitement of the successful questor. But what he was feeling was absolutely dreadful. Almost tearful, which was, of course, ridiculous.

23

Regent Street was awash with people, and they stood at the top of the steps climbing up from the underground at Piccadilly Circus and looked along the curve of the street, trying to catch their breath. For Jessie it wasn't just the crowds that made her feel breathless and anxious; it was the harsh glitter of the Christmas decorations that draped the shop windows, the flapping garlands and lights and the fat and singularly vacuous-looking Mickey Mouses and Donald Ducks simpering down at her which made her feel so curiously uncomfortable, and she drew a little nearer to Ben and said, 'Heavens, but I feel so provincial! I can't remember the last time I was in London, and all this makes me feel the complete country cousin.'

'Such nonsense!' Ben said. 'Of course you're not provincial.' He looked down at her, standing there in her neat buff raincoat with its collar up against the cold and her hands thrust into her pockets, her head uncovered and a little wind-blown, and then laughed. 'Though I suppose I do know what you mean. Looking at some of these people and their extra-ordinary clothes, I do feel I've got straws in my hair.'

'Perhaps we shouldn't have come up so early, after all. It seemed like a good idea at the time of course, but now . . . .'

'It was a good idea and it still is. We've been tied to that place for so long we've forgotten there's anywhere else. And I'd have gone mad sitting there all day thinking about tonight. This way I won't be able to think about it so much.'

'If you believe that you'll believe anything,' she said. 'I haven't stopped worrying about it since I woke up this morning. Nor have you – be honest.'

He laughed again. 'Well, no. I was so sick with it I couldn't eat any breakfast.'

'And now it's lunchtime. Come on. Let's find somewhere and then plan how we deal with the rest of the day. We don't have to be at the studios till eight, do we? We've plenty of time to kill. What about Christmas shopping?'

They were walking north now, along Regent Street, and Ben grimaced. 'I suppose I could . . . I hadn't given it a thought, to be honest. I don't usually. I mean, there's only June and I usually give her a cheque and she can do what she likes with it. Buys stuff for Timmy, mostly, I think. She'd rather do that than anything else. If I did something different she'd get into a state over it, I imagine. So . . . .' He stopped talking and walked a little faster so that she had to scuttle, almost, to keep up with him.

'Then get something for Timmy,' she said embarrassed now, and aware that he was too. 'It'll please June if you do, and give us something to do – it's years since I had to buy toys.'

'Something for . . . well, I suppose I could. I've always left that to June.'

'Well, get something on your own account. From all you say, she'll be delighted, and of course so will Timmy and we have nothing to do and all day to do it in.'

'So we might as well spend money. All right, then. Something for Timmy.'

They went to Hamley's toy shop and spent the next thirty minutes wandering, half-dazed by the noise, past piles of expensive toys, picking their way through the mobs of children who ranged from being obviously totally bored to being hysterically excited, and emerged at last with a box of plain wooden bricks.

'June has strong views on what's suitable for a child of his age,' Ben said. 'She reads all the books on child development and care and all that. I think it'd be more fun to get one of those electronic things that bleep and flash lights and that he'd break before breakfast, but she's all for durability and play value. I think she'll approve of this.'

'But will Timmy?' Jessie said without thinking, and then blushed. 'Heavens, I'm sorry. That was very rude of me.'

'Not at all.' They were back in the street now, walking towards Oxford Circus. 'It's a fair comment. The trouble with June is she doesn't think about children as people exactly. They're just children, you know? I hope she'll be as attached to Timmy when he grows up and stops being quite so obviously dependent and charming, but I don't know – there are teenagers living in the house next door to ours, and she seems to dislike them.'

'I don't blame her,' Jessie said. 'Mark when he was small was rather nice. Now he's . . . .' She shook her head. 'If I were to be honest, I'd say he was repellent. I feel I hardly know him. And what's worse, I don't really care whether I do or not.'

'That sounds healthy to me. Being able to see your child for what he is, I mean, rather than just as someone labelled My Child and Therefore Adorable. That's what worries me about June. She doesn't seem to see any life for herself unless she has someone she can label that way. She makes do with Timmy, I know, but it's her own child she wants – I just can't seem to get her to see that it isn't the end of the world if she never has one.'

'Look, there's a place there we could have lunch,' Jessie said quickly, and steered him towards the kerb so that they could cross the road. This conversation was getting even more embarrassing and she didn't like it. It created a closeness between them that was frightening and she thought – I shouldn't have agreed to come up so early today. I should have realized, said I'd stay at the lab till the last possible moment . . . .

'What do you think we'll have to do tonight? Did they give you any sort of idea about their plans?'

'Not much.' He seemed as glad to abandon the talk about June as she was. 'They said they wanted to discuss with you the work with the animals and how they were kept, but they wanted me to talk about Contravert. I . . . .' He shook his head as they reached the restaurant and there was a little flurry as they made their way to a table and ordered food. Once the waitress had gone and they could talk again he said abruptly, as though their conversation had never been interrupted, 'I should have stuck to my guns, somehow. I said I didn't want to talk about it, that it was premature . . . .'

'Then why didn't you, Ben? I must say I was surprised when you told me you'd agreed.'

He made a face. 'Because they told me they'd get Lyall Davies in to talk about it if I didn't. The brass gall of that man! He's marching round, carrying on as though it was his stuff and that he had as much to do with it as I did, when the old fool knows damn all about it. He's just climbing on to the publicity bandwagon. He makes me sick, he really does.' He grinned then. 'It was worth saying I'd do this damned programme just to see how furious he was that he wasn't doing it too. He wanted to get on to it in the worst way – got his secretary to ring the studios, you know, to tell 'em he was available! Fortunately I'd already told them how little he had to do with it, so they didn't take him. All the same, I wish I didn't have to do the wretched programme. I'm shaking over it all more than I did when I did my final exams, and I thought that was the ultimate in panic reactions.'

'Why didn't you tell them to drop it? That it's too soon to talk about it and that's that?'

He laughed at that. 'Now you're *sounding* provincial, Jessie, and you ought to know better. If there's one thing I've learned since all this fuss began – it feels like months rather than weeks – it's that you can't control these people. They decide they want to write a newspaper article or do a TV programme and that's all about it. No one can stop them, no one can even tell them how to do it so they get it right. Did you see the garbage they ran last week? I have to speak to the bloody people, like it or not, to try to get the facts right. If I don't they just guess and their guesses are the wildest you ever heard. We're caught in a great big sticky trap and there's not a damned thing we can do about it.'

He was silent for a while as their food arrived and they began to eat. 'I'll tell you what's the worst thing about it,' he said eventually. 'It's a bloody seductive trap. I may be scared about tonight's programme but I'm elated too. It's all so marvellously exciting, you see, isn't it? On one level I may be revolted by the whole mishmash of journalists and photographers and TV interviewers and all the rest of it, but I'm absolutely fascinated too. I'm enjoying all the drama. It's different, and it's exhilarating. Sitting here eating lamb chops with you, that's different and exhilarating. Being in London with all the hubbub out there, all the rush and the drama – I *like* it. I don't know how long I'd go on liking it if I had to put up with it all the time, but right now I'm enjoying it in a masochistic sort of way. And that's the most worrying thing about the whole business. The perverted pleasure I'm getting out of all the attention.'

She had been sitting staring at him as he talked, startled by the rush of words and the passion he was putting into them, and now she said quickly, 'It's nothing to be ashamed of. Why shouldn't you enjoy it? You've worked unbelievably hard for so long that you're entitled to it. You've had no attention at all. No one cared or shared any of it . . . .' She stopped, once again aware of the embarrassment she felt when June seemed to come into their conversation. She didn't want to talk about her at all, least of all wanted to seem to criticize her, yet over and over again it just seemed to happen.

'You do,' he said, and smiled at her. 'I haven't said it properly, but I really must. I'm so bloody grateful to you, Jess. This last year of the work's been so much easier, because you've been there. I chose well when I chose you for the job, and I keep on congratulating myself on my acumen. I've had more support this past year than I would have thought possible in the first three. So, here and now, it's on the record. Thank you.'

There was a little silence and then she said simply, 'Thank you. I . . . .' She managed a rather shaky laugh. 'I like attention too, you know. It's marvellous to be told you're doing a good job. It's all I want, just the job, and knowing that . . . well, thanks. And . . . .' She leaned forwards and put her hand briefly on his. 'Don't worry about tonight. All you have to do is be honest, tell them what you want to tell them, and no more. You'll be in charge, won't you? It's not like those things when people are recorded and they cut bits out and mix them up and use them the way they want to. This programme goes out on the air while we do it, doesn't it? It's live – so you can say what you like, and more important, needn't say what you don't want to. And I'll back you up all the way, I promise.'

'And I'll back you,' he said. 'You'll need that, Jess. They're going to go on about the use of animals in research, you see. It's really a totally different subject – I mean, there's enough to talk about with the Contravert, let alone the ethics of using animals, but that's what they're doing, so . . . it might be rough. You know how the anti-vivisectionists go on about cruelty.'

'I know,' she said, and made a face. 'And I know that sometimes they're right – look, let's not talk about it now. It makes me feel more scared than ever. Bad enough we'll have to do it tonight. Let's talk about something else. About what we'll do when all the fuss is over and we can get back to work properly. Have you a plan?'

Gratefully he pushed his plate aside and leaned forwards with his elbows on the table. 'Yes, you're right. Let's plan. I've been thinking about it. I'm going to make some use of that old fool Lyall Davies. If I can't get some research money out of him and his department after all this, I don't deserve the name of researcher. And the fact that we've had a single success in a human trial should help. I want to do some tissue work as well as animal work, side by side. I'm a bit worried about the possibility of chromosome effects and . . . .'

'Chromosome effects?'

'The stuff derives from prostaglandins and hormones, remember. For all I know it could be teratogenic – there's always that risk with all drugs that act directly on cells the way Contravert does, but it seems to me there may be an added risk in using such sensitive material. So, I want to set up a series of tissue cultures and use the stuff on those, as well as another series of animal trials. The people out at the factory . . . .'

'You're saying that Contravert could damage unborn babies?'

'I don't know. That's the point. As I said, there's always that risk, especially with something that's based on hormones. There was that evidence that babies born of women who went on using the Pill after they became pregnant, because they didn't realize they were pregnant, had a higher incidence of birth defects.'

'That was just anecdotal. There was never a full trial, was there?'

'Of course not. How could there be? The evidence has to be anecdotal – you can't deliberately feed hormones in heavy doses to pregnant women – where are your ethics, Jess? The point that's worrying me is that there may be an effect like that with Contravert and that's why I want to do some tissue cultures as well as other animal trials. It's all right to use the stuff on the non-pregnant, of course – at least I think it should be. Though maybe it isn't – maybe it could have an effect on gonads in young people, do damage that could affect their ability to conceive and carry normal infants? You see what a problem this side-effects issue raises? Why it is that I have to be sure? So, there's that work to do. And maybe all this publicity won't be such a bad thing after all. It might mean that I can get more research money – might even be able to give up the path. job, get a pure research berth somewhere, really get my head down on it . . . .'

She felt cold in her belly suddenly. 'You'd leave Minster Hospital?'

'Just watch me go, given half the chance! I've done all I can in pathology. It bores me now – I just go through the motions. It's the research that matters, not the damned post-mortems and blood tests and histology and all the rest of it.'

'Oh,' she said, and then with an effort added, 'I'd miss you if you went.'

'But you'd come with me, wouldn't you? I'd have to have my own assistant wherever I went. You don't imagine I'd leave you behind after all the work you've done this year? Be your age, Jess!'

'Thanks for the reassurance,' she said, trying to sound sardonic and succeeding in sounding only happy and grateful. 'I'll keep you to that. I can't imagine not being involved with this work. I'd be . . . there'd be nothing left worth bothering about.'

There was a silence again and he didn't look at her, and then lifted his head and stared at her very directly. 'Are you leaving him, Jessie?'

'I don't know.'

'But you're not living with him at present?'

'You know I'm not. I'm bunking down at the hospital. But that can't go on. I've got a local estate agent looking for a furnished flatlet for me. Nothing much. Just a room and bath'd do.'

'Then you're going to leave him.' It wasn't a question, but a statement.

'I told you, I don't know.'

'Why not?'

'That's a stupid question!' she said hotly, and then bit her lip. She knew he was right, of course; she couldn't push away consideration of her situation much longer. She'd been managing to cope a day at a time, concentrating only on work, refusing to think about Peter, but she'd have to think about him soon.

'Try it this way, Jessie. Are you going back to him?'

The word came out before she even realized she was speaking. 'No!'

'Then you *are* leaving him, aren't you?'

'I suppose so. I just haven't thought about it. It's all so . . . it's not easy. Over twenty years we've been married. You can't throw that away just like that. Twenty years . . . .'

'I had a lecturer once who told me always to beware of people who told me they'd had twenty years of experience at something, and that that fitted them with the ability to do whatever it was they wanted to do. Mostly, he said, they've just had the same year of experience twenty times over and learned nothing at all from any of 'em.'

She was silent for a long time, and he said, 'I'm sorry if I'm being impertinent.'

She shook her head. 'No, you're not. I hope you're speaking as a friend. And friends aren't impertinent. Just interested . . . .'

'Got it in one. A friend. I don't want to meddle, of course I don't, but . . . I can't help but notice how much happier you've been these past days. Since you moved out to stay at the hospital.'

'Have I?'

'Very much so. You've been so much happier that you've made me think about myself.'

Now there was nothing she could dare to say.

'I've been happier too. Staying at the hospital, not going home at night. Phoning June sometimes. Not much of a marriage, is it?'

Still she said nothing and he said very deliberately, 'I feel more married to you. Together as we are so much . . . .'

'No!' She said it quickly, and began to gather her gloves and bag together. 'You really mustn't talk that way.'

'Why not? It's true.'

'Then it has no right to be.'

'Again, why not? This is the age of the modern marriage, Jess. People divorce and remarry every five minutes as far as I can tell . . . why not me? Why not you?'

'No.' She shook her head again and stood up, not looking at him.

'No, you don't want to talk about it. Or no . . . what?'

'No, I don't want to talk about it. Please, Ben, don't make things any messier than they are! I'm happy as I am. Working and . . . just working. Please don't make me confused. I get my head in enough of a tangle as it is thinking about Peter. Don't make it worse.'

'I won't.' He stood up too and picked up the bill the waitress had left for him. 'Come on. We'll go and walk round Covent Garden till it's time to go to those damned studios and offer ourselves up on the altars of the television gods. I'm sorry if I confused you. Put it down to my own confusion and the peculiar effects of being in London. I'm safer in Minster, I dare say, where everything's rather dull and ordinary . . . .'

'Dull?' She stood outside the restaurant, staring out at the jammed traffic in the road and the pushing crowds on the pavement and took a deep breath of the diesel-scented air. 'No, it's not dull in Minster. It's the place where Contravert happened, so it can't be dull. Covent Garden, you say? That'll be nice. Do we go by underground or do we take a bus?'

And they went, and said not another word about themselves or about June and Peter for the rest of the afternoon. But that didn't mean that Jessie at least didn't think a great deal about their conversation, nor that she didn't feel remarkably elated by it. She knew she ought to be distressed and anxious, ought to be worn down by the messy state of her marriage, and by the state of his, but she felt none of that. She just felt good and happy, enjoying the roasted chestnut smells and the street entertainers and the gaudy stalls and raucous sounds of Covent Garden with all the abandon of a girl on a first date with a man she found exciting.

24

The studio had arranged to send a cab to collect them at six o'clock, but by a quarter to, Jessie was already in the lobby waiting for it.

They had come back to the hotel from their afternoon in Covent Garden at five, to have time for a shower and a rest before the real business of the day started, but she hadn't been able to rest at all. The excitement and her anxiety about the coming ordeal and an undertow of confusion about her closeness to Ben had coalesced into a queasy mixture of sensations that made her feel actually sick, and only moving about fairly briskly controlled that, so move briskly she did. And now, in the lobby of the rather pretentiously decorated hotel near the Park, not far from Paddington, she couldn't sit quietly waiting. She had to move about, prowling from jeweller's display window to bookstall, from the reception desk to the doorway, under the sardonic eye of the clerks and the hall porters; and suddenly embarrassed by their cool stares she pushed her way out through the revolving doors to stand on the damp pavement outside and breathe the cold evening air.

Above her head a series of flags snapped and rattled their ropes in the night breeze and ahead of her the traffic sulked its viscous rush-hour way along the Bayswater Road and she stared at it and at the people hurrying along the pavements, their heads down against the December bite, and felt a great wave of loneliness and strangeness. What was she doing here in this great soulless mass of buildings and people who didn't give a damn whether she lived or died? She ought to be in the warm moist animal room at home, smelling the dusty comforting smells of corn and hay and laboratory chemicals, with Castor and Pollux chattering softly at her from their corner cage and the rabbits rustling contentedly in their straw, not here in this horrible cold place where everyone was a suspicious stranger; and she thought desperately, I must ring Errol, make sure he remembers that Castor needs extra vitamin capsules, and to see that Pollux doesn't steal them the way she usually does, and almost turned back to the hotel to find a phone.

But she stopped, controlling her own foolishness with an almost physical effort. Errol would do it right, of course he would. For all his apparent insouciance he was a sensible chap, and knew on which side his bread was honeyed. She wouldn't give him a penny of the five pounds she'd promised him for taking care of the monkeys in her absence unless she was certain all was well with them, and he knew it; phoning him wouldn't help at all, even if she knew where she could reach him at this time of day. He'd have settled the pair of small creatures for the night by now, and gone home, or wherever it was he disappeared to at the end of his working day. Ben had once said that he suspected that he went down a manhole as he left the hospital, only to reappear the next morning from the same place; no one ever saw him or his Rastafarian friends anywhere about the town, so where else could he be? And she smiled, now, remembering that silly conversation, and turned back to the pavement, hunching her shoulders inside her coat. She really must stop being so stupid, fussing herself this way. It was all going to be over soon anyway: they'd go to this silly television studio, do this silly programme, spend a silly evening, and tomorrow they'd go home, back to the hospital and its safe certainties, and she could put on her white coat again and have nothing more to worry about than the work, the lovely comforting reality that was work, and she actually shivered with pleasure at the thought.

A black taxi drew up at the pavement and the driver got out and peered at her in the half-light. 'You waiting for me, lady? BBC? Mrs . . . ah . . . .' He squinted at a piece of paper in his hand. 'Mrs Pitman?'

Her face flamed immediately, and she said loudly, too loudly, 'No! I mean, yes. I'm waiting for a cab from the BBC, but I'm Mrs Hurst . . . Dr Pitman will be out soon, I imagine. I don't really know . . . we're not together. I mean, he's in room 431 and I'm in 458. Ask them at the desk to call him . . . room 431, remember . . . .'

As if, she told herself furiously as the driver went lumbering into the hotel to find Ben, as if it mattered tuppence ha'penny what a wretched taxi-driver thinks! Why did I have to go to such lengths to tell him we have separate rooms here? What does it matter? Who gives a damn?

You do, her secret voice told her sardonically as the door revolved again and the taxi-driver came out, followed by Ben. You bloody well do, but she shook the little voice away, and managed to smile brightly at Ben.

'Hello! I came down early to get a little air. It'll be stuffy, I imagine, at the studios?'

'I expect so,' he said and his voice was crisp and a little remote and she thought – he's as nervous about all this as I am. Oh, hell, I wish I'd refused to do it. I wish I wasn't here. Is there still time to go home, forget all about it? But she got into the cab obediently as Ben held the door open, and settled herself in the corner against the window, staring out at the street and saying nothing.

He sat in the corner on his side, as far away from her, it seemed, as he could get, and the sense of alienation and loneliness deepened in her, made her feel cold inside and she thought – do it the way you did when you were at school, and you had to face frightening things. Pretend it isn't you at all, that the real you is sitting in a corner, high up in a corner, watching this foolish creature down below going through it. Watch and laugh and you'll feel none of it. Just be separate from it all – and that helped, made her shoulders relax, made her breathe more easily, and she could lean back and stare out of the window as though she really cared what was out there.

The taxi rocked and bounced its way westwards, along the Bayswater Road, through the crowds at Notting Hill Gate, and still they sat silently, listening to the crackle of the driver's radio call system, paying little attention to anything but their own silent thoughts, and then the driver said, 'Three nine . . . three nine . . . what? Yes . . . yes. Oh, like that, is it? Right, I'll use the other side . . .' and then reached behind him to push on the already open glass partition behind his head.

'Got to take you to the other building,' he said. 'Trouble at the main one, it seems.'

'Trouble?' Ben said sharply.

'Some demonstration or other,' the driver said and peered at them in his rear-view mirror. 'What you done, then?'

'I've done nothing,' Ben said stiffly. 'I don't know what it's about any more than you do.'

'Well, you must ha' done something,' the driver said with an air of great reasonableness. 'I mean, they don't do that all that often, send messages like that, I mean to take passengers somewhere different because of demonstrators. Not Irish, are you?'

Ben laughed at that, sounding really amused, and in the darkness Jessie relaxed her shoulders even more. 'I wish I were,' he said. 'I'd be having more fun than I am. Just a bloody doctor, that's all.'

'Doctor, eh?' The driver manoeuvred his cab on to the big roundabout at Shepherd's Bush. 'Abortion and that? Or experiments on babies? Lots of demonstrations over that this year. Popular for demonstrations, that is.'

'No!' Ben looked at Jessie in the lights thrown by the shop windows they were passing as they inched their way through the heavy home-going traffic and said quietly, 'This'll be those damned animal freedom people, Jessie. Will you be all right if we do get mixed up with them?'

'I'll have to be, won't I?' she said, and then added, almost violently, 'as if I'd do anything to hurt Castor and Pollux! As if I would! I've been worrying about them, damn it. Why don't these people understand? We don't hurt them . . . we never would . . . they're our animals . . . .'

'They're not thinking about individuals like Castor and Pollux. They're thinking about principles. It's easier to get agitated about principles . . . .' And again he lapsed into silence and stared out of his window and she looked at his profile, etched against the light of the glass, and thought confusedly; I wish I didn't think about individuals, I wish I didn't think about you . . . .

The radio crackled again, and the driver answered, clearly enjoying the small drama in which he was involved. 'Change of . . . right. Well, on their own 'eads be it. So much as a scratch on the body-work and I'll throw the bloody book at 'em. BBC can afford it . . . .' Again he reached back to push uselessly on the open partition. 'Got to go through it, it seems. No sense in going to any other entrance on account there ain't one they haven't covered. They really got it in for you, haven't they? Animals, is it? You one of these bloody vivisectionists, that it?'

'Since you were obviously listening to us, you know, don't you?' Ben said savagely.

The man sniffed loudly, and said, 'Cruelty – that's one thing I can't be doing with. Politics, that don't matter two hoots, they're all bloody liars and thieves, but cruelty's something else. Can't blame people getting upset over that . . . .' Very deliberately he reached back again and this time slammed his partition shut.

They could see the little knot of people at the main entrance to the television centre as the taxi rumbled up the road towards it. There were one or two home-made placards which they couldn't read in the poor light, and even through the closed windows they could hear the sound of chanting voices in a ragged chorus, so ragged that what they were saying was as unintelligible as the placards. Jessie shrank back against her corner as the taxi took the curve into the building's entrance, stopping at the barrier that was across it, and waiting stolidly. The barrier lifted at once, but still he sat there, his engine chugging noisily, as the group of people surged towards them and Ben leaned forwards and rapped urgently on the glass and shouted, 'Get in man, don't hang around!' But the driver sat lumpishly, not turning his head until at last a man came out of the little glassed-in lodge beside the gates, moving with obvious unwillingness towards them.

Around them the people pushed and shoved and faces were pressed against the glass, hideous in their distortion, and Jessie pulled herself even further back, staring at them with a sort of mesmerized horror. They didn't look like people at all; they were caricatures, gnomes out of a mad Disney film of the most frightening kind, and she cried out and lifted her hands to her face as the cab rocked slightly under the pressure of pushing hands.

'Get on, you bloody idiot!' Ben was shouting at the driver now, and at last, slowly, urged on by a gate-keeper who was clearly as angry as Ben was with the man's tardiness, the cab moved in past the barrier and it came down behind them, holding back the pushing crowd.

'You made that worse than it need have been!' Ben shouted at the driver as at last the cab pulled up at the foot of the steps that led to the door to the reception area and they could get out. 'You didn't have to sit there like that, you bloody fool!'

'You mind who you're calling a fool, mister,' the driver said and glared at him. 'Let the bleedin' dogs see the bleedin' rabbit, that's my motto, and if you don't like bein' a bloody rabbit, that's too bloody bad, ain't it? I don't suppose you give your bleedin' rabbits much choice, do you, *doctor* . . . Some fuckin' doctor . . . .' And he put the engine into gear with a crash and went off, leaving them standing there, Ben shouting furiously after him.

'Ben, don't.' Jessie held on to his arm as behind them someone came out of the swing doors towards them. 'Ben, don't come down to his level, please, Ben . . . .'

'I really would agree,' a voice said behind them, and they both turned to look. A tall young man in an open necked shirt and tight jeans and holding a clipboard under one arm was standing there and he smiled at them very widely and held out his hand. 'I'm Giles Stetler. Researcher for J.J. Sorry you had so unpleasant an experience getting here. We heard what was happening, tried to find another way to get you in, but these wretched people have settled themselves at every entrance we have. It's remarkable how they operate – get all sorts of information, don't they? One's amazed, really amazed. Do come along, now, and we'll get you a little something to restore the ailing tissues. I'm sure you can use it . . . .'

'I really think I'd rather we left now,' Ben said. His face was white with anger in the yellow light thrown through the entrance door, and he was holding Jessie's elbow in so firm a grip that she wanted to wince with the pain. But she didn't. 'I came here to . . . to provide information, accurate information about the work I'm doing. It's important work, and of great . . . and I didn't expect to be faced with this sort of . . . I thought I could trust the BBC to treat us fairly and . . . .'

'But my dear chap, of course you can trust us!' Stetler raised his eyebrows. 'You can hardly blame us for the fact that a group of hotheads gather at our gates, can you? Hardly our fault . . . .'

'But you've got a bloody camera there filming it all!' Ben said, and Jessie looked up at him, startled. 'Oh, yes, I saw them! Right there, whirring away, filming it all! Will it make a good start to the programme for you, is that it? Did you want a bit of excitement just to prove that . . . .'

'My dear Dr Pitman, you really must calm down! I can understand your distress at being faced with that sort of thing, but you really can't accuse us of setting it up, you know, you really can't . . . .'

'Why can't I? Isn't it the sort of thing you television people do?'

There was a little pause and then Stetler said crisply, 'No. Any more than being unnecessarily cruel to animals is what researchers do. It's because people have stereotyped notions like that that we're doing this programme tonight. We want to change that false belief, you see. We had hoped you'd realize that.'

Ben stared at him in the half-light, his face still angry but less passionately so now. 'Well, that's as may be. But why are you filming that rabble at the gate, then?'

'Because we have to reflect what people feel about important issues,' Stetler said promptly. 'They appeared there, at our feet, as it were, and we could hardly ignore them, could we? We had to use 'em – and they aren't exactly a rabble, you know. A bit over-heated, perhaps, but they have a valid point of view, and it's one, I must repeat, that we have to reflect. You're pretty heated yourself, after all . . . .'

'Because we were threatened,' Ben said, and Jessie heard the defensive note in his voice and felt a wave of desolation fill her; Ben angry and attacking had been a protector, someone she could rely on to say the right thing at the right moment, but Ben on the defensive was suddenly a weaker, more frail creature, one in need of help, and she tightened her arm against her own body to squeeze his hand against her, and said quietly, 'We'll have to do it, Ben. Now we're here. And getting angry won't help. We've got to explain what we're doing and why . . . haven't we?'

'Very wise, very wise indeed,' Stetler said, and began to make ushering movements, leading them towards the entrance. 'Come and have a little drink, restore the old tissues, you'll feel much better about it all. Meet J.J., you know, check out the areas you're going to cover, make sure he knows exactly what it is you want to talk about – we want to give you every opportunity, you know, to state your case, get it all clear in the public mind . . . .'

They had reached a bank of lifts by now as Stetler hurried them past knots of curiously staring people and Ben stopped short as Stetler pressed the call button.

'What do you mean, state my case? I'm not on any sort of trial here, you know! I agreed to come and talk about my research, that's all. Jessie agreed to come to explain how the animals are used and protected in the lab, and to warn people of the risks they run because those idiots let them out and . . . .'

'Of course, of course,' Stetler said soothingly. 'Absolutely, got it in one – well now, shall we go into hospitality? Then I can show you to your dressing rooms if you want to use them, and then after that a little bit of a drink and a sarnie or two – though we'll give you some real supper later, of course – a swift visit to makeup to damp down the shine and all that, make Mrs Hurst look lovelier than ever, you know, then the meeting with old J.J. and it'll be over before you know it, really it will . . . do come along, now.'

And after one more long moment of hesitation while he stared at Giles Stetler's bland face, Ben allowed himself to be led into the lift, and Jessie, her moment of illogical hope withering away, the hope that they would after all turn and go and leave the whole wretched business behind them and return to Minster, followed him. There was nothing else she could do, though every instinct in her, despite her earlier urging of him to do the programme, was now urging her to turn and run, and take him with her.

25

She could see the sweat on Ben's face clearly from where she sat on the far side of J.J. Gerrard, could see the trickles gleaming in the powerful lights that washed all the reality out of the scene they were inhabiting, and she wanted to get up and go over to him and dry his face for him, as a mother would dry a weeping child's tears, and she was glad of the fact that she was virtually tethered to her seat by the microphone cable that had been pushed up under her skirt so that the small microphone could be pinned to her lapel. Ben wouldn't thank her for fussing over him, badly as she wanted to do it.

'So, let me get this clear, Dr Pitman,' J.J. Gerrard said, and he smiled at Ben with great benignity. His tanned wrinkled face under its thatch of beautifully waved steel-grey hair seemed open, devoid of expression, but Jessie could see the sharp-eyed malice that was in him, and feared him. He's not interested in us, in what we're saying, she thought. He's only interested in his own cleverness. I don't like him. I'm afraid of him. Don't trust him, Ben, he's after you – but Ben didn't look at her and she knew her silent message couldn't reach him.

'Just for my own satisfaction,' J.J. went on. 'You set out to find a cure for all the virus infections that afflict mankind, a cure as far-reaching in its effects as the antibiotics? A lifesaver of the sort that Fleming developed? You wanted to be a great man like Fleming?'

'Actually it was Florey and Chain who developed penicillin,' Ben said. 'This tendency to deify Fleming always irritates me, when you consider the work the Oxford people did and . . . .'

'Well, that's by the by, Dr Pitman, by the by. We're interested in *you*. You set out to produce something as important as penicillin . . . .'

'Well, yes, you could say that . . . .' Ben shook his head, irritated again. 'I mean, I didn't set out to be some sort of . . .

I'm not interested in fame, you know! I just saw an area of research that interested me. I thought, if I can find a substance that will trigger a cell-mediated response to virus attacks, then there could be a considerable value in it. Not just the obvious things like the common cold, or flu, but possibly the slow viruses – we don't know for sure how much multiple sclerosis, for example, is a virus-triggered problem – and then there are the cancers. Some of them implicate viruses, of course.'

J.J. pounced on that. 'You were looking for a cure for cancer as well as the common cold? In one magic bullet?'

'No!' Ben said it almost despairingly. 'You really mustn't see it in such simple terms, Mr Gerrard! Magic bullets and . . . science just isn't like that . . . it's a long painstaking piecing together of bits and pieces of information, until you have a full enough picture to apply what you've found to some of the problems that we have to deal with in modern medicine. I must make it clear I wasn't looking for any . . . any personal glory or . . . I was just looking for one piece in a major jigsaw puzzle . . . .'

'And you seem to have found it,' Gerrard said with an air of triumph. 'Going by what happened to Andrea Barnett, you found it!' He whirled and stared directly at the camera that was right in front of him, holding up a warning hand at Ben as he opened his mouth to speak. 'At this stage we'll stop our discussion here in the studio and show you some film, a very remarkable piece of film, that was taken only this afternoon at the hospital in the small seaside town of Minster, a piece of film that I believe will be an historic one. Over to our reporter Carolynn Lauderdale in Minster . . . .'

Above their heads the monitor screens blanked, showed a series of rapidly flashing numbers and then the image of a girl with long hair hanging over her shoulders and framing a face on which was an expression of great earnestness. 'Here at Minster Hospital,' she said, staring firmly out at them, 'I have had the opportunity to . . . .'

'Three minutes, twenty seconds, studio!' shouted a man in earphones who had been jumping about busily ever since they had come into the studio. 'Audience, this is a good chance for you all to get your coughing over and done with!' And he flashed a grin up at the rows of seats that banked one side, and the faces of the people there grinned back at him and obediently broke into a rattle of coughs that almost drowned out the voice coming from the monitors, and Jessie had to strain to hear it.

'This child when she arrived here was in a desperate state . . . but let the specialist in charge of her case explain it all . . . .' The image of the girl diminished as the camera pulled back from her to take in the person beside her, and there, grinning with a vast self-satisfaction, was Lyall Davies, and Jessie stared at that so familiar face with amazement. *Was* that Lyall Davies, the man she knew so well and found so foolish? Or was it just an actor, a simulacrum of the real Lyall Davies, posturing there, so obviously pleased with himself? But there was no mistaking that thick voice with its plummy overtones and she listened horrified as he seemed to describe himself as a great physician of world-wide repute – was he actually saying all that or just implying it? It didn't matter, because the sense of what he was saying was clear enough – he had seen this desperately sick child brought to him, had looked upon her with deep compassion and had turned to his colleague in the laboratories for help in her care.

'I knew about his stuff, of course,' Lyall Davies almost purred it. 'Knew he was beavering away down there in his little cubby hole, and I venture to say I had perhaps a clearer view of the clinical possibilities than he did! Remarkable scientist, of course, remarkable, but not the . . . ah . . clinical acumen of we physicians. Not the experience, of course, but bless the man, there he was with this magical stuff of his! And I knew, absolutely knew we had to try it. Child was dying, don't you know. It was pitiful to see, dying! So after some persuasion . . . .'

He smirked and at once there was the image of the greatly caring physician, almost on his knees to the ice-cold researcher who didn't really care about people at all, only about his science.

'At last my little bit of commonsense prevailed! He was cautious, of course, properly so, but sometimes one has to be brave, wouldn't you agree, and take the bull by the horns, so to speak, make a major effort for the sake of a sick child – and that was my small contribution.'

And again he smirked and this time the picture he projected was one of a selfless, self-effacing, all-caring doctor, who always put others' needs before his own; and watching that grinning image Jessie felt nausea and turned and looked at Ben who was sitting staring up at the monitor with the same look of disgust on his face that she knew was on her own. 'Bloody man!' she said aloud and didn't care that J.J. Gerrard flicked an interested glance at her before turning back to the makeup girl who was crouching at his side and patting his face with a piece of chamois leather soaked in eau-de-Cologne.

The scene on the monitor shifted and showed Ward Seven B and Jessie leaned forwards, fascinated, as the camera moved lingeringly over the rows of beds in the cubicles and then closed in on Andrea Barnett. The child was sitting up in her bed looking both nervous and excited, and though she was pale was clearly in basic good condition. Looking at her, Jessie tried to see the way she had looked that day when they had started using the Contravert on her, tried to see those eyes now darting brightly about as the half-closed white-rimmed blanks they had been; and couldn't. That child, that Andrea had been almost lifeless. This one was as alert and alive as Castor and Pollux were, when they swung eagerly towards her as she came to their cage with her hands full of nuts for them . . . .

'Thirty seconds, studio!' bawled the man with the earphones and the makeup girl scuttled away, ignoring the streaks of sweat on Ben's face, as J.J. Gerrard again settled himself in his seat, and then the whispers that had been going on around them stopped as the earphoned man lifted his arm and looked at J.J. warningly. The red light flicked on on the camera facing him and then he was saying smoothly, as though he'd been talking to them all through that film, 'A remarkable story, a very remarkable story! A child who should have been dead, from all accounts, now clearly very much alive and well and living in Minster! How did you feel, Dr Pitman, as you watched that piece of film?'

'It wasn't quite like that,' Ben said uneasily and flicked a glance at Jessie. 'Actually it was my assistant Jessie – Mrs Hurst, here – who suggested that Contravert could be useful in the child's treatment. I was dubious, because of the possibility of side-effects, you see . . . .'

J.J. Gerrard had turned to Jessie for a moment at Ben's words but now he whirled his chair back in order to look hard at Ben again. 'What's that? Side-effects? You mean this drug could be dangerous?'

'We don't know,' Ben said. 'That's the trouble with all this fuss you people are making. It's too soon to be publicizing it, you see! We need to do any number of tests in animals, in people, long-term trials – you really can't go off half-cocked like this!'

'But when lives are at stake, Dr Pitman, it isn't easy to withhold a lifesaving drug . . . .'

'Sometimes you have to,' Ben said, and set his mouth mulishly, and Jessie wanted to call out to him, to warn him of the effect his expression could have on the people watching. Already she had seen all too horribly clearly how Lyall Davies had managed to show himself as a person he most certainly wasn't, and she wanted passionately to shout to Ben, to cry out, 'Don't let them show you as something you're not! Be careful, these bloody cameras are hunters, they'll hurt you, they'll damage you, be careful!' But she said nothing, silenced herself by her awareness of those voracious cameras, waiting there in her chair, her hands folded on her lap, tensely watching him.

'The mention of possible side-effects to your drug is a timely one, Dr Pitman,' J.J. was saying silkily. 'It brings me to another vital question. What about the side-effects of your *research*, rather than of your drug?'

'Of my . . . I don't understand you?' Ben said and stared at him, clearly confused by the change of tack.

'Of your use of dangerous strains of viruses in animals, Dr Pitman,' J.J. was sounding silkier than ever. 'You have already explained to us, have you not, that you do your research by deliberately infecting laboratory animals with a dangerous flu strain – 737, you call it, I seem to remember – and then treating some of the sick animals with your drug Contravert, and letting the others die of it . . . .'

'Wicked bastard!' someone shrieked from the audience and there was a little flurry from the banked rows of seats as some of the floor staff went hurrying up towards the source of the disturbance. 'Wicked, cruel bastard, why don't you give yourself your stinking diseases and . . . .'

J.J. held up one hand and smiled with an air of great imperturbability. 'Your opportunity to join in the debate with Dr Pitman will come!' he said with great joviality. 'Let me have the privilege of getting the facts clear first, if you please!' And there was a little spatter of applause from the rest of the audience as J.J. turned back to Ben.

'As I was saying, Dr Pitman, the side-effects of your research are risky, too, are they not? Now these animals infected with this deadly virus have escaped and . . . .'

'Damn it, they didn't escape!' Ben exploded, and this time Jessie leaned forwards and held out one hand towards him, needing to silence him, wanting to do anything to stop him showing himself in so bad a light, as an irascible and difficult person. 'They were deliberately stolen and released by a bunch of idiots who hadn't the least idea what they were doing . . . .'

'Humane people, not idiots!' screamed the voice from the back of the audience. 'You're the idiot, deliberately giving vile diseases to helpless little animals. You're the wicked one . . . .' There was a louder scuffle as the objector was clearly physically removed and with magisterial patience J.J. Gerrard waited till it had subsided.

'I take your point, Dr Pitman, that you had no intention of permitting your . . . ah . . . subject animals to leave your laboratory alive, but the fact remains, does it not, that you were dealing with lethal bacteria here . . . .'

'Viruses,' Ben growled. 'At least get the facts right. Viruses, not bacteria. They can be dealt with via antibiotics. Viruses can't.'

'I stand corrected,' said J.J. Gerrard, and cast a droll look at his audience. Clearly those who dared to correct the great J.J. were few and far between. 'But the essence of the situation is the same, surely. Lethal viruses, now loose in the community, could spread the disease to a great many other children like Andrea Barnett, who we saw in that historic piece of film?'

'It could,' Ben said unwillingly. 'It could . . . but we can't know that it *has*. The first cases of this current epidemic started before my animals were released, so we can't be *sure* it's due to the organism I was using. I know that cleaner woman might have picked it up and . . . but we don't know, do we? There's a great deal of flu of one sort and another going round at the moment. Probably several different strains are involved – why pick on *my* research to be blamed? The evidence is so flimsy . . . .'

'But it's possible?' Gerrard said and leaned forwards to stare more closely at Ben. 'It's possible?'

'I don't know.' Ben was sweating even more now. 'I'm trying to tell you. I don't *know*. No one could know.'

'But the possibility is there?' J.J. was clearly very pleased with himself, well launched now on his famous *Probe* technique of nagging an interviewee until he capitulated. 'The *possibility* is there?'

'It's what I'm afraid of,' Ben said at last in a low voice, and J.J. leaned even more closely towards him and said, 'I beg your pardon?' and this time Ben shouted it. 'It's what I'm afraid of!'

'You are afraid of it,' J.J. now had a note of great seriousness in his voice. 'You are afraid of it. But were you not afraid of your virus while you were using it in your laboratory? Was there no fear in you then of the possible outcome if the virus escaped, by whatever means?'

'No. Why should there be?' Ben looked at him with a sort of helplessness in his expression. 'How can I explain to you who know nothing of what hospitals are, and how they're run and what it's like to do research on a shoestring, how can I possibly make you, or anyone, understand? It's . . . we shouldn't be talking about all this! It'll only alarm people unnecessarily! If I hadn't had it forced on me I'd never have used Contravert outside the laboratory and I'd never have agreed to come here tonight! All you're doing by making all this fuss is creating anxiety . . . it's all wrong . . . .'

'But surely people have the right to know what goes on in the medical world? You wouldn't suggest you scientists should be allowed to do whatever you like with no references to us, the people? We live in a democracy, surely, Doctor, and doesn't that democracy's rules and standards apply to you as much as to anyone else? Aren't you as accountable as anyone else?'

'Of course I am!' Ben said, sweating more and more heavily now. The streaks on his face could be seen clearly on the monitor above her head, and Jessie could have wept for his obvious misery. 'Of course I am – but not like this! This isn't being accountable – this is being pilloried. You don't know what you're talking about, you put a set of loaded questions to me, based on all sorts of false assumptions and then ask me – can't you see how unjust all this is?'

'I can see how distressed you are, Doctor,' J.J. said with great courtesy. 'Let's give you a little time to recover your composure while I talk to your assistant Mrs Hurst . . . .'

Here we go, Jessie thought. My turn. And suddenly she remembered the time, all those years ago, when she had had to have her tonsils out, had had to lie in a bed in a hospital ward which smelled horrible, watching other children wheeled away on long white beds and then brought back smelling even more disgusting and with their faces all bloodied, waiting for her turn; and that image and the fears it recreated in her were so powerful that she hardly realized that he was asking her a question and that she was answering it.

But she was, and she sat there automatically responding to the man who was staring at her, aware only of the brightness of the light behind his head which wrapped it in a hazy nimbus, and the swell of his unctuous voice, and hardly thinking about what she said at all; and then, slowly, realized that she must be doing rather well. There was a little rattle of applause after she launched herself into an impassioned account of the lives that had been saved by the use of medical progress made via animal research, talking about the dogs that Banting and Best had used to develop insulin, which had saved millions of human lives, of the work done by Jonas Salk on animals when he prepared his poliomyelitis vaccines, and she caught a glimpse of Ben looking at her, his face approving and almost happy for the first time since they had come to this hateful building; and she began, suddenly, to feel better.

J.J. was asking her to describe the lives the animals led in the laboratories and this time the image that rose to her mind was of Castor and Pollux – of the way those small black wrinkled hands would reach for her, to cling to her and to go seeking in her pockets and around her hair for titbits and how she stood and laughed and played with them when they behaved so – and without any sort of conscious planning to impress her listeners, she spoke of what she was seeing in her mind's eye, of the way she cared for her animals, of the affection that they created in her, and spoke too of the bitter sense of loss she had felt when the intruders had taken them. And to her amazement there were tears in her eyes when she stopped talking and the audience was applauding her.

'You see?' It was Ben's voice that rose above the sound of the fading applause and the camera swung to pick him up. 'We aren't cruel and uncaring! You've heard how the animals are looked after! How can anyone think we ill-treat them after listening to J . . . Mrs Hurst? And I assure you she's telling the truth. Of course it's sad when some of the animals die because of our research but we do all we can to make sure they don't suffer pain, and we do it only to find a worthwhile object. It's not as though we were trying to . . . to make a new shampoo or were looking for ways to make cigarette smoking safer. That sort of use of animals is greedy – it's wasteful. But our research is different . . . .'

'After Mrs Hurst's splendid account of what you do there at Minster, Dr Pitman, who can doubt it?' J.J. Gerrard said. 'But it's time now to go over to our studio audience, and to our wider audience who can phone in – the number is on your screen now – to get their opinions on this vital topic of our time. Now, to help you all, let me just recapitulate the case that we have heard outlined here tonight. Dr Pitman, as part of a research project which might, just possibly, reveal a cure for cancer as well as for the common cold and the more dangerous forms of flu and other virus infections which we suffer, has worked with animals in his laboratory. Some of those animals have been removed from the laboratory and released and may be carrying a dangerous epidemic with them . . . .'

He held up his hand as Ben tried to protest. 'No one blames Dr Pitman for this unfortunate state of affairs – but it is a state of affairs that exists and it can't be denied that it exists. Now, what we must discuss are the ethics of this complex situation. Have the researchers the right to expose us all to dangerous germs as part of their research into cures for those germs? And have they the right to use helpless animals, who can't plead for themselves, for the work they do? That's the nitty gritty of it, ladies and gentlemen, and I open the floor now to you, the people! Now, our first speaker is . . . who? Ah, you there, sir, in the middle . . . I believe you are a member of the Souls against Science Group? Yes . . . well, let's hear from you. The airwaves are yours . . . .'

26

The hubbub in the hospitality room was clearly a jubilant one; the people who worked on the programme – of whom there seemed to Jessie to be an inordinate number – were congratulating each other excitedly, recapitulating with glee the various points J.J. had made, chortling over some of the idiocies perpetrated by the members of the studio audience who had participated, laughing hugely at the phone-in man who had got his wires crossed and thought they were talking about homeopathy cures for sick animals, and Jessie sat in the corner, her hand curved round a glass of wine she didn't want, listening to it and trying to get clear in her own mind what had happened.

Ben beside her said nothing, staring down at his own untouched glass of wine as the chatter rose and fell around them; now the programme was over it was as though they were no longer there. The people involved wanted to talk only to each other, not to outsiders, and they sat there, a little forlorn, until Jessie broke their silence by murmuring, 'Can we go now, Ben?'

'Mm? I suppose so. No point in staying any longer – Jessie, did I make as much of a fool of myself as I think I did?'

She thought for a moment. 'Not a fool, Ben, no. But you didn't do yourself justice. I kept wanting you to explain more about how much you worry and . . . .'

'Thank God for you,' he said and managed to smile at her, a twisted little grimace that made his eyes look more miserable than ever. 'You were bloody marvellous. You took a lot of the fury out of those people, you know. You heard what they said when they started talking – and how the Animal Freedom Brigade lot were howled down . . . .'

'I can't think why they weren't arrested as soon as they said that's who they were,' Jessie said indignantly. 'The damage they did at the lab and . . . .'

'You weren't listening properly, Jess. They're organized on a cell system. None of them know each other. They only deal with their own immediate group, so they can't be held accountable for what other groups do.'

'They ought to be,' Jessie said and her voice rose a little with her anger. 'They ought to be, and then maybe we'd . . . .'

'Now, we can't have you two sitting here on your own!' Giles Stetler was beaming down on them. 'Do come and collect a plateful of food. Nothing too fancy, you know – the hospitality budgets are being cut to ribbons these hard times, I'm afraid – but the chicken legs are edible. I promised you you'd feel better once it was all over and done with, didn't I? Well done, both of you. You were absolutely superb, you really were. Excellent television, it really was – if those bloody reviewers don't give us the accolade tomorrow, well, I don't know *what* J.J. will say. He's delighted about it all right now – he's in his dressing room – but he'll be along in a few moments. Do come and get some victuals – you've more than earned it . . . .'

'I'm not so happy about how it went,' Ben said bluntly. 'I don't think I gave a fair picture of what I do, and what the problems are . . . .'

'But you were splendid, splendid!' Stetler said heartily, and then added with an edge in his voice. 'You can't deny you were given every opportunity to say what you wanted?'

'The questions . . . .' Ben said and then stopped. 'I never realized before how difficult it is to give the right answers if you don't get the right questions.'

'But you were given the right questions!' Stetler said, more sharply now. 'There was that long briefing session you had with J.J. – you talked for at least ten minutes – and he told you the areas he would cover and . . . .'

'I know he did. But the way the questions were framed it just wasn't possible to make it clear. I kept being sent off at tangents . . . .'

'Forgive me, doctor, if I say that's no fault in J.J. He doesn't control your answers, you know – this was a live programme, you were free to say what you liked! No one was trying to catch you out.'

'Then why do I feel as though they were? Why do I feel so uneasy? Why did I never feel I was in control of my own . . . .'

'Oh, that's just the effect of television! I'm sure that you'll

feel much better when you see the video. I'm sure you
arranged for someone to video it so that you could see yourself
tomorrow?'

'No,' Ben said, and frowned. 'It never occured to me.'

Giles shook his head, amused. 'Then you're very unusual.
Most of our studio guests do that. Can't wait to see how they
performed.'

'I'm not a performer, I'm a doctor,' Ben said. 'Perhaps I
should have remembered that before I agreed to come.'

'You're being over-sensitive, my dear chap!' Giles put his
arm soothingly across Ben's shoulders. 'Now, do relax and
try some of our delicious BBC supper! I have to call it that in
case anyone from the DG's office is listening, though between
ourselves I can't deny it's pretty ghastly . . . oh, Jenny. Are you
looking for me?'

The girl in leather trousers and a heavy sweater, in spite of
the heat in the room, who had come pushing through the
crowd towards them was grinning from ear to ear. 'No, Giles,
for Dr Pitman. My dear, the drama! We've only been off air
twenty minutes and the phones have been positively
humming. Jammed the switchboard, I'm told – and there's
already someone here from *The Times* wanting an interview
with you for tomorrow's paper, and I dare say there'll be
others yet! J.J's over the moon about it – it's been ages since we
had a programme that got them like this one has. Not even the
Warnock Committee report got under their skins the way this
one did – you can't beat animals, can you? It always gets 'em
where they live – the reporter's over here. Will you come with
me, Dr Pitman?'

'No!' Ben said. 'I've talked enough for one night to last me a
lifetime. Not another damned word . . . .'

'But you must!' Giles said. 'You've become a person of
considerable importance, my dear chap. You really must . . . .'

'I *must* do nothing of the sort,' Ben snapped. 'I'm leaving.
Now, Jessie?'

At once she nodded. 'As soon as you like, I'll get my coat –
it's in that dressing room place . . . .'

'But you can't say no to *The Times*,' the girl Jenny almost
wailed it. 'I mean, it's not as though it's the *Sun* or something
– this is the man from *The Times* . . . .'

'I don't care if he's from bloody Timbuctoo. I'm leaving.
My coat as well, please. If someone would get it and arrange

for a taxi to take us back to our hotel . . . .'

He was white about the mouth again and Jessie felt better; Ben once again in an attacking mood was a great comfort in this alien setting, and she moved a little closer to him, grateful for his physical bulk.

'Would this be Dr Pitman, then? Yes, of course, I recognize you. Watched the programme. And Mrs Hurst too . . . how convenient. Perhaps we could find a quiet corner, somewhere, Dr Pitman? Just a few minutes of your time before the hordes descend on you . . . .'

'This is the *Times* journalist I told you about,' the girl Jenny said, looking at Ben with an imploring expression on her face. 'Jimmy, Dr Pitman's a bit tired, as I'm sure you'll understand and he said . . . .'

'I am not tired,' Ben said furiously. 'But I do not intend on any account to . . . .'

'Have you heard about the death, Dr Pitman?' The journalist was standing looking at him with his head tilted to one side, his eyes bright and birdlike in a rather pallid round face. 'Very unfortunate, isn't it?'

'What death?' It was Jessie who asked, pushing forwards a little from Ben's side. 'What are you talking about?'

'Three children in Dartchester,' the *Times* man said, never taking his eyes from Ben's face. 'They live in the same house – two brothers and a cousin, it seems. They showed signs of a flu attack early yesterday morning, apparently, and the grandmother who looks after them called the doctor, who didn't come. She found the youngest dead in her bed this morning. Little girl of seven.'

'Why are you asking Ben about it?' Jessie's mouth was dry.

'Because Dartchester isn't that far from Minster, and because the symptoms are, I gather, similar to those the child at your hospital had – the one you cured with your Contravert, Dr Pitman. It seems likely, according to the local GP, that the children picked up the virus from your animals – they'd been playing in a field near the town where there are a great many rabbits and . . . .'

'Dartchester's an enormous distance from Minster when you're talking about rabbits. The animals from our lab couldn't have gone that far – it's almost forty miles!' Jessie was standing in front of Ben now who was still silent, staring at the journalist. 'They're much too small to travel forty miles,' she said passionately. 'Much too small and much too weak. They're probably dead by now, if those people let them loose in the open. They're not used to fending for themselves, they can't have got that far. Whatever those children had, it can't be the same, it can't . . . .'

'It must, Jess,' Ben said quietly and everyone looked at him. Around them the room had quietened as people turned and listened, craning to see and hear over each other's heads. 'Viruses can transmit great distances quite quickly. It depends on the availability of vectors and there are a lot of rabbits and small mammals of all sorts in the country. They cover a big area. Has the child had a PM? Post-mortem examination?'

The journalist lifted his brows. 'I don't know, Dr Pitman. No idea. Would you care to comment on the situation?'

'No,' Ben said shortly, and began to move forward, pushing aside the people clustered round them. 'Not enough information. I can't comment – not enough to comment on. Just a supposition . . . .'

'You said yourself that the virus could be from your animals . . .' the journalist said, and Ben turned and blazed at him.

'I bloody well did not! I said only that a virus could be transmitted the distance in the time that's elapsed since my animals were stolen and released. That is all I said, and I have witnesses here. You report me as saying anything else, and by God, but you'll pay for it!'

'Fair enough,' the journalist said pacifically. 'Sorry, I misunderstood. But you don't deny that these children *could* be affected by the virus which you had infected your animals with in your laboratory, Dr Pitman? The ones that were later stolen and released by a cell of the Animal Freedom Brigade?'

'I neither deny nor affirm,' Ben said, and now his rage seemed to have left him, for he spoke with a weariness that made Jessie reach out and take hold of his arm. 'I only said that I don't have enough information to make any sort of useful comment, so I make none. That is what I said, it's what I say again, and if you report me as saying anything else, I'll . . . I'll sue. There has to be some legal protection against the sort of distortion you people go in for . . . .'

'No one is distorting anything,' Giles Stetler said loudly. 'If that comment was directed at the way this programme was produced, then I oppose it categorically. We've done all we can to give you a fair hearing, an open forum, and if you damned yourself out of your own mouth, that isn't our fault, is it?'

'And no one could ever think *The Times* would misreport you either, Dr Pitman,' the journalist said and smiled at him, again tilting his head winsomely. 'I'm sure you didn't mean to suggest otherwise.'

'I'm glad you're sure. Jess, are you ready? Mr Stetler, our coats if you please . . . .' And he began to push towards the door even more determinedly.

'One last question, Dr Pitman!' The journalist came pushing along behind them. 'Will you be willing to provide some of your Contravert for the remaining children of that family in Dartchester? They're very ill, it seems, and a request has been sent to your hospital for supplies . . . .'

Ben stopped short and stood staring ahead of him, his eyes blank. Then he turned and looked at the *Times* man.

'I'll consider the request as soon as I receive it,' he said carefully, enunciating each word very clearly. 'I can't make any decision in the absence of information. I can't decide here, in a TV studio, what would be good medical practice at Minster Hospital. Can I? As soon as I get back to the hospital tomorrow morning, I'll see the request and decide then. That's all I can say. Goodnight, gentlemen.' And this time they let him go, with Jess close beside him.

Long after they had said goodnight and parted, she sat on the side of her bed at the hotel, her dressing-gown pulled round her, staring at the floor between her bare feet, thinking.

The taxi journey back from the television studio had been a grim one, because the driver had a radio on, and the news bulletin that started just after they got into the cab led with the account of the death of the child in Dartchester, and warnings that a severe epidemic seemed to be building up as a result of the releasing of the laboratory animals.

'Speaking on the BBC programme *Probe* tonight,' the newsreader had said in cheerful tones, 'Dr Ben Pitman, whose research involved infecting the released animals with the lethal virus strain known as 737, said no blame can be attached to the hospital at which he did the work, nor to his department. The Animal Freedom Brigade, who claim responsibility for releasing the animals, similarly deny all responsibility for the threatened epidemic, pointing out that they did not infect the rabbits in question with the lethal germ . . . .'

'Damn them, damn the ignorant bastards for . . . . Why do they keep calling 737 lethal? Are they trying to put the fear of God into everyone? It's the most irresponsible business I . . . .'

'No sense in getting agitated, Ben,' Jessie said, trying to sound calmer than she felt. 'The story's out and there it is. And it's no use saying 737 isn't dangerous because we know it is. Look, let's not talk about it any more tonight. You're exhausted and so am I, and we've talked ourselves into a state of bewilderment as it is. So, tomorrow, when we get back, then we'll be able to think it through properly. Right now, you're just getting upset and that'll get you nowhere.'

And he'd agreed and had lapsed into a silence that he barely broke even when they reached the hotel. He'd collected his key from the desk, grunted a goodnight to her and gone, and she had watched him as he let himself into his room along the corridor and then gone into her own.

She had thought she was tired, thought that all she wanted was sleep, but she was wide awake now, in spite of a hot bath and a straight double whisky from the little refrigerator in her room. She didn't drink much normally, but tonight, she'd told herself, she needed a sedative. And whisky would do as well as anything else.

But still she sat there at the side of the bed, her senses preternaturally alert, her eyes wide and unblinking, unable to rest, thinking only about him. She imagined him, there in his room, a few doors down the long corridor outside her door, as alone and as wakeful and miserable as she was, and the image made her restless, made her get to her feet to prowl around the anonymity of this pink wallpapered box of a room in a box of an hotel in the middle of this noisy box of a city that she so hated.

Below in the street she could hear traffic, and somewhere in the distance a police siren began to wail excitedly, lifting waves of fear in her, and she pulled her dressing-gown even more tightly around her, even though she wasn't cold, and opened her door and went out into the corridor. Being shut in that square featureless room, with its ominous lack of any personality at all, was suddenly more than she could bear. Even walking up and down the dusty overheated corridor outside would be better than sitting here, she told herself, and began to pace along the strip of carpet in the middle of the narrow way, setting her feet in front of each other very deliberately, the way a child does when she fears stepping on the lines between the paving stones, the way she had walked herself when she had been small and there had been so much in the world to be afraid of. Just as there still was.

She hadn't meant to go to his room, she really hadn't, or so she told herself. But there she was, staring at the gilt numbers. 431. The four was slightly askew and she looked at it and then put up one hand, wanting to set it straight, and then pulled away, furious with herself for her own foolishness. As if it mattered that the number was crooked; who cared? And she made herself look away from the upper part of the door and so saw that the key to the room was still in the lock. He'd left it there when he'd let himself in, and she stared at it and then, very deliberately, put out her hand again and this time grasped the key and turned it so that the door opened on the dark room inside. And she went in.

27

She woke in the bed in room 458 suddenly, one moment deeply asleep and the next wide awake with her heart thumping heavily in her chest, as though something terrifying had happened to her. It was dark in the room, though a faint glow came through the curtains from the floodlighting that criss-crossed the front of the hotel, and she peered at the faintly luminous face of her bedside travelling clock, squinting to see.

Half past six. She collapsed back again into her pillows, trying to puzzle out why she had woken in such fear; and then it started again; the wail of a police siren getting closer and closer, and she knew at once that it was that which had woken her before, and turned on her side, to settle to sleep again. No need to get up for another half hour yet . . . .

And then she remembered and lay very still, staring out blankly at the dark room and its bulky shadows of dressing-table and luggage-stand, trying to convince herself that it hadn't happened, that she'd dreamed it – which in itself would have been worrying enough, surely? – that it had all been a figment of her whisky-fed imagination.

But of course it hadn't. She knew perfectly well that it had all happened. She had behaved extraordinarily oddly, God knew: she, the passive obedient wife of Peter, who had never even told him how she felt about his sporadic and clumsy lovemaking, to have behaved so? Had she really walked calmly into another man's bedroom last night and taken off her nightdress and slipped her naked body into his bed beside him? She contemplated the enormity of her own actions and then, as she remembered the startled way he had responded to her – his moment of total stillness and then the urgent reaching for her – her mouth curved and she was grinning with delight in the darkness of her blank hotel room, going over and over each movement he had made, each movement she had made

231

herself, enjoying it all again, reliving it so that her skin moved across the muscles of her belly at the memory.

It had all seemed so normal, she told herself, now, so natural and right. If anyone had ever asked her how she might react to making love with a man other than Peter, she would have been unable to answer. She had never shared a bed with any man but her husband, going into marriage with him as a virgin – a fact about which, she had later discovered to her chagrin, he had boasted a good deal – and had never even considered the possibility. She had told herself a long time ago that she was one of the more fortunate of the world's women, not unduly perturbed by sexual needs, and had been grateful for that. To hunger after sex when married to a man like Peter could be a recipe for some unhappiness; as it was she had never felt particularly deprived, and had never thought of any other man in that context.

Until now, and she looked back down the corridor of her memory at last night and marvelled at how much urgency there had been in her and how she had been able to unleash it at his touch. Had she really rolled about beneath him in that abandoned fashion? Had she really made those extraordinary sounds, and above all, had she really gone on and on after she had reached the peak of her excitement so that wave after wave of delight curled through her? She who had more often than not felt little more than gratitude it was over and done with when Peter had made love to her, and who had only a few times in her life with him reached any sort of climax – and meagre ones at that – to have reacted with the strength she had showed last night? It ought to be unbelievable, she told herself, but glory be, it wasn't, and she turned on to her back, abandoning any thought of sleep now, to lie with her hands linked beneath her head, staring at the ceiling and remembering, over and over again.

When the phone shrilled on the table beside her she knew it was him, never even considered the possibility that it might be the waking call for which she had asked. She picked up the phone and turned on her side again so that she could sandwich the instrument between her ear and the bed and said softly, 'Good morning!'

There was a little silence and then he said, 'Why did you leave me? I turned over and you were gone.'

'Put it down to old fashioned morality.' She smiled into the dimness. 'Didn't fancy being caught with you by a hotel chambermaid.'

'Hypocrisy,' he said and she could hear the smile in his voice, too.

'It's the same thing. Did you sleep well?'

He laughed softly. 'Eventually. Eventually.'

'I know. You snore. Did you know that?'

'I'm not surprised. Always had a funny nose. Does it worry you?'

'Not in the least. It's a useful signalling system. Told me when it was time to leave.'

'Then I'll have to get my nose fixed and the snore abolished. It wasn't . . . agreeable to wake up and find you gone.'

Now she was silent. 'You're assuming there'll be other times.'

'Aren't you?'

'I haven't thought about anything apart from the now. Last night and now. And now it's time we got up, had breakfast, caught that train . . . .'

'Not yet. If I can't have you here beside me, let me talk a little longer at least. Why shouldn't I get my nose fixed for you?'

She sighed, and turned on her back again, holding the phone to her ear. Now it was all over, the glory of the night shattered and the last glittering shards fell into the darker recesses of her mind. Now it was a time for sense.

'Because we're going back to work, Ben. Because this is London and nonsense and unreality and what happens here is . . . . different. Nothing to do with real life or with us.'

'Everything to do with us.' His voice was sharper now, as though he was alarmed. 'Everything . . . .'

'No,' she said it sadly but definitely. 'We're going back to Minster, Ben. There it's different.'

'Why should it be?'

'Because of Peter. I am married to him, you know. Whatever I decide to do about him in the future, I am still married to him and I'm . . . a tidy soul, I suppose. I need to have things right to feel right.'

'Didn't last night feel right?'

She took a deep breath. 'Yes, last night felt right. Here, in London, in this horrible hotel, it felt marvellously right. That's my point. It wouldn't feel right in Minster, not for me.

233

I've got to get things tidy first. And there's June, isn't there?'

She heard the deep intake of breath that mimicked her own. 'Yes, I suppose so,' he said after a moment. 'I suppose you're right. What's the time, Jess?'

'Just after seven.'

'What time's the train?'

'Eight thirty. Just time to get up, get some breakfast, get packed, go to Paddington . . . .'

'To hell with breakfast. Talk a little longer, make it last a little longer. We can get coffee at the station.'

'All right.'

There was a silence again, and then he said carefully, 'It's the guilt, isn't it?'

'Whose guilt? Mine or yours?'

'Both, I suppose. Mine most of all, though. You've no reason to feel guilty about Peter. The man's a bastard, hit you, treated you badly . . . .'

'That's not entirely fair . . . .' She made a face in the darkness. 'I mean, yes he did, but I think it was as much my fault as his.'

'How can it be? You aren't saying you believe all that nonsense some people trot out about victims being to blame for their own pain?'

'To an extent. After all, I've lived with him for twenty years, haven't I? I agreed to a view of life through his eyes all that time. Did it his way. You can't entirely blame him for being so . . . for reacting as he did when I confused him by changing, can you?'

'I can blame him. By God, I can.'

'Then you're being unjust. I colluded with him all these years, let him think I was one kind of woman when I wasn't. I lied to him, if you like. Put that way, how can you blame him?'

'For beating you?'

'He lost his temper. It wasn't a real beating.'

'For Christ's sake, Jess, why are you defending him? Are you trying to tell me you love the man? I don't believe it . . . .'

'No, I don't love him. I thought I did, but I didn't know what loving someone really felt like, so I couldn't help my ignorance, I suppose. But that wasn't his fault . . . .'

'Then why not . . . why not let me get my nose fixed and the snoring stopped?'

She laughed softly. 'It's a nice snore. Melodious. I liked it.'

'I'm glad to hear it. Jess, why not?'

Now she had to say it. 'Not because of my guilt, Ben, and you know it. It's your guilt that's the problem, isn't it? I've left Peter, in effect. I've only got to tidy things up and then I'll be free and I won't be guilty about it — though I might be regretful. For the wasted years and for him. Poor Peter. But it's different for you, isn't it?'

He was silent and she wanted to reach into the phone, to push her finger in and touch him there somewhere deep inside it, as though she were a child who had to have her fantasies made real.

'Ben?'

'Yes.'

'I am right, aren't I? You've got to deal with the way you feel about June.'

Again the silence and then he said, 'Yes. Oh, God damn it, yes. I suppose I do.'

'I . . . I shouldn't ask, but I have to. Do you love her, Ben?'

This time the silence frightened her, and for the first time since she had woken she felt a stab of shame. She had seduced a man who loved someone else. It shouldn't matter, not in these bright shiny 1980s when no one gave a damn about love when it came to sex, but it did matter to her. For her the two were indivisible and always had been: it was because she had been able to face up to the fact that any feeling she might have had for Peter was a dead one, and certainly not love, that she had been able to allow herself to love Ben, and having allowed that, been able to give that feeling a natural and physical expression. To hear in his silence now the possibility that he had taken her love from her while giving his own to someone else made her feel, just for a moment, sick.

'No,' he said then, and she blinked.

'What did you say?'

'I said no, I don't love her. I did, once, and I've gone on trying to for a long time. But I don't.'

It was as though someone had switched on the light in the dark room, and she closed her eyes against the brightness and said, 'Are you sure?'

'As sure as I can be. How can you tell when something starts to shrivel? How can you tell when the shrivelling's complete and there's nothing left? It's been shrivelling for years, the way she has . . . .'

'You mean she doesn't love you?'

'Not really. Not me as Ben. As a husband who might give her a child – ah, that's something else.' The bitterness in his tone was very clear. 'As a stud I'm an important part of her life and her schemes. But as myself – no. She has only one passion, and she keeps it in her bloody uterus.'

'She can't help that, Ben.' She needed to defend her lover's wife, needed to try to make him attack her more. 'It must be hell on earth to want a child and not be able to have one.'

'Do you think I didn't care about it?' he said almost violently. 'Do you think I never felt deprived? I'm on the way to fifty, Jess, and I'm not exactly likely to have children of my own now. It matters to men too, you know. It matters to men. That's what makes June such hell. It's as though she can't imagine it mattering to anyone but herself. It's as though I don't exist except as a pair of balls . . . .'

She couldn't help it. 'You're certainly that, whatever else you are,' she said and then caught her lip between her teeth. And when he laughed let her own breath go into a husky chuckle. 'I'm sorry. That was frivolous and cheap of me.'

'No, it wasn't, and you bloody well know it wasn't. Don't be coy. It doesn't suit you, Jess.'

'I'm sorry,' she said, mock-apologetic. He laughed again and then said with a sudden urgency, 'Jess, we will again, won't we? Last night was . . . incredible. I needed you and it was as though you knew, and you came here and . . . it can't just be once, Jess. I won't let it . . . .'

'June . . . .'

'I'll think about June. Whatever you say won't make any difference, you know. I mean, whether you agree to go on with what we've started or whether you come the Victorian madam and cast me into the outer moral darkness for ever, it's the end of the road for June and me. It has been for ages, but I was too busy to notice or care, I suppose. Now I care. So, Jess, can we? Go on as we've started?'

'Ben, we'll miss that train if we don't get going soon. I'll see you in the lobby in three-quarters of an hour. Then we can get a cab over to Paddington. We can talk another time. Not now. It's impossible now. No need to rush . . . please?'

'On the train then. We can talk on the train.'

'Yes,' she said and stretched her other arm above her head,

luxuriously arching her back, feeling the lingering traces in her body of the sensations that had filled it last night. 'Yes. We can talk on the train. Don't be late – three-quarters of an hour to meet downstairs and then an hour and a half on the journey. Lovely.'

But there was no time to talk on the train, after all.

28

June sat on the window seat staring out at the sooty wet garden, listening all the time to Timmy's breathing and trying not to panic inside. He was all right; it was no more than a nasty little cold he'd picked up. She should never have taken him on the bus into town, should have got a taxi and to hell with the cost; shouldn't have taken him into town at all really, but then he'd wanted to see Santa Claus in his grotto so much and she had wanted to see him there, his little face alight with the excitement of it all.

She bit her lip and turned back into the room. Timmy was still lying fast asleep on the sofa, and she looked down at him, trying to see if he was feverish, whether he was really ill, but he looked all right; his face was a bit rosy perhaps, and he was breathing noisily with his mouth open because of his blocked-up nose, but he wasn't restless, showed no signs of the fretfulness a real illness must surely bring with it . . . . Carefully she bent, and moving with infinite care, pulled the blanket over him more securely and then tiptoed to the table to sit and make paper chains for him. She'd promised him they'd hang them up at her house this afternoon, and though she was getting more and more doubtful about the wisdom of taking him out of the warm flat, a promise was a promise. You mustn't ever let children down, mustn't destroy their confidence in their little world by breaking your word.

As she sat down she saw the newspaper again, and felt once more that swoop of terror in her belly and had to close her eyes against it and hold on to the edge of the table. Why had he told her to read the papers? Why hadn't he left her in happy ignorance? Why had he set out to frighten her like this, spoil all her time with Timmy? She hated him for it, hated him, *hated* him – and thinking that helped, made it easier for her to open her eyes and look at the headline that screamed its alarm in inch-high letters. If she hated the source of that alarm, then it

238

meant it was false. There couldn't be anything true about someone you hated, could there?

And yet . . . and despite herself she leaned forwards and picked up the paper and smoothed it on the table and began to read it again. A dead child in Dartchester, a considerable number of children admitted to hospital with severe symptoms, and heaven knew how many in their own homes with slightly lesser symptoms. Clustered in the south west, but some cases beginning to appear further afield; some reported in London, not a few in the Birmingham area, and a suspected one as far north as Gateshead . . . .

And side by side with the ominous reporting of this plague of the children, as the newspaper persisted in calling it, the excited comment on Contravert, Ben's Contravert, her husband's Contravert, the man she hated's Contravert – I don't hate him really, she told herself, staring at the page. I don't, but I'm so frightened, so frightened – and across the room Timmy stirred on his sofa and she lifted her head and looked at him anxiously, but he didn't wake and she returned to the paper.

There was a lead article as well as the excited front-page report, and almost against her will she turned to it and began to read. '"The Mills of God",' said the article portentously, '"Grind Slowly, but they Grind Exceeding Small." In other words,' it went on in some confusion, 'it was clearly meant that this great new British cure should be developed just at the time it was most needed for a dread new disease that threatened all our children. The fact that the epidemic that is clamouring for large supplies of Contravert to deal with it was itself caused by the research that developed the wonder drug adds to the poignancy of the scientific dilemma facing Dr Pitman – which,' the article allowed handsomely, 'is well understood by every intelligent person, of which, of course the readership of this newspaper is entirely composed and one with which said intelligent persons must deeply sympathize. But . . .' and now the article took on a hectoring tone. 'Dr Pitman cannot be left to make this decision alone. He might in a spirit of scientism want to tread the slow and laborious path of the perfect scientific method and test his drug further before making it freely available, but with a child killer plague loose – a plague, it must be remembered, engendered by the work of Dr Pitman himself – it is action that is needed. We live not in the Groves of Academe,' the article boomed, 'but down in the mud and struggle of the real world. Dr Pitman must therefore listen to us when we demand that he releases his great discovery for immediate use to save those children whose lives hang by a thread and . . . .'

Why won't he? June sat and looked at Timmy and tried to puzzle it out. Why was Ben being so stupid, refusing to let people have the Contravert, if it was all that was needed to save children's lives? Why was he refusing – as the paper said he was – to talk about the stuff, let alone let people have any of it? Was it because there wasn't enough?

She lifted her chin at that thought; not enough, it had to be that, surely? She tried to remember what he'd told her about his work, about the things he did and the way he got his materials, but she had never listened to him properly, finding it all too boring, had sat and thought about all sorts of things of her own, nodding brightly but never really listening, and now she just couldn't remember . . . .

But it had to be that. Not enough, that was the problem. But there was some. They'd used it for that little girl from Bluegates School, hadn't they? The paper had said so, and that doctor on television last night, he'd said so. So there had to be some at the hospital. In Ben's own laboratory? Where else would it be?

Timmy opened his mouth and began to wail even before he opened his eyes, and at once she ran across the room and picked him up, crooning to him soothingly to make him cheer up. If he woke up cranky he stayed cranky all afternoon and that made both of them feel dreadful; and she crooned and rocked and rocked and crooned and he stopped crying and buried his hot damp face in her neck and she held him close and thought about the Contravert that had to be somewhere in Ben's lab, and the shortage of it and what she would do if Timmy got the plague.

'Mr Clough isn't here,' the girl on the phone said, and looked appealingly at the old man, but he shook his head at her ferociously and she said it again, despairingly. 'Honestly, he's not here. No, I don't know anyone else who can help, no one at all. I'll take a message if you like . . . yes, Dr Lyall Davies, I'll tell him . . . .'

'Good girl! Say that to all of them,' Don Clough said, and

turned and went out of the small cluttered office he shared with her. 'And don't let no one in here, neither. I'll show the buggers. No one's telling me what I ought to do and what I oughtn't to do, and that's about it . . . .' And he went stumping out across the yard to the worksheds and she watched him from the window and then went sulkily back to her desk.

It was too bad of the old man, she told herself resentfully. Nothing interesting ever happened in this mouldy old place and now, when for the first time there was a bit of life, he went and ruined it all. Why shouldn't she talk to the newspaper people who kept phoning up? What harm would it do him if she had her name in the papers? Perhaps he was too old to be interested, but she wasn't. It might even get her on the telly, if she was lucky – but she knew she was wasting her time even thinking about that. He'd got those men to stand by the gates and wander round the fences so no one could get in, and certainly no one with a camera. Boring old fart that he is, she thought, and reached in her desk drawer for a Mars bar. Boring old fart with his boring old invoices. I shan't type them, not till I'm ready and he can go and stuff himself . . . .

In the big clattering shed where the extraction work was done, Clough was shouting at the top of his voice to make himself heard above the din of the machinery.

'It's the second time I've seen the buggers,' he bawled. 'They've been hanging around asking questions a bit too much, so I'm taking it seriously. They're after us, and they're after the place at Podgate where they breed the animals for Dr Pitman. I warned 'em I was being watched, told 'em to keep an eye out themselves, and they've seen 'em too. Bloody loiterers hangin' about – must think we're half-wits, don't know trouble when we see it. Well, I do, and I'm not putting up with their bloody meddling. And I'm buggered if I'll give 'em the satisfaction of making me do anything other than what I want to do. I want to go on extracting this stuff for Dr Pitman until such time as he says don't. Now, if there's any of you don't fancy working with me on account of the way things are, then say so now and your wages'll be made up and no bad feelings. But Gawd help anyone who stays on and then tries to come the acid afterwards. Do I make myself clear?'

The three men who worked in the shed looked at each other and then at him, and then one of them said, 'What sort of things is it you think they're up to, Mr Clough?'

'Oh, the usual shit. They'll come and burn the place down on account of we work with animal exploiters, that's the way these buggers think. I ask you, animal exploiters, us! The stuff we're using here comes from women, so if they called us women exploiters they could be right. But animals? What've we got to do with bloody animals?'

'Dr Pitman does though, don't he? I was reading in the paper this morning that he experiments on rabbits and monkeys and that. Doesn't seem right, really . . . .'

'Experiments, my bloody foot,' Clough said. 'He just uses 'em, that's all. I've seen his animal room, been over to Minster to see him, many's the time, and I can tell you he treats his animals a bloody sight better than some men treat their wives. You a vegetarian then?'

'Eh?' The man blinked his bewilderment.

'You a vegetarian? D'you live on lentils, only wear plastic shoes, then?'

'No,' the man said and shook his head at his two mates. Old Clough was off his rocker for good and all, now, obviously.

'Then don't you go talking about people ill-treating animals when you eat them, and walk on their tanned skins, all right? Anyway, there it is. It's my belief these Animal Brigade people plan to get in here, that they're watching us to find out our weak points, and get in and wreck the place, and I don't reckon it, I don't reckon it one little bit. I've got a half dozen blokes taken on temporary as guards around the fences and at the gate – if you don't fancy staying, in spite of precautions like that, then like I said, sling your hook. Now.'

'I'm with you, Mr Clough. Don't like other people deciding whether I work or not, not these days. No one's got any right to interfere with anyone else, that's how I see it. If I was a miner I'd be bloody working, and I'll go on working here too an' all . . . .'

'No one's talking about strikes,' Clough growled. 'Just about protecting the job.'

'That's what I mean,' the man said triumphantly. 'Protecting the job. I'm on. Stay overnight if you like . . . .'

'It might be an idea at that,' Clough said. 'I'll be staying here myself for a couple of nights, to be on the safe side, but if anyone else fancies doing it – it'll be worth double time. I make a good product here, all above board and legal, and no one's going to tell me I'm an exploiter or stop me running my business any way I bloody want. As long as Dr Pitman can use his stuff and I can get the materials, then I'll make sure there's plenty of it. No matter who prowls around spying on us.'

'It's not my bailiwick,' Dan Stewart said, and then said it louder as though that would help. 'Nothing to do with me! I can't release the stuff . . . I don't even know where it is! You'll have to wait till Ben Pitman gets back . . . .'

At the other end of the phone Lyall Davies swore under his breath and then said cajolingly, 'Look here, Stewart, you know the way his mind works as well as any. Always been a friend of his, haven't you? Yes. Well, I dare say if you put your mind to it you could work out where in his laboratory he keeps the stuff, and go and find it? Then I'd take full responsibility for . . . .'

'I'm sorry, Dr Lyall Davies,' Dan said loudly. 'Can't be done. Got to go, I'm afraid. Afternoon!' And he cradled the phone with a clatter and then scowled at it. Bloody man. He'd do anything, anything at all, to get more glory over this damned business, and he for one wasn't about to let the old faker get away with it. He was right about one thing though; finding Ben's Contravert wouldn't be all that difficult a thing to do. He knew the lab pretty well, knew where Ben kept the refrigerator keys and so forth – seen him lock up and put them away more times than he could remember – and it might be just as well to get the stuff out and tucked away somewhere safer. With Ben away, anything could happen there . . . .

He found the laboratory working apparently as usual when he walked in. Errol was washing petri dishes at his sink in the corner, jigging to the muffled dance of the earphones clamped over his ears, his woolly hat a glorious splash of colour in the ill-lit space, and Moscrop and Harry Gentle were both busy at their benches while Annie sat beside the centrifuge, ostensibly waiting for it to stop so that she could unload it, but in fact using the time to file her already perfect scarlet nails.

'You too?' Harry Gentle looked up at him sardonically. 'I'd have laid odds you wouldn't come beating the path to the magic door, but there, I was wrong. Can't win 'em all, I suppose . . . .'

'Talk sense, Harry,' Dan grunted and leaned against the bench beside him. 'What are you doing?'

'Got so many complete blood work requests we're

swamped in 'em,' he said cheerfully. 'So I've stopped worrying. We'll get through as many as we can and when the boss gets back, *he* can worry about the backlog. Right, Moscrop?'

'Right.' Moscrop didn't look up.

'And if we get any more interruptions from people wandering in here asking oh–so–casually where Ben keeps his magic muck, then we'll get even fewer done, won't we?'

Dan flushed. 'I'm only looking for it to keep it away from that old devil, Lyall Davies. He's been pestering me all morning . . . .'

'And half the consultants around the country been pestering us,' Harry said, and bent his head to his microscope again. 'And they're all wasting their bloody time, because it isn't here.'

'Isn't here?' Dan stared at him and then said more loudly, 'What do you mean it isn't here?'

Harry Gentle was clearly enjoying himself greatly. 'What I said. It isn't here, H–E–R–E here. Where it isn't. Eh, Moscrop?'

'Right,' Moscrop said, still keeping his eyes clamped to his microscope.

'Why?' Dan shook his head in bewilderment. 'Why not?'

'Because dear old Ben, trusting soul that he is, decided it wouldn't be wise to keep his precious stuff on the premises, what with break–ins and so forth, and took it somewhere else to be safe before he went to London to feast at the media's lush troughs. Lucky bastard. Why can't I make great medical breakthroughs now and again? Some of those telly bits are real stunners. Very munchy. I'd really get some good out of a trip to the BBC, but old Ben just took Jessie Hurst with him, and much good that'll do him.'

'Where did he put it, then?' Dan demanded.

Harry shrugged his shoulders. 'If he'd told us, that would have damaged the object of the exercise, wouldn't it?'

'You're talking riddles, Gentle!' Dan said, irritation sharpening his voice. 'What are you on about, for Heaven's sake?'

Moscrop lifted his chin for the first time and stared at him. 'He doesn't trust us, Dr Stewart, that's what Harry means. He wouldn't leave his stuff here while he was away, not because he was afraid of break–ins again, but because he was afraid one of us might try to make some use of it. And that would muck up his patents or whatever good and proper, wouldn't it? If one of us managed to get hold of some of the Contravert and work out what it was and we might make it ourselves. I'm told that people who patent new drugs make a lot of money, a great deal of money. So we reckon that's why Dr Pitman took it away and hid it somewhere outside this building. Not because of break-ins, but because of break-outs. Charming, isn't it? All this public concern about people's welfare and all the time thinking of the money . . . .'

'I ought to knock you down, Moscrop!' Dan said very softly. 'You're a bastard, do you know that? I've known and worked with Ben Pitman a great many years, and I know him better than you ever could. And he's no more thinking about his own profit in this bloody affair than you . . . than you ever think of anything *but* your own lousy skin. If you dare say another word like that, so help me, I'll murder you. You hear me? If he took his work away from here, he had bloody good reasons to do it. And they weren't financial. Now, go to hell and stay there . . . .' And he turned and slammed out of the lab so loudly that even Errol jumped at the slam of the door which interrupted his music.

He'd calmed down enough by the time he got back to his own office to be able to be almost amused at the thought of Ben's prudence in taking his precious stuff away from the lab and putting it somewhere else. Dan was certain that Ben would have been thinking solely and wholly of the risk of further break-ins by those idiot Animal Freedom Brigaders, but he'd been at greater risk from his own staff; because there wasn't the least doubt in Dan's mind now that Moscrop would steal anything that wasn't nailed down, given half the chance. He was one of the most devious people he'd ever met, he told himself as he locked his car and went up three steps at a time, to his office. I've got to warn Ben the moment he gets back what a snake he's got there, see what I can do to help him get rid of him, union or no union – but where the hell is the stuff in the meantime? Where could he possibly have put it to keep it safe till he needed it next? Well, only Ben would be able to answer that question, he told himself as he reached for his phone to check on the newest figures for the epidemic. I'll ask him as soon as I get the chance. If I get the chance, the way things are going . . . .

The weather had picked up a good deal by the time Timmy had had his tea and his sniffles seemed a little less than they had been, and he was nagging over and over again to go to Auntie's house and hang up the paper chains; so stifling the doubts she had about the advisability of taking him out, June wrapped him up warmly and strapped him into his pushchair and set off, going via the supermarket in Greenway Road. The fridge at home would be empty, and she must be sure she had something for Timmy's supper. A few fish fingers maybe, and a little potato she could bake in its jacket – and at the last moment she remembered the possibility that Ben would come home too, from London, and added a pack of frozen curry for one. There'd be no time to do anything better, not with Timmy to look after . . . .

When she had got home and switched on the heating to make it comfortable for Timmy, and had taken him round the house to remind him of it, so that he'd be comfortable there, she went to the kitchen to unpack the food and put it in the fridge; it would be dreadful if the fish fingers defrosted before she could cook them, because that would be unhealthy, everyone knew that. But the fridge was full when she opened the door, and she stood there and stared at its contents with her face blank, not knowing quite what to do. Or where to put the fish fingers.

29

'I've asked for police help,' Mrs Cloudesley said. 'They'll do their best, but it seems there's no law against them standing around the gates waiting. There ought to be, but there isn't.'

'I'm sorry,' Ben said. 'I'm sorry the hospital's being bothered with all this . . . .'

'Not your fault,' Mrs Cloudesley said with a gracious air, and then spoiled it. 'Well, of course it is, in a sense, but there's no need to apologize, that's what I meant. You ought to be congratulated really, I suppose. If it weren't for the epidemic everyone'd be cock-a-hoop over your discovery . . . .'

'Not precisely a discovery,' Ben murmured, but she continued as if he hadn't spoken.

'. . . And the hospital would be very proud. Well, we are proud. I just wish we didn't have all these wretched journalists to put up with. It gives the domestic staff ideas, you know. They're all hanging round the gates wanting to be interviewed. As if they'd be likely to have anything useful to say or do!'

'They can do a great deal,' Ben said and got to his feet to peer out of her window at the gates below. 'It was a domestic who caused a good deal of this trouble in the first place.'

'Yes,' Mrs Cloudesley said. 'But what can you expect of women of that sort anyway?'

Ben looked at Jessie, who had opened her mouth to protest, and shook his head slightly, and as though he'd spoken she knew what he meant: they had enough to deal with without getting involved in silly arguments over a silly woman's silly snobbery.

'She didn't make the problem because she was a domestic, but because she was . . .' he said. 'Well, that doesn't matter now. What we have to do is decide how to cope with the extra work there is, as well as all the fuss. I've only been away twenty-four hours and the demands for blood work have almost quadrupled while I've been gone. We're not going to be able to cope with it all, unless we get more people in – and more equipment – or you offload some to Doxford and Farborough. Can you arrange that?'

'I'll have to,' Mrs Cloudesley said, looking distracted. 'I suppose I'll have to. I certainly can't find you new people. Are they willing to work overtime, the ones you have?'

'No,' Jessie said, and Mrs Cloudesley swivelled her eyes at her. She was still irritated by the fact that Ben had brought Jessie with him to this meeting; one of the main rewards of her position for Mrs Cloudesley was the way she spent so much time with men and men only. The presence of another woman detracted from her own importance, and she objected to that. But Ben had brought her and there was nothing that could be done to send her away.

'Oh?' she said frostily.

'They've got some sort of notion into their heads,' Jessie said carefully, speaking more to Ben than to the woman behind the big desk. 'Moscrop in particular. He thinks you're going to make a lot of money out of Contravert, and he's livid.'

'Money?' Ben laughed then, a loud sound full of genuine amusement. 'You've got to be joking.'

'I'm not. Nor is Moscrop. He was bursting with it when we got back. You went straight into your office but he clobbered me as soon as I walked in. Wanted to know where you'd been, whether you'd seen any pharmaceutical firms. Made any deals was what he said.'

'If he'd asked me he'd have got his answer,' Ben said, his face patchily red now with anger. 'How dare he? How dare . . . I'm going back there now to take him apart . . . .'

'No!' Mrs Cloudesley and Jessie said it together, but it was Jessie who went on urgently. 'Don't be stupid, Ben. To have a row won't help him change his mind, but it could give him just the excuse he wants to stop work altogether. And we need him, if we're to get the jobs even half way dealt with.'

Slowly Ben sat down again, for he had got to his feet in his sudden access of anger. 'Oh, God,' he said. 'Why the hell did I start all this? I wish I'd never begun looking for the bloody stuff. I wish I'd never found it. How can it all have turned into such a stinking mess? People thinking I'm a money-grabber and . . . I don't think I can bear it . . . .'

There was a little silence and then Jessie said in a voice that was much brisker than she felt, 'Well, you'll have to. It's tiresome, I know, but it can't be helped. You did find it, it's a marvellous development in medicine, as you'll realize when all this initial fuss is over, and it's downright ungrateful of you to wish it hadn't happened. Anyway, it's silly. You can't unhappen anything. What's done is done.'

He was staring at her and as she closed her mouth with almost a snap he laughed, a hiccupping little sound. 'You sound like a Victorian nanny.'

'You make me feel like one,' she retorted and subsided, rather flushed about the face and caught Mrs Cloudesley staring at her with a more than usually owlish expression in her round eyes.

'Dear me, but you two *are* a double act, aren't you?' She tittered then. 'You want to be careful! You'll have people talking more than they already are, but about different things, if you go on like this!'

Ben threw her a look of cold dislike and stood up. 'You'll arrange with the other two hospital path. labs to take on some of our work? I dare say they're fairly heavily loaded too, but they've got better facilities and more staff than we have. And better staff, too. Come on, Jessie. There's a lot for us to do, and it seems we'll be doing it mostly on our own – unless Harry Gentle's opted for us rather than the repellent Moscrop.'

'Hard to say,' Jessie was on her feet too and following him to the door. 'You can never tell what Harry's really thinking. I'll see how the situation is once I've checked the requisitions and sorted them out – which should I send to the other labs? The full blood counts or the . . . .'

'I'll let you know what they're willing to take,' Mrs Cloudesley said. '*If* they are. But you'll have to be prepared for a bit of overtime, clearly. Not that that will worry you two unduly, I imagine,' and she looked at Ben with her chin tilted at a provocative angle and he looked back, his face expressionless.

'I've never noticed the hours I've worked for this hospital, Mrs Cloudesley, and I don't imagine I'll start now. Good morning. Let me know as soon as possible what I can offload . . .' and he almost pushed Jessie through the door and shut it behind them with what was very close to a slam.

'Bloody woman,' he said wrathfully. 'She's got a mind like a goddammed sink, with her revolting innuendoes . . . .'

'But Ben, she's right,' Jessie said, and she didn't look at him. 'We are . . . I mean, she's right, isn't she?'

He looked down at her and frowned sharply. 'I suppose so, but . . . .'

'I told you it would all be different here at Minster. London wasn't real. Here is real and that changes everything.'

'Spoils everything.'

'Not necessarily. But we've got to think. About a lot of things, about people and work. Mostly work . . . .'

'Yes.' He brightened then. 'Yes. It's a mess, but it's important, for all that. Work, and sorting out what we do about Contravert . . . .' They were walking across the car park now, towards the lab, and Jessie said, 'Those reporters who followed us on to the train and were such pests – did they come all the way here? Or did they get off when they left us? At Doxford, perhaps?'

'No, they're here. I saw them at the station. Got the cab behind ours. I dare say they're at the gates with the rest of the bloody vultures.'

'Perhaps you should have talked to them on the train. Why not talk to them now, Ben? Then maybe they'd go away,' Jessie said. 'I know you've decided to keep quiet, but honestly, I'm not sure it's the right way to handle it. Better talk to them, answer their questions, and then get some peace, get time to talk about . . . other things, and not just the Contravert situation.'

'No. I'm not talking to them now or ever. They can't be trusted. They lie, twist what I say. You saw what happened there on *Probe* last night. You saw what the papers were saying this morning. It's as though they saw a different programme altogether – it's sickening, and talking to them won't make it any better, will it?'

'It might. If you took precautions.'

They had reached the door of the lab now and he looked down at her, chewing his lower lip. 'How, precautions?'

'Well, I'm not sure, but I've seen on the news on television . . . press conferences? Lots of people standing around, all witnesses if you like, to what is said. If you talk to all of them at the same time, then you can say what you want to, and they can't tell lies because so many people will have heard what you say.'

He stood thinking for a while and then nodded. 'You could be right, I suppose. I'll think about it. If the fuss goes on. Thanks, Jessie . . . .' And he bent and kissed her swiftly and then urged her through the door and into the laboratory.

Only Errol greeted them as they came in, waving cheerfully from his overloaded sink where he was clashing away amidst the glass, and Annie looked up and grinned at Ben and said, 'Sorry, I was late this morning – but I sat up late to watch you on the telly. You looked great. Really great. My new fella got ever so jealous when I told him you were my boss . . . did you enjoy it all?'

'Not a great deal,' Ben said dryly. 'I wasn't there for fun.'

'What did you think of what he said, Annie?' Jessie looked at her hopefully; perhaps if someone else – especially someone like Annie – told him he'd done tolerably well on the programme, that she had found his contribution useful and understandable, that would help restore some of his battered self-confidence.

'Oh, I wasn't really listening to all that stuff,' Annie said blithely. 'Get enough of it here, don't I? Very boring. But you looked lovely – you too, Mrs Hurst. Ever so nice. Do they do your makeup for you and all that? That must have been ever such fun . . . .'

'I'll be in the office,' Ben said shortly and went, straight past Harry Gentle and Moscrop, who had been sitting head down over their microscopes with an air of great industriousness.

Harry looked up as he passed and said briefly, 'I saw it.'

Ben stopped, but didn't look at him. 'Oh?'

'Seemed to make sense to me.' Harry grinned then at Jessie. 'Though as Annie says, I've heard it so often already. But it made sense. You too, Jessie. Liked the way you stood up to those bloody animal nuts.'

'Thanks. And they're not nuts. Not all of them,' Jessie said, and went over to look at the pile of request slips and the trays of blood samples beside Harry's bench. 'What can I take over, Harry?'

'As much as you like. There's a million of 'em. Help yourself . . . .' And he returned to his microscope. Moscrop went on working, paying no attention to anything that was going on around him, apparently absorbed in what he was doing.

'I've got some things to sort out in the office and then I'll be out to do some as well,' Ben said. 'Got to call Clough at Charringtons, sort out the placentae situation from maternity, but I shouldn't be long.'

'You'll talk to Podgate about some more animals?' Jessie said.

'No,' he said after a moment. 'No. Right now, I've enough to do without starting new trials. That'll have to wait. It's all going into cold storage for a while. Till this fuss dies down and I can do the work properly. No one can do useful work under the sort of circumstances I'm in. So I shan't try. But we'll get back to it. I may get a bit low sometimes, but I know that much. I shan't give up. Not yet, anyway.'

'Then why are you talking to Charringtons? If you're putting it into cold storage, as you say, then you don't need any more supplies, do you?' Moscrop's voice was sharp and Jessie turned to look at him, but he still had his eyes glued to the microscope.

'Because I don't want to leave him in the air,' Ben said loudly, too loudly. 'Because I operate as honourably as I know how, and I booked all the capacity the man could give me till the end of the year. I have to take what he's got, make sure he's got raw materials to work on, see the contract out. After that, I think again. Are you satisfied?'

Still Moscrop remained at his microscope. 'Am *I* satisfied? As if that mattered. It's what you're getting out of all this that's important, isn't it? And I'll bet you're satisfied and over the top.'

'You bastard.' Ben said it softly, so softly that Jessie thought for a moment she hadn't heard it, and then she cried out as Ben propelled himself across the room to haul on Moscrop's shoulders and pull him to his feet.

'Careful, Pitman,' Moscrop said, and his eyes were bright and excited, like an eager dog's. 'Hurt me, and you'll really be in the shit. Oh, it'd look great in tomorrow's papers, wouldn't it? Medical hero beats up his laboratory staff. What else has the man to hide beneath his façade of devoted scientist, seeking cures for all the ills that afflict us? Could it be that he *isn't* the wonder-man after all? Could he be as greedy and as selfish as everyone else in the normal world? Who'd ever have thought it?'

Both Jessie and Harry were holding on to Ben's arms now, preventing him from moving, and Harry said, 'Come on,

Ben. This'll get you nowhere. Send the man home on sick leave or something. Can't be doing with all this around the shop, now can we?'

At last Ben let go and Moscrop stood rubbing his arm where Ben's fingers had gripped him, his eyes still glittering.

'You'd better go,' Ben said thickly. 'Tell the union there's not enough work for you, tell the pay office, tell anyone you like . . . we'll manage without you. I'll see to it they pay you as usual – pay you myself, if I have to . . . .'

'You'll be able to afford it, I dare say,' Moscrop said, and moved across the laboratory to collect his things from the lockers in the far corner. 'The sort of money you're going to make in the future, what'll my few quid mean to you? Will you kick anything back to the NHS for the amount of time you used here to do the research?'

'Get him out of here!' Ben roared it and Harry shot him a quick look and then jerked his head at Moscrop.

'Go on, big mouth,' he said, and his easy-going voice was for the first time sharpened and had none of its usual jocularity. 'Enough is enough.' And Moscrop looked at him consideringly and then shrugged and turned and went, slamming out of the door, leaving them all in silence behind him.

It was Ben who stirred first. 'Why?' he demanded. 'Why the bloody hell are people so malicious? What did I ever do to that man that justifies that sort of behaviour?'

'You're cleverer than he is,' Harry said and now he sounded his normal mocking self again. 'Thou shalt never be better than anybody at anything, that's the rule for these modern times. No one likes an original thinker. Too frightening. They only believe in original sin – they can understand that. There are millions like Moscrop who'll see what you've done only in terms of what's in it for you. Money, fame – all that. The rest of 'em'll want to see you as some sort of angel – no one'll see you as an ordinary chap with rather more brains than are comfortable for him, doing his best to do what's right in the middle of all his cerebration.'

There was a little silence and then Jessie said, 'He's right, Ben. It's not just Moscrop. Those journalists in the train this morning – they were the same, weren't they? More subtle about it, but the same. Kept trying to dig out the real facts, they said – couldn't understand there wasn't anything nasty to be dug out. Simple stories of work and . . . they just don't believe them.'

'And now Moscrop'll go and tell God knows what sort of tale to them all at the gate, and they'll love it. The real dirt, they'll reckon. The Contravert spirited away God knows where, and you fighting with your own staff . . . .' Harry looked at Ben quizzically. 'Hope you've got the strength for it all, old man. Wouldn't be in your shoes for a pension, I wouldn't. Great discoveries – they're just great headaches from where I sit. Why bother to find cures for people when most of 'em are such bastards?'

'Because I don't believe that,' Ben said. 'And damn it, Harry, you're as bad as the bloody journalists.' He was calming down now, and his hands, Jessie noted, had stopped shaking as his colour returned. 'Thinking that people set out on research with high-minded notions about great cures and . . . all I did was work out that there might be an answer to virus infections. That was all. There was no . . . I wasn't having any visions of myself shoved up on a pedestal, or making extra money . . . .'

'Tell that to the marines,' Harry said. 'They'll believe it before anyone else will.'

'Jessie, what do I do?' He was looking at her now, and it was as though there were no one else around them, as though Annie sitting staring with her mouth half-open and Errol, still wrapped in his earphones and oblivious of what was going on, didn't exist. 'You told me to have a press conference, but where would be the point? If Harry's right and what most people want is either to think you're a self-seeking bastard or God Almighty – where's the point?'

'I don't know,' she said after a long pause, while she stared at the floor, trying to think. 'Don't put it on me, Ben. I can't think for you – I feel for you, God knows I do, but you have to make up your own decisions. For good or bad, you've got to make your own.' She did look up then at his tired anxious face and couldn't bear to be dispassionate any longer. He needed real answers, not considered fence-sitting. 'I can tell you what I'd do but no more than that . . . .'

'What would you do?'

'I'd talk to the Press, once and for all. I'd carry on with the work as though none of the fuss had happened. And I'd ride it out. They'll get bored eventually, leave us in peace. That's what I'd do. But I'm not standing in your skin. I don't know what it feels like to get that sort of . . . to have to deal with people like Moscrop. I can only guess.'

'You'd better make your mind up soon,' Harry said, and sat down again at his microscope. 'Because the next thing that'll happen is you're going to be asked to use your precious Contravert on another kid somewhere, if you haven't already, that is. The way this epidemic's going . . . .' And he put out a hand and rifled through the pile of request slips. 'The way it's going, there are going to be a hell of a lot of kids who need it, aren't there? And then what'll you do?'

He grinned at Ben then, over his shoulder. 'And while I'm asking questions, where is the stuff? It sure as hell's bells isn't here. I've looked.'

30

'I took it to my own fridge at home. It seemed the most sensible thing to do,' Ben said. 'I meant to talk to you about it, but in the drama of that day, and the fuss about the Press and that damned TV programme, I didn't. I just collected up all the supplies I had and took them away.'

'Why?' Jessie stirred her coffee and began to drink it, cupping the beaker between both hands, needing to make sure she had a firm grasp of it. She was so tired she could hardly sit up straight, let alone hold a beaker in one hand.

'I'm not sure.' He was tired too; it showed in the dark smudges beneath his eyes and his red-rimmed gaze and in his unkempt hair. He looked like a man who would willingly crawl into a corner to die, if he could. 'I think it was because of the break-in, or maybe it was because of Lyall Davies. I don't know . . . I just thought . . . there it isn't really mine. At home it is. So I took it home. No reason why not. June isn't there, so it wouldn't get in her way, make no problems. Jessie, how much more is there to do?'

'Nothing,' she said firmly, and carefully put down her beaker. 'Not tonight. It's nearly three, for God's sake. We can't do anything else useful today. Go and get some sleep, and I'll do the same. Tomorrow in the morning we'll see how things are going. By then Mrs Cloudesley might have some news about what we can offload, but right now, it's enough. Come on.'

And he let her pull him to his feet and lead him to the old sofa in his office and she pushed him down on to it and then hauled his legs up on to it, and covered him with the blankets from the corner cupboard.

'I'll bring you some coffee and toast in the morning,' she said, as she stood at the door, her hand on the light switch. 'Sleep well . . . .'

'What about you?' He said it thickly, as though he were half-asleep already, and she didn't answer but waited, and within a moment or two his breathing changed, thickened, and became a soft snore, and she nodded to herself in satisfaction and switched off the light. Now she had only to drag her own exhausted body across the yard to the nurses' quarters and see if she could find an unoccupied room to curl up in for what was left of the night. She'd managed on hardly any sleep often enough in the past; she could do it again. As long as she was around when he needed her, that was all that mattered; and as that thought came to her mind she made a face. It sounded so trite, so sentimental, like the worst kind of pop song; and yet it was true and she didn't know which was worst; the banality of the thought or its accuracy.

She slept heavily and woke feeling surprisingly refreshed, which was fortunate, for the day began at top speed and seemed to accelerate from there. First, there were the Breakfast Television programme and the radio news broadcasts, about which all the hospital's staff were agog, and she felt she was running a barrage of stares and whispers when she went to the night staff canteen to collect coffee and toast to take to the laboratory for breakfast. And then there were the newspapers: now every one of them was devoting two or more pages to the story of the epidemic, with heartrending accounts of individual children all over the country who were in desperate straits, and strongly worded demands that Dr Pitman be forced to give his new drug over to other doctors willing to use it if he was unwilling to do so himself. There were interviews with such doctors – among whom Lyall Davies figured prominently – saying that it was his Hippocratic duty to do so; while interviews with others said they agreed with Ben that it was dangerous to use untried but powerful drugs, especially on children. One woman, a consultant endocrinologist from a London teaching hospital, ranged herself on that side, to Ben's considerable relief, explaining in some detail in one paper just what the risks were.

'Some children,' she was reported as saying, 'might possibly suffer damage to their gonads – the organs that make the cells that in due course create new life. Any drug derived from hormones and prostaglandins, as I gather this substance is, could carry that risk. I wouldn't use it on my own patients, not unless it were fully tested first.'

'There, Jessie, you see?' He looked up from the paper, and,

for the first time for what seemed like weeks to her, managed something that looked like a smile. 'I don't have to talk to the bloody Press. Not while there are sensible people around to do it for me.'

'Whatever she says, it won't mean as much as if you say it,' she said. 'More coffee? I brought four cups over.'

'No, that was great, thanks. How are things in the hospital? Did you pick up any news?'

'The Barnett child's leaving today,' she said. 'The night staff were agog, because the TV people'll be at the gates to film her and heaven knows what else. Lyall Davies is getting himself fitted for a new wig for the event, they're saying.'

'He deserves every bit of the bitching he gets. Look, Jessie, I don't want anyone to know I'm here. Can we arrange that, do you think? I'll stay here all day – I've got Clough arriving with some more Contravert . . . no, don't worry. He's bringing it in the back of his own car, and it won't look like a delivery at all – and I want to be here for that. Otherwise I want to keep out of sight as much as possible.'

'I don't see why not . . . .' She stood up and began to clear the detritus of their picnic breakfast from his desk. 'Where will you put the new stuff?'

'Eh?'

'Will you take it home? Like the rest of it?'

He considered for a moment, and then shook his head. 'No. And now I'm going to be here all the time, I'd better get the stuff that's at home back here too. Look, Jessie, would you mind getting it for me? I'll give you the keys and . . . .'

'Of course,' she said. 'I'd feel better if it was here, too. Ben . . . .' She hesitated at the door. 'Is there no way that you'd let anyone use it at present?'

'Oh, Jess, not you too!'

'I'm not being like everyone else!' She jumped to the defensive. 'It's just that reading about some of those children . . . they're as ill as Andrea Barnett was, fit to die, and now she's going home today.'

'It can't be helped,' he said and stared at her with his reddened eyes blank with stubbornness. 'I shouldn't have agreed to that use, and I wish to God I hadn't. My God, but I wish I hadn't.'

'It was my fault. I suggested it.'

'And I acted on it.' He shook his head irritably. 'Can't you understand, Jessie? I'm dying to use it. I'd love to try it on any number of these children, but I daren't. And the more people go on about it and the more badly I want to use it, the more important it becomes that I stay firm and don't. Can't you see that?'

'Yes,' she said. 'I suppose so. I'll go and get the stuff from your house, then.'

'Yes. Go and get it. The keys are here somewhere . . . .' He began to scrabble in his desk drawer.

'June won't be there?'

'No . . . at least I don't think so. I haven't spoken to her since . . . .' He rubbed his face. 'Not since before we went to London. I lose track of time these days. I should phone her, I suppose.'

'Yes,' Jessie said. 'You should.'

'Well, I'm too busy, and I'm too tired and I . . . I can't. I just haven't the reserves right now to deal with June going on about Timmy. Lay off, Jessie, I don't want to talk about her. Go and get the stuff from the fridge in the kitchen and get back here as soon as you can, and we'll get the work going again. The deliveries of yesterday's requests'll be here soon, and then God help us . . . .'

She was puzzled when she got to Ben's house. She'd expected to find everything blank and feeling empty in spite of the presence of furniture, the way an uninhabited house is, but the heating was on, and in the kitchen there was a lingering smell of hot toast and a comfortable cluster of dishes on the table: a sticky porridge dish with a picture of Pigling Bland on it, an empty shell in a Peter Rabbit egg cup, and a half-empty mug of milk with Jemima Puddleduck on its side. She stood there and looked at them and then round at the neat kitchen with its flowered curtains and pine dresser adorned with blue and white china, the epitome of cosiness and security, and then back at the child's special dishes, and she felt her face actually redden with shame. She had abused the owner of this snug domesticity, had robbed her as surely as if she had knocked her down and taken the contents of her pockets. She, Jessie Hurst, was one of those Other Women she had always rather despised – if she'd thought of them at all – and that realization was a hateful one. The fact that she stood here in this inner sanctum of another woman's life, with keys of admittance that had been given to her by that woman's husband – it was horrible, and she wanted to turn and run away, to go back to Ben and tell him he must fetch his Contravert for himself, she couldn't fetch it for him; but then she shook that thought away. It was ridiculous. Whatever had happened between Ben and herself had nothing to do with the job in hand. It was just fortuitous that doing this particular piece of work meant encroaching on June's territory; it meant nothing in any real sense, and very deliberately she turned to the refrigerator.

The six big bottles of Contravert were there, lying on their sides, their tops carefully fastened on to prevent spillage, and she lifted them out, one by one, and stacked them on the kitchen table. They stood there gleaming dully in the thin winter sunshine thrown through the pretty curtains and she looked at them and thought – children's lives. How many children's lives are in there? And then had to push that thought away, too. Ben said he couldn't use the stuff, no matter what, and had good reasons. She couldn't, shouldn't think about it any more. Thinking didn't help, and she moved about the kitchen purposefully, looking for something in which to carry the bottles. She should have brought something, she told herself irritably, hating the way she had to pull open drawers and pry into cupboards to make her search, grateful when at last she found, neatly folded in a drawer, a stout plastic carrier bag.

Before she left she hesitated, and then took a piece of paper from a wooden doll-adorned wall rack, and the pencil that the wooden doll held in one carved hand, and wrote swiftly, 'Dr Pitman sent for the bottles in the fridge. As you weren't here, I helped myself. I tried not to disturb anything.' And she stopped before signing it and then very deliberately left it without her name on it. What was the point? Why tell June her husband's lover had been prowling round in her kitchen? Why make it worse than it need be for her?

Illogical thought, crazy illogical thought, she told herself angrily as she got back into Ben's car and started the engine. June doesn't know what happened in London. I'm not sure I do. That was yesterday, a lifetime ago, in a place that isn't real. Maybe it never happened, and anyway, how could June know? And she backed the car out of the drive and into the road, and turned its nose towards the hospital.

Quite when the thought came to her she wasn't sure, but she

was half way back to the hospital when she passed the top of a main road that led to the estate of houses where Purbeck Avenue was and without stopping to judge the sense of the thought, she steered left into it. There were things she needed, she told herself, extra underwear, a few sweaters against the colder weather that must surely be coming, odds and ends like that; it's not so that I can go into my own kitchen again, exorcize that experience of trespass in June's kitchen. It isn't that at all, of course it isn't . . . .

The house seems to have shrunk, she thought, as she stopped the engine and got out of the car. She hadn't parked it in the drive, feeling oddly that she had no right to, now that she'd left, but left the car at the side of the road a few yards down, and walked towards number 30 trying to see it as it had seemed to her in the long years she had lived there. But she couldn't see anything but the here and now: a square, uncompromisingly dull house, in white Snowcem with bay windows with a few panes of coloured glass let into the fanlights, and neat cream curtains, and a garden scrubby in the winter sunshine with dead roses on weeping bushes and unpicked late dahlias. A totally anonymous, dead house. Twenty years of her life had been given to washing that house's paintwork, polishing its floors and weeding its garden, and yet looking at it now it could have been a stranger's house for all it said to her, and as she pushed open the gate she was startled by its familiar double squeak.

Her key turned smoothly and the front door opened, and for a moment she stood there, surprised. Peter was in his office at this time of day, of course. Had he become so disorganized since her departure that he didn't lock up as carefully as he usually did? The single lock had been the only one that held the front door, not the mortice and chain as well, which was how the door was meant to be fastened when everyone was out. Peter had always been very fussy about that; perhaps, now, he didn't care any more. Peter not caring about his possessions? It was a warming thought and she felt a glow of softness at it, a sort of pity for him in his loneliness, and she thought – I must see him. I'll call him, tell him we must talk, make him see that it's just the inevitable passage of the years, not a fault in him or me, just that we've outgrown each other. We don't have to part enemies, we can be civilized, sensible people the way they are in books and films, not childish and sulky the way I've been; and she stepped over the threshold of the door and closed it behind her, warmed and strengthened by the resolve she had made. She felt a better person already, a wiser and more caring person, and that was a good way to feel.

She stopped and looked into the living room and that hurt. Here it was familiar, the furniture that she had chosen, the pictures she had found for the walls, but it all looked forlorn and dusty and she tried to see it the way she had been used to keep it, fresh and clean and alight with fresh flowers, but it was impossible. All there was to see was there: the crumpled weary look of an uncleaned unloved room.

The kitchen was worse; a dead emptiness that made her feel actually cold, even though the house was warm. If there had been dirty dishes in the sink, evidence of a messy person using it and not bothering to clean up afterwards, she wouldn't have minded. That would have been human and attractive, somehow. As it was the place was bleak with its dusty work-tops and bare kitchen table and gaping, blank sink and she shivered, and turned away to step out into the hall again and go upstairs to fetch the things she had come for. The sooner she got out of the house the better . . . .

And came face to face with Peter. He was standing very erect and tidy in his navy blue office suit, his shirt as white and neat as it always was, his tie as tightly knotted and his hair as smooth above his forehead. He was well shaved and she could smell the cologne on him and yet for all that he looked somehow bedraggled and ill-kempt. It was nothing she could directly identify, no detail that showed he was not the man he had always been, but she knew. He was a hollow version of the Peter she had lived with for twenty years; there was none of the certainty that had been so much a part of him. The sleek assurance that had always been his hallmark was quite gone, and she felt the pang of pity again and held out a hand impulsively.

'I'm sorry you feel so bad, Peter. I've been thinking . . . we've got to talk . . . .'

He still stood there staring at her, his face quite blank, and then he said, in a voice that was rather higher than it usually was, 'You're what? Did you say you were sorry?'

'Not precisely. I'm not apologizing, if that's what you mean. I said . . . and I mean it . . . I'm sorry you feel so bad.'

'I feel fine. Do you hear me? I feel fine.'

'I hear you.'

'I don't feel bad.'

'All right . . . you don't. I just thought, looking at you . . . .'

'What are you doing here?'

'I came for some of my things.'

'What things?'

'I don't know . . . just some clothes. It doesn't matter . . . I shan't bother, after all . . . .' She began to edge past him, wanting to get away, suddenly frightened. There was something about him that was different, almost a smell of threat, and it filled her with uneasiness, an uneasiness that was increasing, congealing in her arms and legs and her belly, making it difficult to move. 'I won't bother . . .' she said, and then was past him, and in the hallway, and she ran for the front door, scrabbling for the fastening urgently, wanting more than she had ever wanted anything to be out, out in the air, away from the house and from him.

But of course he caught her, and as the blows started, rhythmic vicious blows to each side of her head in turn, and as she tried to put up her arms to shield herself she knew that what was happening was inevitable, and knew, too, that there was much worse pain to come.

31

It wasn't until Annie got to her feet and announced loudly that she was worn out with all this extra work, if no one else was, and she was going over to the hospital for her lunch and wouldn't mind fetching back sandwiches for anyone who wanted them and asked nicely, that Ben realized that the morning had passed him by. He had settled himself beside Harry Gentle at Moscrop's microscope and worked with every atom of concentration he had, doggedly making his way through request after request, and now he lifted his head and stretched his stiff shoulders and said, 'Mm? I'll have a couple of ham sandwiches, then. And coffee . . . what'll you have, Harry? They're on me . . . and where's Jessie? Tell her it's my shout and see what she wants.'

'Not here,' Annie said. She was prinking at the mirror in the corner by the lockers, pursing her lips at herself and turning her head from side to side to admire her own profile. 'She went out this morning . . . took your car, didn't she? And she's not back yet.'

Ben frowned sharply and looked at his watch. 'But it's after one! That means she's been gone . . . it must be almost four hours. She ought to be back by now. Now, why do you suppose that . . . .'

'Hope she hasn't pranged your car the way she did her own,' Harry said. 'Remember? That was as fancy a piece of vehicle demolition as I've seen since I was eighteen and an expert in the field. Regularly used to put my car into a state of irrevocable buggeration, I did . . . .'

'Thanks for the reassurance!' Ben said savagely, and got to his feet. 'I'll go and see if the car's back.'

'Well, she'd hardly be sitting in it in the car park, would she?' Harry said reasonably, but Ben had already gone, slamming out of the door, and almost sending Tomsett flying off his feet.

The old porter was coming in with a couple of requests to be signed which would allow post-mortems to be transferred to Farborough, and he turned and stared after Ben venomously and shouted, 'Goin' ter get me on the way back, then, are yer?' But Ben paid no attention, running out of the building and on into the car park with his white coat flapping around his knees.

And he found her there. He saw his car parked in its usual place and stopped to look, to see whether it was occupied, and saw the shadow of her head and knew she was still in the driver's seat, and waited, expecting her to get out and come towards him. But she didn't move. She just sat there, her head silhouetted blackly against the rear window and he began to move forwards again, anxiety sharpening in him.

He bent to peer in at the front window as he came up to the car and there she sat, very upright, staring ahead, quite still, and he crouched so that he could get nearer to her and bent his head so that he could look up into her face.

'Jess, for God's sake, what's the matter? Are you ill? Don't just sit there – tell me what's the matter.'

Her eyes, glazed and blank, seemed to shift and then focus and she looked at him, and now he could see her face clearly. It was a sickly white, with dark violet smudges beneath the eyes, and her lids were swollen and reddened. She stared at him for a long moment and then her lips moved. 'Ben? Did I get back then, after all? Ben?'

'Jess, for heaven's sake . . . .' He stood upright again and putting his arm behind her back tried to turn her so that she could get out of the car, and she winced and cried out, but he persisted gently, bending to lift her legs out of the car and then carefully urging her to her feet until she stood swaying slightly beside him.

The effort had brought some colour back into her face but she still looked pale and drawn and he put his arm round her shoulders and said softly, 'What is it, Jess? What's happened?'

'The stuff . . .' she said, and tried to pull away from him to look into the car. 'Is it all right? I was so frightened. I drove over the kerb, bumped badly . . . he ran after me, you see. I had to almost run him down to get away, it was . . . is it all right?'

He followed her as she scrabbled at the tailgate handle and helped her open the car and there it was, jammed into the corner and supported by the pile of road map books he kept there, a bulging black plastic carrier, and he reached in and picked it up carefully.

'Are they broken? Are they all right?'

She was looking at him piteously and he looked into the bag and shook it gently and said reassuringly, 'It's fine . . . absolutely fine . . . now, come on, love. Come over to the lab and sit down and tell me what's upset you so much.' And again he put his hand out to take her arm, her left arm this time, and again she winced and cried out, flinching away from him and weeping, and he set the bag of Contravert bottles carefully on the roof of the car and then turned back to her, his face set and almost as white as hers. 'You're hurt,' he said. 'Now tell me what happened, at once, and let me see your arms . . . .'

He unbuttoned her coat and slid it back over her shoulders and she stood very still, trying to hold herself rigid as though doing that would stop any pain, and as he slipped the coat down her arms he could see the marks through the thin sleeves of her blouse: great spreading blue lakes of pain, running from shoulder almost to elbow, with the deeply gouged prints of fingers showing darkest of all. She twisted her head to look, and stared, almost surprised, as though it was someone else's body she was examining, not her own.

'How did that happen?' Ben said quietly.

She looked up at him and said, 'I'm so sorry . . . I shouldn't have, I suppose . . . I didn't think . . . I went home, you see, thought I'd collect a few things on the way back . . . I shouldn't have gone there. I'm so sorry . . . .'

'Stop apologizing, for Christ's sake!' He shouted it and the sound of his voice whipped round the car park and came buffeting back and again she winced. 'There's nothing for you to apologize for.' He spoke more quietly now. 'This was Peter again.' He said it as a fact, not as a question.

She bent her head and stared at the ground like a guilty child. 'It was, wasn't it?' he said again. 'Isn't that what happened? You went home and he was there and he beat you?'

Still she didn't answer, and again he reached to take hold of her and remembered in time and let his hands fall. 'Tell me what happened, Jess,' he said softly. 'I can't help you if you shut me out. It's no shame on you that he beat you. The man's a bastard – that doesn't make you bad.'

'It wasn't the beating,' she said then, and now she looked at him. 'It was . . . .' She drew a long shuddering breath. 'He

266

raped me. Ridiculous, isn't it? The idea of a man raping his own wife. But he did. I couldn't, I really couldn't . . . but he got worse and worse and pushed me over and then, in the hall, it felt so . . . it was crazy. Peter raping me . . . I didn't believe it. I still don't . . . really, he couldn't have, could he? But he did, honestly he did and when I pushed him off and got up and got out of the door and ran . . . and then he ran after me and I still don't believe it . . . Ben, tell me he didn't.'

But Ben didn't answer. He had put her coat round her shoulders and picked up the plastic bag of Contravert from the roof of the car and now he began to lead her not towards the laboratory block, but towards the hospital.

'Can you walk? It's not too far, Jess. Lean on me and see how you get on . . . .'

'Where are we going?' Obediently she began to walk, though obviously she was in pain at each step.

'Accident and Emergency,' he said briefly. 'No, don't argue, Jess. You need to be checked, looked after. That's it, love. Lean on me . . . you're doing fine, absolutely fine.'

The Accident and Emergency Department was blessedly quiet when they got there, and he took her straight into one of the curtained cubicles and still moving very gently, helped her up on to the couch and pulled the red blanket up over her. She took the edge of it in both hands and hung on, clearly glad of it, for she was shivering a little now, even in the heat of the big room.

'I'll get someone to see you right away,' he said, and looked down on her face, pinched and tired against the pillow. He whispered softly, 'Oh, Jess . . . I am so sorry . . .' and bent and kissed her mouth gently. Her own mouth moved against his and then she turned her head to one side and wouldn't look at him and he stood for a moment, knowing what she was thinking and hating the man who had made her think that way.

Once the registrar on duty had gone in to see her he went over to the laboratory, carrying the plastic bag of bottles, to lock them in the small fridge in his own office. It was one he used rarely, because of its small capacity, and it had dwindled into being more domestic than anything else; the department's tonic water and occasional cans of beer were kept in it, and he knew that apart from Harry Gentle no one else in the laboratory really knew of its existence. And he felt that despite his off-hand air there was something dependable about Harry. He could be trusted – and anyway he wouldn't be told the stuff was there. He, Ben, would carry it in unobtrusively, put it away quietly, and then he would go back to Accident and Emergency and see what needed to be done for Jessie. All the way back through the car park, past his car and along the corridor he concentrated his thoughts on that small timetable, on what he had to do, telling himself that the most important thing was just to tuck away his Contravert safely so that no meddling physician such as Lyall Davies could get his hands on it, and then to make sure that Jess was all right – anything rather than think about what had happened to her. Because if he did he knew his rage would slide out of his control, and if that happened – and again he refused to think about anything except the here and now, and what he had to do.

Harry didn't look up from his microscope as he came in and said casually, 'Find her?'

'Mm?' Ben managed to sound relaxed and off-hand. 'Oh, yes. She'd just got back.' He was holding the bag in his right hand, shielding it with his body, and he walked over to his office door in the same deliberate off-hand manner, praying that Harry wouldn't look up, and he didn't, but went on working.

'Errol's gone to lunch, and Annie too. She should be back soon. I told her to get salad sandwiches for Jessie. That's her usual, isn't it?'

'Mm? Oh, yes . . . I'm sure that'll be fine.'

'I gave her the money.' Now Harry did look up but Ben was in his office by now. 'You owe me . . . .'

'Fine,' Ben called as he tucked his precious burden into the fridge and locked it and then sat back on his heels. 'I'll give it to you now.'

Why was it so important that he hide the Contravert? he found himself thinking, as he remained there staring at the blank white door and the big padlock that fastened it. What the hell does it matter anyway? Why not just give it to the bastards, let them get on with it, leave me in peace? If I'd never started on this bloody work, none of this would have happened. Jess wouldn't have . . . .

But that was stupid thinking. The war between Jessie and her husband had nothing to do with his work on Contravert, had it? How could he blame it for that? And yet he did, feeling that somewhere, if only he could perceive it, there was a pattern that consisted of his research and his job here and June and Timmy as well as Jessie and Peter. The whole was interlocked in some way, with the Contravert itself the pivot on which they all turned: it was because he needed help with it that he'd advertised for an extra staff member, and so pulled Jessie into the pattern, and it was because of his research that Jessie's husband had become so . . . he scrambled to his feet, refusing to think further along that path. There were things to do – things to *do*, and the next was to go back to Accident and Emergency, see how Jess was, assess the damage to her, take care of her . . . .

He went outside to find that Annie had come back and was unpacking sandwiches under Harry's critical eye. 'All the ham was gone and so was the salad, so it's corned beef all round,' she announced. 'There's the change from the fiver . . . .' And she dropped a handful of silver and copper on the bench.

'Corned bloody beef and soggy white bread,' Harry said disgustedly. 'Call this a health palace, and I don't think, the garbage they feed you . . . where are you going, Ben?'

'Over to the hospital. I'll be back soon.'

'You owe me!' Harry bawled but it was too late; Ben had gone and Harry lifted his brows in resignation and started on his sandwich.

In the Accident and Emergency Department the Registrar was waiting for him, and as soon as he appeared told him that Jessie had been admitted to the side ward on the main gynaecological ward to recover.

'No more than a lot of bruises,' he said. 'Her thighs and the vulva – the bastard must have been an ox. It doesn't bear thinking of. But she says she won't talk to the police, though I tried to persuade her. Won't say a word about what happened, so we can't do a thing. I do all I can to get these cases properly reported and dealt with, but if the women won't talk – can you persuade her?'

'There's no need,' Ben said, and his voice was flat, with no expression in it at all. 'I know who did it. And I'll deal with him.'

'Hey, now, look, that's not on!' the Registrar said anxiously. 'You can't go coming the vigilante, Pitman, really you can't!'

'Can't I?' Ben said. 'Well, if you say so. When will she be fit to leave the ward, do you think?'

'Tomorrow, really, if there's someone to take care of her. The bruises'll take a few days to subside, even a week or two, but there's no structural damage otherwise. But she's shocked and she shouldn't be left alone.'

'Can you arrange to keep her here longer? You're senior on the gynae firm, aren't you? Control the beds?'

'Yes, of course I do. Why?'

'Keep her here for a week, then. As long as you can. She's been overworking lately anyway, and . . . she needs a rest. Can you fix that? She hasn't a home to go to, really, you see. She . . . she left her husband and . . . .'

'Is *that* who did this to her, then?' The Registrar was looking at him with bright birdlike eyes, and Ben looked away from the glitter of interest in them. In spite of the man's clearly real concern for his patient, in spite of his anger at what had been done to her, still there was a salaciousness in that gaze that was inescapable; he was excited by what he had found out and Ben felt his carefully controlled anger shift inside him, move towards this man at his side.

'That's none of your business,' he snapped and the Registrar reared back slightly and his face hardened.

'Anything that affects a patient in my care is my business,' he snapped back. 'If I believe a crime has been committed it's up to me to decide whether I notify the police or not. I think this woman was abused and I want to do something about it. She's hospital staff. She's entitled to better from us than shrugged shoulders.'

'I know that – and that's why I'm asking for a week's care and protection here for her. But that's all. I'll deal with the rest of it. She's one of *my* staff, remember. I can take care of things very well on my own.'

'Like I said – vigilante stuff isn't on. If I thought that you were going to . . . .'

'Well?'

There was a sharp little silence between them and then the other's gaze shifted, and he turned away. 'All right then. I'll arrange for her to stay in the ward for a while longer. It won't do her any harm and our waiting lists aren't too bad, considering. Mind you, if we get any urgent stuff pushing in – cone biopsies or difficult abortions – we may need the bed. You understand that.'

'I understand and . . . thanks, old man. Sorry if I sounded . . . well, I was upset. It's a nasty thing to happen to . . . to one of your staff.'

'Very nasty. No need to apologize. I'll tell her you'll be in to see her then?'

'Yes. Later today. I've a few things to sort out first.' And he turned and went and the Registrar watched him disappear in the direction of the car park and after a moment went back to his cubbyhole of an office and picked up the phone. He was as angry as any doctor would be at the sight of a beaten raped woman – it was sickening to see the sort of injuries that had been inflicted – but all the same, as a responsible citizen he couldn't let Ben go and take the law into his own hands; apart from any risk to the man he was seeking, what about the risk to himself? Pitman could be letting himself in for more than he bargained for; after all, this woman's husband was clearly a very violent person. And he sat and waited for the police to answer their telephone, rehearsing in his mind all that he would tell them, and feeling rather excited at the posture in which he found himself, as one who dealt not only in sickness and in health but in law and order. It was an interesting way to feel.

32

There was no one at the house in Purbeck Avenue. It wasn't just that no one answered his repeated rings on the doorbell; it was the silent emptiness of the place that proved it, an emptiness the house seemed to exude, and after a while he turned and went back down the path to his car. It would have to be where the man worked, then, and he took from his pocket the sheet of details he had collected from his office file on the path. lab staff, and peered at it in the already darkened afternoon. She'd entered her husband as her next of kin, and had given his working address and phone number, and he nodded with a sort of satisfaction at that, and turned the ignition key. Soon . . . I'll be there soon, and then he'll know how I feel, what Jessie feels, what it feels like to be the attacked rather than the attacker.

He felt better than he had for a very long time; it was quite extraordinary, he thought as he drove the car smoothly through the dwindling afternoon towards the town centre. There was none of the weariness that lack of sleep had induced in him all morning, none of the sense of heavy depression that he seemed to have been carrying around with him for so long; just a sense of resilient muscular power, of strength and general wellbeing. He was on his way to a confrontation that would be, at the very least, a very disagreeable one, yet he felt like a kid on his way to a tennis tournament he knew he was going to win. Extraordinary!

He parked without any problems – another ingredient to add to the mix of good feelings which were getting stronger by the moment – and ran up the steps into the Civic Centre with all the energy of a teenager, and would willingly have walked up the seven flights of stairs the man on the reception desk told him lay between him and his quarry if there hadn't been a lift ready and waiting for him; and he stood in it staring at the floor number panel above his head winking and changing as it purred upwards thinking – quarry, yes, that's what he is. He's my quarry and I'm hunting him. My God, but I feel good about this!

Big double doors, an expanse of carpeted floor, a wide desk heavily cluttered with pot plants, and behind it a narrow-faced woman who stared at him woodenly as he came towards her.

'Peter Hurst,' he said firmly. 'I have to see him urgently.'

'Have you an appointment?'

'I told you, it's urgent. I . . . I've come from the hospital. It's about his wife.'

The woman's face lost its wooden expression, took on a look of deep concern mixed with excitement, showing a relish for bad news that set his teeth on edge.

'Oh, she's not ill, is she? There, I knew there was something up. He came in late, and he never does that, and he looks dreadful. I'll tell him you're here, then . . .' And she reached for the telephone.

'No,' Ben said swiftly. 'No, better not. You know how it is . . . he'll need . . . better I just go and talk to him quietly. You know? Which is his room?'

The woman pointed down the corridor. 'Third door on the right. Oh, dear, I *am* sorry. Will . . . er . . . will she be all right? Was it an accident or something?'

Ben nodded at her affably and said nothing, just unbuttoning his raincoat as he went purposefully along the corridor. It was warm in here, and anyway he didn't want to be trammelled by his clothes. He took the coat off as he reached the door the woman had indicated and dropped it on the floor beside it, and then moving with sure direct actions, opened the door and walked in.

Peter Hurst was standing at the window with his back to the room staring out into the street. Because of the bright lighting in the room the sky looked darker than it should at this hour; almost indigo, with gleams of light from the street lamps far below reflecting and winking on the tilted fanlight which was open at the top. He didn't turn as the door opened, but he lifted his head and said in a voice that was clearly meant to be loud and authoritative but which sounded only husky, 'I won't be needing anything more tonight, Miss Price. You can go now if you like – I'll sign your time sheet for the full day.'

Ben said nothing, just stood there waiting, and after a moment Hurst turned round and looked at him. He was a stocky man, square-faced but with a layer of softness blurring his jawline and making him look like a wax doll that had been left out in the sun too long. It wasn't only his jawline that had that melted look – so did his pouched eyes and his drooping mouth and his ponderous cheeks – but down one of those cheeks there were three red swollen welts, and Ben thought with satisfaction – good girl. She managed to do some harm of her own then.

'Who are you?' Hurst said, and moved towards his desk to reach for his telephone. 'I see no one without appointments, and . . . .'

Ben moved faster than he did and jerked the phone away from Hurst's reaching hand, and he whitened at that action, looking down at the phone and then at Ben's face; and what he saw there seemed to frighten him, for he began to bluster and shout.

'Who the hell are you coming in here unasked, interfering with . . . who the bloody hell do you . . . .?'

'I'm Jessie's boss. Yes, that's what I am. Jessie's boss,' Ben said and came round the desk towards Hurst, who began to back away from him. 'It's high time we met.'

'I see no reason why . . . I really have nothing to say to you, or you to me,' Hurst said in a high voice, and tried to straighten his shoulders, to put on an air of being in control of the situation, and for one brief moment Ben was able to pity him. The man was obviously terrified and yet he was trying to show courage – it was almost admirable.

'I've nothing to say to you either,' Ben said, and reached forwards and took his shirt and jacket in a tight grip. 'Nothing to say, lots to do . . . .'

The absurd thing was that Ben had never been a physical sort of man, had never expressed his anger in any way other than verbally. As a schoolboy, at university, at medical school, he had never been one of those who joined in a fist fight with whoops of delight like some of the other men around him. He'd always dismissed people who did that with contempt – in the same way that he dismissed people who took pleasure in violent body-contact sports – regarding them as mindless lumps of muscle and little more, but now he knew for the first time what it was that fired such people. The way his knuckles stung and then burned as they made contact with Hurst's face, squeezing that pudgy flesh against the cheekbones beneath; the pleasure he got from the way the man's neck snapped backwards, the satisfaction of hearing the grunting, weeping, gasping noises he was producing as Ben thumped him and then thumped him again, using both fists in sequence; the way he crumpled at his feet, now weeping in good earnest and trying to hold off Ben's flailing fists with both arms held protectively over his head – it was, Ben found, exciting and exhilarating, almost sexually arousing, and he wanted to shout and jump and scream that excitement the way he had seen spectators do at boxing matches and rugger games. But he had no breath to do that, needed all the energy he had to go on hitting the pulpy creature who was now crouching at his feet and keening rhythmically.

He heard the door open behind him but paid no attention at all. He had now pulled Hurst to his feet again and had him pinned against the desk with one knee held in his crotch while he pummelled his belly, though the blows were slowing down now as the muscles across his shoulders began to protest and his own breathlessness made him gasp. The scurry of footsteps across the room meant nothing to him until he felt hands grabbing at his shoulders and pulling on them; and though he tried to go on hitting Hurst, the grip of the interloper was too much for his exhausted muscles to resist, and he stopped hitting and straightened his back and his leg and let go of Hurst, who slid down the desk to sit on the floor, still wailing loudly.

'What's going on here, for Christ's sake?' The voice came from the door and Ben turned his head, trying to see who was holding him behind, but couldn't, and looked back to the door instead, blinking through the sweat that was now running into his eyes, trying to see how many people there were to deal with.

'He said he came from the hospital . . . said Mr Hurst's wife was ill or something . . .' the voice behind him cried shrilly. 'So I let him in . . . the police are on their way . . . called them as soon as I heard what was happening . . . .'

'Good for you, Miss Price!' The man at the door came in, carefully, watching Ben at every step he took, but Ben was now standing still, concentrating on his breathing, his shoulders as lax as Miss Price's grip would allow them to be, and his head drooping forwards. 'I always said you had more guts than any man in the place . . . well, really, poor old Hurst

. . . beaten up in his own office! Whatever next?'

He crouched beside Hurst, who was still sitting on the floor and moaning, and shook his head. 'You poor old fella, Peter! Nasty, very nasty you look. Can you get up? Come on, old chap . . . on your pins . . . that's the way . . . .' Ben turned his head and looked blearily at the man whose head now appeared over the edge of the desk as the other lifted him to his feet.

Hurst turned his own head as he was half-led, half-dragged to his chair and caught Ben's gaze, and for an appreciable moment the two men stared at each other, Hurst's eyes gleaming dully through the visibly swelling flesh around them and Ben's wet with the tears of his exhaustion. It was as though for a moment, they spoke to each other. As though Ben had said, 'That's it then. Now you know,' and the other had replied submissively, 'Yes, now I know.'

There was more noise at the door and Ben turned his head to look, and it was a great effort to do it; his neck ached, his eyes ached, every part of him ached, and he blinked to clear the sting of saltiness from his eyes and saw a cluster of people there, girls staring with wide awestruck eyes, a couple of young men and then, pushing through them, a couple of uniformed policemen.

And Ben looked at them and began to laugh, a silly hiccupping almost giggling sound, and the woman behind him, who was still holding his arms, shook him slightly, clearly disapproving, but he couldn't help it. All he'd thought about had been getting to Hurst and dealing with him. He'd given no consideration to what might happen afterwards. And now here he was, about to be arrested.

'And back in the news again,' he said and hiccupped once more. 'Back in the bloody news again.'

They left him sitting alone in the green painted bareboarded room for a very long time, and after a while he folded his arms carefully on the rather rickety wooden table, spreading his blood-encrusted and painful fingers wide, and rested his head on his forearms, thinking – I'll just rest a little. And fell deeply and dreamlessly asleep, only waking when someone pulled on his shoulder and made his muscles shriek a protest.

'Well, well, sir, clearly you've no sort of bad conscience, have you?' The policeman who was standing there looking down on him seemed to be in a jocular mood and Ben blinked at him and then, moving carefully, drew himself up, letting his now very stiff and painful hands rest in his lap.

'Bad conscience?' he said, and was surprised at how thick his voice sounded. He must be more tired than he realized. 'No, I've no conscience. I'm glad I did it.'

'Personal problem, I take it, sir?' The policeman sat down and leaned back in his chair and grinned at him. 'Something that got up your nose, that this fella did, was it?'

Ben looked at him suspiciously. Were policemen interrogating men who'd attacked other men usually as chatty and relaxed as this? His experience of legal matters was sketchy in the extreme; his only contact with the police over the years had been an occasional search for lost property. He'd never even broken a motoring law, let alone any other, until now; and he frowned. All those films he'd seen, all the TV shows that dealt in police affairs, were all he had to go by.

'I think I'm supposed to ask to see my lawyer, aren't I?'

The policeman grinned. 'Well, now, why should you want a lawyer, sir? Here we are with a chap that it seems you treated to a fair old basinful sitting there but refusing to say a bad word about you, let alone willing to make a proper complaint against you, and since it all happened on what you might call private – certainly enclosed – premises and no harm done or obstruction caused, no need for us to make any fuss. So what would you be wanting a lawyer for?'

Ben closed his eyes and stretched his neck with great care and then opened them and said cautiously, 'Then I'm free to go?'

'Not precisely, sir. Not at the moment. I mean, you did attack another citizen, didn't you? Even if he seems willing to let bygones be bygones, I'm interested . . . well, any man would be, in why that should be. I can guess, mind you. Gather that Hurst's wife works for you. Yes. Personable lady, is she?'

Ben sat up straighter and stared back at the policeman, determined to keep his face free of any expression, but clearly he failed because the man said easily, 'Well, now, no need to get agitated, is there? No. It's none of my affair, I suppose. But I'll tell you what is, and I'd be glad to have my curiosity satisfied!' He leaned forwards chummily and folded his arms on the table so that his face was quite near to Ben's. 'How is it that just after you get here we get this instruction that there's to be no fuss made and no problems about letting you go? It was an easy instruction to follow, seeing that Mr Hurst's behaving so magnanimously, but all the same . . . it's a fair old puzzle.'

'Instruction?' Ben said carefully, and stared back at the pleasant face in front of him. 'Who from?'

'Ah, now that'd be telling, wouldn't it? But I'll tell you, why shouldn't I? Office of the Chief Constable, that's who. And that seems to me to suggest Special Branch.'

'Special Branch? What does that mean?'

Now the policeman looked a little less affable. 'Come on now, sir, I'm not so daft as I look, you know.'

Ben shook his head, and then stopped, wincing slightly. God, but his neck muscles ached. He must have held his own head like a vice to have had that effect on them. 'I'm sorry, I really don't . . . I've always been an ordinary sort of person, you see. Never had any dealings with the law. Except when I bought my house, things like that. I really don't . . . Special Branch? What's that to do with me?'

The policeman leaned back. 'Well, sir, that's what I'd like to know. But if you're not prepared to tell me, what can I do? Not a thing. I've no right to ask, neither, I suppose. Still, I thought I'd try. Curious, you know. Any man would be.'

'If I knew I'd say,' Ben said, and began slowly to get to his feet. 'You say I'm free to go?'

The policeman stood up too. 'I'll check again with the Chief Constable's office. They said they'd call back, but some of those women there . . . right dreamy lot they are. I'll find out, call 'em myself. If you'd care to come along to the canteen, sir, you can have a cuppa. Do you good, that would . . . .'

'Thank you.' Ben followed him out of the room, his body screaming its fury at him, but as he moved the stiffness eased and he began, very slightly, to feel better, less battered and more alert. A cup of coffee would be a great comfort, come to think of it.

He was sitting in the canteen sipping his second cup half an hour later when the affable policeman came back, this time with a tall man in a neat dark suit behind him.

'Well now, Dr Pitman, it's all settled. We've got the clearance we need to let you be on your way, and here's your driver to take you back to the hospital.'

'My . . . who?' Ben looked at the other man who nodded at him in a cheerful way. 'Who are you?'

'Just your driver, Dr Pitman. Will you let me have the keys to your car then? You're parked over at the Civic Centre I think? The chaps here'll give us a lift back to it – but I think I'd better take over now, don't you? You don't really look in any fit condition to drive yourself, after all.'

33

'I don't believe this,' Ben said, and shook his head again. 'I'd have known if people were watching me, for God's sake!'

'But they were and you didn't,' the man said gently. 'I do assure you, ever since the first piece of publicity on this affair appeared, we've been interested in you. Your work, you understand rather than any . . . ah, personal aspects.'

'I'm glad to hear it.'

'Not that we don't know a good deal about you. Inevitable, really. You can't watch a chap, do a bit of vetting on him, without picking up a lot of information about his little ways and his private preoccupations.' He reached into his neat briefcase and took out a green cardboard folder and Ben blinked; his name was printed neatly on the front of it and the man smiled as he caught the direction of his gaze and said even more gently, 'You see? We really do have you well documented.'

'But why? I still don't understand. You turn up out of the blue when I'm in a . . . at a sort of crisis time, announce yourself as my *driver* and then tell me you're a . . . what is it? Civil servant? What sort of civil servant, for God's sake? Are you from the DHSS? Is all this because I've been doing my own research on DHSS premises? Is that it? If it is, and I was wrong, then I'll do what I can to put it right, but all this cloak and dagger stuff – it's bloody ridiculous. Do you people really go about spying on hospital staff to make sure we don't waste NHS money? Because if you do, by God, you're missing some pretty obvious . . . .'

'No, no, no!' The other man was holding up one hand, laughing gently. 'Nothing of the sort. I know damn all about the Elephant House, my dear chap! The DHSS has nothing to do with my department and I have nothing to do with it, I do promise you. You can rest assured about that.'

'Then what is your department?'

'I did tell you.' He sounded reproachful, as though they'd been introduced at a suburban tennis party, and Ben had committed the social solecism of forgetting. 'I'm Richard Franey of Division Seventeen, not that that need worry you.'

'Everything worries me! Look here, Mr Franey . . . .'

'Doctor actually. But call me Richard. So much more agreeable to be friendly, don't you think?'

'You come here, Dr Franey, and you tell me some tale about getting me out of trouble with the police and . . . .'

'But it's true. You really mustn't call it a story, you know! We had cause to know – well, suspect – that you were about to, shall we say express a difference of opinion with Mr Hurst. And when the disagreement became so profound that the police became involved we thought it better to sort things out ourselves. It saves time, you see. Can't have a chap we're interested in turning up in court on charges of causing affrays or inflicting grievous bodily harm or whatever it is these chappies call it. Low profile, that's us. Very low profile.'

'But you still haven't told me who you are!' Ben said almost despairingly. It was impossible to get angry with the man; he was so friendly, answered every question so readily – albeit unsatisfactorily – and seemed so anxious to please that getting angry would have been absurd. But the bewilderment that had filled him ever since the man had escorted him, half-dazed, from the police station to collect his own car and bring him back here to the lab was threatening to become more than he could handle, and he rubbed his head with both hands, forgetting how his fingers hurt and wincing at the effect of his own action.

Franey was at once all concern. 'My dear chap, you must be feeling dreadful, and here I am not offering you any comfort! Have a quick one, what do you say?' And he reached again into his briefcase and this time brought out a silver flask. 'Brandy? Mind you, your opponent probably needs it more than you do. Long time since I've seen a chap quite so satisfyingly flattened. You *were* angry with him, weren't you?'

'Yes,' Ben said, and after a moment took the little silver cup Franey had unscrewed from the flask and filled, and swallowed its contents. They burned his mouth and his throat, made him cough a little, but warmed him.

'It really is very simple, Dr Pitman.' Franey bent over his folder, smoothing out the sheets of paper that were in it. 'We –

the department, you know – are very interested in your work. Very. We can see there is a considerable potential there, and we would like to discuss with you the possibility of working with us. Excellent facilities, you know, and all the resources you need. Just have to write a requisition, and you have it all, staff, materials, the lot. And of course, we'll be able to give you a better salary than the poor old NHS can! I worked it out. It would be eighty-three per cent more than your present income, after tax,' and he handed Ben a sheet of paper covered with neatly typed figures.

Ben took it and stared down at it, and the numbers printed there as income, and as additional expenses on which he could draw, read like telephone numbers, they were so large, and he looked up at Franey and said almost in awe, 'This is a salary scale?'

'Indeed it is,' Franey said, and leaned back in his chair in high good humour. 'And of course that doesn't mention the resettlement cash that's available. You'd sell your house here, of course, before coming North, and you'd need a new one, and the way house costs vary between the areas means you could have something rather more elegant than you now have; I'm sure your wife would love it . . . if, of course she chooses to come with you.' He stopped and coughed, a genteel little sound in Ben's small cluttered office that sounded oddly muffled as the small refrigerator started up its motor behind him and settled to a steady hum, and Ben looked at him, suspicion leaping even higher in him.

'I mean, you may decide that the time has come for a parting of the ways, hmm? We did notice that – how shall we put it – you and your wife aren't as close as some married couples, are you? No. But of course you could take anyone else with you you choose. We aren't interested in private matters, I repeat, Dr Pitman, even though we had to do some vetting, you understand. If you chose to bring your own assistant with you to the job, wanted to . . . ah . . . arrange shared accommodation for you both, well, that's no business of ours. Might in fact have a lot to commend it. A partner who understands one's work, is really in sympathy with its objectives, such a help, don't you think?'

'Why?'

'Why share accommodation? Well, I can't say really! It's entirely up to you. I'm just making the point that you'll be free to do as you choose, and that we offer generous resettlement cash to help you do so and . . . .'

'No, I mean why offer me all this? What for? What do you want me to do?'

'Just what you're doing now, my dear man, exactly what you're doing now. Only better. Trials of your Contravert, large-scale trials of every sort. Animal, then human. All the help you need, access to our excellent computer for all the statistical work, and for some very sophisticated predictions too. It's amazing what the machine can do, I'm told. It's beyond my simple understanding, of course – my doctorate is in chemistry, not the sort of fancy physics these computer chaps go in for – but there it is. I know the results they get and you'll enjoy them, you will indeed. A lot of the donkey work will be taken off your back and you can concentrate on what you do best. Which is getting a really pure source of Contravert that can be given in standard doses and which is safe to use. We're well aware of the fact that you've been working here on a shoestring. Looking around now it amazes me that you've done as much as you have with such limited resources. You are clearly a resourceful man, Dr Pitman, if you'll forgive a bad pun!' And he laughed gently.

Ben bent his head and looked again at the piece of paper in his hands. 'You're offering me all that, and this salary and . . . I don't understand,' he looked up and shook his head. 'I'm probably being very stupid, but I've had a . . . it's been a difficult day and I'm being a bit slow on the uptake one way and another. You still haven't explained fully who you are, who's offering me all this. And why.'

'Division Seventeen,' Franey said and smiled at him. 'That's us, Dr Pitman. Division Seventeen.'

'But that tells me nothing!'

'It isn't meant to.' Franey sat and gazed at him for a long moment and Ben stared back and there was a silence broken only by the hum of the refrigerator and, from the animal room, the subdued chatter of Castor and Pollux, and then Franey sighed and leaned forwards.

'I can see that there's more to you than I thought. I had a distinct impression that you cared only for your research, that given the chance to do more of it, and do it better, you wouldn't care unduly about who you were doing it for . . . .'

Ben frowned. 'Who for? I'm doing it for myself. And I

283

suppose, ultimately, for people with virus infections. Who else would I be doing it for?' And suddenly his face darkened and he got to his feet to stand and stare angrily down at Franey. 'My God, I should have realized this ages ago! I'm a bloody fool – or I nearly was. You're one of these damned pharmaceutical firms, aren't you? Want to get me to make the stuff for you, patent it, make yourselves a fortune? Go to bloody hell! If I get Contravert right it isn't going to be picked up by just one firm and used to make them fat. It'll be available to everyone who wants it, and it'll be made as cheaply as possible and . . . .'

'I absolutely agree, Dr Pitman!' Franey said and again smiled up at him. 'Do sit down, old man, you're giving me a crick in my neck. I agree totally with your views of these multinational pharmaceutical firms. Parasites, some of 'em, downright parasites. Not all, mind you. There are some we negotiate tight contracts with and get excellent materials and excellent products for a very low rate. You'll see if . . . when you start with us. No, my dear chap, I keep telling you, I'm a civil servant! I'm not one of your businessmen. I am here to represent the Government of this country, and telling you that your country has a job to offer you. That sounds rather like a bad American TV show, doesn't it? Your country calling you and all that. But it's true, all the same. I was about to explain to you when you jumped to the wrong conclusion.'

He waited till Ben sat down, again still moving rather stiffly, and then said with a casual air, 'Division Seventeen is part of the MOD.'

'MOD?' Ben repeated stupidly.

'Defence,' Franey said.

Again a silence filled the room as Ben looked at the other man, who looked benignly back at him, and then Ben said carefully, 'Defence. To do with war and weapons, is that it?'

'I'm afraid so,' Franey said with an air of genuine regret. 'Sad, isn't it, that a word that should conjure up images of high walls and nice secure doors and gates actually makes you think of offensive weapons. But that's how it is these nasty days, isn't it? To defend yourself you have to be fairly ferocious.' He smiled again, then, a sly little grin this time. 'As you showed this afternoon. Defending your Mrs Hurst, you see, weren't you, who was treated so badly by her husband, and so you attacked him with great energy, very great energy indeed.

284

Yes, defence means fighting, and we don't pretend otherwise.'

'How did you know that Mrs Hurst . . . .' Ben shook his head, not wanting to be diverted from the questions he wanted answered, but needing answers to everything. 'She didn't make any official complaint, did she? How could she have done? She's been admitted to the ward . . . .'

'No she didn't. But we found out. It's the same way we found out that you were on your way to Mr Hurst in a rather bad mood.' Franey produced his gentle smile again. 'Chap on duty in Accident and Emergency, you see. Thought he ought to behave like a responsible citizen, prevent a crime being committed . . . .'

'The bastard!' Ben said and flushed with anger as the image of the face of the Registrar in Accident and Emergency rose before his mind's eye. 'He had no right! Medical confidentiality – he had no right!'

'I'm sure he didn't. But he did it all the same. So you see, we have many ways of finding out what we need to know.'

'But why . . . what's the point of all this watching and spying and . . . it's horrible!' Ben said. 'You tell me you've been watching me . . . .'

'And all the people you've been dealing with,' Franey said. 'Clough – the chap who does your extractions for you – marvellous fella, really marvellous. Very suspicious he was, got the idea that our investigators were these Animal Freedom Brigade types, set up a complete little army on his premises in consequence.' He laughed with real amusement. 'I wanted to tell him he didn't have to go to that sort of expense, that it was only a highly proper government department that was snooping about, but there, we do have to be careful to keep ourselves out of the public eye, so we couldn't. Maybe you can tell him yourself in a day or two he's wasting his efforts and his money. There's no threat to him. Special Branch worked out who those AFB people were days ago. They'll do no harm to anyone else – well, not at present anyway. They're being watched, you see, and they'll be stopped smartly if they overstep the mark. A little bit of lunatic fringe activity doesn't hurt anyone, and we don't mind it. But if it gets silly and over the top we step in, of course. You see how important defence is, old man? It isn't just a matter of waiting for something nasty to turn up and have a go at you and then telling it to push off. It's a matter of working out what sort of nasties might turn up and then going out and clobbering them before they clobber you.'

'And what good would I be in that sort of activity?' Ben said, and now it was his turn to laugh. 'What possible use can my sort of research be to the Ministry of Defence?'

Franey lapsed again into one of his contemplative silences, and this time Ben sat and watched him and said nothing, leaving it to him to break his own silence, and after a long pause Franey got to his feet and began to walk up and down the little office, no more than four strides in each direction though it was.

'This is difficult to explain to a man with a medical training. You people tend to have . . . well, they've been labelled as sentimental views about medical practice. I prefer to call them highly ethical views. But there's more than one sort of ethic, and we have ours just as you have yours. They may not march, you know, they may not march, but they *are* both ethical standpoints.'

He stopped his pacing and came back to stand above Ben and look down at him. 'This Contravert of yours – it will have the effect of enabling the individual human body on which it is used to fight off any infection; even the most severe of virus infections?'

'That's a very simple way of looking at it . . . .'

'But . . . essentially it's what it does?'

'Yes, I suppose so.'

'And it isn't the Contravert that sees off the viruses, it's the body's own cells?'

'That's right. It's like the auto-immune reaction which acts against all sorts of threats, and not just specific invaders . . . .'

'Precisely. Now, supposing you were able to work on your research with no stops at all, with no constraint of money or staff of any kind. Could you develop, do you suppose, a product that could be given to all the population, as a sort of vaccine? In times of high risk, you know? Suppose a severe epidemic was known to be on its way, could you visualize Contravert being given to everybody, man, woman and child, so that when the epidemic arrived it would simply peter out, not be able to get a hold?'

'Yes, I suppose so. I mean, I hadn't seen it as a prophylactic, more as a treatment, but of course it could be used that way. If

I got the product purified, standardized, produced in huge bulk. It would cost a fortune though, to do that.'

Franey waved one hand. 'That's immaterial. Now, can you see why the Ministry of Defence is interested in helping you develop your Contravert along these lines? What a useful adjunct it would be to the State's protection system for its population?'

'No,' Ben said after a moment. 'No, I can't.'

'You're not interested in politics, Dr Pitman?'

Ben blinked, startled. 'What the hell's that got to do with it? No, not particularly.'

'Then you don't read the political news much, I dare say. Don't worry yourself about strategic arms talks, Star Wars conferences, attempts to maintain a balance of power as regards the possession of major weapons . . . .'

Ben's face cleared. 'I see what you mean. Well, of course I pay some attention to that. You can't fail to . . . the news, the papers, they're always going on about it. But I've never been as interested as I should be.'

'Should be?'

'They asked me to join the Medical Campaign against Nuclear Weapons,' Ben said, and was uneasy suddenly. 'I meant to, but somehow . . . it all seemed so pointless. What good can we do fussing about the damned things? The weapons are there. We've got them . . . we can't just unmake them . . . .'

'And of course when one side possesses them the other must too, for its own protection, you'd agree . . . .'

'I don't know . . .' Ben said, and then exploded. 'For God's sake, Franey! What the hell's this got to do with me? I've had a God awful day, I've no idea what tomorrow's going to bring. I need some sleep and you're standing there blathering on about nuclear bloody weapons . . . .'

'Not as irrelevant as you might think, Dr Pitman. You see, there are other weapons apart from atomic and hydrogen bombs and so forth.'

'I know that! I heard enough from my parents about the last war. They were bombed out, went through the London blitz and the buzzbombs and . . . .'

'Yes, indeed, there are conventional explosives like those. And there are also the group of biological weapons.'

'Biological?'

'There's been a good deal of interest for some time in the possibilities. We have considerable evidence from our Intelligence people that certain groups around the world are showing an increasing interest in them. Infections that attack plants and livestock.' He paused for a long moment and then said smoothly, 'And people.'

Ben lifted his chin and stared at him, his face blank with astonishment.

'Ah,' Franey said with satisfaction. 'Now I see you understand! Yes, Dr Pitman. A product like Contravert could be of enormous value to any country if biological weapons became as important as nuclear ones. And they are rapidly becoming so, I have to tell you. They are rapidly becoming very important indeed.'

34

'I had to talk to someone,' he said. 'And who else is there but you? I know I'm a bastard, coming here and bothering you when you're feeling so lousy . . . .'

'I was feeling lousy only because I was alone and bored and . . . seeing you has made me feel much better. And talking about this is desperately important – I'd have been very upset if you hadn't.'

'You wouldn't have known,' Ben said and managed a grin, and after a moment she returned it.

'Well, no, I suppose not. But I'd have found out eventually and been miserable. Anyway, I've a right to know. If they really want me to be part of it all.'

'That's what he said.' Ben got up from his perch on the edge of her bed and went over to the window to peer out into the wide hospital courtyard and the foreshortened cars in the car park, seven storeys below. 'He said they'd been watching me, too. Do you suppose they still are?'

'That's horrible,' Jessie said and shivered a little, and pulled the blankets higher over her shoulders, even though the room was quite warm. 'To be spied on . . . it would make me feel . . . I don't know. Grubby.'

'It makes me amazed. It's so ridiculous, isn't it? Like a silly film.'

'Life imitating art and all that?'

'Some art! People skulking around, watching me, watching you, even old Clough . . . .' He laughed then. 'That's funny, you know. Old Clough spotting them and thinking they were the Animal Freedom people and turning his place into a beseiged fort, apparently. Just like him.'

'Watching me too, you say?' Jessie said sharply, and he turned to look at her and grimaced.

'I shouldn't have told you – yes, apparently. They've been watching everyone who's had anything to do with me, June and Timmy too. I'm sorry, Jess. I feel sick that you should have . . . .'

'It doesn't matter,' she said, though it did, a great deal. Someone had watched her running out of her own house, her husband after her, watched her behaving like a frightened rabbit instead of turning and fighting back; she was filled with sudden self-loathing at the thought. 'Goddamn it, yes, it does matter. I feel more than grubby when I think about it. I feel . . . I don't know. Polluted, almost . . . .'

'That's an over-reaction, Jess,' he said and came back to sit on the edge of the bed again. 'The surveillance wasn't because there was anything bad about you. Or about me, I imagine, it was just . . . .' He shrugged. 'They wanted to know more about me and mine before they approached me, as I understand it. That was all!'

'I don't think that's true, Ben,' she said levelly. 'Is it? Why else should he have said I could come and live with you in the new house they're offering, if they didn't know? Or at least suspect? You said that was what he offered, didn't you?'

Ben dropped his head and gazed at her for a moment and then said, 'Yes. That's what he said. I . . . oh, hell, I wasn't trying to deceive you, Jess, I just wanted to . . . he's only guessing, after all. He can't know anything about us, but it seems a reasonable guess, after all. I went and had that fight with Peter, and . . . .'

'I suppose so,' she said wearily, and closed her eyes. 'I'm being childish and ridiculous, I dare say. As if it matters anyway. I'm divorcing Peter and everyone'll know about that soon enough. And then the gossip'll really get going here. I dare say the nurses on this ward have done their share of it already. There can't be many people around the place now who don't know I was raped. Christ, but I've got to get away from here! I can't stay to be looked at by everyone, have them thinking . . . .' She began to shiver and couldn't stop, and he set his hands on each of her shoulders and held on, saying nothing, and slowly the shivering subsided, and he let go and stood up again and went to lean against the window with his back to the light, so that his face was shadowed.

'You're definitely divorcing Peter?' he said after a while.

'Are you surprised?'

'No. No, I'm glad. You don't deserve to put up with a man like him.'

'I did it for twenty years,' she said. 'So he can't be all bad. Don't try to make him worse than he is, Ben. I couldn't cope with that.'

'It isn't possible to make him worse than he is.'

'I lived with him for twenty years,' she said again. 'Remember that, and don't . . . just remember that.'

There was a long silence and then he said, 'All right. No talk of the past. Only of the future. Shall we do it then, Jess? Take this job?'

'We?'

'I told you . . . they want you to come too. He . . . Franey seemed to think it would be a good idea. Having my own assistant, someone in sympathy with what I was doing, someone I could trust and rely on, he said. I agree with him.'

Again there was a silence and then she said, 'I'm not sure I would be in sympathy, Ben. I don't think you could rely on me in the same way any more.'

He frowned. 'Not in . . . but you've worked with me on Contravert for a long time, Jess! Now, when I'm given the chance to really get it right, all the time and the money and the resources I need – how can you lose interest now?'

'I didn't say I'd lost interest. I said I wasn't sure I'd be in sympathy with the new job. The work and the job – they're two separate things, aren't they? I can't see myself in a Ministry of Defence set-up.'

'The politics worry you?'

'Of course. Don't they worry you?'

He took a deep breath and then said, 'I don't know. There, I've said it. I don't bloody well know. I've been thinking about nothing else for the past three days, ever since he talked to me, but I have to tell you I just don't know what to think any more. All I can visualize is a decent laboratory and plenty of staff and enough animals and the chance to do proper trials, access to a really good computer, all that. I can't think of much more than that either. And I don't see why I should, damn it!'

He moved away from the window and began to prowl around the small room, and she lay against her pillows and let her eyes follow him as he went from one side to the other.

'What bloody affair is it of mine why I'm being given the chance to do the work? Isn't it the work that matters? What'd the difference be, anyway? Suppose I went on as I am, and managed to get Contravert right, and properly tested, working the way I already do – it'll take years, no doubt – but eventually, suppose I manage it? Then won't these Division Seventeen people take it up anyway? How could I prevent them? And what would I do when the research was complete, anyway? Sell it to a pharmaceutical company? That'd be really moral, wouldn't it? And if I didn't, how would the stuff be distributed to people who need it? And wouldn't they sell it to the highest bidder, anyway, and couldn't that be another country, rather than this one? As I see it, it doesn't make much odds what I do. As long as the research goes on and the stuff's made available, then the way I do it and where I do it are really immaterial.'

'If it goes on,' Jess said after a moment, and he turned and looked at her miserably.

'Yes,' he said. 'I thought about that too.'

'What conclusion did you come to?'

'I didn't. I've been trying . . . .' He shook his head. 'And there are a lot of questions to be asked here, too. Suppose I did say – this is dangerous knowledge, I mustn't do anything more to gain it, I've got to bury it, pretend I never thought of it; do you really think that'd make any difference? I've started, and the idea's been put into people's heads. Franey's head. If I refuse to go on, won't he find other researchers, point them in the direction I was going in, start them off? For all I know he already has, and there are people beavering away on my work, and they'll get there before I do if I don't accept the invitation I've been given . . . .' He went a sudden dusky red. 'And I know that oughtn't to matter, but it does, it bloody well does. I never thought of myself as particularly ambitious, Jess. I used to despise the people I knew who were, thought them . . . oh, I don't know, stupid and rather childish. Wanting to build the highest dungheap and jump on it and shriek, "Look at me, look at me!" I thought they were greedy, too, did it just for money, all that wanting and striving but . . . it isn't like that, is it? It's a different sort of wanting and I'm full of it now, that same need. And it's not to do with wanting to be looked at or wanting money, it's a different thing entirely. I just couldn't bear to see someone else get Contravert right before I do, that's the thing. It's my stuff, *mine*, and I want it to stay that way. So when I think of abandoning the work altogether I feel sick. I don't think I could.'

'I'm sorry,' Jess said after a moment, and he turned and

looked at her and made a small face.

'Apologizing, Jess? What for? For having a mind of your own?'

'No. Commiserating. It's a hell of a dilemma to be in.'

'The doctor's dilemma,' he said and laughed, a short sharp bark of a sound. 'Bloody cliché isn't it? All living's a cliché, I think, sometimes. I keep finding myself in situations that feel like stories. Not real at all.'

'It's real,' she said. 'That's why the stories. They come after the reality – they don't create it. Ben, please, can you wait for me to think some more? About whether to come with you or not? If you really want me, that is, after what I said. I mean I do have . . . difficulties about the politics of it, but the things you've said – they make sense. I need time to think more.'

'Really want you? Are you mad?' And he smiled so warmly that her eyes filled with tears and she couldn't look at him. 'Don't be a bloody fool. Of course I do.'

'What about June?'

'I . . . that's another issue. I haven't thought about that. She might not want to come. Not without Timmy. And I can't see Liz letting him come north to be with June so . . . it might resolve itself.'

'Story time again?' Jess said. 'I don't think it'll be as easy as that, Ben. I think you'll have to make a decision.'

'I know!' he said, and there was a controlled violence in his voice now. 'I know. But there's a limit to what I can cope with at any one time. Let me get my head clear about work, first. And as far as the work's concerned – if I do go, and I'm still thinking about it, I want you to come too. To work with me. I can say that much, can't I? Without compromising your Calvinist conscience any more than it already is?'

She sat and thought, looking down at her fingers interlaced on the sheet in front of her, and then she nodded. 'Yes, you can say that. I need time to think too, though, remember that. And I have to sort out the business of my divorce . . . .'

'Oh, Jess, I'm sorry!' He came back to the bed to sit on it and took hold of her hands. 'I've been as selfish a bastard as a man can be, thinking only of my own affairs and . . . .'

'Oh, rubbish,' she said, making her voice as matter of fact as she could. 'There's nothing much to talk about. I've decided, and that's a comfort. It's all a mess, of course it is, but knowing what you want, being certain of it, that helps a lot. I've talked to a solicitor, got him to come here to see me, to get it all in hand as fast as I can. I heard from him this morning – he says Peter's being very amenable. Not arguing at all, not defending. We're going to court and asking for divorce on the grounds of cruelty, and he's not defending.'

She lifted her head and looked at Ben almost appealingly. 'So you see, he isn't all bad. He could have put me through hell, if he'd decided to defend. I think he's sorry for what he did, and that's why he's behaving this way.'

'You'll never convince me.'

'And on the financial side, too – he's agreed to everything my solicitor's asked for, and wasted no time about it. He's willing to sell the house in Purbeck Avenue, and I'm entitled to half the proceeds of that and also of half our savings and insurances and so forth – my solicitor says he's falling over backwards to behave well.'

'After all he did to you, how can you expect anything else? If he tried to refuse, you could throw the book at him, and he knows that.'

'And he knows I wouldn't,' she said in a level tone. 'I'm not vindictive, Ben. I just want it all settled as peaceably as possible, and he's being . . . co–operative. Don't try to make me feel bad by denying that.'

'Make you feel . . . my dear, as if I care about anything but helping you to feel good. I don't give a damn for Peter or his feelings . . . .'

'I do. So no more, please. Just be glad for me that it's all going to be as painless as possible. My solicitor's making special efforts to get things sorted out fast.' She grinned then, a little crookedly, 'I'll be quite well off, you know. Not rich, but able to think about what I want to do. I can buy a flat, get a car of my own, all that sort of thing. I've never really owned anything before. It'll feel rather odd.'

'You've owned it all this past twenty years, really. Half of the house, I mean and . . . .'

She made a face at that. 'I know I did, technically. But this is *really*. I'll decide what to spend and how to spend, on my own. It'll be . . . odd,' and her eyes were bright as she looked at him. 'Do I sound mercenary? I don't care if I do. It's freedom, you see, money. It's not anything else at all, not status or pleasure or . . . it's just freedom.'

'Yes. Freedom,' he echoed, and lifted his chin to stare at the bright square of the windows again. 'It's freedom to work, too, isn't it? To do the work you want to do? Oh, Jess, what shall I do? I wish I could make up my mind!'

The ambulance, for all its shrieking siren, seemed to go as slowly as a horse and cart, and she sat on the edge of the bunk beside Timmy, holding his hands in both of hers, and urging the vehicle forwards with every scrap of strength she had. Her belly felt as tight and knotted as an old tree trunk, and her legs trembled with the tension in them, and the uniformed ambulance man sitting on the other side of the swaying little box said sympathetically, 'We'll be there soon, missus, don't you fret, now; soon be there. You relax, love. You can't do the little chap no good getting so agitated, can you? You relax now.'

And she tried to, tried very hard, but it was impossible. Every time the ambulance slowed down to take a corner she wanted to shriek at the driver, wanted to rush and take over the wheel herself, to make the great lumbering thing go faster, faster, get there sooner . . . .

'Mind you, they mightn't take us at Minster Hospital, you do understand that?' He said it as though he hadn't already told her twice. 'They might say this is one for Doxford – communicable diseases, you see, they prefer to keep 'em all in one unit . . . .'

'You tell them my husband's Dr Pitman,' she said. 'I told you, he's the pathologist there and they can't refuse us, they can't. You tell them. We've got to be there.' But she didn't tell him why, didn't say anything about the small bottle that was in her handbag, wrapped up in a clean tea towel. As soon as she got Timmy there, as soon as she could talk to Dr Lyall Davies, then it would be all right. But they had to get there, and again she leaned forwards on the edge of the bunk as the ambulance slowed down to take a corner, urging it forwards. But this time it was turning into the hospital grounds and for the first time she began to allow herself to hope that she could, after all, make it all work out right.

35

'Is it the epidemic he's got?' June said, standing very straight beside Timmy's bed, her hands just touching his shoulder. She needed to be in contact with him all the time; as long as she could feel him there under her fingertips she could stay in control of the situation and of herself, she could stop herself from screaming her terror aloud. 'Couldn't it be something else?'

'It's the same infection all right,' Lyall Davies said, and there was a sort of satisfaction in his voice, the sound of a man who knew he was right in all things. 'The bulbar involvement, the muscular weakness, the lot – comatose too, you see? Yes . . . .' And he leaned down and pinched Timmy's finger hard and the child didn't respond, just lying there with his eyes half-closed and his breathing painful and laboured.

'What's going to happen?' June said it loudly, needing to hear her own voice. 'What treatment will he have?'

'There's nothing I can do, my dear.' Lyall Davies looked at Sister standing beside June and lifted his eyebrows, signalling his opinion of her as a stupid woman as clearly as if he'd shouted it aloud. 'I must explain that this dreadful infection involves a virus we just can't control. Far be it from me to point out that it was started by the research your husband does, but there it is, it can't be denied . . . .'

'And what about the Contra . . . the stuff he's been working on? That made that girl better, didn't it? That's why there's been all this fuss in the papers and on the television.'

'Yes, it made Andrea better. She's in excellent health, excellent,' Lyall Davies said, almost preening. 'I knew she would be and so could all the others, as I've told everyone who'll listen to me, but the one person who won't listen is your husband.' He shook his head ponderously and bent again over Timmy, prodding him with the bell of his stethoscope but patently not listening to any sounds that came through it.

'It would be as effective for this child, too, but what can we do? Your husband won't let us have any . . . .'

He straightened and then nodded at Sister and said, 'You go ahead, Sister, and see about making the respirator available for this child, will you? We may need it – I'll stay here with Mrs Pitman . . . .' Sister nodded and went rustling away and Lyall Davies came round the bed to set his arm heavily across June's shoulders. She didn't move but stood there, staring down at Timmy's flushed face, her own expression wooden.

'Now tell me, my dear, how much influence do you have on your husband? He's a very estimable man in many ways of course, but stubborn – I dare say I don't have to tell you that, eh? Yes, stubborn. But it occurs to me that now his own child is affected he may be more reasonable?'

'Timmy's my nephew. Not Ben's child. My nephew,' she said dully.

'Well, yes, m'dear, I quite understand that, but clearly a much beloved member of the family, hmm? Mother away, you in charge – surely your husband will bend a little under these circumstances? If we can persuade him to use the stuff on Timmy, you see, it could not only help Timmy – it could help all those other little children who are afflicted. There are hundreds now, literally hundreds. Some more might die – and if you can prevent that by appealing to your husband to let us use his stuff on Timmy and so prove to him it's safe for others, why . . . .'

'I don't have to ask him,' June said, still not taking her eyes from Timmy's face.

'You . . . how do you mean?' Lyall Davies seemed to sharpen and his voice lost its avuncular tone, became louder and more peremptory. 'Have you already discussed this with him?'

'I haven't seen him for well over a week,' she said, and now she turned to look at him. 'He doesn't even know Timmy's ill. I didn't waste time trying to call him.'

'Then perhaps we should call him now? I can send a message down to the laboratory, get him up here at once . . . .'

'No!' She said it sharply. 'I don't want him to know we're here.'

'Oh!' Lyall Davies peered at her in the shaded light of the small screened bed. 'Well, private affairs, I suppose, private affairs, none of my business. But what did you mean that you don't have to ask him about his stuff?'

'I've got some,' June said, and turned again to look down at Timmy's face. 'In a bottle.'

'You've . . . my dear girl! How did you manage that? I understood he had it all under lock and key, damned near an armed guard . . . .'

'He took it home. Put it in the fridge in the kitchen.' June spoke in the same dull voice. 'I found it there, so I took some. Put it in a bottle I had.'

Now she looked at him again. 'I boiled the bottle of course, did my best to make sure it was properly clean and all that. I thought – if Timmy gets ill, I'll just use it and then he'll be all right and Ben won't know and . . . .'

Slowly her eyes filled with tears and she looked at Lyall Davies appealingly, like a terrified child.

'But then Timmy did get ill and I didn't know what to do. I didn't know how much to give him or anything and then I heard all the time about Ben saying it was dangerous, it could have side-effects and I just didn't know what to do, and then today, when he got so much worse, I thought . . . to bring him here, to the hospital, try to see you, because you don't say it's dangerous, do you? You'll know how to use it, I thought, and now . . . now I just don't know what to do. I've got it, and Timmy's got to get well . . . but if it's dangerous . . . oh, what shall I do? If I give it to you and you use it and it hurts Timmy in some way I'll . . . and if I don't and he doesn't get better . . . oh, what shall I do? I don't know what to do . . . .' She wailed the words, and began to rock herself from side to side, keening like a child, still never letting go of Timmy's hand where it lay lax on the sheets.

'Where is it?' Lyall Davies said, and looked around the room as though it would jump out at him. 'Let me have it.'

'But suppose Ben's right and it's dangerous and could hurt Timmy? Then what? I couldn't bear it if I did anything to hurt Timmy . . . and I couldn't bear it if I had the stuff and he needed it and I didn't use it . . . . It seemed so easy when I took it, it made me feel everything was going to be all right because I had it, and after Ben sent and took the stuff away again I thought . . . I took it just in time, I took it and hid it just in time, and I was so pleased with myself . . . . It seemed so *easy* then, before Timmy got ill. But now . . . now I don't know what to do . . . .'

She was still touching Timmy's hand, but the other one

moved about as though she were trying to wring both hands together, giving her a curiously wild appearance, and Lyall Davies looked at her with an irritated expression on his face and said sharply, 'Now, my dear, don't you worry your head over such things. The important thing is you've got some, and it will help this child. Now, where is it? Give it to me at once and we'll start his treatment.'

Still June stood there, moving her left hand about aimlessly and saying nothing and Lyall Davies said loudly, 'Well, it's up to you, I suppose. He'll die without it, that much is certain. Here I have a treatment that could save a patient's life and you're withholding it. I can't force you, of course . . . .'

June's hand stopped moving and she stared at him with her eyes very wide, and then she said breathlessly, as though she had to rush to get the words out before someone stopped her. 'It's in my bag. Over there, under my coat, in the corner, in my bag. It's wrapped in a tea towel to stop it getting broken. It's a clean tea towel, it was boiled so it's absolutely clean, and I thought it was the best thing to do, to be on the safe side . . . .'

But he was paying her no attention, scrabbling in her bag, spilling the contents everywhere and then straightening up with his face plump with satisfaction.

'Sister!' he bawled at the top of his voice so that June jumped, and then he pushed the screen aside and shouted again. 'Sister!' There was a rush of footsteps as Sister came and shot behind the screens, almost pushing Lyall Davies aside, going straight to the bedside.

'I've got the respirator ready – Staff Nurse is just bringing it . . . .' And then she bent closer and stared at Timmy. 'He's still breathing the way he was,' she said accusingly, and looked at Lyall Davies.

'Of course he is!' He sounded jovial and beamed at her with great good humour. 'No one said he wasn't. I need syringes, Sister, packs of new syringes and a treatment chart. We'll put him on the same regime as used for the Barnett child and we'll get the same result, you see if we don't! And I tell you what else I want. I want you to send one of your nurses down to the main lobby and bring up a couple of the journalists down there. Tell 'em I'll see the man from *The Times* and one other – not the cheap ones, of course, perhaps the *Daily Telegraph* – yes, they're the ones, *The Times* and the *Daily Telegraph*, and they can have photographs too. You won't object, will you,

Mrs Pitman, my dear? It's important news, you see, and I know these journalist fellas, they always insist on photographs too. If they don't have them, you don't get much of a showing, and this little chap deserves all the showing he can get. He's going to get better! Now, chop chop, Sister! No time to waste . . . .'

He was glowing with satisfaction and excitement and June looked at him and then down at Timmy and tried to think about what she'd done, about whether it was right to have done it, whether there was still time to stop him and whether it would be right to stop him; and again her thoughts began to scurry round in her head, over and over again, each thought coming in the precise words and in the same precise order; if he has the stuff it could hurt him, if he doesn't he mightn't get well, what shall I do? And dizziness filled her and she swayed slightly and the staff nurse who had just arrived, pushing the respirator before her, saw her and left the machine at the foot of the bed to hurry to her side and set a hard hand under her elbow.

'You'd better come outside and sit down, dear,' she said firmly. 'You're not feeling well, are you, and we're busy – I've got a lot to do and . . . .'

'No!' June cried shrilly. If there was one thing she was sure of it was the importance of not leaving Timmy, of being always literally in touch with him. 'If you make me go I'll fetch Ben and tell him what I've done and . . . .'

'Let her stay,' Lyall Davies said at once. 'Get her a chair, let her stay. But not a word more, my dear. We've got a lot of work to do . . . .'

It didn't seem possible. There he lay, his eyes properly closed now, and, it seemed, sleeping normally. Her hand was still clamped over his and for a mad moment she considered pinching him hard, the way Dr Lyall Davies had done, to see if that would make him move and prove he was no longer unconscious, but she couldn't do that. She who had never done anything to hurt him, who would do anything to make him well, to deliberately inflict hurt? It couldn't be considered, and she whimpered deep in her throat as once again all her fears and doubts about what she had done rose in her, and then she looked swiftly at the nurse sitting on the other side of the bed.

She had been left there to special Timmy – to check his pulse every half hour and to take his blood pressure – but most of the time she dozed, comfortable in the knowledge that June was there and would wake her if she was needed, and now she sat with her head drooping on her chest, her arms folded across her starched apron front, and didn't stir at the sound.

June looked back again at Timmy and then at her watch on the bedside locker, beside the covered dish where the syringe, already filled with the next injection, sat waiting. Her heart thudded against her chest wall as she saw it. Almost quarter to. At three a.m., in another fifteen minutes, the nurse would have to be woken to give him the next injection, to push the needle into the tube that dangled from the bottle above Timmy's head, dripping its contents steadily into the vein in his arm, and then to push the plunger home and send the Contravert into that small body to fight the infection that had invaded it – June sat and stared at the covered dish, imagining the syringe lying skulking there, seeing the needle glittering on the end, seeing the straw-coloured fluid in it, trying to see equally clearly how it would behave in Timmy's body. Would it travel gently through his veins and arteries, kill the germs that so threatened him? Or would it seep wickedly where it shouldn't, damage those small arms and legs, that round soft belly, the firm little buttocks and the curving nape of his neck that always made her chest tighten when she looked at it – she shook her head, tried to look away from the dish and back at Timmy, but she couldn't, and for the first time lifted her hand from his, and moved it away.

It wasn't that she had actually thought about what she would do; it was almost as though someone else was doing it as very gently she lifted the cover from the dish and set it down softly on the locker top. The syringe lay there exposed, and still moving steadily she dipped her fingers into the dish and, using just her thumb and forefinger, very delicately picked it up.

The syringe lay in her palm, and she looked down at it and then, still with that same steady movement that seemed to be powered by some other brain, not hers, and governed by some other thoughts and certainly not hers, she took it up with her other hand and, moving easily and without hesitation, drew her skirt up above her knees to reveal her thighs. She watched her own hands moving just as she had watched the nurse's hands when she had given the last injections to other people; pinching up the flesh, setting the needle against the bulge, pushing it easily inwards. It hurt, a sharp pain that she liked, almost gloried in, and still with that same steady movement she pushed the plunger home and the sharp pain became a deep dull ache that spread across her legs and made her eyes fill with involuntary tears, but still she moved steadily, pushing on the plunger with her thumb until the piston met the end of the barrel, and then withdrawing the needle.

And now, at last, she felt better. Whether she had done the right thing or not for Timmy, she had shared the risk. That was what had been so dreadful about it all, the possibility that she would be left out of what happened to him. If Timmy were to get better then she had to be part of that, but if he didn't then she had to experience what he did, whatever it was. And if he was to be damaged by the treatment she had instigated – well, now she would be too, and she smiled gently down at the syringe in her hand and felt the pain in her leg as it increased and then slowly eased, and felt her eyelids droop. Now she'd be able to rest a little, perhaps get some sleep. Let the nurse stay awake for a while and give her a chance to rest her head on the side of the bed, so that Timmy's hand could touch her hair, and sleep a little. To sleep would be lovely, and she reached forwards to set the syringe back neatly in the dish, and then, suddenly, the sweet drowsiness that had begun to fill her shot away and she was staring wide-eyed and terrified at the syringe in her hand and at the empty dish. An empty syringe and an empty dish, and she whimpered again, this time with fear at what she had done and what she would do when she was found out, and the nurse stirred and lifted her head and said thickly, 'What's the time?'

June's hand jerked guiltily as a great surge of adrenalin moved through her, and she involuntarily hit the dish on the locker top and sent it rattling across the Formica surface to go tumbling to the floor, and without stopping to think she opened her hand and let the syringe go too, and it followed the dish to the floor, and she moved one foot forwards and managed to stamp on it and felt the glass shatter beneath her heel.

'Oh!' she gasped. 'You made me jump! Oh, heavens, look what I've done! Oh, this is dreadful . . . you'll have to get another syringe, get some more of the stuff . . . oh, I'm so sorry, but you made me jump . . . .'

The nurse was beside her now, crouching to pick up the pieces, and her face was red as she got to her feet again.

'Well, there was no need to be quite so clumsy,' she said sharply, her face blotched and angry. 'I mean, I only asked the time – well, no need to fuss. There's plenty in that bottle – I'll get another dose drawn up and we'll say no more about it. What no one knows about can't make problems can it? If you say nothing, I'll say nothing.'

'Yes, yes, of course,' June said gratefully. 'Not a word. Anyone can have an accident, can't they? Not a word – but do get it. It's time for his next one, isn't it?' And she looked anxiously at Timmy and squeezed his hands and bent her head closer to see how he was.

And this time he reacted to the pressure of her hand. She felt his fingers move under hers, and he rolled his head and made a small noise in his throat, and she stared at him and then up at the nurse and her face was blazing with excitement.

'He's getting better . . . he is, isn't he? He's getting better? Oh, it was right to use it, it was . . . it hasn't hurt him! Oh, please get the next one, as fast as you can. He's getting better. My Timmy's getting better!'

36

'Younger child, you see,' Lyall Davies said, beaming round at them all, but making sure his face was most directly presented to the men with the cameras. 'Faster rate of recovery. It's most gratifying, really most gratifying. It's as remarkable a recovery as the Barnett child's, only faster. He's not asked for scrambled eggs, mind you. It's rice crispies he's tucking into! Day before yesterday damn near dead, and now chasing rice crispies round a plate. Remarkable, really remarkable . . . .'

'Did Dr Pitman work with you in the use of the Contravert this time, doctor?' one of the journalists asked. 'Is there any chance he'll come and give us a comment too, this afternoon?'

'And what about the mother? Can we talk to the mother?'

'Mother's in America,' Lyall Davies said, carefully avoiding looking at the first questioner. 'It's his aunt who's in charge of him.'

He stopped and gazed at the woman who had asked the second question with an oddly smooth look on his face, and then said with an air of great casualness, 'She's a Mrs June Pitman. I don't know if she'll want to talk to you. You'll have to ask her yourselves.'

'Pitman? Quite a coincidence.' The man who'd asked whether Dr Pitman had been working with Lyall Davies pushed his head further forwards through the press of his fellows. 'Isn't it?'

'Not really,' Lyall Davies said, and smiled widely. 'She's Dr Pitman's wife.'

He couldn't have been more delighted with the effect of his words and his pleasure showed in every line of his body as he stood there smiling at them, enjoying the sudden silence that had fallen. As one of them said in a voice that was tinged with awe, 'Are you telling us that this child is a relation of Dr Pitman's? That he's *agreed* to the use of his drug on this child when he's refused it for all the others?' his smile widened even more.

'Now, don't you go putting words into my mouth! I didn't say and I do not say now that Dr Pitman agreed to the use of Contravert on this child, who does indeed happen to be his nephew. Wife's sister's child, as I understand the relationship. All I said was that it had been used, that the child is better, and that if you want to know more you'll have to talk to Mrs Pitman. She can explain a good deal more than I can.'

'It's Dr Pitman I want to talk to,' one of the journalists said grimly. 'I've got three kids under fifteen, and I've been worried sick about 'em with all this going on. It's Dr Pitman I'd like a word with.'

'If you'll take my advice it's his wife you'll talk to first,' Lyall Davies said jovially, and began to move forwards, pushing his way through the crowd. 'Now, I've got work to do, other patients to see, and I can't stand here chatting with all of you all day, splendid chaps though you are! Good afternoon!' And he was gone in a flurry of flashlight photographs, marching along the lower corridor towards the main ward block, leaving the journalists behind him talking among themselves with considerable energy.

'And if that doesn't persuade the man to part with his stuff for the rest of the people I'd like to use it for, nothing will!' he told Sister on Ward Seven B ten minutes later when he recounted, with great gusto, his version of dealing with the Press men downstairs. 'And don't you look at me like that, Sister, so po-faced. You know as well as I do that the stuff's good, it's a lifesaver, and Pitman's got to be made to see he can't go on sitting on it like a broody hen. If he doesn't know the good of what he's got there, there are others that do . . . .'

'But what about the long-term side-effects he's told you about?' Sister said, tilting her chin at him stubbornly. 'Why aren't you worried about them? Doesn't it concern you that you could be doing irreversible damage, using an untested drug like this? If those children grow up to be sterile, or to give birth to congenitally damaged babies, what then? That's what I want to know. *Sir.*' Arguing with Lyall Davies was an essential part of her daily life, and had been ever since she'd taken this post, but now his new self-satisfied sleekness and his passion for talking to journalists was making argument even more necessary. 'He's the man who made the stuff and he should know. If he says it could be dangerous in that way, then he's got to be right. I'm sure I wouldn't let anyone use it on any child of mine.'

'Well, that's a dilemma you'll never need to face, is it?' Lyall Davies said spitefully. As her face flamed he added smoothly, 'He's just being over-cautious, Sister. You really ought to be able to judge the difference between these laboratory wallahs and their neurotic fussing and the demands of real clinical medicine. If you can't, you oughtn't to be working in an acute ward, certainly not one of mine. I'm made in the good old heroic mould of doctors, Sister, and I'm not ashamed to say so. Nothing ventured, nothing gained, and you can't deny that so far I've gained two young lives that would have been down the drain without me. As for what happens to them twenty years from now – the important thing is they can now look forward twenty years, isn't it? Better than being dead. Think of that if you want to ease your conscience. And remember – if you can't stand the heat of the kitchen you'll be better off playing in the garden. That's what I say.'

'And I say that heroism isn't what good medical care is about,' Sister snapped, and stared at him challengingly. 'These children could have lived without the stuff, given the right nursing. You never gave us the opportunity to see the boy through – just gave him the drug. Well, if he finishes up with damaged testes because you've been pumping him full of stuff you don't understand, I hope you'll sleep sound of nights. I'm sure I wouldn't be able to, in your shoes.'

'Piffle!' Lyall Davies said, even more pleased with himself now he'd managed to make her so angry. There was nothing that enlivened the day more than a fight with this boring old spinster. 'I never go to bed with my shoes on!' And he laughed and reached for the charts and wrote on Timmy's treatment schedule in his usual sprawling hand instructions to continue using the Contravert for another twenty-four hours.

'To be on the safe side, Sister!' he said, and grinned. 'It wouldn't do to stop the treatment too soon, would it?'

June sat and worried all day about it. She'd have to tell him, and the longer she left it the worse it would be, but the thought of his anger made her shiver. She knew she'd done the right thing of course; looking at Timmy sitting there in bed playing with his plasticine and listening to the music coming from the earphones he now refused to take off, who could doubt it? Two days ago he'd been unconscious, flaming with fever, struggling to breathe, and now he was Timmy again. But all the same the thought of telling Ben made her feel sick.

She had in fact been feeling sick all day, and now, as the trolleys carrying the patients' suppers came into her ward smelling powerfully of macaroni cheese and tomato soup she felt her gorge rise more insistently than ever, and got to her feet unsteadily and smiled at Timmy as cheerfully as she could and said loudly, 'Just going to the bathroom, darling.' And Timmy looked at her vaguely and returned to his plasticine, clearly unworried by her departure, and she almost ran to the sluice at the far end of the ward.

One of the nurses came in behind her and found her bent over the basin retching miserably, and leaned over her with professional competence and took her forehead in a cool firm hand, holding her steady, and that helped; and after a little while she lifted her head and said shakily, 'Thanks, nurse. I'm all right now, I think . . . .'

'I think I'll just check your temperature and pulse, Mrs Pitman,' the nurse said briskly. 'You're the colour of old boots, but you're a bit flushed over the cheeks as well. We can't have you going down with the same infection, now, can we, and not notice it? That'd never do. Come and sit down in the treatment room and we'll check things . . . .'

'No, really, nurse, I'm fine. It's just nervousness and worry about Timmy, I expect and . . . .'

'Well, yes, that's as may be,' the nurse said, urging her along so firmly that June couldn't resist her. 'I know all about these psychological effects, but in my experience people who get sick and look flushed when they've been nursing children with infections are very likely to have a good physical reason for their symptoms. Now you just sit there, and we'll pop a thermometer into your mouth and see what's what. Can't have one of our own consultants' wives being neglected, now, can we? That'd never do. Especially one who's getting so much attention at the moment . . . .' And she pushed the thermometer into June's mouth, filling it with the taste of chemicals and making her want to retch again, and seized her wrist to count her pulse.

June leaned her head back against the tiled wall behind her and closed her eyes. No point in arguing with the girl; if she wanted to think she had an infection, let her. June knew she hadn't for her throat wasn't sore and her nose didn't itch at the back the way it did when she caught a cold or the flu. This was just worry, worry about Timmy and worry about what Ben would say when he found out she'd taken the Contravert from the fridge and, deep inside her, the lingering fear about what she might have done to Timmy allowing the stuff to be used on him. But it was a very small fear, that one now, she told herself. It had to be, because wasn't Timmy fine now, sitting playing with plasticine and listening to music on his earphones?

'Well, your temperature's normal!' the nurse said, and sounded a little disappointed. 'And though your pulse is a little fast, it's nothing to worry about. That could be due to anxiety, I grant you. But the vomiting – have you been eating anything unusual this past few days?'

'Eating?' June opened her eyes and looked up at the girl's round face a little hazily, and then managed a smile. 'To tell you the truth, I've hardly eaten a thing for days. I was too worried. Tea and toast and so forth. No, it's nothing I've eaten. Honestly, I'm sure it's just worrying about Timmy and what Ben'll say when he knows what I did . . . .' And she shook her head and tried again to smile but all that happened was that she retched again and the nurse once more had to hold her head over a bowl.

'What about your periods then?' June leaned back again as the wave of nausea left her, and tried to relax, and the sound of the nurse's voice seemed to come from a great distance.

'Mmm?' she said.

'I was just wondering – some women get sick when they have painful periods. Do you have painful periods?'

'No,' June said and then, very slowly, opened her eyes and stared at the nurse. 'What did you say?'

'I said that some people get sick when they have dysmenorrhoea – painful periods . . . .'

June moved then, made herself sit upright, and stared again at the nurse, her eyes very wide.

'What's the date?'

'The date? My dear, I know you've been worried about your little nephew, but even so, you can't have forgotten it's nearly Christmas. December 21st today, that's what it is. Christmas next Tuesday . . . .'

'Oh, my God,' June said. 'Oh, my *God*!' and she began to laugh, softly at first and then more and more shrilly until she was hiccupping with it, and that made her retch again, and yet she went on laughing.

The nurse bent over her and took her shoulders in both strong hands and said loudly, 'Now, Mrs Pitman, you must calm down! You really must relax and . . . .'

'Oh, it's all right.' June managed to stop the laughter, managed to get the words out. 'It's really all right. It's just that I . . . I can't believe that I hadn't noticed, you see. Me, not to notice! The last one was . . . let me work it out . . . it was November 13th. I remember that . . . November 13th. I knew I was in the fertile phase, and I called Ben and . . . .' She stopped and reddened and then smiled at the nurse. 'You know how it is when you're trying . . . you sort of . . . my last period was October 30th, that was it, because my periods are dreadfully erratic and I do my best to remember all the dates and I worked out I was fertile on November 13th. It was a Tuesday and I remember thinking, maybe this'll be a lucky date for me . . . .'

'Then you're coming up to missing your second period,' the nurse said matter of factly. 'I dare say that's what it is then. Lots of women get sickness all day, and not just in the morning in early pregnancy. Presenting symptom, really. I did my midder last year, so I'm well up on it.'

June was sitting very erect and gazing at her with the pupils of her eyes so dilated with excitement that they seemed to be black.

'I wouldn't have thought I could . . . I mean I've been trying for years. Years and years, and now when I miss a period, not to notice? It just doesn't seem possible . . . .'

The nurse laughed. 'It's possible. It's amazing what women can forget, when it suits 'em. I had a friend who managed not to notice she was pregnant for almost three months, because she so badly didn't want to be. Only faced up to it just in time to get herself aborted, but it was a near thing . . . .'

'But I do want to be pregnant! I want it more than I've ever wanted anything in all the world . . . and not to notice . . . it can't be possible . . . .'

'Well, if you've had a lot to worry you, it could be,' the nurse said practically. 'It certainly seems like you've managed it. Would you like me to check your breasts, just to see if they show anything?'

'Yes . . . oh, yes, please . . . do anything you like . . . just tell me I'm not imagining it . . . .'

'Why should you be? You're almost two months overdue,

you're being sick . . . that's real enough. Let's have a look at those nipples then . . . .'

June fumbled for the buttons on her blouse and sat there stiff and tense as the nurse prodded her breasts and peered at her nipples, and then sat very still when the girl straightened up and said almost casually, 'Well, yes, no doubt about that I'd say. Nice big Montgomery's tubercles, looks quite dark there – had any tingling or discomfort?'

'I don't know,' June said, staring up at her, almost distracted with excitement. 'I mean, I've been thinking about Timmy a lot, worrying about him in this epidemic and everything . . . .'

'That's what they told us when we did our clinic weeks – infertile women who adopt or foster get pregnant sooner than those who sit around worrying about it. I do congratulate you, Mrs Pitman. It's nice for you – I'm sure Dr Pitman'll be thrilled too,' and the nurse beamed down at her with a proprietorial air, as though she had played a direct and personal part in creating the pregnancy. 'Would you like me to sit with Timmy while you go over to the path. lab? Sister's off this evening and we're not so busy I can't spend half an hour with the little lad!'

'Yes . . . yes, I must go and see Ben,' June said, still staring at her. 'Oh, God, I must go and see Ben. I've got to tell him what I've done . . . .'

The excitement was ebbing away now and the knowledge of what she had done came pushing back up through her mind from the depths where she had tried to bury it, bringing waves of cold fear with it. She could see her own hands as though they were someone else's, see how she had pinched up the flesh of her thigh, how she had set the syringe against the bump and pushed the needle in. She closed her eyes tightly and heard the nurse say anxiously, 'Now, just take it easy, Mrs Pitman, head between the knees, *that's* right . . .' as a hard hand pushed her head downwards. 'You'll be fine, just take it easy. Everything's going to be fine . . . .'

But it isn't fine, June thought despairingly. It isn't. I've ruined everything, destroyed everything and there's nothing I can do about it.

She began to cry, deep retching sobs that shook her whole body. There was nothing she could do.

37

It had seemed a mad idea when he'd first suggested it, but now, she thought, as the train came into Minster station only half an hour late, she had to admit he'd been right. What else could she have done over Christmas, after all? Spending it at a health farm had actually made her feel a good deal better. She'd had time to recover physically from her bruises, she'd been able to avoid the hazard of eating too much – always part of the family Christmases in the old days at Purbeck Avenue – and above all she'd been thoroughly drained of any traces of self-pity. Seeing the other people who had nowhere else to spend the holiday, the loneliness, the tedium and the emptiness of other lives, had made her grateful for her own problems. They at least gave her a sense of being a real person with a real life to live, unlike the people she had shared saunas and gymnasia with this past week.

And there had been the freedom from the pressure of the news, too, she thought as she caught a glimpse of a newspaper hoarding for the *Advertiser* as she came through the ticket barrier. That had been one of the promises the place had made in its brochure. 'Plenty of video entertainment to choose from,' the glossy pages had trumpeted. 'But none of the depression of the bad news at Flinders House during this truly traditional festive season.' At first she had been appalled by that. How stupid could people be, trying to withdraw from reality to a never-never world where there was only entertainment and cosiness, and none of the real living pain of the here and now? Pretending that a place was Dingley Dell and that all was for the best in the best of all possible worlds didn't get rid of fear and danger and cruelty and stupidity – and yet it had been comforting to spend a week without a newspaper or a television newscast. She felt fresh and new and agreeably bored. Ready to go back to work.

But still with her mind not fully made up about the new job she had been offered with Ben. It was as though her intelligence had gone into abeyance while she'd been at Flinders: shut away

311

from reality by the place's policy, she had allowed her own mind to be manipulated away, too, and had given no real thought to what she should do. That decision still lay ahead of her, and she settled herself in the corner of the taxi taking her to the small hotel near the sea front where she had decided to stay until she had finally settled on a flat of her own, and thought – as soon as I can I'll contact Ben, see how soon we can meet and talk. Maybe he's already decided for himself, and that has to affect what I do . . . .

The hotel room was small and dull and devoid of any personality, and that was a relief. Flinders House had been so ferociously tasteful and welcoming that it had been intimidating. Here she could think properly and find herself again, and she unpacked the few clothes she had taken away with her and put them away and then sat down at the small desk in the corner with her bank book and the letters her solicitor had sent her. Before she did anything else she needed to work out her long-term finances, to see what her needs would be. To take the job that was being offered just because of the attraction of the high salary it carried – and though no specific sum had been mentioned, it was obvious it would be high, going by the offer to Ben – would be wrong. She needed to have all the facts clear in her head first so that she made her choices for the right reasons. That was a refreshing and comforting thought. After so many years of not making decisions at all, of having Peter tell her what was to happen to her life, there was a deep pleasure in having to be so definite on her own account.

She emerged from her computations feeling rather light in the head. She was, she decided, very well off. She had known that Peter was a thrifty man who had saved carefully and that the house had gained greatly in value during the years they had lived in it, but she had not expected her share of the spoils salvaged from the wreck of twenty years of marriage to be so substantial; and she looked at the neat columns of figures and the totals they came to with something approaching awe. There was no question of making the wrong decision about jobs on purely financial grounds, that was for certain.

She ate a frugal supper in the bleak hotel dining room, and then, on an impulse, decided to wrap up warmly and walk to the hospital. It was a good half hour's trudge through the town, but an agreeable one, and regular exercise was something she'd got used to over the past few days; it would be a pity to let her healthy regime go too soon, she told herself as she pulled on boots and a thick coat and gloves. And he might be there, whispered the little voice inside her head, mightn't he? And you're aching to see him – but she refused to think about that, and pushed her fists deep into her pockets and started to walk.

It was an agreeable walk though there was a melancholy about it too: the houses she passed with their brightly lit windows were heavily decorated with trees and lights and Santa Clauses pasted to the panes, and the occasional glimpse of family groups inside staring at the flickering bluish screens that occupied the corner of every room she looked into made her feel the pinch of loneliness; and there was another ingredient to the sense of sadness that filled her. She would be leaving this town soon. She knew that, even though she hadn't yet decided what to do about the new job that hung over her like the shadow of last night's dreams, impossible to shake off. Whether she went north with Ben to work on a defence project – and the thought of that made her cringe inside, a reaction that told her that surely she had, after all, made her decision? – she would not be able to go back to the old days. The comfortable year of working with Ben in that shabby ill-equipped corner of a shabby ill-equipped path. lab in a small provincial hospital was over. No more time would be spent with Castor and Pollux scolding her from their corner cage as she fed the rabbits snuffling and rustling in their pens, no more long hours would pass bent over microscopes or writing reports for Ben. It was over, and her eyelids pricked and she walked faster, bending her head against the sharpness of the winter night, hating herself for being so mawkish. It was as well she was going to see him now, she told herself. She wanted him to be there; not for any emotional reason, but to sort this business out, once and for all. A new year was hovering just over the horizon, a mere handful of hours away. Now was the time to make new plans, settle new decisions, start out on new roads. Yes, she repeated firmly to herself, that's the only reason I'm hoping he's there, the only reason I've set out like this. It's because I need to know what's going to happen to my life. Not because of him, as a person, at all.

The light was on in the corridor that led to the lab, and she pushed open the glass doors and stood there, smelling the familiar scents of pine disinfectant and formaldehyde and laboratory chemicals, and felt a great wash of nostalgia engulf her, and was furious with herself for it. To be nostalgic for the

313

here and now – it was crazy. And yet it wasn't, because wasn't this all now part of the past, a yesterday that was just as far away as if it had been years ago? It didn't matter how far behind you an experience was; once it was over it was dead, and regret for it could be just as poignant within hours of the loss as after years, and she shook her head at her own muddled thinking and moving purposefully went into the lab and across the big shadowed space to the office door beyond. Her heels clacked on the terrazzo as she went and she thought – I hope he hears me. I don't want to startle him, I want him to be expecting me . . . .

But he didn't move as she came in, sitting at his small desk, his head bent over what he was doing, and she stared at him and took a deep careful breath, to control the lift of pleasure the sight of his rumpled hair had created in her, and said as casually as she could, 'Hello, Ben.'

At first she thought he hadn't heard her, because he went on sitting in exactly the same posture, and she opened her mouth to speak again, but now he straightened and turned and looked at her, and her words died in her throat. He looked dreadful, and impulsively she moved forwards, pulling off her gloves as she did so, and said urgently, 'Ben? Whatever is it? You look ghastly – what is it? Are you ill?'

He looked at her for a moment and then smoothed his hands over his head, and then stood up and stayed there at his desk, looking at her awkwardly.

'Oh, Jessie . . . I didn't think you'd . . . I'm fine. A little tired, because I'm so busy, but you know how it is . . . did you . . . was it a good break?'

She stopped short, staring at him, no longer wanting to be near him, and he stared back, his eyes a little red-rimmed as they always were when he was tired, and she said uncertainly, 'It was fine. Great. Very restful – Ben, what is it?'

He shook his head and looked away from her, down at his desk, and then after a moment sat down a little clumsily. 'Nothing, Jessie, really. It's just there's a lot to do to sort things out . . . .'

'I see,' she said after a moment, and moved away from him to stand leaning against the door jamb, well away from him. He didn't want her to be near him; that much was very obvious. 'Then you're going north?'

'Going north?' he said, still not lifting his head.

'You're going to work on that defence project?' She knew her voice was sharp and she couldn't help it. There was something in her that was growing and she knew it to be disgust and anger, and neither of those were feelings she wanted to direct at him. Not at Ben who had made her feel so good, so sure that she could, after all, find pleasure in a man's company and a man's touch.

'No,' he said after another pause and this time he did look at her. 'No, I'm not.'

At once she felt a wave of guilt and closed her eyes and said impulsively, 'Oh, thank God for that! I've been trying so hard to see a way it could be done, and . . . but I'm so glad. It was a horrible idea, horrible. You can't let them have your work, and I'm so glad you . . . .'

'No one's going to have my work,' he said loudly, and she opened her eyes to stare at him. 'I'm not doing it any more.'

'You're . . . what did you say?'

He took a deep breath and began to speak very rapidly, looking at a point a few inches above her head. 'Jessie, I had hoped to be able to get a message to you before you came here. I was going to arrange . . . I thought it would be better if we met outside the hospital so that I could explain properly. It isn't easy here. It's damned near impossible . . . .' And for a moment he was Ben again, the man she had worked with for so long and had thought she knew so well, instead of the chilly stranger who had been sitting in his place. But it was a momentary change, because now he said in the same rapid, rather high voice, 'I'm afraid your job here doesn't exist any more, Jessie. It's all . . . there just isn't a job here for you. I'm very sorry.'

'You . . . you're stopping work here? Where are you going to do it, then?'

'I'm not,' he said, and again turned away from her. 'I've decided not to do it at all; I've burned the notes, disposed of the last of the 737, destroyed my batch of Contravert, Clough's destroying the rest and tomorrow they're collecting Castor and Pollux to take them back to the breeders.' He lifted his chin and stared at the closed door that led to the animal room. 'We've been short of storage space for the lab's records for some time, so we're having that room made over for them. It'll take a bit of the pressure off the space outside and help us a lot.'

'But . . .' She shook her head, bewildered. 'You mean you're not leaving here? Just giving up the research?'

'I couldn't have said it more clearly,' he snapped, and slid his eyes over her face and away again. 'I've spelled it out as simply as

I know how. The research is finished so I don't have a job for you any more. It should be crystal clear.'

There was a long silence as she took it all in, and then she said carefully, 'I think after all the work I did, I'm entitled to know why.'

'I've decided, that's all.'

'No, it isn't all.' Again anger was bubbling up in her. 'It bloody well isn't all! That work was part of me, too. Those notes you say you burned – I worked on those as much as you did! I was as much part of this project as you. Now, tell me why. I have a right to know. Was it the publicity? The pressure to use it too soon? The epidemic? Was that it? Christ, Ben, I know it was hell, but the worst of it was over! We only had to decide where to go next, that was all! The pressure was easing off . . . .'

'Like hell it was!' he blazed. 'Like bloody hell it was! Haven't you seen the publicity this past week? Haven't you heard what they're saying ever since Timmy . . . .' He stopped and took a deep breath and then said dully, 'I'm sorry, I'd forgotten. You mightn't have heard at that. That place made such a point about no newspapers, no TV newscasts . . . .'

'What's happened? What have I missed?'

'Oh, Jessie, where do I begin?' And again he rubbed his head with both hands and now he really was back, her Ben again. The cold, shrill, angry man had gone and left a shell of himself behind. 'It's June. She . . . it's the stupidest thing. I should have realized that she . . . have you ever thought about weak people, Jessie? How much harm they do just by being what they are? I thought June was weak and feeble and . . . I'd come to despise her, do you know that? I was sorry for her, and I wanted to take care of her still, but I despised her for being so stupid and helpless. Helpless! Christ, but the power she has is unbelievable. She's changed everything all on her own. Changed and ruined everything.'

'You haven't explained.'

'She stole some of the Contravert. She gave it to Lyall Davies when Timmy got ill, and she was afraid he had the infection. I don't know if he actually did have it, though I gather he was quite ill – anyway, Lyall Davies of course used it, with all the fanfare and the noise he could, bloody nearly called the TV cameras in to watch him give the injections. And when it got out that I'd let the stuff be used on my own nephew – oh, Jessie, it's been hell all week.'

'Oh, Ben, I . . . .' she began, but he shook his head.

'That's not all. She took some of the stuff herself. No, don't ask me why. She gave me some long garbled rigmarole about the risk to Timmy of using it, and feeling better if she took it too and shared the risk – absolute rubbish, believe me – but she did it. And then . . . .' He laughed then, a thin ugly little sound. 'There really has to be some sort of God somewhere, after all. And he hates me, that's for sure. She's pregnant, you see. You remember the time Peter first hit you and I told you what happened to me? I did, didn't I? Well, it doesn't matter now. Because she's pregnant and she took some of my Contravert. So there you are. I've burned the notes and destroyed it all. What the bloody hell else could I do?'

'But . . . .' She took a deep breath. 'But Ben, what about the *good* use of the stuff? What about all those children who might die? Shouldn't you have kept the Contravert for them?'

'And expose them to the same risks that June has exposed herself to, and Timmy? If it's bad for them, it's just as bad for the children who are ill. Maybe they'd be better off if they died of the bug – who am I to say? Christ, Jessie, what do you think I am? I'm just a bloody pathologist – I'm not a god. It's not for me to sort out all these rights and wrongs. I'm not *capable* of it. Ethics – they confuse me. Always have. It's easier to walk away from the whole problem. I created it – or I might have, we still don't know for sure this bloody epidemic has anything to do with my animals or my 737 strain – and I can't solve it, so I'm walking away. It's not admirable, it's lousy, and I just don't care. I'm not capable of caring any more. I'm worn out . . . leave me alone. I've had enough. I've had *enough* . . . .'

'Even if more children get ill?'

'Even if they do. I've told you. I can't handle it any more.'

'Then let someone else do it. Give the Contravert to another researcher or another doctor and let . . . .'

'Another doctor? A Lyall Davies? And what sort of sop to a conscience would that be? I'd still have to sit and watch and wait for the time bomb to explode. Some children might survive, yes – but some might get appalling diseases later. Like the girls whose mothers were given Stilboestrel to prevent them aborting and who died in godawful pain, in their twenties, of cancer – wouldn't it have been better for them if they'd died in infancy? Wouldn't it be better if this epidemic now was left to peter out by itself? It will – it has to. They always do.'

'So you'll let children die for fear of what might happen . . . .'

She had to try to understand, had to try to make him understand, but he shook his head, furious again.

'I've told you – I'm not God! If they live or die, that isn't my responsibility. It wasn't mine that the 737 escaped in the first place – how could I legislate for a thief stealing animal food and then going to work in a school? How could I protect my work against people like those Animal Freedom Brigaders? My only guilt is that I started the work in the first place. If I hadn't – well, I did, but now I just have to stand aside and stop meddling. I've done enough harm. I don't want to do any more. Whatever I do now, I do the wrong thing. The way I've chosen I believe is the lesser wrong. I can't be sure – Christ, if only I could! But I've tried to do the best I can . . . now leave me alone.'

There was nothing more to be said, and she stood there against the door jamb with her hands in her pockets and her head bent so that her hair half-hid her face, trying to think of what she could do to comfort him, seeking a way out of the maze for him, but there was no way. He was caught in the most complex of traps and there was no escape for him at all, and after a moment she said lamely, 'You're staying with June, of course.'

'Of course.'

'You'd rather I left the town, I imagine. Not just the job. The town.'

Again there was a silence and then he said, 'Yes.'

She nodded, still not looking up. 'Very well. I'll leave as soon as I can get away.'

'Jessie, I . . . .'

Now she did look at him, and for a moment it was there, the need for her, the feeling she had been nursing for him all these months there for her, too. It was too late but it was there and she smiled at him and said gently, 'Never mind, Ben. Put it down to bad luck. That's all. Bad luck.'

She turned and opened the door, and beyond it the laboratory looked big and dark, and behind her she heard Castor and Pollux wake up at the sound of the opening door and begin to chatter, and she looked back over her shoulder and said, 'Well, Ben, thanks for . . . I'm glad I did it all, you know. I'd never have got away without the job, so at least that much has come out of it all. It may sound selfish to say so, but still – at least you don't have to feel bad about me.'

'Of course I do,' he said, and though his voice was flat and colourless she could hear the pain in it. 'Of course I bloody well do.'

'Don't. It's worked out quite well for me, after all . . . I've got a lot out of these past months. A lot.'

'You're trying to make me feel better. Don't. It only makes it worse.'

'It's true, Ben, it really is. I've found me, you see. Without this job I'd still be Mrs Hurst of Purbeck Avenue, wouldn't I? As it is, I'm Jessie Hurst of nowhere in particular. I like that. It's . . . it's exhilarating, really. All sorts of things are possible for me now.'

'I'd like to believe that.'

'Then do. Because it's true.'

'I'll try.'

She moved forwards out into the shadowy laboratory, and he stood and watched her, and she said quickly, 'Ben . . . I hope the baby's all right. It would be dreadful if . . . I do hope it's all right.'

'Yes,' he said, and then laughed suddenly and she looked back at him once more, startled by the sound, and he said, 'Isn't it ridiculous? It'll be the last of the human trials on Contravert, won't it? How's that for devotion to original research? Doing a human trial on your own child! Oh, I'll certainly go down in the annals, won't I, Jess? I certainly will go down in the annals . . . .'

'You could,' she said. 'But not for that reason. Let me know when you're ready to start again, Ben. You will be one of these days, I think. You'll find it again – your . . . I don't know . . . courage, I suppose. And when you do, I'll be interested to know. You can find me through the bank. I'll tell them to forward letters. Goodbye, Ben.'

He said nothing, just staring at her, and she pulled the door closed behind her and moved across the dark laboratory surefootedly, avoiding the hazards, knowing every bench and every stool intimately, and on out into the corridor and then into the dark car park. In the distance she could hear the traffic in the main road and she thought – I'll buy a car tomorrow. Buy a car and pack my things and call Peter and Mark, it's only right to say goodbye, and I'll go away. I don't know where, but I'll go away. There has to be something for me to do somewhere. I'll go and find it.

And she pushed her hands into her coat pockets and set out to walk back to the hotel. It felt rather good, being on her own. It was the first time she had been completely alone in all her life, the first time she had had no one to rely on but herself. And it felt better than she would have thought it possibly could.

BESTSELLING FICTION FROM ARROW

All these books are available from your bookshop or news-agent or you can order them direct. Just tick the titles you want and complete the form below.

☐	THE COMPANY OF SAINTS	Evelyn Anthony	£1.95
☐	HESTER DARK	Emma Blair	£1.95
☐	1985	Anthony Burgess	£1.75
☐	2001: A SPACE ODYSSEY	Arthur C. Clarke	£1.75
☐	NILE	Laurie Devine	£2.75
☐	THE BILLION DOLLAR KILLING	Paul Erdman	£1.75
☐	THE YEAR OF THE FRENCH	Thomas Flanagan	£2.50
☐	LISA LOGAN	Marie Joseph	£1.95
☐	SCORPION	Andrew Kaplan	£2.50
☐	SUCCESS TO THE BRAVE	Alexander Kent	£1.95
☐	STRUMPET CITY	James Plunkett	£2.95
☐	FAMILY CHORUS	Claire Rayner	£2.50
☐	BADGE OF GLORY	Douglas Reeman	£1.95
☐	THE KILLING DOLL	Ruth Rendell	£1.95
☐	SCENT OF FEAR	Margaret Yorke	£1.75

Postage _____

Total _____

ARROW BOOKS, BOOKSERVICE BY POST, PO BOX 29, DOUGLAS, ISLE OF MAN, BRITISH ISLES

Please enclose a cheque or postal order made out to Arrow Books Limited for the amount due including 15p per book for postage and packing both for orders within the UK and for overseas orders.

Please print clearly

NAME..

ADDRESS..

....

Whilst every effort is made to keep prices down and to keep popular books in print, Arrow Books cannot guarantee that prices will be the same as those advertised here or that the books will be available.